THE DRAGONS' REDRESS

The Vasara Chronicles, Book 2

Roland Capalbo

I0564090

For all those who have ever sat under a tree in a field or wood as they read a story, letting the magic of the tree and the words combine to bring to life something truly amazing.

Chapter 1

The river was an angry tempest, matching Andy's mood as he stared out across the water from under the eaves of the ruined house. The feeling of betrayal was strong, and he never felt more alone in his young life than he did at that moment. He looked up as the first stars began making their appearance. It seemed like an age ago when he first stepped onto this island and was transported to the wild and wonderful world known as Vasara. There he was both human and dragon.

Now that he was back in his own world, he could sense the source of the five gods, but he could not touch it, and therefore could not transform. The source was the power of wizards and dragons. His sharp hearing and keen eyesight that had been awakened in him when he first became a dragon were still there, as well as his ability to talk mind to mind. Looking up he saw deer walking along the road that cut into Storm King Mountain across the river. He felt very hungry.

Andy could feel the man he called father in his mind long before he reached the house ruins. Emilia had given Redlin a broad overview of what had transpired in Vasara while Andy stood here and brooded. He turned to look at him.

Redlin was taller than both Andy and Emilia. His mane of black hair rested just above the top of the neck line. Not exactly the style of the day, but it seemed to fit him. His shoulders were broad and his brown eyes had an ageless look. Andy had been shaken terribly by the fact that his father was the third wizard of Vasara that had gone missing some fifteen-hundred years ago, by Vasara reckoning.

"Can we talk?" Redlin asked.

Andy bowed his head and idly kicked the stone at his feet without answering.

This is not becoming of you Andros.

Andy suddenly felt hot anger that he should be addressed in this manner of communication by a man he thought had no knowledge of dragons or magic.

"Why?" Andy asked hurt and angry. "And have you always known?"

Redlin put a comforting hand on Andy's shoulder. "Let's go sit over there," he said pointing to some rocks lying by the trail.

"So I assume our last name isn't Lidzi, and your first name is not really Darren," he said as they walked over.

As Andy sat down, he looked out across the river to the twinkling lights from the waterfront buildings of Newburgh. The heat of anger started to dissipate from his body.

"It is but it isn't. Throw my middle initial W in there, you were always good at those puzzles in the newspaper, can't you see it?"

Andy thought on it. His eyes opened wide as he realized the letters were jumbled. In a different arrangement, Darren W Lidzi became Wizard Redlin. He laughed in spite of everything, but then grew quiet as the situation came back to him.

"Are you my father?" Andy said without looking at Redlin, dreading the answer.

Silence.

"Look into my eyes Andy, and tell me what you see,"

Andy stared long into his eyes, as if seeing into the past. Redlin was somehow able to show Andy the moment of his birth. Standing in the hospital room was the wizard, looking exactly as he did now. His mother was holding him, wrapped in a blanket and tickling his chin. A very young Emilia stood next to the bed, peering up at him. No wings or pointed ears, just a normal looking girl.

The scene changed. Andy was sitting in the baseball stadium at his first Yankees game. He was five years old. His father was with him, sharing a Coke and a hotdog. Now he was twelve and he was up at bat in his Little League All Star game. It was one of those situations when it is the bottom of the ninth and the game winning run is on third base. Andy saw himself get a hold of one and drive it into deep right-center field. He could see his entire family jumping up and down, yelling during his triumphant moment.

Many times the vision changed. Showing his life played out, both the joys and the pains. And there, through it all was Redlin, his father. He knew beyond a doubt that this was his father and the elation he felt made him collapse in Redlin's arms as he wept.

"It's all right lad," his father said stroking his son's hair. After a moment, Andy pulled away and wiped his eyes.

"How is it that you still have your magic?" He believed he could not have seen those images without some kind of magical help. His father reached into his shirt and pulled out a medallion that hung on a chain around his neck. Stamped on its surface was the image of an open scroll. It was gold in color and had strange letters engraved on it. Andy felt his own medallion that Paolo had given him before he left and wondered at how similar they were.

"I'm very confused with all this."

"Let's go sit with your sister and Abby, and maybe we can make some sense of it all." They stood up and Redlin put his arm around Andy's shoulder as they walked back to where the girls sat on a log with a small fire burning in a shallow pit.

As they got closer, Andy looked at his beloved with a lump in his throat. Her blue dress that she wore when they left Vasara seemed almost black in the darkness. The firelight danced off her golden hoop earrings. He believed her the most beautiful girl in the world, and they were joined by a bond that neither of them understood.

Emilia looked up, and Andy could see her green eyes glowing like a cat. The pearl comb that would transform into the staff of the goddess gave off a white luminescence against her black hair. Her Summoner clothes had vanished when they arrived back on the island. Emilia now wore a garment of white with a red sash. She had explained that everything that belonged to the Dragon Summoner would stay in Vasara. The pearl comb was different, and Braylynn had told Emilia she must keep it with her always.

"Are you all right Andros?" Abby asked concerned.

"I'm better, though I still have many questions."

"Sit down," Redlin said. "We will share information, because believe it or not, I have some questions as well."

"How did you know?" Andy asked his sister. Emilia had affirmed Abby's proclamation that their father was the wizard Redlin.

"Do you remember when Braylynn gave me my memory back?"

He did remember. He and the goddess had been standing at the source not long after Andy thought Devon had killed Loki. The faerie he knew as Donella joined them there. It was then that Braylynn allowed Andy to see the Dragon Summoner for who she truly was, his sister.

"Yes," he answered.

"I had gotten all my memories back," she stated, "including the ones from my time as a child, living in the remote north of Vasara, with my mother, the faerie princess Luel, and my father, the wizard Redlin."

"So Mom is a faerie princess," Andy said rubbing his forehead. "Why didn't you tell us any of this?" he asked his father.

"I think it would be best if I tell you the story from the beginning," Redlin said.

"Oh boy!" Abby said rubbing her hands together in anticipation.

"Why are you all excited?" Andy asked her.

"Because, no one in all of Vasara knows what happened to the mighty Redlin," she smiled with mirth.

"I'm not sure I would use the accolade of mighty, but thank you, Abby," Redlin smiled.

Andy watched as his father ran his fingers through his hair, thinking of where to begin. "Just before Devon seized power, the god Trystan told me to take your mother above Lake Pleasant to the foothills of the Macedon Mountains."

"I thought the gods left long before Devon came to power?" Abby asked puzzled.

"They did, but I am able to communicate with Trystan through this." He held up the medallion he showed to Andy.

Andy had not told his father of his own medallion, but upon seeing Redlin's, Emilia jumped up in surprise.

"Why, that is just like ours," she exclaimed.

"What are you talking about?" the wizard asked sharply.

Emilia took out her own medallion and showed her father the image of the white swan. Andy figured he'd better follow suit and withdrew his own, the black pyramid with lightning bolts emanating from it.

"How is it that you have these," Redlin said recognizing them immediately.

They told their father the story that Paolo had relayed to them. How a Queen of Vasara had been carrying twins and was killed in order to have both her babies brought out at the same time, creating two bloodlines, since they both shared the title of the eldest child and heir.

The King and his eldest have the ability to open the crypt where the medallions had lain. Paolo had given Andy and Emilia the medallions, so they would take them out of that world, denying their capture by that other bloodline. The power of a god and goddess resided in them.

After their story was done, Redlin told them how Trystan had made his medallion at the same time he crafted the others, the god pouring a small portion of his own power into it.

"This tale really begins with me and your mother. Maybe it is best I start there instead."

Redlin told them of how he and Luel had been friends since forever. Whenever he was in Laurel Hollow they would take long walks through the talon woods. But then he would have to leave, because he belonged to all of Vasara, and not just the kingdom of the faeries.

"Luel hated the time between visits," their father told them.

"Why didn't she travel with you?" Abby asked.

"Because she was a faerie princess and felt obligated to remain."

"I remember the portrait in Valencia's study," Emilia remarked. "Although at the time I didn't realize it was her. In the painting she smiled, but it was not reflected in her eyes."

"Her nobility weighed heavily on her," Redlin continued, "but in the end, a disquiet in her soul caused her to leave Laurel Hollow."

He paused as an owl's screech cut the air. Andy watched it alight on the top of the turret, slowly scanning the ground for prey. His father took up the narrative once more.

"What happened when Luel left Laurel Hollow?" Abby asked.

"She disappeared for almost a hundred years."

"I never knew that," Emilia exclaimed. "Where did she go?"

"I don't know," the wizard said soberly. "And she told me to never ask."

"Our family is full of secrets," Andy said.

"I believe the time of secrets will soon be coming to an end," he said putting a firm hand on Andy's back. "But you must understand that any secret, knowing or unknowing, was necessary."

"When did Luel find you again?" Abby asked, trying to get the story moving along.

"I was coming out of the Border Lands when she met me on the road outside the guard station. I remember being so taken aback from not seeing her for so long that when she all of a sudden appeared in front of me I couldn't speak for a few moments. On her head was a thin gold crown with a blue ice crystal embedded in the center. Once I found my voice, I asked her where she had gotten it. Again, she would not tell me. I have not seen the crown since that day."

"Was I born shortly after that?" Emilia asked.

"About ten years later. After Trystan told me to take your mother and disappear into the mountains. He told me not to contact Devon or Loki. The god must have known something was afoot."

He paused and looked skyward, as if speaking of his brothers stirred old memories. Andy thought he saw regret and loss play across his father's face.

"That was why I had no immunity to skull spiders," Emilia said. "I was born in the mountains and lived there until we left."

"What is that about skull spiders?" Redlin asked.

11

Emilia told her father of her trip through the Parma Wilds, and two days out of it had taken on a burning fever that almost consumed her body. Most faeries are immune to skull spider venom because they are usually bitten as children and their bodies are able to handle it.

"Sweetheart, I am so sorry," her father said with tears standing in his eyes thinking of the pain and almost near death experience of his only daughter.

"It's okay Dad, Braylynn was looking out for me," she smiled.

"What happened after you vanished into the mountains?" Abby asked.

"We stayed there until shortly after Devon had murdered the king and queen. I then went looking for Kendra, a healer and Rafael's priestess at the time. I charged her and every successor after her to watch and protect Taiyo's descendants, for they would be the rightful rulers of Vasara. We then left Vasara through a door built into the mountainside near where we were living, and arrived at these very ruins."

"That must have been quite a shock," Andy remarked.

"At the time I thought so, but now that you are back it is an even bigger shock to learn fifteen hundred years has passed in Vasara."

"What do you mean?" Emilia said.

"Devon's murder and betrayal is only sixteen years passed for me. That is barely a wink for someone who has lived several thousand years."

"It shouldn't be that much of a shock," Abby said pushing a lock of hair behind her ear.

"Why do you say that?" Andy asked her.

"Because your father wrote about it here," she said as she pulled a book out of the satchel she had brought from Vasara.

Andy read the title. "Parallel Worlds by Wizard Redlin."

"Lyson let me take that when we first went to his house."

"May I see that?" the wizard asked. Abby passed the book over to him. Redlin ran his fingers over the binding, as if seeing an old friend with his eyes and hands.

"It was a long time ago that I wrote this, and most of it was just theory."

"Yes, but the part that I believe you got right was that the time between worlds run totally independent of each other."

"What does that mean?" Emilia asked.

"That sixteen years here does not necessarily equal fifteen hundred years in Vasara," her father responded. "Because it happened in this case does not mean that it always will. The way time runs in Vasara with respect to other worlds I believe has a great deal to do with the needs of the living prophecy than anything else."

"So if we ever went back any amount of time could have passed, or none at all. Is that what you're saying?" Andy said.

"Exactly."

Something else had been bothering Andy, and he felt now might be a good time to bring it up.

"Dad, did you know I was a dragon?"

"No. Daughters of a faerie are faerie, sons are human. I didn't know until I saw you wearing the clothes of a dragon in human form."

"That is something I have been struggling with," Andy said. "How is it possible that a faerie and dragon are brother and sister?"

"I don't know. Loki is the master of dragon lore, I'm sure he would have a theory."

"When I first met him, he did say my spirit had to have been created in Vasara."

Redlin seemed to ponder that for a moment. "He might be

13

on to something. I always thought it odd that there were only nine dragons. Not very symmetrical if you know what I mean." He looked over at his son. "Maybe there were always ten."

"What do you mean?" Emilia asked.

"I think Loki is right. Andy's dragon spirit was created in Vasara, but I think the prophecy decided how he would come into the world. It would be the only way you two could share that special Summoner and dragon bond."

"My legs are starting to cramp," Andy stated. "I'm going to walk around for a little bit."

"All right," his father said looking at his son with some concern.

Andy's legs weren't really hurting that badly, but he felt he needed to take a break and let his mind rest a little. He was getting a serious headache between his eyes from all these revelations. Walking up the trail and passing the house, he found a small clearing with an unobstructed view of the river. Andy sensed the presence he knew would be coming.

"Are you all right Andros?" Abby said reaching him and encircling his waist with her arm.

"I'm okay, I just needed to walk away for a moment to regroup." Andy could feel Abby's happiness and positive energy flowing from her being. He was amazed by it, far different from his own reaction when landing in a foreign world. "How are you, now that you are here?"

"Well, I haven't really seen anything yet but this island," she replied. "But the fact that we are here together makes me feel very content. And your father seems like a great man."

Andy had to chuckle. "I have a feeling that you know more about him then I do."

Abby looked at him with a serious expression. "Listen to me. I only know the history of the wizard Redlin. I know nothing about the father of Andros."

Andy thought hard on that statement. It was true. There was not a person alive or dead in either world who knew what it was like to be Redlin's son. That history, that part of the man belonged to Andy alone. He smiled thinking what a wonderful young woman he had come to love. She could see right through to his heart on just about any matter.

"What of your own father?" Andy asked her. "We really have only spoken of how he died. What do you think he would say about you being here?"

Abby's eyes took on a hurt look for a moment, thinking of her father always did this to her. But then she smiled.

"He would say 'You go Abby, and live the adventure of a lifetime!'"

"I'll bet your dad was a really cool guy."

Abby looked at him quizzically. "I'm not exactly sure what that means, but he was very special. He was a scholar, but he was also in tune with all things around him. He used to tell me that books and nature had a certain harmony with each other. Words have a living force of their own and will sometimes combine with the physical world to make wonderful things happen."

Andy could see Abby's eyes sparkle as she told the story of the man, her father.

"You could say he was almost a wizard. And I loved him more than anything." A couple of tears came out of the corner of her eyes and slid down her cheek.

Andy gently wiped her tears with the back of his fingers and cupped her face with both hands as he kissed her lips.

"Do you think your mother will like me?" Abby asked.

"Are you kidding? She'll adore you."

"I hope you are right. What is she like?"

Andy thought for a moment before responding.

"She's very smart. She taught literature at the high school

before leaving academic life to do community work. My mom really likes helping whomever she can."

"Sounds like a very giving person," Abby said. "How were your parents able to learn the ways of this foreign world so quickly?"

"I'm sure my dad cheated with some magic," Andy replied smiling. It felt good to smile he thought. And to also be resolved in whom his father really was.

Abby had turned away from Andy to look south toward the hills of West Point Military Academy. The moon had risen over the mountain and cast a silver glow across the valley. The illumination was enough that Andy could see the head of the dragon mark peeking out above the top of Abby's dress. His body still felt a surge of anger when he thought of Tolbert pushing the hot branding iron onto Abby's skin, all because she would not marry him.

He started to trace the outline with his finger. At his touch, Abby turned and smiled at him.

"There are healers in this world who could fix this."

"No!" she said with vehemence.

Andy was so startled by her outburst that he stared at her wide-eyed.

"I'm sorry," he stammered. "I just thought…"

"Forgive me," Abby said touching a hand to his cheek. She looked down for a moment choosing her words. The crickets in the brush by the river seemed very loud in the pause before she spoke.

"When Tolbert first gave me this mark it made me feel ugly. I hated it. I cursed the gods who allowed such a thing to happen. But time does heal all wounds, physical and spiritual. It was an evil act of an evil man, and the gods had nothing to do with it. I can't say I was ever actually fond of it, but I no longer loathed it." Abby paused for a moment and took Andy's face in both her hands smiling.

"But then something wonderful happened," she continued. "There has always been a feeling of stiffness where the mark is, but after the first time I saw you, it went away. The only times that the stiffness returns is when you walk the forest paths to the source of your power."

"What does that mean?" Andy asked scratching his head.

"You blockhead, don't you get it. We share a connection through this mark. As long as I feel no pain, I know you are alive."

"And if you feel the stiffness, I'm at the source?"

"Or dead," she said soberly.

"Well I certainly hope that is never the case."

"Hey, you two coming back?" Redlin called.

Abby and Andy walked back to the fire.

"Dad, there is something I wanted to ask you," Andy said.

"Ask away, as I said, secrets are over."

"Did you know the other dragons?"

Redlin's mouth was slightly open as if he suddenly realized something.

"I had forgotten all about that. They are your brothers."

"That is what Loki told me. Nearly knocked me off my feet when I found out I had nine brothers."

"By the gods!" Redlin exclaimed.

"What is it?" Emilia asked concerned.

Redlin looked at his daughter. "It just dawned on me. The dragons are equal, one to another, but there is a kind of hierarchy. It has to do with the first letter of each dragon's name. The dragon with the letter closest to the beginning of the alphabet is the leader. That was Brion"

"Was?" Abby said.

Redlin looked at his son. "The chief dragon is Andy now, or Andros as is his true name."

"That's why Braylynn said I would be chief among them," Andy exclaimed. "And the thing about the alphabet brings up something else that has been puzzling me. Why do we have the same language here as they do in Vasara?"

"Abby?" Redlin said directing the question to her with a self-satisfied smirk on his face. Andy thought his father looked just like Loki right before the wizard believed he was about to dazzle everyone with his brilliance.

"Well, according to the mighty Redlin," Abby said playing to the wizard's vanity, "in his book of 'Parallel Worlds', he fosters the theory that worlds that touch, suffer what is known as 'the bleed through effect', which means cultural aspects will tend to overlap."

"What are the other dragon's names?" Emilia asked. "Even with my memory loss, my powers as Dragon Summoner allowed me to 'feel' Andy's name. I could sense no others though."

"Not surprising," Redlin said. "Wherever Devon sent them, I doubt you would be able to make contact. He would have made sure of that. Although Zana killed Layla, the Summoner at the time, Devon was not sure that Braylynn wouldn't anoint another faerie to be her Dragon Summoner."

"Loki told me the dragon names," Andy said. "But he never mentioned this leadership order."

"I'm sure he figured you had enough things on your mind without having the added responsibility of being the chief dragon," Abby chimed in.

"Their names," Andy began, "are Brion, Caleb, Daragh, Elek, Finn, Gael, Herve, Irwyn and Jace. It's funny, I have no idea what they look like, but when Loki told me what they were called, their names seemed as familiar as my own."

"Well, as to their appearance," Redlin added, "I can tell you their dragon colors."

"They are not all black, like Andy?" Emilia asked.

"No. Brion, Caleb and Daragh are red, Elek, Finn and Gael are gold and Herve, Irwyn and Jace are silver."

"And chief among them is Andros the Black," Abby said using the name given to Andy by the Viper captain, Tori.

Andy turned sad eyes on Abby thinking of his friends he left behind, wondering if he would ever see them again. He looked toward the east shore of the river.

"Dad, let's go home."

"Sure," his father said with understanding. "The boat is over here."

They put the fire out and in a few minutes found themselves walking up to the lighted house on the hill. The door stood open and Andy could see the silhouette of his mother in the doorway to welcome them home.

***

The moon, or rather what he called a moon, cast a sickly glow on the dark water. A young man in clothes like dragon scales stood on the rocky shore of the lake's only island. A scraping noise of talons against stone made him turn. Brion looked to see the red dragon form of his brother Caleb.

"He must be wrestling with his dreams again," Brion said to himself.

Seven other dragons lay sleeping in various spots throughout the island. They slept from an enchantment placed on them by Brion himself. It was one of the last bits of magic he could wield before being totally cutoff from the source. He didn't know how long Devon would imprison them here, but he was pretty sure his brothers would starve to death long before any help came.

Brion had a gift that did not require contact with the source.

The gods had given it to him at the moment of his creation. All dragons had a gift that was their own. Brion's was the ability to go a thousand years without food. He knew that time had long since come and gone. Starvation had started to settle in, and he felt weaker with the passage of time. Should he succumb, there would be no one to wake his brothers, and one by one, they would die.

There was a shield of power surrounding the island, preventing the dragons from flying out. On the shore he could see nine hooded figures. Brion could not tell if they were men from this distance. There used to be ten, but one had disappeared not too long ago.

The only other thing discernible was the faint odor of sulfur brought to him on the errant breeze.

Chapter 2

Andy and his father had been sitting at the kitchen table as the morning sunlight poured through the window. Two years had gone by since arriving back from Vasara. Andy and Abby were set to graduate high school in a few days' time. Abby, with a little help from Redlin, was brought up to speed on the academics of this world. The former library curator was a born intellect, and she soaked up the information like a sponge.

"How did this happen?" Redlin asked his son.

"I don't know. It may have been building up and I just never noticed. What are we going to do?" Andy said scratching his head.

"Abby's her own person my boy, if she chooses the dark path there is nothing either one of us can do."

"I was supposed to protect her Dad. I've failed."

Just then the object of their conversation came striding into the room. Abby was wearing jeans with a white short-sleeve button down shirt. The shirt-tail was pulled out and the two top buttons were unfastened. Her brown hair was loose and spread out on her shoulders. Andy still thought she looked like a pirate when she dressed this way.

But it was what adorned the top of her head that had prompted the early morning discussion. Sitting above that lovely face was a baseball cap with the logo of the Boston Red Sox affixed to it.

"I could hear you two in the living room," Abby said placing her hands on her hips. "You Yankee wimps need to get used to the idea that this is not just a one ball club home anymore."

Andy and Redlin cast sidelong glances at each other, not saying a word lest they unleash a tongue lashing from this Dragonsgate scholar.

"Well?" Abby said raising one eyebrow.

"Nothing," Andy said shaking his head quickly before he said something he would regret.

Abby started to turn and walk back into the living room. She paused, looked back and leveled a gaze at Redlin.

"I have been reading master wizard that the Sox were once under a hundred-year curse. You wouldn't possibly have had anything to do with that would you?"

"Abby! I'm shocked that you would even suggest that. Besides, that curse was in place long before I ever got here."

Abby, feeling she had tormented them enough gave them a winsome smile and glided out of the kitchen.

"That smile of hers is deadly," Andy remarked.

"That it is. I think if she wanted, we would be converted to Red Sox fans on the spot, and we would be powerless to stop her."

All of a sudden there came a rich musical laugh from a side room.

"Luel, not so loud, she'll hear you, and that will only encourage her."

Andy's mother came walking in suppressing her mirth, but not very well.

"You are too much, the both of you."

"I'm sure I don't know what you're talking about," the wizard replied haughtily.

"You take this baseball thing way too seriously. Eighteen years ago you never even heard of baseball."

"Well I…" Redlin sputtered.

Andy smiled as his mother and father bantered back and forth. It was good to be home. When they arrived at the front door two years ago, Luel gave her son and daughter such fierce hugs that Andy felt they would never be allowed out of the house for the remainder of their days on earth.

Andy thought back to that night. He remembered the image of his mother vividly. Luel had been standing framed in the doorway. Her brown hair cascading down her back the way Emilia's did. His mother was the smallest in the family. It was from his mother's side that Andy received his hawk-like hazel eyes, for hers' were identical, and she would almost float the way Emilia did when she walked. He could easily imagine her with wings and pointed ears.

He told his mother everything that night and into the predawn hours. Luel just adored Abby, and was overjoyed at their love for each other. She had kissed Abby and gave her a faerie blessing, much to Andy's delight. That was one meeting he had dreaded. How do you tell your mother you had fallen in love with someone from another world? But as it turned out, Andy was really the one from another world.

"Mom, what happened?" Andy had asked her that night.

"What do you mean?" Luel replied in her sing-song voice.

"I mean everything."

Luel had been wiping the counter after making a sandwich for her son, and then paused in mid-wipe.

"I think everything would take a long time to tell," she said continuing her cleaning.

"How about some highlights?"

Luel smiled at her son and went over to sit in a chair at the table.

"What would you like to know?"

"Well, for starters, what about my grandparents."

Luel's eyes took on a fearful look.

"Why do you ask about them?" she said with dread.

"I know you told me they died, and maybe they have, but

23

not here. Mom, I know you and Dad felt you had to lie to protect us, but there is a big hole inside of me wondering who I am and where I came from."

Andy's mother was silent for the longest time that he wondered if she would even answer.

"Of all the questions you would ask, it would be that one."

"I'm sorry," Andy said. "You don't have to tell me if there is too much pain."

"No, I believe it is time I got this out in the open. Let's go find the others, they should hear it as well."

Andy and his mother made their way to the backyard, where set off by the edge of the grass and at the top of a slight incline stood an open air gazebo. In the center of the gazebo was a fire bowl with several leather high back chairs situated around it. A little table was off to the side with various forms of food and drink.

Redlin, Emilia and Abby were sitting with their feet propped up and staring at the fire with a drink in hand. Redlin was smoking a pipe not unlike the ones Andy used to see Loki use. Redlin turned his head to see Luel and Andy's approach.

"Come sit and enjoy the fire dear," Redlin called to his wife.

Andy could tell his father suspected something was wrong by the way his eyes narrowed as they stepped into the gazebo.

"What's wrong Luel?" the wizard asked with concern.

"Your son is asking after his grandparents," she replied.

"Oh," he said with understanding. "This is that subject you've asked never to be questioned about isn't it?"

Luel nodded.

"But I think you all should know now. And with everyone I love here, I believe I can bear it."

Luel sat down in the chair her husband offered while he fetched a folding chair for himself. Emilia had poured her mother some wine and Luel swirled it around in her glass as she looked into the fire as she thought of where to begin. Andy wondered if he wasn't pushing too hard, having his mother reveal something that obviously had caused her a great deal of sorrow.

"My mom was my best friend," she began, "We would do so much together. One time, my mother and I ventured into the Parma Wilds looking for a rare herb. She worked closely with the healers, and was always on the lookout for any new plant or root that might have healing properties."

"What was her name?" Abby asked.

"Brya," Luel replied. "Searching for days, we finally found it. We were on our way back when a band of Alfar attacked us." Andy remembered the story his sister told of her own encounter with the Alfar, wild wood elves seeming no bigger than a child but lithe and extremely fast. They made their home in the heart of the Parma Wilds, protecting their territory fiercely with their bows and poison arrows.

"Oh my!" Abby exclaimed.

"What happened Mom?" Andy asked

"My mother took a poisoned arrow in the chest protecting me as we began to fly out. I started to go after her as she fell, but she yelled at me to flee. I could see the beasts swarm over her as she hit the ground."

Andy watched as his mother's eyes burned with hatred for the Alfar. He believed if one stood in their presence with Luel holding a talon dagger, that Alfar would be shrieking from the sudden loss of its skin.

Emilia had come over and put an arm around her mother. "I'm sorry Mom," she said with great sympathy.

Luel patted her hand. "It's all right dear, she's in Braylynn's paradise now."

"How did your father react," Andy asked her.

Luel's face took on a despairing look.

"Sweetheart, you don't have to tell us," Redlin said seeing the anguish written all over his wife's face.

"No, I want to tell it and be done." She took a moment to compose herself and then began. "His name was Eriyn," she said for Abby. "He was a Border Lands blacksmith. As a matter of fact, Eriyn was the chief blacksmith and the best the Border Lands had seen in a thousand years, and more than that he was an artisan. He could work his hands on any raw material. He adored my mother, and would fashion all kinds of jewelry for her out of the most precious gems. This was one of them."

Luel pulled up her pant leg to reveal a golden anklet, but instead of the common chain link, the anklet was formed by swans in flight, touching wingtip to wingtip. The detail on the miniature birds was remarkable.

"That is the most beautiful thing I have ever seen," Abby exclaimed.

"It is beautiful, but it is only a shadow of what he could create. The weapons he made were not only ornamental, but deadly and without peer, which made him sought after throughout all of Vasara. It was for my mother that he created his greatest works. He once told me she was the reason he drew breath."

"It sounds like he loved her more than life," Andy commented.

"Yes, and it proved his undoing."

"What do you mean, Mom?" Emilia asked.

"When I returned, Braylynn and I told him what had happened. His eyes went vacant, and he stared at nothing for the longest time as if he had fallen into a trance. Then his head turned slowly and his eyes focused on me."

"You killed her!" he shrieked at me. "It is your fault she's dead!"

"Braylynn tried to reason with him, but in the end he cursed her. He told her what good was a goddess that couldn't even protect her own people. My father snatched up his sword of godstone and ran screaming my mother's name into the Wilds. Grief stricken and without hope I thought that would be the last time I would ever see him."

Luel stopped as she looked over at her husband. Tears rolled down his stubble cheeks. Andy could see some shell had broken in his mother as his father came over and knelt next to her. She wrapped her arms around him and let the sobs come.

"No matter what he said, it was not your fault Luel," he could hear his father whisper, soothing her. Andy understood. His mother had blamed herself for her own mother's death and had carried that guilt around for the gods knew how long.

It was awhile before anyone spoke. Luel's tears were spent and had laid her head on Redlin's shoulder as she watched the flames of the fire dance. The last statement of his mother's made Andy wonder about what happened to his grandfather.

"You said when your father left that you 'thought' that would be the last time you saw him."

His mother looked over at him and the determination to finish it came into her eyes.

"Yes, unfortunately the tale did not end that day. And it got worse."

Luel told them how rumors had been coming out of Parma of what people were calling an avenging shade. For several years Alfar would turn up dead along some game trail.

"Your father?" Emilia asked.

"I believed so, but I never went to investigate. Then all of a sudden, the killings stopped and all was quiet for hundreds of years. My father being mortal, I assumed he had died."

"He lived on, didn't he," Abby guessed.

Luel nodded in affirmation.

"At first I did not think it to be him, but Alfar started turning up dead again. Only this time they were killed in a very brutal and ritualistic manner, almost as if someone were using the bodies in some kind of magical spell."

"I'm not sure I want to know what happened next," Andy said with dread.

"Well, whatever you're guessing, it's much worse."

Luel launched into the account of how she left Laurel Hollow to try to learn what she could of these strange events. She was restless at home, and with Redlin out in the world, Laurel Hollow was turning into a prison for her. She threaded her way into Parma, avoiding as many confrontations as she could.

"You must have been very brave to enter Parma alone," Abby said.

"I am not totally defenseless Abby. I have a certain gift that offers me protection, of a sort."

"What gift is that?" Andy asked.

"I remember!" Emilia exclaimed. "I hadn't been thinking about it, but it came to me just now, color."

"Color?" Andy said clearly puzzled scratching his sandy brown hair.

"Yes," his mother went on to explain. "I can change the hue of my skin and hair to any color I want, my wings as well."

"Wow," Abby said, "kind of like a rock salamander."

"What is that?" Andy said.

"Like a chameleon," Redlin answered.

"Oh," Andy said understanding. "And this allowed you to slip through the Wilds almost invisible."

"Exactly," Luel responded. "But the Alfar have keen eyesight, and they are not fooled for long. Many times I stood absolutely still, blended into my surroundings as a troop of Alfar passed right by me, only to have a poison arrow come flying back a minute later. I spent many years in the Wilds. Sometimes Pan would come across my path and help me search for a while. I even ran into Diminitus a couple of times, but he was in such a cranky mood that he wasn't much help."

Emilia burst out laughing at that. "That sounds like him alright. But he was invaluable when he traveled with me."

"I always believed that gruff exterior was more for show than anything else," Luel said.

Andy felt old friends popping into his head as his mother's tale unfolded. Pan, the king of the fauns, and Diminitus, the seemingly mortal man who lived forever in the Parma Wilds which normally was home to the magical creatures of Vasara. Both had been instrumental in his quest to defeat the wizard Devon.

"So did you keep searching, or give up?" Andy asked.

"I was about to leave the Wilds and go find the mighty Redlin," she said smiling at her husband.

"Since you didn't find me, I'm guessing this is when you disappeared for a hundred years."

She nodded, affirming that his guess was correct.

"Braylynn visited me in my dreams that night when I was set to leave Parma. In her cryptic way she told me what I sought was in the sacred mound of the Alfar, which of course was in the heart of their territory."

Luel told them of the weeks she played cat and mouse with the Alfar in order to lure them away from the mound. She explained how she finally deemed the time to be right as she turned her flesh the color of sky and clouds and flew for the opening that was the mound's entrance.

"Once inside, there was no light of any kind. Even the natural sunlight seemed to die at the mound's mouth." Luel turned toward Redlin. "I need to ask something of you, husband."

"Anything," he responded without hesitation.

"Can you use your medallion and make my thoughts and memories appear in the flames? It would be easier in the telling I believe."

"Give me your hand love."

Redlin pulled out his medallion from the god Trystan, and holding his wife's hand concentrated on the fire. The flames grew higher and coalesced as if they encircled a beach ball. Soon images of an opening in a hillside started to appear. Everyone could see, hear and feel everything Luel was doing, as if they were living her ordeal through her eyes.

***

The darkness was absolute. Luel could not even see her hand in front of her face. She was in an entryway of sorts. The height of the ceiling could only be guessed at. Taking her spear off her arm, she extended it and thrust above her head, but it met with no obstruction. Luel felt for one wall than paced off the distance to the other; ten paces. She had room to move, and fly if necessary, although she wouldn't attempt that except in extreme need. Flying, without being able to see, was the easiest way a faerie could kill herself.

She started walking. How long, she could not tell. It may have been days or it could have been years. There was no sense of time there.

On three occasions the floor disappeared from beneath her feet. With wings outstretched she would descend for hours. After her last descent she could see pinpoints of light up ahead. Upon exiting what she had come to call the 'tunnel', Luel was standing on a precipice. The sight that greeted her eyes nearly brought her to her knees.

"By the gods!"

What she saw was neither land nor sea, but a vast expanse of stars. She saw entire universes, planets, and streaking comets. The immensity of it made her feel insignificant and small. Many worlds were here, and only the gods knew what kind of life may be on them. As she stood staring, a golden disc big enough for a person to stand on came floating toward her. Something stirred in her breast, telling her it was all right to step out.

She tentatively stretched a foot across the space between the precipice and the disc. When her foot made contact, she pushed on it to make sure it was stable and would not flip, dumping her into oblivion. She brought her other foot to rest next to its mate and the disc proceeded to glide through what she assumed to be the heavens. Again, time had no meaning, and she had no idea how long she traveled. She started to come into a patch of blackness. Her pointed ears listened for any errant sounds.

Silence.

She came to a stop next to a roughhewn cave mouth. Torches were embedded into the rock on either side of the lichen covered entrance. Luel approached with stealth. She was about to open her spear to be ready for anything, when a voice in her head whispered, "Not yet."

Her brow furrowed in puzzlement, but she heeded the voice and pulled her talon dagger instead. Luel's body and wings took on the color of the cold rock as she moved forward, deeper into the cave. Every hundred yards or so there was a torch burning, dimly illuminating the path she was traveling. It wasn't before too long that she came upon the last thing she would have expected in a cave, a wooden door. Symbols and swirls were carved into its surface. She had seen markings like this before and her heart sank. Luel could recognize the artistry of her father anywhere, and she knew without a doubt that he had made it. She also knew the key to open it. Her father had taught her the pattern long ago. Tracing the design in the proper order she then pushed and the door opened.

Sunlight greeted her eyes as she looked out onto a lush green valley. In the center was a small lake with a house made entirely of black stone situated on the water's edge. Attached to the house by a breezeway was a workshop and forge. She saw no movement anywhere. Turning the color of grass, she skimmed the ground as she glided up to the side of the house.

She could hear the sound of a hammer striking an anvil. She pressed herself against the stone and took on the hue of obsidian. Being nearly invisible she slowly approached the opening to the forge and peered in. Her worst fears were realized. She saw the familiar form of her father as his muscled arm rained down heavy strokes onto a piece of steel.

As if sensing someone watching him, Luel's father halted in mid-swing and quickly turned his head toward the door. Luel ducked back, but not before noticing that the eyes that peered back at her were the color of night.

The hammering resumed again. After a few minutes, Luel risked another look. To her astonishment the hammer was floating in mid-air as it descended without the aid of the human arm that had wielded it only a moment ago.

Quick as a flash, a thickly-muscled arm slammed into her head and dazed her. Then a hand, with a grip like a vice encircled her neck and lifted her off of the ground. She made gurgling sounds in her throat as she struggled for breath. Her head started to clear somewhat, and she could make out the features of this man she once called father. Aside from the black eyes, his face was hard and angular. Eriyn's mouth was drawn in a thin line, and his brow was furrowed in a menacing scowl. She caught a faint whiff of sulfur on his breath. Recognition seemed to slowly dawn on him as he released her, allowing her to fall to the ground.

Luel gasped for as much air as she could get into her lungs.

"Why are you here?" Eriyn said, his voice carrying the echo's of the dark hereafter.

"Father...," she started to sputter.

"Do not call me that!" He screamed insanely. "Wife killer!"

She had finally gotten her breath back, just in time for his words to make a deeper cut into an already open wound in her heart. Tears slid down her cheeks as she looked up at him.

"What are you doing here?" she asked.

"I will make them pay," he started muttering. "I will make them all pay. That goddess will be made to suffer, and before I kill her, I will make her restore Brya to me."

Luel could tell her father was insane. But there was something more. The odor of sulfur led her to believe that Eriyn had made a pact with a demon in exchange for power.

"You need to come back with me," she said poised to defend herself lest her father strike out at her for commanding him so. Instead, he started to cackle.

"You think you have the strength to do it?" he said getting his mirth under control. "I think you should see something."

He started to float into the air. Luel watched with open mouth as he slowly turned with upturned palms. Lightning split the air as it shot out of his hands and streaked across the sky. It was then that she realized a demon lord possessed her father's body.

She started to slowly back away. Luel knew she was no match for a demon lord and tried to make good her escape. She hadn't gotten far when a circle of fire erupted all around her.

"Where do you think you're going?" Eriyn's voice boomed as he descended to where Luel stood watching him. She tried to plead with him.

"Father, please! You need help. Let me help you."

"Ha! I have new friends now. I do not need or want your help. Do you know where you are?"

She stared at him blankly.

"That is the forge of Trystan!" Eriyn said triumphantly pointing back toward the building in which he labored. "I forge new weapons now. Talisman's of power to challenge the gods themselves. I shall be a god!"

Luel knew she had to flee and warn Braylynn. She launched herself straight up, but her father, anticipating she might try something like this quickly reached out a hand and grabbed her by one of her wings. He yanked, and with the might of a demon lord to aid him, the wing made a ripping sound like a sheet torn in two as it separated from her body.

Luel let out a skin-crawling wail, the like of which was never heard from a faerie. Her body crashed to the ground and set off sparks in her head as the blood pooled around her. She tried desperately to stand before he killed her, pushing up with her hands only to have them slide in the blood soaked grass. She looked over her shoulder to see her father standing above her. His brow seemed to alternate between an expression of puzzlement to one of extreme hate, as if two forces battled within him. His hand would slowly rise like he was about to perform some action, but then would lower back down to his side. Luel was feeling weaker and she fought to stay conscious.

"Father…"

Something in that plea made his head jerk slightly, and quickly, before that other being within him took control, he pressed a burning hand onto his daughter's open wound, cauterizing it.

"Ahh!" Luel cried out in pain.

The blood flow had stopped, but the demon had the upper hand once again. Unsheathing the sword at his side Eriyn raised it high, intending to lop her head off.

Now, a voice in Luel's mind whispered. She knew what it meant. Snatching the spear off her arm, she pointed at her father's chest, and lifting it as high as she could, pushed the spot that would make it extend. Now a normal talon spear would be little use against a demon lord, and would have a difficult time penetrating any chain mail her father would have made. But this was not a talon spear. Eriyn had made this spear for his daughter. Mixing godstone and a rare rock he discovered called moonstone, for he believed it fell from the sky ages ago, he melted them together to make the spear Luel now held. It was the color of silver birch and the points on either end were honed to such a degree that they would slide through any armor defense. Proof of this was the fact that one end of the spear was bloodied and protruding out of her father's back.

Eriyn looked down dumbly at the shaft that had so neatly penetrated his chest and pierced his heart. The sword fell from his grasp to land at his feet, as he fell to his knees. All of a sudden his head snapped back and his mouth opened wide in a silent scream. Issuing from that orifice was a black vapor that rose and was carried away by the breeze. Luel was transfixed as she watched it disappear from sight. A quiet, gentle voice brought her back to the moment at hand.

"Luel," her father said weakly.

She looked at his face and could see that his eyes were no longer black, but the warm brown color she remembered from her youth.

"Father! Father, I'm sorry. What have I done?" She grabbed the spear and was about to pull it out.

"No!" Eriyn said with what little strength remained to him. "If you pull it out, I will be dead before it leaves my body. I am going to die regardless, but I need to tell you something."

"I have to get you out of here and free of this place."

"You have set me free Luel. That demon and madness are gone." He started to cough. Blood and spittle ran down his chin and onto his chest. "I haven't much time. The demons have a plan...made a pact..." He coughed harder this time. Luel was worried he wouldn't stop. "In the forge...crown...." His chest started making a rattling sound. Eriyn gripped the spear with both hands as his eyes went wide. "Don't...let...." He turned toward his daughter, but Luel didn't think he could see her. "Sorry..."

The life that animated Eriyn's body was gone.

She woodenly stood up and made her way to the forge. Her mind was in total shock, and she was moving on basic instinct alone. Following the last words of her father she walked into the forge and started moving her head left and right. She forgot what she was seeking. Her mind was teetering on the abyss.

A flash of blue caught her eye. She looked more closely and sitting on a wooden dummy head was a gold crown with an ice blue crystal embedded in the center. Luel walked over and thought this must be what she sought. She placed it on her head and then stood with her arms stiff at her sides. Her heart broke, and she slowly sank to her knees and hugged herself, rocking back and forth as the uncontrollable sobs racked her body. She felt totally alone as she closed her eyes and let the grief and darkness take her.

***

Everyone felt sore, numb and tired from having witnessed what Luel had gone through. There was not a single dry eye.

Andy got up and walked over to his mother and hugged her with all the love a son could give. The trials and pains that Andy had endured in his short life were nothing compared to the pains his mother had to overcome. And in spite of all that, life had not left her bitter.

After several minutes in silence, Emilia asked her mother what happened to her afterwards. She told them as far as she knew Braylynn must have gotten her out and had given her a new wing. None of the other gods would have been able to do it.

"What became of that crown?" Abby asked.

"I hid it in Vasara, do not ask me where. What you do not know cannot be forced from you."

"It is powerful then," her husband remarked.

"It is. Although I do not know all it can do, one thing it does is show the wearer visions; past, present and future. The kinds of visions you see depends a lot on the person you are looking at, as well as any possible connections you have to that person." Luel looked sidelong at her husband.

"You saw something about me when I met you outside the Border Lands," Redlin said.

Luel nodded mutely.

"What was it?" Emilia asked.

"Your father's death," Luel replied looking her husband full in the face. "I have not worn it since that day, lest I see the death of others I love."

"Sweetheart, future events can be changed. What you saw was a possible future, that is all."

"That was enough. After that I hid it, before it had a chance to fall in the wrong hands."

***

A snapping in front of his face brought Andy back to the table where he and his father sat. The snapping was his mother's fingers.

"You sleeping?" his mother asked. "I think you were a million miles away just now."

"No, I was just thinking back on the story of your parents."

His mother looked at him with understanding.

"Have you ever been back to that forge?" Andy asked.

"No. I would have to go through the land of the Alfar again, and the goddess willing I will never enter a second time."

Andy had a sinking feeling in the pit of his stomach that Braylynn's will was going to be very different from the wishes of his mother. His experience in Vasara had taught him one thing. If you wanted something to happen, wish for the opposite.

Chapter 3

It was a beautiful spring day at Vassar College. The plant life around the campus was bursting with color. In the courtyard just beyond the main gate, students lounged on the grass or sat on the various benches spread throughout. Some studied for final exams, and others were soaking in the sunshine or lying beneath a shady tree.

One student was sitting on a bench in the corner of the courtyard closest to the library. She sat in the middle of the bench but couldn't get comfortable. A raised plaque fastened to the bench was poking her in the back. Strands of her long black hair kept getting snagged between the wood and the metal. She turned and read the words as she slid down to one end, "Class of 1958, Fortieth Reunion June 7, 1998."

She glanced up at the castle-like structure that is the main library building. Affixed to the walls and attached to the top of the rain downspouts were stone dragons. The girl smiled, thinking how her brother laughed when he first saw them on one of his visits.

"Dragons don't look like that," Andy had said.

Andy should know, Emilia thought. As a matter of fact, she knew dragons quite intimately as well, being the Dragon Summoner of the faeries. She reached behind her head and adjusted the pearl comb Braylynn had given her. Emilia could not transform it into the staff of the goddess, but she always kept it with her.

The term was almost over. She had two more finals this afternoon and one tomorrow. She would just make it in time for Andy and Abby's graduation. They seemed to be destined for each other she thought, smiling to herself. Andy can be a handful, but there were no doubts Abby was up to the task. Her posture took on a melancholy slump whenever her thoughts wandered towards love. She couldn't help thinking of what Lyson might be doing right now. The Border Lands general had worked his way into her heart more than she cared to admit, even to herself.

Emilia let her eyes scan the courtyard. She always found peace here among the various types of trees that populated the space. It was the practice of the graduating class to plant a tree. There were Norway maple and spruce, pin oak, red horsechestnut just to name a few. An enormous London plane tree occupied the center of the yard. Emilia wondered what the view would look like from the top. It was moments like this that made her regret that she could not fly in this world.

As she stared at the uppermost limbs, she thought she caught some movement among the branches. Squirrels she thought. They must've been moving fast because she could see rustling of the leaves half-way down the trunk.

"Oh my!" she gasped.

Several other students who were close by glanced in her direction. She recovered quickly and looked down at her books. Keeping her head lowered but raising her eyes she saw her classmates had gone back to their earlier activities prior to her sudden outburst. What had caused her to be startled was not a squirrel jumping from limb to limb in the big tree but the flash of a human leg peeking out from under a branch.

When she returned her gaze back to the tree, Emilia could no longer detect any movement. Out of the corner of her eye however she saw a flash of silver hair. Then streaking out from the base of the tree on the other side were two girls who seemed to be chasing each other. They circled in and out of the trees in the far corner of the yard. Giggling and laughter came floating back to Emilia. She smiled to hear it. They appeared to be quite young, and Emilia wondered where their parents might be, for all she saw were students like herself.

Just then the taller of the two girls slipped and fell, the other smacked her on the head.

"Catch me if you can!" she shouted as she ran in the opposite direction.

"Tera! That's not fair!"

Emilia's mouth suddenly dropped open at what she had just heard.

"No, that's not possible," she said aloud shaking her head.

The girls were headed her way. The smaller one indeed had silver hair. There was only one child-like person she knew with hair that color, and she was a whole world away. But the name she heard was unmistakable.

"Donella! Help!"

"You can't do that!" the other girl screamed. "She's not part of the game!"

There was no doubt it was Tera, but without her wings and pointed ears. She assumed the other girl was a faerie as well, but Emilia knew they had never met. She was taller than Tera and her hair was brown, coming down just below the shoulders. Her brown eyes were like a deer, soft and reflective of the world around her.

"Tera!" Emilia exclaimed incredulously. "What are you doing here? How did you get here?"

Tera forgot the game and flung herself into Emilia's arms.

"Donella! How have you been? This is a beautiful place. Is

41

this where you live? Where is Andy and Abby? It is so strange to have no wings. How do you stand it?"

Emilia burst out laughing. Tera would never change, thank goodness.

"Slow down sister, who is this with you?"

Emilia cast her glance over to the girl who had been chasing her silver haired sister. Mischief played in her eyes like Tera's, but it was much more planned and calculated, like a chess player always looking three to four moves ahead.

"Oh, this is Emma, my good friend. It was because of her that we were able to get here."

"It is an honor to meet you Summoner," Emma exclaimed excitedly. "Tera has told me all about you, though I must admit some of her stories seemed quite incredible. Did you really fly down Devon's throat and pull his heart out?"

Emilia gave Tera a sidelong glance with one eyebrow raised quizzically.

"We are sisters Emma, please call me Donella, and it didn't exactly happen as Tera says."

"But you have to admit, it sounds more exciting," Tera said smiling.

Emilia still could not believe they were here.

"How is it that we did not meet in Vasara?" she asked Emma.

"I was in the forest archives of Akron," Emma explained. "Akron is an island that is about a day's sailing from the Mistral Islands. Thousands of years of tree lore is stored there." Her eyes sparkled as she said this.

"That is Emma's gift," Tera chimed in, "she can speak to the trees."

"I assume that is what you meant when you said it was because of her that you were able to get here," she said thinking of how they came to be in the tree.

"Exactly!" Tera said jubilantly.

"How do you talk to the trees?" Emilia asked mystified.

"Well, talk is not entirely accurate," Emma replied reaching behind her head to gather her hair up into a ponytail. "I understand their words as they pass from tree to tree, carried on the wind, and I am able to make my thoughts known if I am physically touching them."

"This is all happening so fast. Why are you here?"

"Braylynn sent us," Emma said. "Everyone needs to come to Vasara right away."

"I don't understand," Emilia said with concern.

By now, students that were close to them began to take an interest in their conversation, glancing over with concerned frowns. Emilia could tell these were things best discussed out of earshot.

"Let's walk over by the chapel," Emilia suggested. "There are fewer people."

As they started to walk away, Emma cried out.

"Oh, wait! I almost forgot." She ran back to the London plane tree and hugged the trunk.

"What is she doing?" Emilia asked Tera.

"I'm sure she is thanking the tree for bringing us through."

"You'll have to explain how you did that."

"Better ask Emma, I haven't a clue."

Reaching the chapel, they found a comfortable spot on the grass where no one would hear them. Emma explained that some trees have the ability to let their roots spread across worlds, but only if a tree spirit takes up residence inside.

"In Akron there is a tree very much like this one. Their roots can touch, and at Braylynn's insistence I was able to convince their spirits to give us passage."

"That is truly remarkable," Emilia said astounded.

"Yes, but you should know it only works coming here, not back. We need to find another road to Vasara."

"I imagine we could go by way of the castle, that seems to work both ways."

Emma's head came up. Her eyes took on a distant look as she tilted her head slightly to the right. She seemed to be listening.

"What is it Emma," Emilia said concerned, touching a hand to her shoulder.

"I'm not exactly sure. Just when you mentioned this castle, the trees started humming with agitation, as if something was wrong."

Emilia did not like the sound of that. But the thought of going back to Vasara sent a thrill up her spine. Not just because of Lyson, although that might have been a large part of it, but she longed to see her faerie sisters again. Just seeing Tera brought that hole in her life back to the forefront. She needed to see Braylynn and Leah. She wanted to be back in the house of the Dragon Summoner, and waking the path to the glade where she trained. Above all, she wanted to fly again. Then her face took on a horrified look.

"Donella, what is the matter," Tera asked seeing her expression.

"Tera, how long has it been since we left?"

"Don't worry sister," Tera said knowingly with a smile. "Lyson doesn't have any grey hairs yet. It has only been fifteen years since you walked through the door in the White Castle. Besides, out of all humans, warriors have a much longer life span. Part of Fallon's gift for the job they must do I suppose."

Emilia breathed a sigh of relief. She understands now some of the turmoil Leah went through with Dain before he was chosen to bear the mantle of wizard.

"Oh, that reminds me!" Emma said jumping up and patting herself all over.

"What are you doing?" Tera said.

"Wait...Ah, here it is," Emma said holding up a rolled parchment like a trophy. She held it out to Emilia who took it and looked at the wide band of red ribbon wrapped around the scroll. Recognizing Lyson's crest immediately, she opened the scroll and read his words.

Dearest,

I am giving this to Braylynn in the hopes she may be able to get it to you. The goddess and I have spoken at length. It has been more than a year since I've smelled the sweet fragrance of your hair or gazed into the tranquility of your green eyes. Needless to say beloved, part of my heart left with you when you departed. Braylynn has told me of the time shift between worlds, and that if you should come back, I may have already exited this mortal life. One would think that such a thought would throw a man into despair, but it is hard to be downcast when love fills your heart, and though I may never lay eyes on you again in this world, I shall never love another. Be well my beloved and know your knight awaits you, if not in this life than the next.

Forever yours, Lyson

Emilia stared at the scroll for what seemed like an eternity. She did not want to look away lest the moment be lost. His words had reached across time and worlds and opened a piece of her heart that she had carefully kept guarded. Not allowing true love to take root, because to love at such a depth left one open to vulnerability and possible hurt. But Lyson had shown he would never give her cause for pain. She gave her heart totally in that moment and the tears started to slide down her cheeks to moisten the grass at her feet.

Emilia felt a touch on her shoulder bringing her back. It was Emma. An idea came into Emilia's mind.

"Sister, can your trees take a message back to Vasara?"

"I'm not sure, but if any could, the tree that brought us would be the one to try. What would you like me to say?"

She thought about it. The trees would not be able to speak to him directly so it had to be short and to the point.

"Lyson. Donella. Love."

Emma nodded in understanding and ran to the London plane tree. Emilia did not know if it was possible, or if the trees could make Lyson understand, but she felt she had to try.

When Emma came back, Emilia asked them if they knew why Braylynn wanted them.

"All she said was that it had to do with Andy's brothers," Tera explained.

"The other dragons? I wonder what that could mean?"

"I'm not sure," Emma added, "but she made it sound dire if you did not get back in time."

Emilia felt everything was about to change. She looked back towards the main building and regretted not being able to finish her term, but if Braylynn sent Tera and Emma across worlds, it had to be an emergency. She stood up and gazed once more at the peace and serenity of her college campus, wondering if this was the last time she would look upon it.

"All right, let's go," Emilia said finally.

After a thirty-minute bus ride, the three girls arrived at the house. Luel was out front digging in her flower bed when she saw them. Wiping her hands on her pants she ran to the end of the driveway to greet them.

"Emilia!" Luel exclaimed hugging her daughter. "I thought you were staying on campus until finals were over."

"I was, but there has been a change in plans."

Luel looked past her daughter to the two girls behind her. Seeing her mother's questioning glance, she began the introductions.

"Mom, this is Tera and Emma."

Luel's eyes went wide.

"From Vasara?"

"Yes ma'am," Tera said excitedly. "It is such an honor to meet the mother of the Dragon Summoner, and also the first faerie to ever snare the heart of a wizard."

Luel smiled and hugged Tera. "My daughter has told me a lot about you." She hugged Emma as well and welcomed them both as her faerie sisters.

"Oh, I almost forgot," Emma said patting herself down.

"Not again," Tera exclaimed.

"Ah, here it is." Emma produced a scroll not unlike the one she gave Emilia and handed it over to Luel.

Emilia noted the seal. A faerie in flight, just like the image on the coin Braylynn had given her when they needed to persuade Diminitus to come on their journey to retrieve the vestments of the Dragon Summoner from Zana. Emilia watched as the color drained from her mother's face when she read the words of the goddess.

"Mom, what's wrong?"

Wordlessly, Luel handed her the scroll.

Beloved Daughter,

The realm of the faeries has need of thy royal blood. But I must warn you, the road to Laurel Hollow passes through darkness. Andros and Donella will need your guidance through the mound of your nightmares, and you must once more adorn the crown made by thy father's hand. The brothers of the chief dragon must be rescued soon, lest their spirits pass forever into shadow. Make haste my daughter, make haste.

Love and affection,
Braylynn

Emilia looked up from the scroll. "What does it mean? I only understood parts of it."

Luel had a question of her own that she directed toward Emma and Tera.

"Who rules in Laurel Hollow?"

"There is a small council headed up by Brie to help manage the day to day issues," Tera said, "but no queen."

The conversation she had with Valencia came back to Emilia's mind; "*I do not believe anything will happen to you Valencia, but I think that should the need arise, a successor will be revealed.*" Emilia looked toward her mother. How could she have forgotten.

"I need to speak to your father," Luel said walking back toward the house.

"Will she be alright?" Emma asked.

Emilia watched as her mother walked up the steps, back straight and head erect. "Yes. She may not like it, but my mother will do what she has to, you can count on that."

"Em?"

Emilia turned to look down the driveway to see her brother and Abby approaching. They must have been walking by the river because they were barefoot and their pant legs were rolled up. Andy kept brushing the sandy brown hair out of his eyes. He had been letting it grow longer she noticed. She was about to call out a greeting but Tera went flying down the hill towards them.

"Andy! Abby!" Tera shouted as she bowled into them. Luckily they had just started to walk on the grass when Tera jumped causing all three to wind up in a heap on the lawn.

"Tera, is that really you?" Abby said stunned.

Emilia and Emma, laughing at the sight, walked over to where they were picking themselves up. Seeming like the most natural thing in the world, they all sat down on the grass in a circle as Emilia brought Andy and Abby up to date on what had been happening.

"Loki said I would eventually come back," Andy remarked. "Though I must admit, I was looking forward to receiving my diploma from high school."

"Couldn't we wait a few days?" Abby asked.

"I don't think so," Emma said sympathizing. "Braylynn seemed to impress upon us to leave as soon as we spoke to you."

"Very well," Andy said getting up off the grass. "Let's go see what plan Dad is cooking up."

Their father's plan was simple. Take the boat out to the castle and enter through the portal that had begun all of their adventures.

Everyone climbed into the motor boat Redlin had purchased from their neighbor two summers ago. As they got closer to the island, Emilia noticed the castle had a sickly orange glow.

"Ah!" Emma screamed holding her ears.

"Emma, what is it?" Tera asked frightened for her friend.

"The trees, they are screaming in pain! As if something were sucking the life force out of them."

Just then Emma's eyes rolled up into the back of her head as she slumped unconscious into the bottom of the boat while at the same time every tree on the island exploded in flames.

"Dad, watch out!" Andy yelled as burning timber came hurtling through the sky.

Redlin steered the boat hard away from the island.

"Andy, take the wheel." Redlin raced to the rear of the boat and perched precariously on the back seat. Holding his medallion in one hand, he extended the other and began making circular motions on the air. Eddies of air current started to form into a shimmering dome creating a protective barrier around the watercraft.

"Look!" Luel exclaimed.

Standing on the walls of the crumbling castle were five hooded figures. Their faces could not be seen, but the faint whiff of sulfur was carried on the breeze. They lifted their hands over their heads as fire bolts shot out of their palms.

Beads of sweat poured down Redlin's cheeks as he struggled to remain focused.

"Can't you fire back?" Emilia asked over the din.

"No, the magic of the medallion is limited in this world. Andy, head down river!" the wizard yelled.

Andy steered west to put some distance between themselves and the island before heading south through what was known as the northern gate of the Highlands. As they approached the part of the river known as West Point, the fireballs ceased. And whether they couldn't or chose not to, the hooded figures did not give chase. This was the narrowest part of the river, and the deepest. Andy skimmed across the whitecaps as he steered east to maneuver around the point.

"Pull into the docks by Constitution Island, there is cover, and we will see to Emma," Redlin said.

Constitution Island was a small piece of land once owned by a couple of sisters who used to row their boat to the military academy on the other side of the river to teach religious classes to the cadets. Upon their deaths the land was given to the Academy so the cadets would have a weekend retreat available to them forever. It was quiet, and no one was about as they climbed onto the dock. A small white house was in the distance with gardens leading up to the residence. It was the perfect picture of serenity. Emilia heard chirping noises. She looked up to see a goldfinch perched on the branch of a cherry blossom tree. The bird looked side-longed at the band of travelers. Emilia wished Brie were here, she would know what that bird was thinking.

"What do you think dear?" Luel asked her husband as he leaned over Emma's body.

"I believe she is just stunned. The screams of those trees must have been extreme agony for her to lose consciousness this way." Redlin looked over at his son. "Were those creatures like the one that attacked you in Albion?"

Andy nodded mutely.

Emilia thought back to that time at Bella's inn. She could feel Andy's life ebbing away through the Summoner link as that... thing was choking him. Luckily Tori was there that day to dispatch it. Emilia didn't know if she would had made it in time.

She looked down at Emma and wished she had the use of her staff. Emilia would have been able to heal her in no time. Her father had Emma's head in both of his hands. His face was fixed in concentration. Redlin seemed to be mumbling something, but as Emilia listened more intently she could tell the mumbling were words in a language she had never heard before. As she watched her father's mouth move, it was as if the words became little wisps of vapor floating on the air and descending into Emma's nostrils.

Emma did a sudden sharp intake of air as her eyes sprang open wide, regaining consciousness.

"Emma, are you all right? Speak to me, say something."

Emma stared at Tera as recognition dawned on her. Her eyes were full of tears and with a raw voice tried to explain what she felt through her gift.

"What do we do now?" Andy asked his father.

"We head down river, to Lyndhurst Castle."

"How far is that?" Tera asked as she reached back and tied her silver hair into a ponytail much like Emma's and as is the fashion of faeries as they go into battle.

"About thirty minutes if the water is calm."

"Why Lyndhurst?" Emilia asked her father.

"I will explain when we get there. Right now, we need to get out of here. Are you able to travel Emma?"

"I can make it," Emma told the wizard rubbing her eyes and looking exhausted as if she hadn't slept in a week.

The time down the river seemed to fly. Once past West Point, the water was like glass, not even a ripple. Andy had the throttle full open as they exited the southern gate of the Highlands and the river opened up onto Haverstraw Bay. After going beneath the Tappan Zee Bridge, they found a spot near the shore not too far from where the castle stood. It was dusk, and there didn't seem to be a soul on the grounds. Large weeping willows with sweeping branches dominated the yard. Emma, with dark circles under her eyes and leaning on Andy looked up at the largest tree in the place.

"Andros, take me to that willow over there," Emma said pointing.

Emilia watched as Andy and Emma disappeared from view underneath the branches. A couple of minutes later they emerged and Emma looked rested and refreshed.

"How did you do that?" Emilia asked clearly amazed.

"We have trees like this in some of the more remote areas of Vasara. Emotions run strong in them, all emotions, which gives off a power that I can sometimes tap into for healing. I thought it might be the case with these," she said smiling with the rosiness of her cheeks restored.

"Quickly, let's get inside before someone notices us."

"This castle is not very big," Tera remarked glancing up at the turrets.

"Technically it is a mansion in the design of a castle," Redlin explained. "The stone and marble facade, as well as the inside is faux."

"What does that mean," Tera asked.

"It means fake," Abby said.

"It was the style of the time," Redlin expounded. "Follow me."

Redlin walked up to the outside door that led into an enclosed outer entry to protect people from the elements while they wait for a tour. The wizard gave a twisting motion with his hand and the door's lock gave an audible click. Once inside, they came to the mansion's true outer door. He unlocked this one as well, and they quickly slipped inside. The foyer was not ornate by any means but gave off a classy if somewhat modest signs of wealth. Proceeding forward to the hallway, two head busts stood guard on either side of the entryway to the main hall. Redlin turned right and then immediately left into what looked like a study. The carpet and chairs were a forest green in color which looked striking against the white wall. In the far left corner was a door that Redlin was studying.

"What is so special about that door?" Abby asked.

"Go into the room on the other side of this wall and look," the wizard said.

Tera followed Abby into the next room and looked into the corner to where the other side of the door should have been.

"There is no door on this side!" Tera exclaimed.

"What does it mean?" Emilia asked.

"I remember when I first visited this castle and the guide told me it was a door that led to nowhere. That struck me as very odd. I waited until everyone had moved into another room and snuck back here to run my hands over the door. When I did, visions of Vasara filled my mind. I assumed it was a portal, but I dared not open it lest Devon find his way to this world."

Redlin ran his hand along the outer edges of the door. It was made of a dark reddish wood. Emilia thought the color was akin to the talon trees of Laurel Hollow.

"This is it," Redlin said. He grasped the doorknob and gave a turn. It opened silently, and to everyone's amazement they were greeted by a white wall.

"That's it?" Tera exclaimed expecting something grander. "I am unimpressed master wizard."

Redlin looked side-longed at her and smiled mischievously. Without breaking eye contact he shoved his hand into the wall, setting off a conflagration of color and light. Tera clapped and squealed in delight.

"You and Loki are definitely brothers," Andy said shaking his head. "You both have a flair for the dramatic."

"Follow closely behind me," the wizard said. "I'm not sure where we will come out."

One by one they passed through the door. Emilia stood last, hesitant to pass through. The last time she went into a portal her memory left her, but she knew she had to go, so in she plunged. Her stomach tightened in fear as the world around her went black and she felt herself falling. She thought she heard someone screaming her name as the darkness sucked her down.

Chapter 4

Andy was spitting out sand. After walking through the door he fell face first onto a glaring white sandy beach. The ocean surf came to within four feet of where he lay. He pushed himself up brushing his pants and looking around. Andy did not see the others.

"Mom, Dad?" he called out. He ran down the beach a short distance to some tall rocks that were jutting out of the sand. "Em, Abby?"

Andy started feeling a prickly sensation down the middle of his back. At first it wasn't noticeable, but now if felt like an itch he could not scratch. Then all at once, realization flooded his brain. It was the source. He could touch it, grasp it and wrap himself in it like a blanket. He turned his thoughts inward and saw his dragon form. Pouring himself into it he made the change. Now, standing on the beach where a young man had stood was the enormous form of a black dragon. The angular head, with horned spikes protruding from the brow and sweeping behind, swept back and forth. Huge wings, like sails the color of midnight opened to catch the breeze blowing in over the ocean. The long neck lifted the head higher as the mouth with serrated teeth opened and jets of flame spewed forth.

I can't believe it! Andy exclaimed to himself. *It feels like it has been so long.*

In his excitement he leaped into the air, his powerful wings beating out a rhythm against the wind lifting him higher and higher. He slowly rotated his body, letting the sun warm the scaly hide on his stomach. He righted himself and started scanning the beach. He could see Abby, Tera and his mother about three hundred yards down from where he landed. His father and Emma he spotted climbing over some rocks heading to where the others waited.

Where is Emilia? he thought. Just then out of the air a figure materialized, black hair streaking toward heaven as the body made contact with the water.

Em! Em!

Andy folded his wings along his sides as he plunged to the ocean below. Like a sea serpent, he glided through the water until he came upon Emilia's limp form. Gently grasping her with his claw, trying hard not to cut her wing with a talon, he rushed to the surface then swam for the shore. Once on the beach he changed his form back to human. He stood above Emilia in his black dragon scale clothes, trying to think of what he should do.

"I don't know how to heal with the source," he said aloud.

Luckily he didn't need to. Emilia started coughing, and vomited a half gallon of sea water. It then hit Andy that he just as easily could have used standard CPR.

"Em, are you alright?"

"I will be in a minute," she said coughing, her voice scratchy. "I just hate traveling that way. I hate it!"

She sat up, and for a moment closed her eyes. Andy watched as Emilia slowly raised a hand and ran it along her pointed ear. A tear slid down her cheek as she moved her dark green wings. She reached behind her head and pulled the pearl comb out of her hair. Bringing it in front of her face she concentrated. With a loud snap and flash of bright light, the staff of the goddess was gripped firmly in her hand. Her clothes had changed as well. On her head was the dragon crown, as well as her ring. She also had on the dress of the Dragon Summoner, except it was slightly altered. The sleeves cut off at the shoulder and green leather bands encircled her biceps and forearms. Emilia looked up at her brother.

"We're back," she whispered as if speaking louder would dispel the entire moment as nothing but a dream. Then more loudly she exclaimed, "Andy, we're back!"

She sprang from her sitting position in a flurry of beating wings. Andy watched as she skimmed just above the water at an incredible speed. She then shot straight up, staff held aloft while streams of light shot in all directions.

"Emilia! Come back," her father shouted when he and the others reached the spot where Andy stood.

Emilia came gliding in and lightly touched down on the sand.

"What's wrong Dad?" Andy asked wondering why his father called Emilia back with such urgency.

"We don't know where we are or how the state of affairs stand in Vasara. I just assume we don't announce our presence yet."

Andy couldn't argue with that logic. The others arrived shortly after Emilia had landed.

"What happened to your dress?" Andy asked her. "It didn't look quite like that before."

"I made some alterations," Emilia said. "When I first retrieved the dress from Zana, Layla had told me not to worry about the size, that it would fit no matter what, as long as I was the true Dragon Summoner. So I figured if it could change size, I may be able to make it change in other ways. And I was right. This is much more comfortable," Emilia said holding her arms up and turning as if she were modeling. Andy just shook his head.

"I hope your goddess doesn't have a fit about it," Andy said looking up in the sky just to make sure Braylynn wasn't going to send a lightning bolt down on them.

"What should we do now love," Luel asked her husband.

Andy did a double-take. This was the first time he had seen his mother as a faerie in the flesh as opposed to just an image in a fire. It was a little unnerving seeing the pointed ears and brown wings. The only other person Andy had never seen in faerie form was Emma. Her wings had streaks of different colors. There were reds, greens, orange, gold and many others. They were stunning. Upon closer inspection he saw little brown lines, like veins running throughout. Then it hit him. "They're leaves," he said aloud.

"What are you talking about?" Abby asked

"Emma's wings," Andy said pointing. "They are the color of leaves in every season."

"Yes," Emma said proudly, slowly moving them back and forth. "It makes sense I guess, given my affinity for trees."

"Not to take away from your moment, sister," Tera said in her whimsical fashion, "but I echo Luel's sentiment. What do we do now? I see nothing but water and island."

"I think Andy and I should go to the source and see if we can contact Loki or Dain," the wizard said.

Luel nodded in understanding. "We'll keep watch."

Andy and Redlin were walking the forest path toward the source. Bird song filled the air, but in a quiet respectful tone, as if the sound came from a great distance. Andy stopped for a moment and bent down to run his hand along the carpet of green grass. He used to love coming here when pressures from the outside became a little too hard to handle. His hand brushed against something and he parted the grass to reveal a tiny red mushroom. Little tingles of electric shocks went up his arm as he ran his thumb across the top. Looking down, he saw tendrils of mist snaking over his hand and between his fingers. He marveled at it for some moments before looking back the way they had come. The entire path was shrouded in fog. Turning to look at his father, panic started to seize him. The only thing in front of him was a wall of white.

"Dad! Where are you?" His call sounded dead and muffled. Andy started walking what he assumed was forward.

So mighty a dragon, a voice spoke to his mind with giggling sarcasm. It was female.

Who is that? Show yourself! He looked around trying to pierce the fog with his dragon eyes but to no avail. Andy was starting to get annoyed. He had hardly been back and someone was already trying to play games with him. He started to draw power from the source.

"There is no need for that," she said sensing his intent.

The voice spoke aloud and to his left. Andy whipped his head that way and saw the fog start to coalesce into the figure of a person. A red glow emanated from behind the girl as she emerged from the fog. Her hair was dark and rested above the shoulders. She wore a red dress, the hem touching the floor hiding her feet. The sleeves covered her arms and terminated to a point just past her wrist. A black belt of discs in the shape of crescent moons linked together circled her slender waist. Her skin was pale, and pink rosy cheeks lit up her face. But the thing most startling to Andy were her eyes. They were hazel like his own, but when you looked into them, they had an almost hypnotic quality. That if you stared too long, you would be unable to look away and be forever lost in them. A deep knowledge was present there and Andy had to admit that it unnerved him just a little.

"Who are you?" he asked, poised to latch onto the source should she make any sudden moves. Andy had no idea what kind of being this was. Her hair was pulled back showing rounded ears, so he knew she was not a faerie.

"My name is Samara," she replied with the slightest upturn of a smile as if she knew some secret she was never going to share with him.

"Samara, may I call you Sam?" Andy figured he would try and put things on a friendly footing. Samara's eyebrows drew down dangerously as she cast dagger eyes at him. "Okay, I guess not. Can you tell me how is it that you are able to be in a place where only wizards and dragons are allowed?" She gave him that slight smile again.

"Technically we are not in that place. Did you not brush your hand over my red mushroom?"

"You put that there. How...?"

Samara raised her hand to pause Andy in his questioning. "I did not put it there, it was carried there by none other than your own father many ages ago, though I doubt he realized it at the time. My sojourn with you is brief and explanations will have to wait for another time. I can read the stars and the prophecy just as well as wizards can, and it just so happens you are going to need a certain talisman for the success of your quest. Hold out your hand."

Andy did as he was instructed, not exactly sure why he was obeying this total stranger, but those eyes, he couldn't help himself.

"Hold your hand open and do not move it," Samara said. Into the center of his palm she laid a small steel object. It was a tiny dagger piercing the top of a skull with the tip emanating from the mouth. Andy thought it felt very light for steel, almost insubstantial. Then a feeling he had not had in over three years exploded in his hand, traveling up his arm and setting his brain on fire. He immediately grabbed the source

Roland Capalbo

to help quell the pain as he looked down at his palm. Perfectly seared into his flesh was the outline of the skull and dagger.

"Damn! By the gods, does everyone feel the need to brand something into my skin! What next, will someone etch a lightning bolt onto my ass. Damn!" he exclaimed again one more time for good measure.

"You will need the death dagger if you are to succeed," she said ignoring his pain. "The prophecy has shown this, and I am the one who has it."

Andy had fallen to his knees and was cradling his hand when the pain hit. Samara took a knee beside him and whispered in his ear.

"I will give you this talisman, Andros the Black, but for a price. And I promise, you will pay it. Ha, ha!" she said standing up, her dress making a flourish as she turned and disappeared into the mist, her ghostly laughter floating back as Andy lost consciousness.

"Andy! Andy!"

Redlin was shaking his son, trying to get some response. The wizard had been walking toward the source when he saw Andy bend down and brush something with his hand, then suddenly he vanished. A few minutes later he reappeared but unconscious. He was curled up in a ball and cradling his hand. Redlin kept shaking until a low moan emanated from Andy's mouth.

"Thank the gods! What happened lad? Are you alright?"

Andy looked up at his father, his eyes red and watery from the pain. He held his palm up so the wizard could see his new brand.

"Do you happen to know a strange girl named Samara?"

Redlin was staring at the skull and dagger mark when the name Andy mentioned registered.

"Samara? Did she do this to you? Tell me everything," Redlin said earnestly.

61

Redlin listened as he told him all that happened from the time he touched the red mushroom until he sank into oblivion. The wizard didn't ask a single question, listening intently. "What is she Dad?"

"A witch," he said. "Her powers are very similar to your sister's. She draws not from a source like we do, but from the earth and every living thing in it. And even sometimes, the dead. She has been around as long as I have, but I do not know her origins. I asked Trystan about her but he would tell me nothing and forbade me from ever bringing the subject up to him. I felt something from him though when I first mentioned her."

"What was that?" Andy asked, the pain in his hand subsiding.

"Guilt. What did she mean that I brought her mushroom here?"

"I don't know," Andy replied.

Redlin was staring absently at the source, deep in thought. Andy's next question brought him back.

"Who's side is she on?"

"Her own, and whose ever side follows alongside hers. Which makes her very dangerous and not to be trusted. The fact that she is willing to give you this talisman means you have something she wants to further her own aims. I do not like this at all."

"I think she may just come in on our side Dad," Andy said. "I got the feeling when her hand touched mine that deep down she wants someone to trust her."

"I hope you are right son, and I hope the price for that trust is not more than we are willing to part with. Come on, let's go to the source and see if we can reach anyone."

Andy and Redlin watched the power of the gods slowly rotate. The orange sphere with its five radiating arms, representing the five gods had a very soothing and relaxing effect on the mind. Redlin had sent his thought out to Loki and Dain, hoping at least one of them would heed his call.

"How long do we wait?" Andy said picking at the dead skin around his new mark. "Abby is going to love to see this."

"I have a feeling she is going to want to go after Samara herself," the wizard said smiling. "As to your question, we will wait five more minutes before heading back." No sooner had he said this when there came a call from back down the path.

"Andros!"

They turned and saw the one-time Border Lands general and faerie queen protector, now newly appointed wizard of Vasara, run and scoop Andy up in a fierce hug.

"Dain!" Andy exclaimed as he set his feet back on the ground. "It is good to see you."

"And I you," Dain replied. Even though he was now a wizard, Dain still had his serpent hilt sword strapped to his waist. "You've hardly changed a bit. The years have been kind to you."

"Actually, it has only been a couple of years for me since I last saw you."

"By the gods! This must be the mighty Redlin, welcome home brother."

He extended his hand and Redlin grasped it in a firm shake.

Dain looked the same from what Andy remembered. With the one exception, that his eyes no longer betrayed his age which seems to be the mark of all wizards.

"Thank you brother," he said with emotion. "My son has told me a lot about you. The Five made the right choice in their selection. There is much to catch up on, but first, where is Loki?"

Dain seemed reluctant to speak.

"He has been taken," Dain replied sadly.

"What? How? By who?" Andy said incredulously.

"Andy, take it easy. Dain, why don't you start at the beginning."

Dain told them how six months ago, the beings not unlike the one that attacked Andy on his first visit to Vasara, had overwhelmed and captured the White Castle.

"All manner of dark creatures and demons inhabit it now. Kensington is a ghost city, everyone has left."

"What of the King and Queen?" Redlin asked.

"After ordering the evacuation of the city, Paolo and Acacia escaped into the crypt. Brayton, the heir to the throne was already away, and was ordered by his father to stay at sea, accompanied by Cathal. How his father got word to him is a mystery. It is rumored he seeks the hidden grove of the Unicorns."

Redlin was rubbing his hand under his stubble chin. "It may be time."

"What do you mean Dad?"

Redlin explained to Andy and Dain how the unicorn is the symbol of Taiyo's house, from which the royal line is descended. They both knew this, but what they did not know is that one day a royal heir would call the unicorns to battle, becoming the fabled Unicorn Master.

"Perhaps it is Brayton," the wizard said.

Andy liked Brayton. After the battle for the White Castle, they became fast friends. Brayton had the same tan features as his father except for his hair which was dark like his mothers'. Brayton could match his father in strength, but he also had the speed and agility of his mother which sometimes gave him an edge when father and son would practice the sword. He would be a dangerous foe on any battlefield. One thing puzzled Andy. "Who is Cathal?"

"That's right, forgive me, you wouldn't know. He is the son of the King's knight, Nyle. None of us knew he even had a son until he had arrived at court with him one day after Devon's overthrow. Cathal's upbringing was not a pleasant one, and I think Nyle wanted to set things right. The tale is a long one and would probably best be told by someone with more knowledge than I."

Andy was startled to hear that. Nyle, the ex-Raptor captain, had helped Andy escape by fighting Tolbert after Andy and Emilia had blinded Devon during the battle to re-take the stone of Fallon. Restoring the stone to the Pillar of Fallon had freed the Border Lands warriors to fight in the war against the demon wizard. In proving his loyalty and battle prowess, Paolo had made Nyle his first knight. It was hard to imagine him with a son.

"But why would Nyle's son go with Brayton?"

"Just as Nyle protects the king, his son protects the heir," Dain explained. "They are the best of friends, brothers almost."

"Dain, do you have any idea what these creatures are after?" Redlin asked of the beings who had captured the White Castle.

"No," Dain replied. "That is what Loki tried to find out when he was captured."

"I would love to know how they managed to do that," Redlin exclaimed. "Loki is a tough wizard to catch let alone hold."

"Before contact was cut off, he told me they had him in the rebuilt tower where Devon was killed."

Andy winced, as he always did whenever he remembered that moment. He looked down at the scar across his forearm from one of Devon's strikes. They had carried the day, but the cost had been high.

"Where are the Border Lands warriors?" Andy asked. "Surely they could have retaken the castle."

"Probably, if they weren't busy chasing demons all over Vasara."

"Do you mean they have breached the corridor?" Redlin said.

"No, these demons crop up sporadically. We do not know how they are able to do this." Dain ran his fingers through his hair, suddenly looking tired. "Loki thought they must have control of some gateway that they are able to move around and pass through whenever they choose. Cleo, Tori and their Vipers ride the kingdom endlessly confronting them. Leah is with them."

Andy could picture Cleo in his mind, her twin swords cutting a wide swath through a line of demons as she stood up in her stirrups. The saddles the Vipers used had a mechanism that when you hit the saddle bow another set of stirrups slid out horizontal to the ground, allowing the rider to stand up.

Redlin scratched his chin thinking. "We are going to need to start moving soon. The way I see things right now, there are at least three tasks we need to accomplish."

"One I assume being the rescue of Loki," Dain said.

"Yes," Redlin replied. "There is also a witch we need to locate." Redlin told Dain about Samara's visit and everything it entailed.

"I ran into her once," Dain said, "shortly after I became a wizard. Not much was said. She told me her name and that we would meet again soon. Do you know where she lives?"

"No, we may have to search the old writings to find where she resides I think."

"Why didn't she just tell us?" Andy asked.

"I'm sure it amuses her to watch us have to puzzle these things out," his father explained.

"What is the third thing?" Dain asked.

"There are other elements associated with it, but lastly we need to find and free the nine dragons otherwise they will die. Braylynn sent some special emissaries to bring us back for that very reason."

"Oh, who was that?"

"Tera and Emma," Redlin replied.

"By the gods! How did they manage that?"

"I'm sure Tera will love to tell you the whole thing in detail," Andy said smiling.

Dain laughed. "I am sure I will receive the more dramatic and enhanced version."

"What have you heard from Braylynn?"

"Nothing in quite some time. I spoke with Brie and she says the same. I fear we are alone on this one."

Redlin turned to contemplate the source again. Andy knew his father, and even though he was calm and composed, his mind was running like a well-oiled machine. Taking in all the data, sifting it and looking at it from every possible angle. Like a chess game he would think three to four moves ahead, weighing each possible outcome.

"This is what we will do," Redlin began. "Make your way to Fenner and meet us there, we will find a way back to the mainland."

"Why Fenner?" Andy asked.

"We need horses. Not all of us have the gift of flight," he said with a wink.

***

Emilia sat on a sand dune listening to the waves crash against the shore. The sun felt good on her face as she let the wind gently push her wings. She sat in a lotus position with her eyes closed, her mind sifting the sounds brought to her on the sea breeze. Gulls screeched as the wind amplified the sound of the surf. The tall sand grass rustled nearby. She could hear the sound of feet crunching sand as they walked. The ruby ring on her finger was glowing. Emilia was feeling the connection of her life's blood with the immediate forces of nature.

"Emilia!"

Her mother's voice. She slowly and gently let go of the energy she had been drawing into herself. Her eyes opened and she could see her mother flying up the beach.

"Your father and brother are back; it is time to make plans."

Everyone stood in a circle on the beach as Redlin told them of their meeting with Dain, and Samara. The wizard had guessed Abby's reaction correctly when Andy showed her the skull-dagger mark.

"I think we need to go to Albion," Abby said after most of her anger dissipated.

"Why there?" Emilia asked her.

"Do you remember that book I found written by the Alfar, Lorcan?"

"What is this?" Luel asked with an edge to her voice. The death of her mother at their hands still made her wince with anger at the mention of that race.

Abby explained to everyone who did not already know of the book she found under a hearth stone in the library at Albion, 'The Betrayal of Parma as Chronicled by Lorcan of the Alfar'.

"It is a big tome," Abby continued, "with hundreds of years of early Vasara history. While skimming through it I came across Samara's name. It could be some of her history is recorded in it."

"That sounds like a good place to start," Redlin approved.

"Not to rain on your party master wizard, but how are we to get off this island?" Tera piped up. "I don't know about you, but I don't want to test the limits of how far I can fly across unknown open water. I don't swim very well, if I did I would be a fish, not a faerie." She crossed her arms and tried to stare him down. After a few moments, Redlin burst out laughing.

"Do not worry Tera, I will think of something."

Chapter 5

In the end, it was agreed Andy would fly out for as far as he saw fit in an effort to see what was nearby. After three hours in the air and spying nothing but open ocean, Andy caught a tiny flash of something like a mirror reflecting sunlight off to his left on the horizon. His huge wings banked toward, what after thirty minutes, was undoubtedly a ship. The nearer he got, Andy smiled to himself. Written on the stern was the name Grey Morning, and on the quarter deck waving madly was Captain Bowen.

"Ho Edward," Bowen yelled as Andy got closer. The captain liked to call Andy by his middle name, which was the name Andy used when first traveling through Vasara.

Andy hovered over the ship and changed form. Upon landing, he ran up the steps and embraced his old friend. Andy could feel Emilia, so he knew she was seeing what he was seeing through the dragon's eye in her crown.

"It is so good to see you lad! By the gods, what are you doing here?"

Andy thought Bowen seemed as fit as ever. His black curly hair had some grey streaks and his beard and mustache were gone, giving his entire face that coppery look all seasoned seaman have. Andy told the captain how glad he was to see him and the story of how he arrived and where the others were.

"But why are you out here, Captain?"

"Let's go to my cabin and I will show you."

Andy sat at the table in the captain's quarters as Bowen pulled a map from a trunk at the foot of his bed. Rolling it out, Andy could see the familiar Kensington coast with the Mistral Islands, but beyond that the various lands and seas labeled were foreign to him.

"What are these places, these names are unfamiliar to me."

"And me as well," Bowen stated. He went on to explain how after Andy and the others left, Brie had come to give him a present from a grateful goddess. "Now mind, I know any gift from Braylynn has two sides to it, so needless to say I was wary. But so much was going on at the time that I put it in my trunk and forgot about it. Then a month ago we were making a run up the Tear river when a huge bird alighted on my main mast. It looked like a hawk, but I can't be sure. In its beak was a piece of paper that it let drop to the deck before it flew away. Wait a minute."

Bowen want back to his trunk and returned with a tiny rolled up paper that he handed to Andy. Andy unrolled it and read what was written.

> *"My dear Captain, seek the treasure and great rewards will be yours."*
>
> *Braylynn*

"So does that mean this is a treasure map?"

"Indeed lad! And this is the island we are sailing for."

Andy looked to where the captain pointed, and he started to have a sinking feeling. "Where are we now on this map Captain?"

"Right here."

Andy's suspicions were confirmed. The island Bowen was sailing for is where they had landed after coming through the door at Lyndhurst Castle. Andy scratched his head as he looked sympathetically at Bowen. Bowen saw the look.

"What?" he asked with apprehension.

"I think you have been duped by a goddess, my friend."

Andy told him that the ship was headed for the island where the others waited. He took it pretty well, all things considered. Only a couple of pieces of furniture lay broken on his cabin floor. He flung himself into his oaken chair rubbing his head and laughing.

"She is a pirate, make no mistake. She dangled the hook out in front of me with just the right bait and then landed me. So apparently you are the treasure, and I am here to provide ferry service back to the mainland."

"Sorry."

"No need to be sorry lad, it is always my pleasure to escort Andros the Black and his family. Besides, the men will be going crazy at the thought of Abby singing again, and it will be a treat for the new sailors we have signed on." Andy remembered Abby can bring Bowen's crew to tears, as she proved on their first trip aboard the Grey Morning while sailing across Lake Pleasant on their way to the Border Lands. It took Bowen the better part of a day and a half to reach the island. Once everyone was on board and introductions made, Bowen set sails and pointed the Grey Morning towards the Fenner coast.

The fifth day out found Andy sitting on a pile of ropes watching his beloved standing on the main deck in a circle of candles with sailors ringed likewise, mouths open in stunned astonishment. Abby was singing. Bowen came up behind him, taking a seat on the sails' locker.

"I tell ya laddie, I could just sail the oceans forever and just listen to that lassie sing," he sighed deeply. "Have you ever seen such a moonstruck crew?"

"I can't say as I have, Captain," Andy replied smiling.

"If she ever needs employment, there will always be an

officer's position for her, officer of morale."

Andy laughed at that. Abby always had the look of a pirate about her. "She would fit right in," he thought to himself. "How much longer until we reach land," Andy asked.

"If we don't hit any rough weather, we should reach Fenner in four days."

Just then Redlin came up on deck and joined Andy and Bowen.

"Evening gentlemen," the wizard greeted them.

"A pleasant evening to you master Redlin."

"Bowen, please, I get enough of that teasing from Abby. For some reason, she finds some great delight in it."

"You are the wizard of the curator's Dad," Andy said smirking. "So I guess you've kind of brought it on yourself."

"Now see here young man...What the..."

What had interrupted Redlin was the sound of furious pounding on the port side hull. Andy had heard that sound before, and smiling ran over to the rail and stood next to Abby who had just concluded her song.

"You thinking what I'm thinking?" Andy asked her.

Abby nodded. "Tagen." Just then Emma flew up and peered down to where they were looking.

"What is it?" she asked folding her wings as she settled to the deck.

"Watch," Abby told her as four streaking underwater comets suddenly shot out and started doing intricate circles twenty yards from the ship.

Andy took off his shoes and shirt and climbed up on the rail.

"Andy, what are you doing," his father yelled running over.

Andy smiled back, then dove in, just as his mother and all the rest reached the spot he dove from.

"Has he gone insane?" Tera asked no one in particular.

"Just watch," Abby reassured them.

Once in the water, Andy sent his thought out to the dragon-like sea horses. He could feel them just before they struck the ship, so he assumed they must have sensed him as well. Suddenly he could feel the water current circling around him. With his dragon eyes he was able to pierce the dark colored ocean.

He saw them, spiky hair streaming from their heads and down their backs like a horse's mane. Their golden underbelly reflecting in the sea. He waited, motionless, until one of them was brave enough to glide up to where he floated. The first time he saw the Tagen, his initial thought was wondering what it must be like to ride one of those magnificent creatures. Holding out his hand and sending soothing thoughts, Andy slowly stroked its head. Feeling he had gained the creature's trust, he glided onto its back. The Tagen's eyes suddenly grew wide and frantic looking at having something on its back, a feeling it had never experienced before. It immediately started to thrash in an attempt to dislodge its rider. Andy was amazed at the amount of force these creatures could muster underwater. He sent more calming thoughts and the Tagen started to respond to Andy's gentle stroking. Giving images of riding into the mind of this sea-dragon, Andy grabbed on tight as he felt the desire take hold inside the mind of the Tagen.

The water felt like a sluice had opened and was rushing past Andy's body as the beast picked up speed beneath the sea and made its ascent to the surface. They broke through as if punching through glass, water droplets falling like sparkling crystals as Tagen and rider took to the air. At its apex, the Tagen did a backwards somersault before dropping back to the ocean. The speed and raw exhilaration was intense. After several more acrobatics, Andy did a free fall at the height of the Tagen's last jump, making a tremendous splash.

As his head broke the surface, Andy was yelling and laughing from the sheer pleasure of that ride. Being mind-linked with the Tagen, Andy felt the creature's joy in the experience as well. Floating in the water, he started feeling a nudging in the small part of his back. In his mind, Andy could sense that the Tagen knew the fun was over and it was pushing him back towards the ship. Folding his arms across his chest, Andy sat in the water as the beast came up underneath and started to propel him forward, the way a dolphin pushes a beach ball with its nose. To those watching on deck, Andy appeared like a king sitting on his throne with his posterior resting on the head of a sea dragon. With a flick of its powerful neck, Andy was thrown through the air high enough to grab onto the ship's rail. Looking down, Andy saw no trace of the Tagen. They had silently slipped away.

"He doesn't look insane," Tera remarked tilting her head sideways as she looked into Andy's hazel eyes.

"I'm not crazy," Andy said slightly offended.

"Actually Tera, this behavior is quite common," Emilia said smirking.

"I'm not even going to respond to that," Andy said pulling himself over the rail and back onto the deck. Bowen threw him a towel and seemed to be smiling funny, as if he was trying to hold in laughter.

"That was amazing!" Emma exclaimed.

"Thank you, Emma," Andy said grateful that someone was on his side.

"Oh, I'm sorry Andros. I meant the creatures. Actually I thought that was the foolhardiest thing I ever saw a human/dragon do," she said sympathetically.

"I think I'll go below," Andy said shaking his head as he walked towards the stairs. He heard everyone burst out laughing as he descended the steps. He couldn't help smiling to himself a little, because he must have had a manic look on his face as he jumped into the water without a word, but it was worth it. That was a ride he will never forget.

True to his word, Bowen struck his sails four days later as the coast of Fenner appeared. It was a totally different view from the first time Andy saw the land of the horse lords. Instead of a sea of grass, a dense forest ran down to the beach.

Leaving the captain to sail back to the Tear River, Andy and the others walked into the woods. It was quite peaceful and quiet under the trees. Emma, would run off now and then to touch some of the various wooden inhabitants.

"Does she do this often?" Andy asked Tera.

"Oh yes," Tera replied smiling. "When it comes to trees, she can be crazier than a dragon that swims with fishes."

Andy decided to let that pass. As he walked a little further, he heard a buzzing sound go past both ears followed by two thunks in the ground behind him. He stood stock still and immediately grabbed the source. Emilia had her staff out and the bright power of the goddess lit up the forest floor. Luel had her father's moonstone spear extended and spinning. The other faeries had the spears Luel had provided spinning likewise. Redlin calmly strode forth and shouted a command.

"Come out! We mean no harm, but if you mean harm to us we are not without resources."

Andy, using his dragon sight, searched the forest in the direction that he felt the arrows had come. Whoever they were, their concealment was flawless. Andy could see no trace of anyone. Suddenly, seeming to appear instantly twenty yards in front of him, he saw two young women, clad in forest green. They were identical in almost every respect, He knew they must be twins. Their hair was the color of wheat and hung loose at the shoulders. With eyes of piercing blue, they stared down the sights of drawn bows.

"Who are you, and what is your business in Fenner?" the slightly taller of the two said. She also had strands of dark color hair among the blond that set her apart from her sister. Andy wondered if it was natural or if she somehow colored it that way.

Their facial features kept nagging at Andy, as if they were somehow familiar to him.

"My name is Edward," Andy said. He figured he would see how things stood before revealing their true identities. "These are my friends. We are merely passing through your lands. I don't want any trouble."

A long look seemed to pass between the two women. Andy braced himself for any sudden flying arrows, but it never materialized. The arrow points dropped a little and the tension on the bow strings slackened.

"Your real name wouldn't happen to be Andros the Black?" This time the smaller girl spoke and her voice was just an octave higher than her sister's.

"It is," Redlin answered for his son, eyeing them cautiously. "How did you know?"

They took the arrows off the string and walked forward.

"My name is Ava, and this is my sister Rhyan." Ava, the slightly smaller of the two, eyed Andy up and down as if measuring him for a suit. "Our father spoke of you often, even about how you met and the name you first gave, Edward."

"Maccus, your father is Maccus!" Andy said realizing how much they looked like him. "How is he? Is he close by?"

Andy saw the sisters exchange sympathetic looks.

"We are sorry to tell you this lord Dragon, but our father is dead," Rhyan said with pain in her voice.

Andy was stunned. A tear escaped his eye as he thought of

the Fenner horse chief. "How?" he asked looking down.

Ava took up the narrative. "Ten years ago we were traveling home from Black River when we were set upon by bandits. There were many. Our father and Bart the archer held the road against them while the rest of us escaped. Both of them perished."

Andy's knees crashed to the earth and he buried his face in his hands as he cried for his friends who he saw only two short years ago but have been dead in their graves for ten. His mind was having a hard time coping. Andy felt an arm encircle his shoulders as someone knelt next to him. Lowering his hands, he saw Abby with tears streaming down her face. Bart had started their adventures with them. Andy always thought of him as his best friend. He knew something like this could happen, but he was in no way prepared for it. How long he sat there, Andy wasn't sure. Looking at his friends and family their faces showed only sympathy and compassion.

"Were they both buried in Fenner?" Andy asked Ava as he stood up.

"Yes, their graves are not far from here."

Andy winced when she said the word grave.

"Follow us," Rhyan said retrieving the arrows they shot into the ground upon first seeing the travelers.

After walking thirty minutes through the woods they entered a small clearing encircled by pine trees. In the center of the clearing were two white headstones glaring in the sunlight. Andy turned to the others, unshed tears stood in his eyes.

"Would you mind if I had a few moments to myself?"

Redlin walked over and put a hand on his Andy's shoulder. "Of course son."

Andy walked woodenly toward the grave markers. Each step bringing the truth of the matter home, his friends were dead. The ache in his heart continued to grow. He stood and looked at Maccus's headstone. Etched in the marble was the figure of a rearing horse. Underneath was written his name along with the words, 'Husband, Father and Protector'. Andy wiped his eyes and briefly smiled that Maccus was able to give his wife and children the one thing that he worked his entire life for, freedom. He kept looking at Maccus's grave for quite a while; because he was afraid to look at Bart's. But he loved his friend too much not to pay homage to the life that had once saved his. Engraved on the stone was the image of Bart's bow and a quiver of godstone arrows. His inscription was simple, 'Bart the Archer, friend of Andros the Black, Chief of Dragons'. Andy sank to a knee as he lowered his head, choking back the sobs for the loss of his friend.

Andy heard light footfalls behind and a hand touched his head. He looked up to see Emma, sympathy and compassion radiated from her soft brown eyes. Taking his hand, she wordlessly helped him to his feet and led him to the far edge of the pine tree circle. She put his hand over her heart and with the other she gently caressed the branches as her wings moved in perfect rhythm.

Suddenly, images started flooding his mind. Images of Bart and Maccus, arms about each other's shoulder as they walked a forest trail. He could tell they were smiling and laughing. Both stopped for a second and looked around, but not from being startled, rather like they felt the presence of an old friend and were looking to greet him. They resumed their walk, but as the last image faded, Andy felt sure he saw Bart look towards his mind's eye, and wink.

Andy's hand dropped to his side and stared dumbfounded at Emma who seemed to be glowing white. When she was her normal self again he asked her, "How did you do that?"

"Pine trees seem to have a special ability to connect with the spiritual forces of all living things," she explained. "I could feel your friends as soon as we entered, and I knew it was a safe bet that the trees had borne witness to their traveling."

"Was that really Maccus and Bart?"

"It is them, wherever they happen to be. I'm afraid I don't know where that is."

Andy felt good knowing they were okay, and his hurt was lessened. The others came forward to pay their respects. Andy saw Ava and Rhyan hanging back. He walked over to where they stood.

"Bart was the one who taught you the bow, wasn't he?"

"Yes, he was," Rhyan answered. "There was no one to match his skill. Ava and I grew up with him, he was like an uncle to us. This is his bow."

Ava smiled, "He would talk for hours, and tell of how he and Andros the dragon defeated the evil wizard Devon and freed Vasara from his tyrannical rule."

"Well, we did have some help," Andy chuckled. It felt good to laugh while thinking of his friend. Bart would be upset with him if he spent his time moody and depressed.

"Oh, that reminds me," Rhyan said reaching back for her quiver. She pulled out a red arrow. Andy knew instantly what it was. The red arrow he had presented to Bart at the Red Bull Inn, as proof that he came from Loki, and the arrow guaranteed his help. Bart of course denied ever giving it to Loki at first, but that was only because of the situation at the time. Bart would prove his loyalty to the bearer of the red arrow later that day by saving Andy and Abby from Devon's elite fighting unit, the Raptors. He held the arrow for a moment and then gave it back to Rhyan.

"Would you mind holding it for me?" he asked her. Rhyan nodded in understanding, putting the arrow back among the others.

"I think it is time to move onto Fenner's main city, Pharsalia," Redlin said as he walked over.

"We will escort you," Ava said slinging her bow over her shoulder. "That way, no one will bother you if we are with you."

The group fell in behind the twins as they wound their way through the woods. After twenty minutes of walking they exited the forest and their eyes were met with rolling hills and green grass. The sun was on its afternoon descent giving the grass a rich hunter green color.

"Beautiful," Tera remarked hovering over the ground and running her hand along the blades.

Just then, Andy heard what sounded like thunder coming over the hill just north of where they were standing. He knew it couldn't be real thunder because there wasn't a cloud in the sky. As he watched, over a thousand horses crested the hill and were galloping like lightning for the woods. With his dragon sight, Andy could see the wildness and fear in these horse's eyes; these animals were terrified. Only problem was, they were directly in the herd's path. Andy was just about to grab for the source. What he would do, he wasn't sure, but he was worried about Abby and Maccus's daughters, who were the only ones not able to leap or fly out of the way of the stampede. It turned out he needn't have worried. Ava and Rhyan stood facing the horses, each had one arm up, palms out, as if that would push the beasts back. Andy was amazed when the horses slowed and eventually stopped to peacefully nibble the grass.

"Okay, let me guess, you are both witches," Tera exclaimed in her whimsical fashion.

Ava and Rhyan exchanged a look, then burst out laughing. Andy liked their laugh, it was almost musical. Unlike Tori's, who was often loud and raucous and more times than not was followed by a 'not to gentle' slap on the shoulder.

"Not at all," Rhyan said smiling. She reached into her shirt and pulled out a black disc on a leather cord that was around her neck. Andy looked closely and saw the image of a white flying horse, much like a Pegasus. Ava also withdrew an identical disc.

"Both of you are the Priestess of Aditya?" Redlin asked, clearly amazed, for he guessed right away what the discs represented. "How is that possible?"

Rhyan told them how when they were born, a man from one of the northern clans visited their home. He had given their mother Lily a small dark wooden chest, with the instruction that she would present it to the twins on their sixteenth birthday. He was Aditya's priest, and he said the god had instructed him to do this. He had no knowledge of what was in the chest, nor would it open for anyone. For sixteen years it sat on a shelf in the back room of their home. On their birthday, golden light shot out of the key hole and the seams of the chest. Setting it on the table, the family gathered around as the lid opened and the discs of Aditya floated out and came to rest around the necks of the two girls. Rhyan said it was bittersweet moment, because even though they were honored by the god, it was also their first birthday without their father. Ava told them that Bart and Maccus would probably be alive today if they had these a year earlier, because maybe they could have averted disaster and controlled the bandits' horses. Andy sensed the twins carried some small amount of guilt about it.

"What caused the horses to stampede in the first place?" Abby asked when they had finished their story.

"It is very troubling," Ava said her brow furrowed. "The images were very jumbled. One moment." She gave three short whistles and a stallion broke away from the rest of the herd and galloped up to Ava. The horse was long and sleek with hair the color of cedar. "This is Cedrus," she said stroking his nose while making soothing sounds. She stared into Cedrus' eye, taking on a distant look in her own. When she turned to them her face was stark white and her pupils totally dilated.

"Ava, what is it?" Redlin said alarmed. At first she did not answer. Her eyes came back into focus and tears escaped from them.

"Death. Pharsalia is burning. The children..." A sob escaped her throat as her legs buckled.

"Andy!" Redlin turned to his son. Andy knew what he meant and immediately started sprinting for open space. Plunging himself into the source, Andy made the change. His black wings clawed the air in their effort to climb quickly. He felt his sister settle onto his back, the staff of the goddess blazing in her hand.

I have a very bad feeling about this, he spoke to Emilia's mind.

"So do I," she agreed.

It wasn't long before they saw the smoke. A few minutes later they saw the fire.

"By the goddess!" Emilia exclaimed. Andy thought this must be how ancient Rome looked when it was burned by the emperor Nero.

We need to put those fires out, Andy said. *You start on the east side and I'll work from the west.*

Andy banked hard to the right as Emilia jumped off his back and headed towards the left. Pharsalia did not have many tall buildings, the biggest ones being at most four stories, but there were a lot, and very close together. The city was laid out in a huge circle, with the terrain flat in some areas and hilly in others, as if they just built the city on the natural contour of the land. The heat was intense. Andy was able to handle it, but he was worried about Emilia. He swung his neck around and glanced back to where she was, suddenly realizing he needn't have worried, because his sister was encased in a transparent sphere, the outline he could just barley discern. She was just hovering, but the hand with the red ring on her finger was lifted towards the sky and glowing. Dark clouds were forming over her head, seeming to appear out of nothingness. He realized what she was doing. His sister was creating a storm.

Feeling Emilia had her task well in hand, he concentrated on what he needed to do. After some thought, Andy felt he would try isolating the bigger fires by blasting a trench with his own fire to keep it from spreading further. It was working quite well as the more troublesome flames were cutoff. It meant sacrificing those buildings, but he realized it couldn't be helped. What bothered him the most was the lack of people running about. He saw some, but none compared to the population a city this size should have. He feared the worst, especially after what Ava saw through the mind of the horse.

Not long after, he saw the others arrive. The faeries flying and the humans on horses. He noticed his father had jumped off his horse and started running into the burning inferno. For a moment he panicked, fearing for the life of his dad, but then he remembered his father is a mighty wizard here. Andy was amazed how easily he forgot that. Redlin would always be dad first in his mind.

Andy circled the city one more time, blasting trenches as he went. The next time he saw his father, he was flying directly over the center of the city. The wizard was standing next to a huge stone well. He had both hands raised and his mouth was moving. Andy started going in for a closer look, when all of a sudden, a geyser of water shot hundreds of feet into the air, but instead of falling straight down, the water appeared to be streaking across the sky forming one huge canopy. Andy didn't fancy getting drenched and as quick as lightning, he flew to the water's edge. When the water encircled the entire city, Redlin released it, causing a deluge, that if it did not put the fires out entirely, severely diminished them. As the water ran off, Andy landed and changed back to human and came to stand beside his father.

"What could you see from above?" the wizard asked.

"A lot of fire and not very much movement on the ground," Andy replied grimly.

"Dad! Andy, follow me," Emilia shouted as she streaked by.

Andy quickly assumed his dragon form and his father jumped on his back as they flew after his sister. They came to where Emilia hovered and Andy pulled up short as the horror met his eyes. Lying below in the field, where undoubtedly the horse herd was kept, were acres of bodies. What hit Andy the hardest was the amount of children among the dead. He understood now what Ava saw.

"Land, son," Redlin said grimly. Emilia descended with them.

They stood on the edge of the field and waited for the others to arrive.

"By the goddess!" Luel exclaimed as she flew beside her husband.

"This is beyond monstrous," Abby said shaking her head in disbelief.

"Dad," Emilia said turning towards her father, "there are Border Lands warriors among the dead. I saw their uniforms from above."

"Why would warriors be here?" Rhyan said with a grim expression on her face. Ava had regained her composure, but her eyes still held un-shed tears. Both sisters had arrows fixed to bows, ready to shoot the first enemy they encountered.

"Andros!"

Everyone turned and looked back towards the city. Running as if demons were behind and her braided dark hair swishing back and forth like a horse's tail, was the last person Andy expected to see, Cleo.

"Cleo!" Andy shouted as he started running towards her. "What are you doing here?" he asked when he reached her.

"No time." Cleo said breathlessly, her cheeks wet with tears. "Tori is dying, I need your help!"

"Take me to her."

Andy followed Cleo through the streets of Pharsalia. The others were close behind as they ascended the steps of what appeared to be a tavern. He took a deep breath and braced himself for the worst, wondering how many more friends he would lose before this day ended.

Chapter 6

Brion sat on a high jutting rock, keeping vigil. The hooded guards had left several years ago, but the magic shield was still intact. His end was coming; he could feel it. He hardly had the strength to stand for any length of time. Brion figured he had maybe a year at most, and then he would be dead. Regret played across his features. As he saw it, he failed in so many ways. He failed to protect the king and queen, he failed to protect Layla, the Dragon Summoner, and worst of all, he failed to recognize Devon's treachery as he led his brother's here to fight an unknown enemy. Caleb had try to tell him to take it slow until they figured out what was going on, but Brion was very trusting of the wizards. It never entered his mind that one of them might betray the dragons. And now with his death coming he would not be able to avenge anything, to redress the wrong that was committed against Vasara. He hung his head as all his failures consumed him.

Are you done beating yourself up?

Brion whipped his head around and found Caleb's dragon eyes staring intently at him.

"Caleb! How are you awake?" Brion asked stunned.

Probably from that damn whining going on in your head. It would wake the dead.

Brion had to laugh. Caleb could always make him laugh.

"I guess as the weaker I get, my enchantment weakens as well," Brion said. In a way, he was not surprised.

Has it been long?

"A long time Bull," Brion replied sadly. Brion most always called Caleb by his nickname, because once Caleb made up his mind about something, he would charge straight into it.

Caleb started to rise, his long neck seeming to stretch to an impossible length. As far as dragons go, Caleb was the longest from snout to tail. He moved his red wings back and forth to get the tightness out of his muscles.

"Best take it slow, you have never slept this long before and your body may need time to regain its strength."

Yeah, I guess you're right. You were always the smart one.

He knew Caleb was not being sarcastic, but his words cut to the core of his being. If he had used his wits, they wouldn't be in this predicament.

I can feel you whining again.

"Sorry," Brion said smiling. He cast his eyes back across the water towards shore. "Can you sense the source?"

Nope. Wherever we are, we have been effectively cut off. During my sleep, I had some wonderful dreams of eating Devon's heart, most satisfying, he said, his long tongue sliding out and smacking against his teeth.

"I will be happy to join you, if no one hasn't already destroyed him."

Caleb swung his long neck back towards his other brothers. *Who do you think will wake next?*

"Not a clue, but I have a feeling that whoever is the last to wake, I shall be the first to die."

We are not dead yet.

Brion knew Caleb was a scrapper in a fight, but his greatest asset was his eternal optimism. The strongest fighter of the dragons was Finn, but unlike Caleb, he was the pessimist of the group. Brion looked over at the golden dragon who was the grouch of the family. He knew a lot of Finn's bluster was due to the fact that he didn't like to let his emotions show, but Brion would catch him alone sometimes just staring at the beauty of a sunset, as if he were remembering a time or person from long ago.

Brion went back to his vigil, but with a little lighter heart, now that he had Caleb awake beside him. He wondered, was that hope stirring in his breast. *Your optimism is contagious Bull*, he thought to himself.

***

As Andy entered the tavern, the reek of death hit him almost immediately. The common room was large and filled with many tables. Each one seemed to be occupied by an injured or dead person. The bar also had several people stretched out on it. To Andy, it looked like a makeshift hospital.

He spotted Cleo moving towards the far corner of the building. Lying on a cot with one hand dangling lifeless was Tori. Sitting next to her with a tired and concerned expression on her face was Leah. Her yellow hair and lavender wings seemed to give off an inner light in the darkened tavern. Blood was sliding down Tori's arm, dripping from her fingers to the floor.

Andy moved closer. Looking at Leah, he could see she had several wounds of her own.

"Andros the Black," a voice barely whispered.

Andy looked down to see Tori's head turned towards him, her eyes open. He started shaking. Blood had pooled inside her eyes, her face was white as plaster. A blood soaked rag encircled her neck. There was a knife slice that ran from her ear, across the jaw line down to the collar bone. Andy was amazed she was even still alive, but he knew she wouldn't be for much longer.

"Don't talk Tori," Andy said soothingly, brushing her blood matted hair.

"No pain Lord Dragon," she said, even managing a slight smile.

"Leah!" Emilia came running to the bedside, followed by her parents and the others.

Leah embraced her sister, although the meeting lacked any joy.

"Can you do anything?" Cleo asked tears running down her cheeks, her facial expression hard.

Andy looked sadly at her. He knew there was nothing he could do, she was beyond his power.

"Em?" Andy asked his sister. Emilia knelt beside Tori.

"No tricks...Summoner," Tori said.

"No tricks," Emilia said smiling down at her.

Andy remembered how Tori was forever the practical joker. Most of the time it involved putting the Viper's pet snake Percy down someone's shirt, of which Emilia was one of the victims. Emilia had gotten even though. Thinking of Percy made him wonder what became of the warrior's mascot. The snake had always hitched a ride into battle. It was then that he noticed Tori's other arm that lay across her stomach. What he thought was a bracelet was in fact Percy coiled around her wrist. The snake raised its head and looked at Andy, his forked tongue sliding in and out.

Andy watched as Emilia, with eyes closed, ran her hands along Tori's wounds. White streaks, the color of moonbeams, shone through her hair as all the healing power of the Dragon Summoner was brought to bear. After several minutes Emilia stopped and looked at her brother. Andy saw the sadness in her eyes and knew there was nothing his sister could do either. Tori started a rasping cough, spittle of blood shooting out of her mouth. Andy couldn't bear to see her suffer like this.

"Couldn't we do for Tori, what Andy and Donella did for

me?" Tera piped up. "Fly her to the Border Lands and get her god, Fallon, to heal her."

Andy recalled the time that Zana, the first faerie to ever murder another, had stabbed Tera when Emilia was recovering the vestments and items of power of the Dragon Summoner from Zana's chambers. The knife wound was mortal.

"What about that?" Cleo asked hopefully.

"We would never make it," Andy said shaking his head. "Ala was there to summon the god Raphael. He was able to slow Tera's heart long enough for me to fly her to Laurel Hollow. And even if Ala were here, I could never reach the Border Lands in time. Not to mention we would need to find Fallon's priest in order to try and get him to heal Tori." Andy ran his fingers through his hair in frustration. He looked at his father, who always seemed to have the answers to life's difficult questions.

"Dad?" Andy asked, hoping against hope his father had something up his sleeve.

Redlin was scratching his chin, his eyes narrowed as he looked at Tori, whose breathing was becoming more labored.

"I have an idea," the wizard said. "I'm not sure if it is even possible, but I believe it is the only option that may have a chance of success."

"Why do I feel like you are going to ask me to move the moon," Andy said warily.

"You are actually not too far off," Redlin said. "We are going to stop the source."

"We are going to what?" Andy said incredulously. "How?"

"Not sure," his father answered. "I wish Dain were here, I could use another wizard."

"Looking for me," a voice called from behind.

"Dain!" Leah exclaimed as she rushed into his arms.

"Thank the gods!" Redlin exclaimed. "Dain, there is not much time. Come with me."

Redlin took Andy, Dain and Emilia off to the side and explained his plan. He told them when the source is spinning as it does, wizards and dragons are touching the power of all five gods at once, giving you pieces of each. But maybe if they could stop it and tap the concentrated full energy of the god Fallon and channel it to Emilia, she may be able to heal Tori.

"It is because you and your sister have the same blood that channeling the source to a faerie is even possible," their father told them. "No dragon or Summoner has ever had that ability."

Redlin looked hard at his son.

"Dain and I will stop the source, but you must be acutely aware of how much and how fast you send that power to your sister. The energy will be so focused and powerful that it will want to run right through you, which will consume your sister from the inside out."

Andy swallowed hard as he glanced in Emilia's direction.

"Try not to fry me little brother," she said smiling.

"Emilia, you know what to do on your end, right?" Redlin asked. His daughter nodded. "Okay, we should go to the source right now, time will slow a little for us there."

Andy, Dain and his father stood before the source as it rotated in front of them. The orange sphere with its five arms of energy always awed Andy. For some reason he felt like what they were doing was a form of desecration. It spun for a reason, and to change that was to court disaster.

"If any of the Five get mad at us for doing this, remember it was your idea, Dad."

"Don't worry, they will never know," Redlin said winking.

"What exactly is the plan?" Dain asked.

"I am going to latch on to two of the arms and try and hold it in place while you do the same with the other two. When we have it stopped, Andy will plunge himself into Fallon's energy."

"Which one is Fallon's?" Andy asked.

"See the one that has a slightly red hue, that is his color. Each god has his own color, but we can talk about that some other time. We need to act now. Is your sister ready?"

"Yes," Andy replied. "I can sense her mind through the link, and she is watching us as well."

"Be quick. The force we will be holding is just as concentrated, and we could burn out. Ready Dain?"

"Ready."

Andy watched as his father and Dain stretched out their hands towards the source, eyes closed. He could see no discernible slowing. Their faces were turning beet red and their hands and arms were starting to shake. He could see it starting to slow now. Andy thought the amount of force and will to accomplish that must be intense. He kept his eye on Fallon's energy, the source was almost still.

"Now!" Redlin yelled. "Hurry!"

Andy wasted no time and plunged in. He was not expecting what hit him. Raw energy, a hundred times more intense than he had ever felt slammed into his being. He had to keep his grasp on it, he could feel it wanting to fly down the link. Aggression filled his mind. The need to fight and kill was nearing a frenzy in his soul as he tried to hold the power back. He could understand why Fallon was the warrior's god.

He could feel Emilia was ready, and he started to slowly release Fallon's source. A couple of times strong bursts would escape his grasp. He couldn't worry about that now. The process seemed to be excruciatingly slow. He knew his limit to holding it back was approaching.

Stop now Andros! came to Andy's mind. He did not know who it was, but he released the power instantly, blackness filling his vision as he crashed to the ground and knew no more.

***

"Andros."

Andy's head felt like cotton, and he had a hard time focusing. He thought he heard someone call his name but maybe he was dreaming. He thought his eyes were open, but all he could see was darkness.

"Andros."

He wished whoever was talking would stop. Couldn't they see he was trying to sleep.

"Andros."

Andy opened his eyes and blinked. It seemed unusually bright as he found himself lying in a bed.

"Finally awake Lord Dragon?"

Andy craned his head around to the source of the voice and saw the last person he expected, Tori. She looked brand new he thought. Or maybe reborn was a better way to put it. Her skin was tanned and positively glowed. With her long dark hair tied back into a ponytail, she leaned over and lightly smacked him on the head.

"Time to get up!"

"Ow! Not so loud." Andy was amazed, there was not a mark on her. No evidence she had been anywhere near death. Then he noticed her eyes. Around the outer edges of those deep brown eyes there was what almost looked like the faint outlines of flames dancing.

"Tori, your eyes!"

"Like them. Pretty cool, I think is the expression you would use," as she batted her eyelids at him. "Must be the residual effect of what you all did to me." She sat down on the bed beside him. "Other things have changed. I have changed, into what I am not exactly sure yet, but my battle skills have increased a hundred-fold."

"What do you mean?"

"Last week I was training..."

"Hold it!" Andy said stunned. "Last week...how long have I been out."

"Three weeks my friend," Tori replied. "Your sister was up and about in a few days. Your father and Dain about a week later. We were starting to get worried about you."

Andy started to rub his head. "Three weeks...It doesn't seem possible."

"Oh it's possible Lord Dragon. According to Redlin you almost burned yourself out."

"And you?"

"I was up an hour or so after you healed me, and for that, I can never repay the debt I owe you, all of you."

"Don't worry about it. You would do the same for me." Tori smiled at him, then mussed his hair. "So tell me what has changed about you."

"It might be best if I show you, stand up." Andy stood up as Tori moved to the middle of the room. She unsheathed both her swords and pointed them at Andy.

"Notice the tips?" Andy looked and saw the points of the sword had red dye on them.

"Yep. Why the..." Andy didn't finish. Tori's arms were a blur of motion as she spun her blades in an intricate dance around her body, never loosing eye contact with Andy. A couple of times it looked like she stepped towards him, but he couldn't really be sure. Suddenly her swords were sheathed and her arms folded across her chest and a smirk on her face.

"That was impressive Tori. I've never seen swords spin that fast."

"Look down at your shirt Andros."

Andy looked down and his heart nearly stopped at what he saw. On his clean-white shirt were thirty or more red dots all around his chest, with a perfect circle of dots over his heart.

"How did you do that?" Andy said with awe. "I'd swear you never got close to me."

"I don't know why it happens, but when I pull my swords, everything around me comes into razor sharp focus. Everyone seems almost frozen, while I can still move normally. Then it feels like every part of my being is more alive than I have ever felt."

"I think you feel the power of Fallon," Andy said rubbing at the spots on his shirt. "It is the same for me when I channel the source."

"Don't ever tell anyone this, but it scares me a little."

"You, scared? I don't believe it."

"Think about it," Tori explained, "I was always part of a team. Cleo and I were closely matched in battle skills, but I have moved way beyond any of them. Different...freak." She turned to glance out the window, her head bent slightly.

Andy understood what was bothering her. She was feeling cut off and alone from her people, and he knew exactly how she felt. He could tell she was really struggling with this by the tears that were just beginning to well up in her eyes.

"Tori, listen. When I first learned I was a dragon, there was an emptiness in the very pit of my soul. I felt I had lost everything about me that was human. I never felt so alone in my life. But there was a man that showed me that no matter what I was or what great and terrible things I could do with my power, I was still the same guy that grew up on the banks of the Hudson, looking for his next adventure that would get him into trouble."

Tori wiped her eyes, ashamed at her supposed weakness.

"You're the same person Tori, you just have greater abilities than most. It hasn't diminished your ability to play pranks has it?"

She gave him a grateful smile as she shook her head.

"Excellent! Now let's...What the..." Andy started shaking and wiggling, smacking himself as if there were a bee in his shirt. "Tori!" he yelled as Percy came slithering out of his pant leg. Tori was rolling on the floor laughing.

After her little prank was over, Andy followed Tori to the common room of the tavern where everyone had assembled. The dead and wounded were gone, the floors and tables cleaned of blood and gore. Sitting by the fireplace were Andy's parents and Abby. Emilia, Leah, Tera and Emma were lounging by a window seat feeling the sun's rays and talking. By the bar, Dain was speaking to Ava, Rhyan and a woman he had never seen before. He did not see Cleo.

"Andy!" Tera yelled as she flew into his arms.

Everyone came over to see how Andy was feeling, asking questions and slapping him on the back, glad he was back among the living. Abby gave him a long kiss and didn't care in the least who saw it.

"I knew you would come back," she whispered in his ear. "My mark was free of pain." Andy remembered that as long as he was alive and not at the source, her dragon brand would cause her no hurt. He stroked her hair and pressed his forehead to hers.

"I love you," he whispered back. Abby gave him a radiant smile in return.

"Andros, this our mother Lily," Rhyan said. Lily was slightly taller than her two daughters with the same wheat colored hair and blue eyes. Looking at her Andy could see where the twins had gotten their good looks.

"Hello," Andy said extending his hand.

"I am afraid that will not do my Lord Dragon," Lily said as she took his hand and pulled him to her in a crushing embrace. Once she pulled back she seemed to study him for a moment as if trying to see something.

"Is something wrong?" Andy said.

"No, my husband spoke of you often, and how there was a stamp of a leader upon you. I now know what he meant," she said with a warming smile. Andy felt slightly uncomfortable under her praise.

"Your husband was a great man. We would not have gotten far without him. As keen as his loss is for me, I can't imagine what it must be like for you. I'm very sorry for your loss."

"Thank you. He and Bart are in Aditya's paradise now, causing the god all kinds of grief no doubt."

To hear her speak warmed Andy's heart, making him think of them on a journey instead of just dead.

"We have been waiting for you to wake up to discuss what has been going on," his father said. "Lily, why don't you start, since you were here when the attack began."

"Of course," she replied. "The morning market shops had just finished opening, and clans from all over we're arriving for the moon market."

"Moon market?" Emilia asked.

"It is held on the longest day of the year. All the shops stay open until the moon rises in the night sky," Ava told her. "Vendors from all over bring their wares to Pharsalia on this day."

"Yes," Lily said taking up the narrative once more, "and that is why there were so many families here. In the center of town, from what looked like a shimmering curtain suspended in the air, more demons than I could count come pouring out. Nightmarish creatures of all different shapes and sizes.

Like ants flooding out of an ant hill they came trampling and killing."

"By the gods," Redlin exclaimed.

"It was horrifying," Lily said with a shudder. "They would have killed us all if the Border Lands warriors hadn't shown up."

"How did you happen upon this Cleo," Dain asked.

"You should ask your beloved, General. She was our scout and alerted us."

Andy almost jumped out of his skin. He never even heard Cleo come up behind him, and she was right next to his shoulder when she spoke. He thought she looked like the old Cleo he remembered, and not the one nearly out of her mind with grief he had met upon arriving in Pharsalia. Her dark hair was braided as is the manner of women warriors before they go into battle. Her leather armor was well oiled and all bloodstains removed. How you remove blood from leather Andy did not know, but Cleo somehow managed it. It hit Andy hard when he realized all the blood had come from the victims of this brutal attack since demons for the most part do not bleed. He looked at her arms and noticed she had black leather bracers with the image of a red arrow etched on them. Andy had the feeling the red arrow was for Bart, he and Cleo had been close friends when he left Vasara the first time, and even suspected they had affections for each other.

Everyone looked to Leah.

"We were in the woods between Dragonsgate and Fenner," Leah said as she pushed her blond hair behind her pointed ears. "I was flying ahead, taking the point, when I spotted a young girl. Her hair was black with streaks like fire, and wearing an ice blue dress as she sat on a rock by a stream. She called my name as I flew down to her." Leah paused for a moment thinking. "She seemed very familiar to me and at the same time, totally alien."

"What does that mean?" Emma asked.

"She may have looked like a little girl, but she was not human. I don't know what she was."

Andy made eye contact with his sister and spoke to her mind. *"Do you think it was Valencia?"*

"It's possible. Leah did say she felt familiar." Andy brought his attention back to Leah.

"I asked her name, but she wouldn't tell me. Instead, she said to take the warriors to Pharsalia, ride all day and night, do not stop." Leah hesitated a moment, sadness in her eyes. "She said we would arrive to see utter devastation, but if we didn't get there in time the destruction would be total."

"By the gods!" Dain exclaimed.

"Yes, I thought the same," Leah said nodding in agreement.

"We rode our horses harder than any other time in their lives," Cleo said taking up the story. Andy noticed her jaw was set and her face hard as she spoke. "The Vipers, with a battalion of warriors, charged in as soon as we crested the hill. We didn't slow or pause, there was no counting the demon horde. Swords were out and swinging as we joined the men of Fenner as they valiantly defended their homes and family. Many paid the ultimate sacrifice. We beat them back, and after they set fire to the city, they fled into the hole they came through." Cleo looked at Andy. He could see her eyes changing to green around the edges, which only happened under extreme anger. "We lost the entire battalion. And of the Vipers, only three remain." Cleo turned her eyes on Tori. "It was almost only two. In any case, the Vipers are no more."

"Dad, how are the demons traveling like this," Andy asked his father.

"I don't know, but I think we need to start making plans."

"I'm all ears master wizard," Tera said as she glided over and sat on a bar stool. Redlin looked at her with a raised eyebrow.

"You'll get use to that," Dain told him.

"Okay, the way I see it, we are going to need to split up."

"Not again," Andy groaned.

"Why do we need to split up dear?" Luel asked her husband.

"Time is running out," he explained. "You need to find your father's crown. Andy needs to get the death dagger from Samara, not to mention we still need to figure out how we are going to free Loki."

"Who's going with who?" Abby asked.

Andy watched as his father seemed to be weighing each person in his mind.

"Abby, Andy, Emma and I will go to Albion. We need to research where to find Samara."

"Why Emma?" Tera asked.

"Because she is a scholar among faeries, she and Abby should be able to find what we are looking for."

"I don't like that Redlin," Tera said with hands on hips. "I don't like that at all."

"Tera, I need you to go with my wife and help protect her."

Tera tapped her chin and narrowed her eyes at the wizard, as if suspecting some trick. Redlin placed his hands on both of her shoulders, giving her a dead serious look.

"You will keep her safe won't you?"

Tera looked momentarily startled at his intensity. "Why, of course I will. Would you expect any less?" Tera stuck her tongue out at him, then hugged him. Redlin winked at his wife over the little faerie's embrace. Luel smiled back knowing her husband had handled Tera just right.

"What about me, Dad?" Emilia asked.

"You need to go with your mother as well."

"I will come with you sister," Leah told her.

"No Leah, I need you, Dain, Cleo and Tori to free Loki."

"I appreciate your new-found faith in me brother," Dain said readjusting the sword on his hip, "but if they were able to snatch Loki, what chance do you think I will have against them."

"You've got something Loki did not have; Leah, Cleo and Tori. Now, as for everyone else I think...Ahhhhhh!" Redlin exclaimed as he put his hands over his ears along with everyone else.

A high-pitched shriek, like claws dragged along a chalkboard, amplified a hundred times cried over the Fenner lands.

"What the hell was that?!" Andy exclaimed once the sound died away, and he could remove his hands from his ears.

"It can't be!" Redlin said as he ran for the door.

"Are we ever going to catch a break," Andy said shaking his head as he dashed after his father to see what new horror they had to face.

Chapter 7

Running out onto the street and shielding his eyes from the bright sunlight, Redlin scanned the sky for something that absolutely should not be there. In the distance he could see a faint outline of a shadowy creature.

"Dad, what was that?" Andy asked.

"That was a shriker, wasn't it," Abby said catching up to them.

"How do you know of them Abby?" Redlin asked her, surprised.

"You should know master wizard," Abby said smiling, "it was in your book, Underworld Creatures Volume I."

"Let me guess, that thing is bad news," Andy remarked.

"Worse than bad news," his father replied.

By now everyone else had joined them in the street. The people of Fenner stared skyward with fear in their eyes. The shadowy form was now just a smudge in the blue sky as it headed West over the ocean.

"So what exactly is a shriker?" Andy asked.

Redlin went on to explain how at the moment of Vasara's creation, a being not unlike a god, tried to wrest control of this young world from the Five and Braylynn.

"His name is Meliakken," Redlin said. "A titanic battle was fought between him and the Five. But it was the added might of a goddess that tipped the balance."

"Are you saying Meliakken could match the Five in power?" Andy asked.

"Yes," Redlin replied. "It was too much for him however when Braylynn jumped into the mix. He was defeated, and they chained him in the underworld."

"What does this Meliakken have to do with shrikers?" Emma asked.

Running his fingers through his hair, Redlin paused before answering Emma. He seemed to be thinking back to another time. "The shrikers are his creations," he finally responded. Looking over at his son, "There are ten, very powerful. They are Meliakken's equivalent to dragons."

"But I thought they were imprisoned with him," Abby said.

"They are, but the bonds must be breaking. How, I do not know, but this does not bode well for us."

"Why was it heading over the ocean," Luel asked her husband as she tied her hair into a ponytail.

"There is an island on which it was created. The Five could not destroy the power Meliakken had given his beasts, but they were able to separate them from it. I have a feeling it is headed there to reclaim that power. We have a small window though. Like all underworld creatures it can only take physical form by passing through the corridor in the Border Lands."

"Unless it comes through one of those gateways the demons used to arrive in Fenner," Cleo remarked.

Redlin looked towards her, the same thought had just occurred to him. "We need to move fast."

***

Redlin scanned the woods as they left the borders of Fenner behind. Andy was scouting up ahead, on horseback instead of dragon form. Abby and Emma were in quiet conversation directly behind him while Rhyan watched the extreme rear. Lily had insisted that her daughters join the wizard on his quest, totally disregarding his protests. Ava went with his wife and daughter.

The hard packed trail had many turns as it wound its way south. Redlin was amazed how much change the land had gone through in fifteen-hundred years, and yet much was still the same. Proof of that was coming into view. Off to the left, where the trail had originally been, stood a solitary tree that was different from any other around it, a talon tree, the only one outside of Laurel Hollow. Redlin had planted it there himself and caused it to grow. One of his attempts to impress the woman he loved by giving her a reminder of home outside of the faerie kingdom. He smiled to himself, Braylynn was not happy about it. The trees were her creation, and she didn't appreciate the wizard taking such liberties.

"All clear behind," Rhyan said riding up next to him.

"Do you sense any horses in the area?"

"No, we are alone. Why does your son not change and scout from the air?" she said.

"I want to try and keep our passing as secretive as possible, and Andy tends to stand out against the sky. May I ask you something Rhyan?"

"Of course," Rhyan said as she adjusted the bow on her shoulder.

"Being a priestess of Aditya, I know you can mind link with horses, but are there any other abilities you have from that role."

"Well, since my sister and I are both priestess to the god, we can also communicate one to another over long distances. Mainly through mind impressions of what we are experiencing at the moment."

Redlin thought it quite remarkable that one of the gods should have two priests. It had never happened that he was aware of, and for Aditya to do that at this time must be a portent for the coming danger.

"That is a great skill to have."

"Well, yes and no," she replied. "The main drawback is all we get are thought impressions, each of us needs to interpret what the other means. Most of the time we are in sync, but once in a while we will be totally off."

"Can you tell where she is now?"

Rhyan closed her eyes and concentrated.

"They are on Bowen's ship still, but too far out to sea for any visible landmarks."

Redlin had asked Bowen if he would sail his wife and daughter, along with Tera and Ava to the northern tip of Parma. They needed to find Pan. Andy had told him how the king of the fauns had disappeared right before the battle to take down Devon. Something about the being that attacked that night at the inn disturbed Pan somehow. They needed to find out what he knew.

"Redlin," Emma said with quiet urgency as she rode up. "Something is wrong."

"What do you mean," he asked her.

"Something evil has passed through here recently. The trees still recoil from it."

"Are you able to discern the danger?"

"No, but...is that a talon tree?" Emma said pointing back to the tree Redlin planted centuries ago.

"Yes it is."

"I'll be right back." Emma rode over to the tree and dismounted. Placing her hands on the bark she closed her eyes, her wings moving as if pushed by a gentle breeze.

"What is she doing?" Rhyan asked the wizard.

"Emma's gift is the ability to connect with trees. I imagine she is gaining some knowledge about what might have occurred here."

After several minutes Emma came riding back, a puzzled frown on her face.

"What is it?" the wizard asked her.

"It is very strange," she replied looking at the ground and shaking her head. "The images from the talon tree showed soldiers of the White Castle. But they were committing unspeakable atrocities. They had prisoners tied to wagons and forced to walk behind." She looked up at the wizard. "Several of the officers had black and orange eyes, which made them seem inhuman."

Redlin did not like the sound of this at all. He scanned the forest with his mind, reaching out to see if he could sense any immediate threat. He could not detect anything.

"Andy!" he called to his son.

Andy rode up on his black mare. A huge beast, but long and thickly muscled, bred for both speed and endurance.

"What's up Dad?" Andy exclaimed pulling his horse to a stop beside his father.

"Keep a close hand on the source. Something is wrong here." Redlin told Andy what Emma had seen from the talon tree.

"Will do," Andy replied as he wheeled his horse around to ride on ahead.

As Andy rode on, Redlin scanned the woods. Reaching for the source he conjured a dome of protection around them. Emma's vision troubled him greatly. Soldiers with black and orange eyes meant only one thing, demon possession. What they were doing with their prisoners was a mystery.

They hadn't gotten too far when Redlin noticed on the trail before them were two rather large butterflies. One was completely black, the other a mixture of blue and green. Their behavior puzzled him, because instead of flitting amongst the flowers or bushes, these two hovered directly in the middle of the path. They couldn't have been there long he reasoned, or certainly Andy would have noticed their odd behavior. As it was, Andy had disappeared beyond a bend in the trail.

Just then, two more butterflies appeared directly above the first, looking like the beginnings of two lines suspended in midair. As Redlin suspected would happen, more and more butterflies kept joining, forming more lines, making a colorful wall.

"Have you ever seen the like?" Redlin asked aloud.

"Actually I have," Emma said scanning the woods. "Bella, come out here! I know you're there."

Giggling came from their left, back in the trees. The branches rustled as a tall slender faerie stepped into view. Her hair was white with purple streaks, coming down past her shoulders which were bare in the silk blue top she wore. Her skin was white, like moon beams, and her wings were a translucent purple, the same color as her hair. Forest brown eyes sat on either side of an aquiline nose, and they carried a mischievous look amongst her quirky red-lip smile.

"Bella, what are you doing here?"

"Emma, perhaps you should introduce us to your friend," Redlin said.

"No need for that master wizard," Bella replied smiling. "My little friends have told me all about each of you."

Redlin turned a puzzled look to Emma.

"Bella's gift is that she can communicate with butterflies," Emma explained. "She has this annoying habit of using them to eavesdrop, since no one would suspect a butterfly in their midst to be listening."

Bella looked a little guilty.

"Now Emma, I only ever did that once on purpose for which I apologized profusely."

"Hmm," Emma said crossing her arms. Abby burst out laughing.

"I'm sure there is a fascinating tale here, but we really must be pushing on," the wizard said.

"Exactly," Bella said. "I have been sent to accompany you."

"Sent by who?" Redlin said eyeing her suspiciously, already knowing the answer.

"Braylynn, she seemed to think you could use someone with my particular skills."

"Did you speak to her?" Emma asked.

"Not directly, no. She hasn't been seen in Laurel Hollow for some time. She came to me in my dreams."

Redlin scratched his head trying to decide if he should go against the goddess's wishes and make Bella stay here. In the end, he figured Braylynn must know what she is doing. He contacted his son through mind speak to let him know of the latest developments. When he mentioned the goddess, Andy did not seem surprised at the unexpected addition to their little party of travelers. The word 'typical' came up a lot in their conversation.

After three hours' travel, they had arrived at a small town. There was a single road going down the middle with houses and small businesses on either side. Redlin did not remember this little village at all. Probably sprang up somewhere in Vasara's history. The wizard spotted a modest inn right in the center of town. Horses were tied up out front.

"Rhyan, what is this place?"

"Prospecting town," she replied. "They are mostly miners living here."

"What are they mining?" Andy asked watching the rough looking group standing outside the inn as they gave them the once over.

"Silver," Rhyan replied. "They mine the hills and streams throughout. These people are very territorial."

"Dad, that bunch over there is watching us intently. I'm having a bad feeling."

The last thing Redlin wanted was attention paid to their comings and goings. Suddenly a wicked thought came into his head and smiled mischievously.

"Oh no," Andy said shaking his head noticing his father's smile.

"What's wrong?" Emma asked.

"I don't know," Andy replied, "but he has that look that means something unexpected is about to happen."

No sooner had Andy finished talking when a cry rang out from the edge of town. A prospector that looked like he had spent a year underground came into view.

"Gold!" he shouted over and over, waving his hands wildly. When he had the attention of most of the prospectors within earshot, he turned and ran back into the hills. The men in front of the inn, looked at one another, then broke and bolted for their horses and equipment, following the man out into the wilderness.

Redlin had a self-satisfied smile on his face when he said, "Shall we proceed."

"That prospector wasn't real, was he?" Andy asked his father, squinting at him.

"Who is to say what is real and what is not," Redlin said giving him a wink.

"Loki kind of said the same thing to me once," Andy said shaking his head. "It's no wonder you're brothers."

The rooms at the inn were adjoining and both doors were open to make conversing easier. Random butterflies kept landing on Redlin's head.

"Bella, I thought butterflies weren't nocturnal," Redlin asked brushing away the one that landed on his nose.

"Most aren't," she replied. "There is one species that will fly in the day or night. They rest when they're tired, doesn't matter when. You can tell which ones they are by the red stripe at the base of the wing. No other butterflies have this."

Looking closely, Redlin could see the red stripe. He had an idea. "Would you be able to send them down to the common room and observe, then have them come back in an hour or so?"

"Easily, master wizard," Bella replied with a smirk as she spoke to one of her little friends. How one speaks to butterflies was beyond him. She held the butterfly to her lips as if she were kissing it. Her voice was a soft soprano. The sound was musical, but Redlin could not understand any words, if words they were. The butterfly fluttered away and down the stairs to its post. Redlin surmised that if this worked, the butterflies could make very decent spies indeed.

"What's the next step Dad?" Andy asked.

"In the morning we continue south to Albion."

"What of the soldiers the trees saw?" Emma asked standing by the fireplace, her wings folded making her look almost like a human girl. "They are still out there, doing only the goddess knows what."

"We can't spend the effort to hunt them down. Time for the other dragons is running out. Should these demon-possessed soldiers cross our path, that's when we will deal with them," Redlin said.

It wrenched at Redlin not to be able to free those poor people, but he saw no other alternative. What he needed was a legion of Border Lands warriors to help deal with this problem, but unless he ran across them on the trail as well, they would be on their own.

An hour later, the butterfly came flitting into the room and landed on Bella's shoulder. Tilting her head Bella listened closely.

"Well?" Redlin asked after several moments.

"There is nothing to fear," Bella replied. "She says there are only common miners. There was one unsavory looking character who had just left when she got down there."

Redlin raised a surprised eyebrow. "Did it really say 'unsavory'?"

"She," Bella corrected, "and yes she did. Butterflies have a more extensive vocabulary than humans."

"Very well, let's get some sleep, we will want to leave early."

The morning turned out to be grey and overcast. Once again, Andy took the point while Rhyan fell back to protect their rear. Emma and Bella would fly in and out of the woods from time to time. Redlin did not know where Bella's butterflies had gone, but one huge black-winged one had decided to hitch a ride on his shoulder. "Lazy," the wizard said to it with his eyebrow raised quizzically. He could swear the creature actually looked offended.

"How much longer?" Abby asked him, bringing him out of his butterfly musings.

"I'm thinking two days," he told her. "We will leave the road soon and take a trail up through that pass over there," he said pointing to a space between two mountain peaks." Redlin looked fondly at Abby. She had become like another daughter to him. His son could not have found a better woman to love, which made him want to protect her all the more, although Redlin knew she had an inner strength and could very well look after herself. She had done it most of her life living in Dragonsgate.

The attack came without any warning. A fireball flew past Redlin's face and impacted with the tree right next to him, setting it aflame. He immediately grabbed the source and threw his dome of protection around himself and Abby. He looked in the direction the fireball had come and spotted a hooded figure like the ones that had attacked them from Bannerman's Castle. It was surrounded by soldiers with black and orange eyes. Twenty at least, demon possessed soldiers. The demon, or whatever it was, had both hands raised, fireballs shooting out of its palms, exploding on Redlin's dome.

"Can you fight back?" Abby asked him, drawing her sword.

"Not without dropping my shield, which will leave you vulnerable."

"Don't worry about me master wizard," Abby said with a wicked looking grin. Redlin groaned inward, she was as bad as Andy.

The hooded being momentarily faltered in its attack. Redlin could see why. Galloping down the trail, Rhyan had her bow shooting arrows at incredible rate as she rode her horse without any use of the reigns. Redlin was sure, as a priestess of Aditya, she could control her steed without the use of her hands.

Andy, we need you, he sent to his son. *We're under attack.*

I'm in the same situation here Dad, they came out of nowhere. Emma and Bella are with me. I shielded all of us, but we can't sit here forever.

Can you change and fly them out?

I don't think so. Not without dropping my shield. It's one of those hooded guys again Dad.

We have one here too, the wizard responded.

Redlin watched as the soldiers started to fan out, encircling them. He looked around, trying to find a weak spot.

"Redlin," the hooded creature hissed like a snake.

The wizard was stunned. He still kept scanning for a way out of this death circle. "How do you know me?" Redlin asked, not dropping his shield even though the fireballs had stopped.

The creature threw back its hood. Redlin gasped. Its face was very much akin to Pan.

Dad! This thing just threw off its hood, it looks like Pan! It even knew my name.

Redlin started thinking fast. Something told him not to get into a parley with this thing.

"Rhyan, get an arrow ready and point it directly between its eyes."

Rhyan did as he bade. Pulling one of Bart's godstone arrows out of her quiver, she drew back ready to fire. The wizard's hope was to distract it long enough to lower his shield and blast a hole through the soldiers ranks blocking the trail. He hated having to kill these innocents, but there was no choice. Hopefully they would get to Andy and the others before that thing had a chance to recover and attack them from behind.

"Now," Redlin said, letting his shield drop, allowing Rhyan's arrow to pass through. The Pan look-alike quickly raised its hands to fire more energy bolts, but as if sensing something, it crossed its arms and vanished as the godstone arrow went through the space it previously occupied. Redlin unleashed wind bursts at the soldiers. With that thing gone, the wizard didn't feel the need to destroy them if it could be avoided.

Galloping through the gap, they flew down the trail towards Andy. He could hear the battle long before he saw it. When they came upon the scene, Andy and the two faeries were engaged with not only one of those creatures, but regular demons as well, not the demon possessed soldiers Redlin had just faced.

Get ready to change son, as soon as we draw its attention.

Demons were crawling and clawing all over Andy's protection dome, they were hardly visible through the swarm of demons.

Dad I can't, I don't have enough room. I will crush my horse, not to mention Emma and Bella.

I'm going to get them to come after me. Once you are clear, have Emma and Bella fly you straight up. When you are high enough, change, we should be able to take care of them.

Great idea Dad, Andy replied.

"We need some distraction ladies," Redlin said to Abby and Rhyan.

"I'm sure I can pull some of them with me through the woods," Rhyan said.

"Can you outrun them?" the wizard asked.

Rhyan patted the neck of her steed. "I doubt these demons can keep pace with Bolt, especially when we start making our own trails through the underbrush."

"What about Abby's horse?"

"She could outrun them as well. I picked these horses myself specifically for this reason."

"Abby, take this," Redlin said holding up a short sword.

"I already have a blade," Abby told him.

"Not like this one." Redlin held the sword in front of him, mouthing some words as he ran glowing fingers along its metal length. "Any thrust you make will cause lightning to shoot out of the tip. Be careful where you point it," He said handing it to her. "Once we start, just ride down the trail getting as many as you can to follow, thrust at anything that moves towards you."

He looked back towards Rhyan. "As soon as you are clear, start sending images of those monsters to your sister. Have you ever met Pan?"

"Yes," Rhyan replied. "Ava and I have ventured into the faun king's territory many times."

"Send her his image as well. Hopefully she will understand that we need Pan's help in figuring out exactly what we are up against."

Rhyan nodded in understanding.

Redlin made a quick move to his left, his horse kicking up lose dirt as it sought to find traction. Once it had its footing, the wizard started shooting energy blasts at what he now thought of as a Pan-demon. The thing fired back, impacting with Redlin's energy causing an ear-shattering detonation.

Rhyan shot rapid fire arrows at Andy's protection dome, scoring direct hits on many grotesque looking demons. A score or more turned and started coming towards her. Kicking Bolt's flanks, Rhyan galloped headlong into the woods with a sizeable demon horde on her tail.

Abby began her assault, lightning shooting out of her sword, cutting through dirt and demons. A great howl erupted as some very large pig-like looking demons came chasing after her. Pulling hard on the reigns, she turned her horse around and began to sprint down the trail, occasionally thrusting behind her to send lightning strikes back to her pursuers.

Redlin could see Andy now, a large portion of the demons having fled to chase after Abby and Rhyan, not to mention the dozens that were headed in his direction. A great fireball shot up from where Andy's dome had been, and he could see Emma and Bella lifting him skyward, their faerie wings a blur as they shot straight up.

"I think it is time to get out of here," Redlin said aloud as he was about to be overwhelmed. The Pan-demon was momentarily distracted as Andy and the faeries took off. Not waiting, he galloped in the direction Rhyan had fled, which turned out not to be the best choice. Just as he started to dash into the woods, he felt a searing hot pain between his shoulder blades, and the feeling of being lifted out of his saddle. A demon had caught up to him, wielding a massive club. Redlin threw up a quick shield to protect his head, but even with that, the impact was so jarring that he could feel himself about to lose consciousness. Just as darkness took him, he thought he could hear a dragon's roar.

Chapter 8

Bowen's ship seemed to be plowing through the water at a pretty fast clip. Luel stood at the starboard rail looking out to sea, her wings catching the breeze as it pushed them back and forth. She felt her daughter's presence behind her even before she uttered a word.

"Mom?" Emilia said gliding up to her.

Luel turned around and smiled at her daughter. She was so proud of her children, at all they have accomplished and what they have become. She could think of no one else she would want by her side as she once again entered the place of her pain. Luel would rather her whole family beside her, but if that was not to be, then it was for a mother and daughter to finish what had begun with a mother and daughter. She prayed her own daughter would not have to see her mother die as she had. The pain was still raw, but Luel felt a true healing process had begun, and her heart was lighter because of it.

She raised a hand to caress her daughter's cheek. "What is it darling?"

Emilia was not wearing her Summoner clothes, but instead wore a comfortable green skirt with a faerie vest to match. The silver comb still adorned the top of her head amongst her black tresses.

"I just wanted to make sure you were okay," Emilia replied.

"I am." Luel took in a deep breath of the ocean air, as if she were breathing Vasara back into her lungs. "I would not have chosen to come back by the route we had, nor under the circumstances that surround us. But it does feel good to be back in our world." She looked closely at her daughter. "Do not think that means I did not treasure the home you and Andy grew up in, or the many friends we left behind. I will miss them all terribly." Luel once again looked towards the horizon, remembering other times when she was Emilia's age, when Vasara was her playground, and she had that indestructible attitude all young faeries have.

"You do not think we will be going back?"

She looked thoughtfully at her daughter. "To tell you the truth, I honestly do not know. We will think about that when and if the time comes."

Just then Ava walked up on deck, followed closely by Tera.

"Your highness," Ava called. Ava had been privy to the scroll Braylynn had sent to Luel and the mention of Luel's nobility amongst the faerie.

"Ava please, just Luel," she told her kindly.

"Yes ma'am," Ava responded. "Sorry."

"No need for apologies dear. What is it?"

"We need to find Pan!" Tera blurted out.

"Oh?" Luel said with a slightly raised eyebrow. "And why is that?"

"I'll let Ava tell you," Tera replied as she smacked Emilia on the head. "Catch me if you can Donella!" Tera proceeded to fly around the mast up to the crow's nest. Emilia gave her an exasperated look.

"In a moment," Emilia replied rubbing her head, "I would like to hear what Ava has to say. It's not my fault you couldn't wait to hear with the rest of us," she called up to her.

Luel was fighting back laughter. "Why Pan?" she asked the priestess of Aditya.

Ava pulled back her blonde hair into a ponytail and tied it off to keep the sea breeze from blowing it all over the place. "I just got a message from my sister."

Luel looked puzzled. "How is that possible?"

Ava went on to tell her the same thing that Rhyan had told Redlin, that as priestess of the god, they can share images across great distances. She told Emilia and Luel that her sister had sent her scenes of a battle with demons and hooded creatures, that when their hoods were removed their facial features resembled Pan. Rhyan had also sent her repeated images of the king of the fauns, which Ava interpreted to be important that they find him.

Luel took all this information in. She did not like that her husband and son were already involved in a confrontation with the enemy. "Could you see the battle's outcome?"

"No, Rhyan did not send that."

"What do you think Mom?" Emilia asked.

"Can you contact Andy?"

Emilia closed her eyes and concentrated. "I can sense him, but he is too far to talk to him. He is alive."

That was something Luel thought. Redlin must have had Rhyan send her message, so she would know Pan had information that would be important to their quest. "Tera, tell Bowen to come here please," she shouted up to the crow's nest.

"Right away your majesty," Tera yelled back. Luel groaned inward. Before they left Fenner, Dain had confided his last trip with Tera. How positively annoying she could sometimes be. Everyone loved Tera and would risk their lives for hers any day, but Tera can try one's patience.

A minute or so later Bowen came walking towards them with Tera circling his head as he tried to swat her away like he would a fly.

"Yes Luel? Tera, will you stop that!" Bowen roared. Tera collapsed on the deck in a fit of laughter, her wings curled up around her body.

"We may need to alter our course," she said looking down at the silver haired faerie attempting to get herself under control.

"I will land you wherever you wish," he said with a bow. Bowen treated her with great respect. She had a feeling that had more to do with being the mother of Andros the Black, and not so much her faerie lineage.

"Can you land us at the southernmost shore of Parma?"

"Let me check my charts, I think I remember an inlet that will allow us to sail partway into the Wilds. I will be right back," Bowen said as he headed below to his cabin.

"What do you have in mind?" Emilia asked her mother.

"We are going to find Diminitus, he knows the way to Pan."

"You know how to find him?"

"I know where his house is, hopefully he will be there."

True to his word, Bowen had found a waterway that took the Grey Morning several miles into Parma. Seeing the land of her pain momentarily wrenched at Luel's heart. She hadn't set foot in the Wilds since that awful day she had to take her father's life. The forest was dense, and one couldn't see but a few yards into it. Tree trunks were thick with moss as multi-colored insects traversed up and down. Birds of every type adorned the branches, lending their song to the musical ripple of the water that was lapping against the bow of the ship.

"This is as far as we can go Luel," Bowen said walking up to her. "The water's depth is almost at the limit of the ship's draft. We will anchor here and put you ashore in the long boats, which I guess is mostly for Ava since you, your daughter and Tera could easily fly to shore."

"Thank you so much Captain, your help has been invaluable."

"It's my honor and privilege. Your family has done more for Vasara, and me personally, that it is not possible to repay such a debt, also friends do not repay one another that which is done out of love. That being said, my ship and myself are always at your disposal without hesitation."

"You are a true friend Captain," Luel said giving him a hug and a kiss on the cheek.

"Umm, yes, well...let me go see about the launch," Bowen said blushing slightly from the attention.

"My turn," Tera exclaimed as she flew into the Captain's arms. Bowen couldn't help laughing as Tera smothered him with kisses.

Scanning the shore for any signs of hostile life, Emilia kept her vigilance from her seat. The last time she rode a river in a boat through the Wilds, a band of Alfar nearly ended their quest before it had even begun. She kept glancing at her mother. Since entering Parma she seemed to have withdrawn into herself if only slightly. Not that Emilia could blame her, especially coming to the place where you watched your mother brutally butchered. Tera sat in the front, watching for hazards hidden just below the surface. Ava was in the stern, one foot on the gunwale perfectly balanced, arrow on string, ready to fire at any movement that threatened to cause them harm. Bowen's sailors kept a steady pace on the oars as they covered the half mile distance to shore.

Emilia had changed into her Dragon Summoner clothes just before leaving the ship. She had taken her comb out and transformed it into the staff of the goddess. She looked through the dragon eye in her crown, but Andy was still too far away to be able to see through his eyes. She also sent her mind roving for any hints of the other dragons, there was nothing.

"Summoner," Ava whispered urgently.

Emilia, sensing Ava had seen something dropped her voice to a whisper as well. "What is it Ava?"

"I see it," Luel said peering toward the bank they were rowing for. Emilia followed her gaze.

"To the left," Ava said. "See the movement."

Emilia could see it now, branches and underbrush rustling from movement of someone or something. Emilia started to focus the power of her staff, ready to obliterate whatever decided to show itself. Just then, a man leading two horses emerged from the wood. It only took Emilia a split-second to recognize who it was. Changing her staff back to a comb, she pushed it into her hair as she flew like lightning to the man on the beach. Those in the boat could only see Emilia tackle the man to the ground. Had they been closer, they would have been able to tell Emilia and this stranger were locked in an urgent kiss.

"Lyson," Emilia whispered over and over in his ear as they broke apart and just held each other.

"Donella my love," Lyson responded.

"So I am assuming this is Lyson," Luel said hovering over them smiling, her spear out and ready, not at first sure of what they were facing.

"Yep, that's him," Tera said with a huge grin spread across her face. She darted down and joined them in a group hug.

Once Ava was ashore and Bowen's sailors had rowed back to the ship, Lyson led them back to the camp he had set up for their arrival. It was set back about five miles into the woods. Emilia rode on the back of Lyson's horse, arms wrapped tightly around his waist as she lay her head on his back. She couldn't believe he was here. His blue eyes still held that soft yet all-knowing look, as if there was nothing they had not seen. His handsome face was devoid of wrinkles and his dark hair held hardly any grey. Tera had been right, Border Lands warriors did not age as normal humans do. Lyson was not wearing his chain mail, or any armor for that matter. Aside from the cloak bearing his family crest. He wore soft leather riding pants and leather jerkin to match. On his hip was his serpent hilt sword which all generals of high rank wear in the Border Lands army.

Ava was on the second horse Lyson had brought. Tera and Luel were flying close behind and in front. Luel had changed her body color to match that of the forest, making her almost invisible. A couple of times Emilia would call out to her only to jump when her voice sounded right beside her. No threats were detected on their short ride back to camp.

Lyson had come prepared, two tents were set up with a camp fire in between and several army campaign chairs positioned around it.

"How long have you been here?" Emilia asked. She sat in a chair next to him holding a glass of wine that Lyson had poured for everyone, swirling its contents and taking a sampling sip.

"A little over a week, although I have been months traveling here."

"Lyson, before we start assaulting you with questions, why not start by telling us where this all started for you," Luel told him.

"Yes, of course Luel."

Emilia noticed Lyson was being very polite and courteous around her mother. Not that he isn't that way, but Emilia could tell the general wanted to get on the good side of the mother of the woman he loves. Emilia looked at the ground and smiled. Lyson saw her and raised an eyebrow, making Emilia's smile even bigger.

"By the goddess!" Tera exclaimed as she watched their exchange closely. "Luel, can't they go into the woods and get all their 'true love' talk out of the way? They're starting to make me nauseous."

Luel looked at Tera, then burst out laughing. No doubt remembering her time when Redlin was courting her. "Tera, sometimes you are positively inspiring. I should have seen that myself. She's right," Luel said to her daughter, "we will wait for you here."

Emilia gave a grateful look to her mother. She knew what Lyson had to say was important for the others to hear, but she needed this time with him. From the time she first suspected he had feelings for her she wanted to keep a silent barrier between them, more for self-preservation from hurt than any real reason. After reading his letter sent by Emma, that fear had disappeared. Giving a gentle thrust of her green wings, she rose out of the chair and settled down next to him. "Shall we sir?" she asked extending a hand. Lyson smiled, and taking her hand led her down the trail that took them from view of the others.

"Donella, stop for a moment please. I want to truly look at you without distraction."

Emilia turned to face him. His blue eyes were penetrating as they drank her in. He looked like he was trying to imprint her very being into his memory, raising a hand to caress her cheek. Emilia closed her eyes, the feel of his firm hand was soft and gentle.

"You are exactly as I remember you," he said with wonder. "Braylynn told me of this time shift, but to actually experience it is something else altogether. You got my message?"

"Yes, Emma and Tera brought it to me. Were you able to get mine?"

"I received no parchment my love. But there was something strange as I entered the Wilds."

"What was that?"

"The trees seemed to be whispering with your voice, calling my name but with such love. It was so faint I felt like I was just imaging it. Or maybe because it is something I so badly desire, I've tricked myself to think that was what it was."

Emilia felt herself flush, and she felt a tingling sensation throughout her body and into her wings. No one had ever told her that they desired her.

"It was no trick Lyson." Emilia told him how she had asked Emma to send her message through the trees. And across many worlds it came to him. The enormity of such a thing staggered the mind, and Emilia felt only love was strong enough to do this. "Don't tell me how you came to be here, save that for when we are back with the others. For now, tell me about your life from the last time I saw you." Emilia folded in her wings and sat down on a fallen tree next to the trail. Lyson sat down next to her.

"Well," Lyson began scratching his head. "I'm not sure where to begin."

"Begin anywhere, it doesn't matter. Just talk, I want to hear your voice." This all felt strange to Emilia. She had given her heart totally over to Lyson, something she had never done with anyone. And if asked when this might have happened, she wouldn't be able to really tell. It was like something so natural and gradual that her heart slipped right into his without her even realizing it. She chose not to think about the impracticality of relationships between humans and faeries. She could see now why Leah was reluctant to acknowledge her feeling for Dain. To love a person you know you will long outlive can be crushing to the soul. But Emilia figured it didn't really matter. It was too late for her, Lyson had her heart for all time.

"After you left to return to your world I went back to Lyonsdale. With all four stones back on the Pillars of Fallon, the Corridor has been a lot easier to manage. No longer did we have to keep constant vigil. It was then that I decided to resign my commission."

"Lyson, no," Emilia said shocked. She could not believe he gave up the only life he had ever known, and one which he seemed to enjoy and was proud of.

"Yes love," he said holding her hand as he looked into her beautiful green eyes.

Lyson went on to tell her that with her gone, the Border Lands had seemed to lose all color. He decided to travel. He sailed for a time with Bowen and saw islands and lands he had only read about. Lyson also told her how he spent a good amount of time in Kensington with Paolo and Acacia, studying in the great library. He always loved to study, but it seemed like he had a hunger he could not satisfy, a hunger for knowledge.

"It was then that my thoughts turned to Laurel Hollow. I felt like I was being pulled there."

Emilia did not like the sound of that. Usually when there is any pushing and pulling of the spirit, Braylynn has a hand in it, and told him so.

"Whatever the reason, I spent almost ten years there. I now know every piece of faerie lore there is, reading every scroll Valencia had in her library and personal study. Braylynn also led me to a cave on the border between Parma and Laurel Hollow. There is a library there that is Braylynn's own. I also know about your mother's lineage and what it means now that she is here."

"Yes, Braylynn's message hinted at what is to come regarding the royal succession," Emilia said. Braylynn had something in mind for Lyson, she could feel it.

Lyson reached a hand up and pushed a lock of Emilia's black hair behind her pointed ear. "Donella, I stayed in the home of the Dragon Summoner, I hope you don't mind."

"Lyson my love, of course I don't mind."

"I could feel your presence there, and it brought me comfort."

Emilia cupped his stubble face in both hands. She was still overwhelmed by the fact that he was here beside her. She lay her head on his chest as he enveloped her in his arms. She felt like she could stay there forever.

"Are you about finished down there?" Tera shouted down the trail.

Emilia, her eyes still closed started to giggle. "By the goddess I love my sister, but she has the worst timing. Let's go back, and you can tell everyone why you are here."

Lyson told them how Braylynn came to him in a dream. He was on his way to Albion because there was a scroll there that he remembered seeing on faerie history the last time he had visited that city, Baron Aidan's own personal copy. The goddess told him he had to make his way quickly to the southern coast of Parma. She didn't say exactly why, but she instructed him to get another horse to bring with him, as well as a pack horse. Lyson assumed he was to meet someone, but she did not tell him who.

"After I had gotten the necessary supplies I thought I would need, I set immediately off for the Wilds," Lyson explained. "It was very strange traveling when I entered Parma."

"What do you mean?" Luel asked.

"I encountered no living soul on the trail until you came ashore. In Parma life abounds, but other than the occasional animal and the birds, the trail was mine alone."

"That is strange," Luel remarked. "At the very least I would have thought you would have been challenged by the centaurs.

They always know when a foreigner enters the Wilds and will go to investigate."

"Maybe Braylynn protected his journey," Ava said as she sat examining the fletching of her arrows.

"Maybe," Lyson said. "In any case, it was pleasant not to be harassed the whole way here."

Emilia kept thinking there must be something else. "Lyson, not that I'm not happy you are here," Emilia said as she smiled at him. "Did Braylynn tell you why she thought you should be here? There must be a reason."

"She did not tell me."

"Typical goddess fashion," Tera said flying slow circles around every one.

"Tera, would you sit down," Emilia said. "You're making me dizzy."

"Why of course, sister dear," she said floating down into Emilia's lap.

"That really is all there is to tell on my part," Lyson said adjusting his sword. "Can you tell me the quest you are on? Maybe I will have a better idea of why I am here."

Luel filled him in on everything, from Tera and Emma's visit to their home in New York to their arrival on the shores of Parma. The fire was built up as night descended over the Wilds. After breaking their meal late in the evening, Lyson took watch outside while the women went to sleep in the tents. Emilia, feeling restless, got up and went outside to pass the night with Lyson. He was not ungrateful for the company.

"Lyson," Emilia said looking over at him. They had been sitting close together watching the burning embers as the fire burned down.

Lyson looked up to meet her green eyes, sensing something in her voice. "Yes my love?"

There was a thought that had been plaguing Emilia since they had first returned to Vasara. She pushed it out of her mind because she didn't want to think about. Now that she was south, in the Wilds, the thought came back full force and knew she must voice it. She had to know.

"Have you seen Zana, now or since, that day?"

After Emilia's confrontation with Zana and then saving her life after Devon tried to destroy them both, and Leah as well, she had watched as Zana fled south behind Devon's ravens. Emilia doubted she had seen the last of her. The prophecy had saved Zana that day, it certainly wasn't how Emilia would have ended it. Now it nagged at her, where Zana might be and what she was up to.

"I have not seen, nor had word of her since you bested her," Lyson replied. He put a hand gently on her shoulder her. "I don't think you need worry about her. She would be crazy to show herself, especially with all of us here with you."

Lyson's words had the desired calming effect. But she knew where Zana was concerned, this was very far from over. If anything, Emilia felt Zana's alliance with Devon was just a prelude to the greater evil yet to come.

Two days after breaking camp found Emilia and the others following her mother as she flew ahead of them, guiding them to Diminitus's house. Once in a while, Emilia could swear her mother would just vanish in front of them. She knew her mother just changed the hue of her skin to match her surroundings, but it was still unnerving to see it happen. Ava brought up the rear, arrow resting on the bow as she scanned the forest for threats.

It came without warning, a buzzing sound followed by a thunk. Emilia looked back to see Ava slumped over her horse, an Alfar arrow stuck out of her neck. The obvious poison already paralyzing her from screaming out.

"Mom!" Emilia yelled. "Alfar!"

"Bastards!" Lyson screamed, wheeling his horse around and racing back to Ava, his sword drawn.

Emilia had the staff of the goddess out, glowing blinding white. She could not see the Alfar, and was hesitant to shoot randomly into the dense forest.

"Ahhhhhh!" Luel screamed as she flew past Emilia, the spear of her father extended as she disappeared into the woods

"Mom, wait!" Emilia yelled after her. "Tera, follow me."

Tera had her talon spear extended in one hand and a dagger in the other settling closely behind Emilia.

The forest erupted in arrows. Emilia projected a shield forward as the deadly missiles ricocheted off. Up ahead she could just barely see her mother. She might have missed Luel altogether if not for the silver spear rising and falling as Alfar after Alfar fell beneath her vengeful fury. The blood lust Luel displayed shocked her. Never in her wildest dreams could she have imagined her calm and gentle mother capable of the ferocity she now exhibited as she dealt out death in the name of Luel's own mother.

Emilia knew it was only a matter of time before sheer numbers of Alfar overwhelmed them. Behind her, she could her that Tera was knocking off arrows coming from the rear. They did not have much time.

"Tera stay right on me!"

Emilia flew like lightning until she was near her mother, and quickly erected a dome of protection over the three of them. Luel screamed in frustration as she was suddenly cutoff from her slaughter, crashing her shoulder into the shield.

"Open it up Emilia! Do you hear me? Now!"

"No Mom," Emilia said firmly. "You are not yourself. We need to get back to Lyson and Ava. They're vulnerable right now."

Luel seemed to soften, but the tightness remained around her eyes as she followed her daughter back out, Alfar arrows following after. Lyson was off his horse when they came upon him with sword drawn. Ava was at his feet unconscious, the horses encircled them. Emilia came to touch down next to him and quickly knelt to examine Ava. Luel and Tera faced the forest, spears ready in case any Alfar gave pursuit.

"Can you heal her?" Lyson asked.

"I don't know yet." Emilia closed her eyes. Moving her ring over Ava's body to see what she may discover. The Dragon Summoner's ring was able to draw power from the elemental forces around it, and she felt this a better tool than the staff. In her mind's eye she could see the poison moving from Ava's neck down towards her heart. She needed to stop its spread until she could figure out what to do.

"I wish Ala were here," she thought to herself. Ala was the healer and priestess of Raphael, who had cured Emilia from her skull spider bite, which had almost killed her.

Luel put a hand on her shoulder. Emilia looked up and saw her mother had returned to her normal self. Gone was the avenging shade who seemed intent on the genocide of the Alfar. "We need to get her to Diminitus. If anyone knows a cure for the Alfar poison, it's Diminitus."

Emilia returned her attention to Ava. The Fenner priestess had taken on a ghostly pallor, her flaxen hair matted with sweat. The wound in her neck was raised and hot to the touch. Lyson had stopped the blood flow after removing the arrow. Emilia could tell she was barely breathing. Her mother was right, they needed Diminitus. He's lived amongst these creatures for eons, he must know something. Emilia flew up and settled onto Ava's horse.

"Lyson, can you put Ava in front of me."

"Donella, what do you have in mind?" Lyson asked her.

"The poison is working its way to her heart. I can hold it in a kind of stasis with my ring so it doesn't move in her blood, but I need to be touching her and it will require all my focus. The rest of you will have to protect us until we reach Diminitus."

"I will lead you to his house, it is about half a day's ride from here," Luel said and lifted off and hovered down the trail for the others to follow.

"I will watch the rear," Tera said with determination, her spear spinning as she took up position behind everyone.

"I will stay close," Lyson said with a hard set to his jaw. Mounting his own horse and drawing his sword, he tied the reigns of Ava's horse to the saddle horn of his own and led them forward. Emilia could tell he was blaming himself for allowing someone in his company to be injured.

The trail was narrow and overgrown. The horses made slow going as they wound through the woods and across marshlands. As the sun was about to set, the forest opened into a wide clearing. In the center was a two story stone house with a thatch roof. A chimney set at one end of the roof line was emanating smoke from the stack, indicating someone was home.

"Wait here," Luel said. "I'm going to make sure it's clear."

Luel, taking on the color of the tall grass, flew low to the ground in a wide circle around the house. She made two more passes before returning to the others.

"We're safe," she said changing back to her natural skin tone. "Let's go."

As they reached the house, Luel walked up the steps to the front door.

"I hope he's not in a cranky mood," Tera said as Luel knocked.

"Who's that?" a voice shouted from inside. "Go away!"

Luel inwardly groaned. "Yep, he's cranky today," Tera said shaking her head.

"Dim, be polite," a woman's voice came from inside the house. Everyone's eyes went wide as the door opened and the owner of the voice stepped into view.

"Oh my," Emilia said shocked to her toes at what she beheld.

Chapter 9

Brayton stood at the prow of his ship, Boreas, the wind pushing his jet-black hair in all directions, his dark eyes scanning the horizon. The name Boreas meant north wind, which seemed appropriate since this wind was propelling him on his journey now. He did not know where he was going, only that his quest involved locating the secret grove of the unicorns, which was never in the same place twice. The sea was not as rough today, although there were significant swells. This did not bother Brayton, he looked like a part of the ship himself as he rode the waves up and down without any movement at all. This balance he learned from his mother. Acacia had taught her son at a young age the nimbleness and grace of fencing. "To be a great fencer," his mother told him, "one must master focus and agility, and above all, balance."

In his forty years of life he had traveled to almost every corner of Vasara. He was now at the age his father was when he had taken the throne. Paolo had hinted to his son that it may be time for him to step down. Still vigorous and more than capable of ruling, he had told Brayton it is not always a good thing for one person to rule for long periods of time. "Things tend to go stale and stagnant," the king had said. Brayton never felt that way during his father's tenure. The kingdom had flourished and had known nothing but peace, until the invasion.

Brayton had been abroad with his wife and son when Kensington was overrun. And of course Cathal was with him.

His best friend and protector was always near. Cathal's father, Nyle, being champion of the king, made it seem only natural that his son would be Brayton's champion. A tradition that would link the two houses for many future kings to come Brayton surmised. Cathal's son Zane was already assuming that role with Brayton's own son, Fenris.

Brayton first met Cathal a year after Devon's overthrow, on what happened to be Brayton's sixteenth birthday. His father brought him to the palace to live. Cathal's life before Brayton knew him was not the kind to be sung in halls, and a life one would not expect of the son of a Raptor captain. But it was because he was a Raptor that Nyle had left Cathal and his mother, thinking himself unfit to be a father, nor wanting to have leverage used against him giving his vocation. Nyle had many enemies at the time, and family attachments would only destroy him. Not to mention that Devon would not have hesitated to use them against Nyle if it furthered his aims.

Cathal's mother died when he was very young, and in fact had very little memory of her. Moving amongst aunts and uncles on his mother side, Cathal more often than not made his home in the streets, mastering a life as a thief and connecting with most of Kensington's unsavory underworld, of which every city had one. But since his transformation with Andros, and his elevation to King's champion, Nyle wanted to redress the wrong he had done to his son.

Cathal's first meeting with the prince had set the tone for their friendship almost immediately. That tone being the two of them constantly getting into trouble. Who knew there were so many secret passageways throughout the White Castle, and Cathal was happy to explore them all with Brayton.

Two boys with a love for adventure, Cathal was all too eager to show his new friend the wonders of Kensington crime life.

Brayton always considered it his duty to get to know the lives of all the peoples he would one day rule, and that included the criminal element, so he justified in his head at the time. Not to condone their lifestyle, but in hopes to come to understand their plight and do what was in his power to affect a change for the better in their lives.

When not running the streets, the boys would study side by side, both book knowledge and skill at arms. Brayton felt he had known Cathal all his life and could not imagine a life of which he was not a part. As if thinking about him brought him to mind, Cathal appeared on deck and was heading towards him.

"We are making good time your Highness," Cathal said in a good humor. His long sandy blonde hair was pulled back and tied off, keeping it out of his ocean blue eyes.

"How can you tell?" Brayton asked him smiling.

"I can't, but if the gods are involved at all in this venture, you can bet we will arrive at exactly the time we are meant to."

Brayton burst out laughing. "I cannot argue with that logic my friend."

"What does your compass say?"

"Only that we are heading in the right direction." Brayton pulled out from under his shirt a charm he wore around his neck. It was a golden unicorn's horn. Right now it glowed. Brayton had found the horn totally by accident, if accident it was, many years ago, not long after Cathal had come to the castle.

Thinking about it now, he couldn't help feeling that he was meant to find it. He had been in the crypt under the castle studying the scrolls stored there, mainly about lands beyond the known seas. As he was putting a scroll back, his foot stepped on a scroll-tube that had fallen, sending Brayton flying backwards, crashing into a glass case. The case held a replica of a rearing unicorn, not unlike the statue in the village where he had grown up. He had wondered that he had never seen it before, not that there was much left of it now, but he could still tell what it was. As he was picking up the pieces and trying to figure out what he would tell his father, something had fallen to the floor. It was the very necklace he now wore, except the horn was partially separated. Brayton knew it must open. Gently he twisted and the horn came apart. Hidden inside he found a small rolled up scrap of paper. Written in script were the words;

In Vasara's need
Let the horn guide you
T

Brayton wondered who 'T' might be. Taiyo? Or Trystan maybe. What did the horn guide you to, and how? Brayton had closed the horn and fastened the chain around his neck. For now, he would wear it as an heirloom from the house of Taiyo. He would need to tell his father.

Paolo had told him of the Summus Re'em, the Unicorn Master. It is said an heir from the line of Taiyo would rise and lead the unicorns in a great battle at one of Vasara's greatest needs. "Maybe this horn is linked to that," Paolo said.

"How does it guide you?" Brayton had asked his father.

Paolo, putting a hand on his son's shoulder told him, "If the time comes, and you are the one, I am sure it will be revealed to you." On that count, Paolo had been correct.

As soon as Brayton had word of Kensington being overrun, he had felt a burning sensation on his chest. Pulling out the horn it was glowing and hot to the touch. It seemed to have gotten heavier and was pulling at his neck. He found that if he started walking in a certain direction, the horn would continue to glow as long as you were on the right path, stray from that path and it would stop. Then began the arduous task of trying to find it again. This happened a couple of times until he had found himself standing in front of his ship as it was tied up at the dock in the harbor. Making arrangements for their families, Brayton and Cathal set sail, with nothing but a glowing horn leading the way.

"Are we insane Cathal? Who heads out into open ocean with no destination, no charts?"

"Us," Cathal replied smiling. "Wouldn't be the first fool thing we ever did, that's for sure."

"You have a point there," Brayton said slapping his back.

"Ouch! Easy you big ox. I mean, you big ox, your Highness," Cathal said bowing.

"Much better," Brayton said trying to look dignified. They both burst out laughing like the overgrown boys they were.

"Your Highness!" a call came from the quarter deck.

"What is it Captain?" Brayton called back as they started walking to where the captain was standing. Even though the boat was Brayton's, he did not captain it, preferring to leave that to others, along with the authority being a captain entails. Brayton's captain for the past ten years was a man named Colton. Bowen had recommended him, and he had been a blessing.

Colton was a man in his fifties. Born to the sea, he had spent most of his life on it and could read the waters like a book. Colton was tall and thin; his face bronze from years in the sun, his hair totally white and clean-shaven. "What's the point of whiskers?" he had once said. "They're a nuisance and constantly getting food stuffs caught in them."

"We appear to be coming into shallow water, pretty soon we will hit the limit of our draft," the captain told Brayton. "I've lowered the main sails to slow us down a bit, but I don't know how much further we can go."

"Could we sail around it?" Cathal asked.

"We could," Brayton replied. "But then there is no telling how long it will take to find the route again."

Brayton looked out at the rippling waves. Hidden only a few fathoms below their draft, the ocean floor was rushing up to meet them. Practicality would suggest to just sail around it. But something in his gut nagged at him.

"Brayton?" Cathal looked at his friend.

"We stay on course," Brayton said with a determined look in his eye.

"But your highness, we are many leagues from any land mass. Even if we did run a ground and managed not to sink, we could be stuck out there for days, weeks even," Colton explained.

Brayton looked at the captain and smiled. "Sometimes Colton, you just have to put everything in the hands of fate and have faith she will deliver you to where you mean to go."

Colton looked skeptical. "I just hope she doesn't smack us upside the head for the idiots we are," the captain said sourly.

Brayton and Cathal both roared with laughter.

Chapter 10

Brion kept hearing a buzzing in his ears. He thought it some insect, flying around pestering him. He tried to swat at it but his arms didn't seem to be moving. He looked around trying to locate the source of the annoying sound. For some reason everything was dim, as if in a dark grey haze. Then he realized.

Wait a minute, he thought to himself. *Why aren't my eyes open?* Try as he might, he could not lift an eyelash.

"Am I dead?"

After further thought, he came to the conclusion he was not. *The gods wouldn't leave me in this perpetual limbo, unable to move. Surely they would not be so cruel.* Brion just wished that persistent buzzing would stop. It was getting on his nerves. It wouldn't go away, and he found himself starting to focus on it.

"Were there words in that buzzing?" he asked himself. He focused his attention harder.

Brion?

That sounded like Caleb.

Is that you Bull? Brion asked.

Oh! Thank the gods! We've been trying to reach you for days.

Where am I? You sound far away.

Where am I? Caleb said incredulously. *I'm standing right over you. You're horizontal on the rock you've been sitting on for the past thousand years. You toppled over, and you have been in some kind of coma ever since.*

I guess I'm still in it since I can't see or move.

Hold on, I'm talking to him, Caleb said.

What? Brion said.

What? Oh, nothing. I have the others talking in my head at the same time asking about you.

Others? Who's awake?

All of us my brother. Apparently when you checked out, the rest woke up. Brion, we are going to starve soon if we don't get out.

The hopelessness of the situation was settling into Brion's consciousness. No one knew where they were, and even if they did, it was doubtful anyone could break the enchantment of their prison. Darkness was starting to overwhelm him, and he could feel his spirit shrinking inside of him. He had nothing for Caleb, no help and no hope. They were all going to die, and the blame was his.

I can feel you beating yourself up again, Caleb told him. *Listen, I haven't said anything to the others yet, because I don't know if it's real or not.*

What are you talking about?

I had a visit from her worshipness.

You know Braylynn hates it when you call her that.

So she's told me many times, Caleb said laughing. *Anyway, she came in my dreams as I slept. You know how she likes to do that. Can't come face to face and say things directly, quite annoying actually, I wish…*

Caleb, get to the point, Brion said frustrated. *It's hard enough to follow your thought in this state.*

Oh, right. Sorry. Anyway, in my dream, vision or whatever, she said the Chief Dragon was coming, and the Summoner rides him. Caleb paused. *I thought you were Chief Dragon and that Layla was killed at the hand of Zana.*

Brion thought on this for a moment. *It's possible Braylynn has chosen another of her faerie to be her anointed Summoner.*

The Chief Dragon is puzzling, but I do remember Loki telling me one time that he thought it odd that the Five didn't create ten of us, given their love of symmetry. All this is starting to make my head hurt, and I can't even feel my head!

Easy Brion, Caleb told him. *You were always the hopeful one, I never put much stock in it myself. But if there was ever a situation that warranted it, it's this one. You know I am not one to give up on life. So for this once, I'm taking it as a sign of hope that we are going to get out of here.*

Brion could feel rage and anger coming through on Caleb's next thoughts.

And when we do get out of here, Caleb growled, *I'm taking my revenge on those life-sucking beings that held us. Alone if need be. There will be no mercy, brother, not from me.*

The coldness in his brother's thought, chilled Brion. When the time came, he would need to keep an eye on Caleb, lest he do something that in the end would make him lose himself. For now, he would follow Caleb's example, and hope.

Chapter 11

Dain looked out from under the cover of the trees toward the great city of Kensington. There was no movement that he could tell on the Palatine Bridge that spanned the great chasm. Closing his eyes and reaching for the source he sent his mind probing. He could sense nothing. Something was blocking him. He could not feel Loki at all.

"Anything?" Cleo said walking up behind him. Her dark hair was braided, as it always was when battle was imminent, resting between her two short swords in their silver scabbards.

"No, something or someone is preventing me from seeing."

Just then Leah came flying in, Tori riding not far behind and arriving a few seconds after.

"After Devon, I thought I was done trying to sneak into the White Castle using stealth and magic," Leah said crossing her arms and folding her lavender wings, staring across the fields with the others. Her long blonde hair, like Cleo's was battle ready and tied into a ponytail. Tori dismounted and came to stand beside her.

The once bright city seemed colorless and drab to Dain. The air had hints of sulfur, and black smoke rose from various points in the city. Devon at least wanted a kingdom that flourished, he did not want to have to keep dealing with despondent subjects. It did not take away from his evil, but he was pragmatic. These things that occupied the White Castle now only seemed to know ugliness and destruction.

"Okay master wizard," Cleo said smiling at Dain. "Any ideas?"

"Cleo, please," Dain groaned. "I get enough of that from Tera."

"She brings up a point dear," Leah said to him, testing the point of her talon dagger with her finger. "How do we get in there?"

Dain looked over at Tori. She was very reticent ever since her healing. Andros explained the concerns she had before they left, that she at times might feel cutoff and alone because of what she had become. The dragon had told him in confidence, so he could be aware and look for any signs that she might be slipping into melancholy. Before his life as a wizard, Dain was a Border Lands general. He knew how incapacitating it can be for a warrior if despondency takes hold. But he also knew the quickest way to snap out of it was a good fight. He felt it time to put Tori's powers to the test and see what she was capable of.

"Tori," Dain said.

"Yes General?" Tori responded. She couldn't help falling back into a formal mode of military address.

"You up for a fight?"

Tori smiled at him as her face lit up. This is the reaction he had hoped for.

"Dain, may I have a word?" Cleo said stern faced.

"Certainly Cleo."

They walked a little way into the woods when Cleo rounded on him.

"What the hell do you think you are doing?" she said with some heat.

"Cleo, calm down. I know your concern, but Tori needs this."

"What do you mean 'she needs this'? We have no idea of her stability, or what might happen. And you want to just throw her right into the thick of things with no preparation. Are you mad?"

Dain knew Cleo was frightened for her friend and sister warrior. He also knew what it was like to lose every warrior under your command, all too well did he know it. It made you gun shy and hesitant to commit another soul to battle. And there was only one cure, send your warriors out in spite of it. Eventually you realize you cannot control the destinies of others, and it is only madness to try. He had come to that realization many years later in Valencia's court, and it had taken the help of a goddess to see it.

Before Leah had found him wounded, bleeding and nearly dead, Dain and his company of warriors had fought a running battle from the Border Lands to Laurel Hollow. A mass of demons had broken out of the corridor and headed south, and the warriors pursued. There were many pitched fights, but the demons kept retreating. This should have alerted him, but he was too caught up in the rush of battle and glory, that he totally missed it. They rode heedlessly and before they knew it, galloped into a narrow gorge with rising cliffs on either side. It was the simplest of ambushes. The vile creatures descended from hiding upon the unsuspecting army. It was a slaughter, total and complete. Had Dain not appeared already dead, he was sure they would have finished him. Such was his shame that he could never face his people again, which made it easier to accept Braylynn's offer to be the chamberlain to the faerie Queen.

Yes, he knew the pain and anguish Cleo felt. And he knew this test was as much for her as it was for Tori.

"This is my decision Cleo," he said sternly leaving no room for argument. And he knew Cleo, being the warrior she was would not debate the point. It was several moments before she spoke. Dain could tell she was angry the way the corner of her blue eyes would turn green. Lyson had told him of this feature of his sister.

"Very well, but she doesn't go alone."

"Understood." He knew arguing this point with Cleo would be useless. She would accompany her shield captain into battle.

Returning to the others, Dain laid out his plan.

"What do you think of our chances Boss?" Tori asked Cleo as they rode toward the bridge.

Cleo looked over at her best friend. "We should be okay," she replied. "It's only a quick scouting mission."

The plan was to ride out across the bridge to see what resistance they would encounter. Dain didn't think the appearance of two riders would suggest anything to the enemy about what they were really after.

"Where's Percy?" Cleo asked.

"Over my heart," Tori said patting her chest.

Tori noted Cleo's sad smile. Of the once mighty Vipers, all that remained was riding to what could potentially be their last mission. So many good warriors lost. *May they rest in peace in Fallon's paradise*, Tori thought to herself. Tori scanned the wall for any signs of archers. Her mind turned to Bart, and how she wished he was here. Tori had visited his grave with Cleo while the others were recovering from their encounter with the raw power of Fallon. She really missed that bowman. No one could equal his skill, and as far as man friends that Cleo had, Tori knew that Bart had gotten the closest to her heart.

Tori still did not know of all that she was capable yet. One of the things she discovered with her new red eyes, was the ability to see much farther than she had ever seen before, and with greater clarity. She could see all the way to the great towers of the White Castle. Nothing stirred. They trotted gently across the field to the chasm, an all-out gallop might seem too aggressive Dain had thought. Tori had a feeling that whatever inhabited Kensington these days already knew they were here.

Finally, they reached the Palatine Bridge, the sun reflecting brightly off the white stone.

"Be wary," Cleo said drawing her swords and letting the reigns fall, her horse knowing what to do.

Tori followed suit, and the drawing of her blades brought everything into sharp relief. Every nerve in her body was instantly alive and quivering with energy.

It was then that they came. Demons of every size imaginable, both crawling and flying, came up from under the bridge and swarmed over like ants spilling out of an ant hill. Cleo hit her saddle horn, extending the upper stirrups of her saddle, and sliding her feet in, stood up to become an extension of her horse as she charged.

All of this seemed to be in slow motion to Tori as she opened her stirrups as well. Giving silent salute to Cleo, she sped forward, but even though Tori had new-found abilities, her horse did not and it was suddenly cut out from under her. Tori jumped and somersaulted, landing in a thick mass of demons. They clawed at her, trying to get at her neck to rip her head off. Again, all of it seemed to be in slow motion, and Tori released all that energy that had come alive in her body. She didn't even know what she was doing, as there seemed to be a loud detonation followed by a huge fireball, sending the demons scattering, some obliterated in the blast.

She looked over to Cleo who was holding her own against several flying monsters swooping down to dislodge her, her swords cutting a path along the bridge as demons vaporized into nothing. Tori was doing the same, cutting demons down ten at a time, never knowing what hit them. But it seemed no matter how many she cut down, many more were there to take their place.

She happened to glance in Cleo's direction when she saw her friend go down. A hideous beast with four arms and wings like a bat lifted her off her horse and started to carry her up into the sky. Cleo drove her sword up into where its heart should be, if these vermin had hearts. The thing vanished and Cleo was in a free fall to the hard pavement below.

"Cleo!" Tori yelled as she raced over to where Cleo had landed. Like insects on dead meat, the demons covered Cleo. Tori was there, like an avenging shade, dealing death with every stroke. She managed to clear the demons off, and slinging Cleo over her shoulder, Tori raced for the bridge's edge.

Tori could see the heat shimmering on the air, like distorted waves dancing in front of her. Again, not sure how she was doing it, Tori drew the heat from the air into herself, and focusing her eyes, she set fire to everything before her. Demons howled in terror as they jumped out of her way, some flinging themselves into the chasm.

Once back on the mainland, the demons did not give pursuit. Either because they feared Tori or were instructed not to, Tori didn't know, but was grateful for the respite in any case. Feeling she had put enough distance between herself and the bridge, Tori collapsed, dropping Cleo onto the ground, causing Cleo to cry out in pain.

"I'm sorry Boss, I'm sorry," Tori said crawling over to Cleo and rolling her over to view her wounds. The demons had ripped through her leather armor, making a gash in Cleo's side that ran from her hip to her armpit. It was not wide, but it was deep and bleeding profusely. She needed to close it or Cleo would bleed out.

"By the gods!" Tori exclaimed. "What do I do? I'm no healer." Dain was too far away and would never get here in time. She knew she must at least close the wound, and the only way to do that was to cauterize it. An idea formed in her head.

"Boss, this is going to hurt like hell, but I don't know what else to do."

She gathered heat from the air. Pulling it into herself the way she did on the bridge. She put her hand on Cleo's hip and released the energy into her flesh.

"Ahhhh! Damn!" Cleo exclaimed as she started to thrash.

"Try and hold still," Tori told her, beads of sweat pouring down her face as she slowly moved her hand up Cleo's side. Cleo shut her eyes and locked every muscle, breathing shallow and rapid as Tori cauterized her wound. At some point Cleo passed out.

Once Tori had closed the wound, she put Cleo on her shoulder again and started to carry her to the forest. Dain and Leah rushed out to meet them.

"Tori, what happened?" Dain exclaimed as he jumped off his horse.

"Get us out of here first," she told him.

"Give her to me Tori, I can fly her back," Leah said. Tori handed Cleo over to Leah as she grabbed Cleo under her arms and flew her low to the ground back to the woods.

Once back at their camp, Tori filled them in on what had transpired.

"I have never seen so many demons in one place," she said. "Not even in the Corridor. And no matter how many we slew, more kept pouring over the bridge, as if there was no end to them. Something is very wrong in the balance of things," she told them.

Dain examined Cleo's wound. "Well I see you've discovered a new talent with your powers. She will live and be in considerable pain for a while. But that will pass with time. She's going to have a hideous scar for the rest of her life though."

"She's a warrior," Tori said. "Scars mean nothing to her. The question is when she will be able to travel. And then how do we solve the riddle of freeing Loki?"

Dain ran a hand through his hair. "The bridge is the only way into the city that I know of, for those of us that cannot fly. And no, you are not going by yourself," he said looking over at Leah.

"Did I say anything?" Leah said crossing her arms.

"I know you my love," Dain said raising an eyebrow.

"What's that?" Tori said jumping up and drawing her swords looking into the forest.

"I heard nothing," Dain said standing up. "Leah?"

"Nope, I see and hear nothing."

"There," Tori said pointing her sword.

Both Dain and Leah looked to where she was pointing. Straining to hear what Tori heard.

"Whatever it is, it's coming this way," Tori told them. They still didn't hear a thing.

Dian looked sidelong at Tori. "Maybe your hearing has been enhanced as well," Dain said. "I will trust that something is out there. Everyone stand ready."

After a few minutes, Dain and Leah could now hear someone or something approaching.

Suddenly, stepping into view was a young woman, black hair with streaks like fire, and wearing an ice blue dress.

"You!" Leah said recognizing her immediately, lowering her spear. "Although you seem a little older since last I saw you. This is the one who told me of the attack on Fenner," she said to the others.

"You need have no fear of us miss," Dain said. "Might we know your name?"

The woman just smiled at Dain and walked past him, ignoring his question and coming to kneel by Cleo's side, examining her wound. She looked up and her eyes met Tori's.

"Well done Cath Priomh of Fallon," she said, her voice musical sounding.

"What did you call me?" Tori asked sheathing her swords. She knew she had nothing to fear from this woman.

The woman ignored Tori's question as well. Instead, she began to run her hand along Cleo's red and raised scar. A white illumination could be seen emanating from her palms.

"Ahhh!" Cleo cried out in pain as the woman kept running her hands along the wound, a gentle smile on her face, as if she were giving a massage. Tori watched in amazement as Cleo's skin turned a healthy pink color, no trace that the scar had ever been. Cleo was also alert. She sat up and gingerly touched her side. Feeling no hurt, Cleo stood up, twisting her torso several times.

"That's unbelievable," Cleo exclaimed. "How…"

"There is no time," the woman said interrupting Cleo.

"What do you mean?" Dain asked.

"Your window of opportunity is closing rapidly. The path you seek is there," she said pointing down the tree line.

Everyone looked to where she was pointing, straining to make out what she might be indicating.

"I don't see…," Dain said turning back towards the woman. "Where is she?"

Everyone turned around. The woman had utterly vanished.

"By the gods!" Cleo exclaimed.

"I'm not surprised," Leah said. "I told you there was something alien about her."

"And also familiar," Dain said scratching his chin. "We can puzzle it out another time. If what she says is true, we need to move now. Any idea what she pointed at, I could see nothing."

"I can see something," Tori said, "about a mile down. It looks like a cairn."

"I will trust your eyes Tori," Dain said. "Cleo, can you ride?"

"Yes. Whatever she did to me, I haven't felt this good in years."

"Dain, wait," Tori said. "What does it mean, what she called me? Cath Priomh."

Dain took his foot out of the stirrup and turned to face Tori.

"I've only seen that name once, in a book Lyson had. It was a story of Fallon's hero, a supreme warrior who was raised up in one of Vasara's greatest trials, infused with the very power of the god. Cath Priomh is the name of this warrior, the supreme Battle Chief." Dain looked long at Tori and placed a hand on her shoulder. "I think the woman was right, you are the Cath Priomh. Don't let this frighten you Tori. Even though we channeled Fallon's power into you, it would never have worked if the god did not mean for you to have the power you've been given, and also if you were not able to handle it."

"Thank you for that," she said gratefully.

"Come, let's go see if we can solve the riddle of how to free Loki."

It took no time at all to reach the cairn. It was about seven feet tall, white flat slate rocks stacked evenly, forming a cone with a diameter of about four feet.

"I wonder why no one has ever seen this before," Dain said gazing up at the structure.

"Maybe it hasn't been here before," Tori said.

"Now what?" Cleo said, her eyes following up to the top of the cairn.

Leah flew around the cairn several times, noticing nothing. As she flew over the top, she saw something. "The top stone is askew," she called down.

"Can you move it?" Dain asked.

"Hold on." Leah grabbed an edge as her wings started to beat out a straining rhythm. She managed to slide it off and let it fall to the ground, causing it to break in two. "There are handholds going down."

"Bring us up," Dain said to her.

Leah carried each of them to the top, where they were able to climb inside. The iron handholds continued on down by another twenty feet below the cairn when they came to the bottom. It was solid rock. Dain reached for the source and created a ball of light to illuminate the tunnel before them, which was wide and tall enough for them to walk through with ease.

"Do you really think this is a good idea?" Leah asked no one in particular. "I don't see how this will get us across the chasm."

"I'm hoping once we get there, the way will be revealed to us," Dain remarked. "In any case, I don't see that we have any other alternatives."

Tori kept an eye behind them. She could still see the entrance of the tunnel lit up from the sun streaming down through the opening in the cairn. After fifteen minutes walking, the tunnel started to veer to the left, sloping down. Tori now relied on her hearing to alert her if someone should be perusing them. So far the way was clear. Another ten minutes of walking had brought them to a wall.

"Well," Dain said scanning the rock face before him, "I'm assuming there is a door here."

"You are the wizard my love," Leah said giving him a kiss on the cheek. "I know you will figure it out."

Dain raised an eyebrow at her. Scratching his head, he brought his attention back to the wall. It was smooth, with not so much as a crack in it.

"I think I see something," Tori said from behind.

"You do?" Dain said looking back. "By the gods!"

"What?" Tori said puzzled.

"Your eyes!" Cleo said with surprise.

"Oh great. What are they doing now?" Tori said exasperated.

"The red around the edges, they're spinning. Like wheels of fire."

"Tori, I want to try something," Dain said as he extinguished his balls of light. "Can you see anything?"

"I can't see a blasted thing," Leah said.

"I can see perfectly," Tori said astounded. "I can see all of you, the wall and the tunnel." This unnerved Tori slightly. She hated being surprised all the time with her new abilities. She wished the god would've just left her with a list of what she could and could not do, and leave it at that. Keep it simple was her motto. This new talent would be most helpful in very dark places she thought.

"What do you see on the rock's face?" Dain asked her.

"Can you light up the tunnel again Dain?" Cleo asked the wizard. "I hate standing around in pitch blackness."

Dain once again conjured up his little energy balls to float above and behind them.

"Tell me what it is you see Tori," Dain said.

"It's a very fine, thin outline, as if it were drawn on the rock. In the center is a symbol." Tori squinted as if not sure of what she was seeing. "It almost looks like one of the stones on the Pillars of Fallon."

"I think this door is meant for you to open," Dain told her. "Place your palm there and push."

Tori did as Dain bid. Placing her hand on the smooth stone over the symbol she started giving a tentative push, not really believing anything would happen. The door did not open out however. Instead, it seemed to melt into the ground revealing the view of the other side of the chasm. The wind howled as it rushed through that rock corridor. Dain looked out and up.

"We are some distance down from the bridge," he told the others, his hair whipping all over his head. He then looked across the chasm and saw another opening not unlike the one they stood in.

"How do we get across," Leah yelled over the noise of the wind.

"Leave that to me darling," Dain said kissing her cheek. Dain closed his eyes and extended his hands. With great effort he was able to channel enough of the source to create a bridge of pure energy. "Quickly, run across."

Cleo went first. Starting out she looked down, which was a mistake. She momentarily lost her balance, but it was enough for the wind to push her off Dain's bridge and into the chasm, whose bottom could not be seen. She screamed some vile oaths as she plunged down into the depths.

"Cleo!" Tori yelled.

Leah was there. She jumped out and down in pursuit of Cleo. Tori lost sight of them in the shadows of the rock face. It seemed like forever, but in reality was only a few minutes when she could see Leah's blonde head emerging from the darkness. As she got closer Tori could see Cleo, held tightly under her armpits by Leah.

"What the hell were you thinking," Tori said angrily when her feet were on the other side of the chasm. "I can't bear to lose any more of us," she said hugging Cleo.

"I'm sorry Tori," Cleo said hugging her back. "That wind caught me by surprise. Thank you, Leah."

"No problem," Leah said winking. "Add it to the tally, I'm sure eventually we will all even out."

Tori knew it wasn't Cleo's fault and that she was just being irrational. They had faced death many times together and beat it back. But ever since they lost all the Vipers, Tori seemed to be overprotective now when it came to her best friend and someone she always viewed as a sister. Percy, during the exchange had popped his head out. Tasting the air with his forked tongue, he decided it was time for a change of scenery and slithered out to curl around Cleo's wrist.

"Good work love," Dain said joining them and letting his bridge disappear. "You alright Cleo?"

"I'm fine Dain," Cleo said. "It's mostly my pride that's hurt. Come on, let's go get Loki and get the hell out of here."

They entered the tunnel and proceeded for another twenty minutes before coming to another rock face. Like the others, it was smooth and without adornment that they could see with a normal eye.

"Tori?" Dain asked.

"Yes, it's there," Tori said, looking at the now familiar markings that only seemed to be visible to her. Placing her hand on the markings, the door was revealed and opened before them.

"Okay, I will go first," Dain said about to move forward.

"Dain wait," Tori said placing a restraining hand on his shoulder. "Let me go. I can see without any light giving us away, and should any threat meet us, I can hold them off until we can retreat back into the tunnel where I will be able to close the doors."

Dain rubbed his chin, assessing Tori's demeanor. In the end he agreed. "Very well. I will place a hand on you as you lead through the dark. Cleo and Leah, keep contact with me and each other. Lead the way Cath Priomh," Dain said smiling.

"Don't get me started wizard," Tori said glaring.

As Dain extinguished his floating balls of light, Tori peered into the darkness and saw the way ahead. The floor was stone, and smooth as far as she could see, so there weren't any obstacles underfoot to cause them to stumble. Leading them on, Tori came to the first turn, which opened up into a circular gallery with four tunnels leading out from it. She wondered which way she should take. The left and right most tunnels had a rotten smell emanating from them. She wondered if the others could smell it, or was this part of her new battle skill set.

The two middle tunnels seemed clean with fresh air blowing down from them. *One of these had to be the way*, Tori thought, but which one?

"Why have we stopped?" Dain asked. Tori turned to look back at Dain.

"Watch out!" Cleo shouted.

Tori turned back just in time to see a fire ball hurtling towards them from the left middle tunnel. Dain jumped in front of her, grabbing the source he was able to erect a shield in time to absorb the blast. The fire was like liquid as it cascaded around them and impacted with the ceiling.

"I guess we know which tunnel," Cleo said drawing both swords and starting to move forward before the next fireball.

"No, that's the wrong one," Dain said heading to the right most tunnel.

"Are you sure?" Tori said doubtfully, wrinkling her nose. "That hole smells like death."

"I'm sure," Dain said smiling. "This time there is a mark I can see."

"What is it?" Leah said straining to see it, her spear extended and held at the ready for any new threat.

"Over the entrance is a scroll symbol with the rune letter R above it. Care to wager who put it there?"

"Redlin, the tunnel making master," Leah said with a laugh. "That wizard has his hand everywhere."

"Let's go," Dain said leading them into the tunnel, balls of energy illuminating the way.

Through the tunnel they ran. Tori did not know how much time they had, but her gut was telling her it wasn't long. The path ran straight and eventually opened up on a wide hall, a thirty by thirty-foot square. Set in the middle of the wall was a door. It seemed to be made of wood, but of no kind Tori had ever seen. Its color was obsidian black. Above the lintel was embedded a clear orb.

"We are at the crypt under the castle," Dain said running his hand along the orb.

"Paolo and Acacia are in there," Cleo said. "You think they would be able to hear us?"

"I have no idea," Dain said. "But they knew what they were doing when they went in there, so I am certain they are safe. In any case, that is not our task." He looked at the others grimly. "We need to locate Loki, fast. I sense a power moving in the castle searching for us. It is only a matter of time." Dain began looking around. "There," he said pointing.

"What?" Cleo said.

Dain walked over to the opposite wall, seemed to peer around, and then vanished into the wall.

"Dain!" Leah called.

"Come on," Dain said sticking his head out, that being the only thing visible.

Tori and the others discovered Dain had walked behind a wall that was overlapping an inner wall, giving the illusion that it was one solid wall when looked at head on.

"Don't do that again," Leah said smacking his head. "That turned my stomach."

"Sorry love," Dain said smiling. "This is the secret passage to the crypt. Paolo brought me down here once. I know the way from here. It will bring us right under where Loki is being held." Dain looked over at Tori. "We are going to need your speed now, to quickly dispatch any enemies before they can raise an alarm."

Tori pulled her blades. "I'm ready," she said grimly.

Dain nodded and started to lead the way up. Three times they had come upon demon possessed soldiers standing guard.

Tori was able to dispatch them before they were even aware intruders were among them. She ran to one of the windows to look out. Looking up at the battlements she saw more demon spawn, but not as many soldiers. Down in the courtyard was the same. It appeared the bulk of actual demons were on the outside, defending against attack from across the chasm, or the sea to the rear of the castle. Possessed soldiers seemed to be all that was employed on the inside. Tori found this most beneficial, because that meant the demons were limited to some degrees by their hosts.

Twenty more minutes of stealth and dispatching of guards brought them to the door of the tower where Loki was. Tori thought it strange that no one was guarding this door.

"I don't like this," Cleo whispered to her.

"Neither do I, Boss," Tori whispered back. "It's a trap, there's no mistake about it."

"Yes it is," Dain said. "And we are going to spring it."

"If you have a plan General, now would be a good time to hear it," Cleo said crossing her arms.

"A shield of some sort is around Loki," Dain began. "That much I know. I also know it has cut him off from the source, or he would have been out of there by now."

Dain looked at each of them as if he were weighing his decisions based on what he saw in his friends. "There has to be at least one of those hooded bastards up there," Dain said with heat. "And who knows how many other soldiers." He placed a hand on Tori's shoulders.

"I believe this is one of the reasons the Cath Priomh is here. I think if anyone can break that shield it's you. How I don't know, but I know you can."

Tori looked doubtful at this. Did she have any choice? None that she could see anyway.

"Let's do this," Tori said drawing her swords.

They opened the door and started to climb the spiral staircase to the top. The tower was tall and the steps were wide as they wound along the wall. It was not a skinny tower by any means. It could double as a banquet hall quite easily. Leah flew up through the center to make sure no one was hiding in the shadows, her talon spear poised to impale any creature that dared to show itself. They encountered no one as the came to the door at the top.

"Tori, your only objective is Loki," Dain said. "Concentrate on nothing else. The three of us will handle whatever else is in there."

Tori nodded grimly.

Dain opened the huge oaken door. The room was empty, save for a solitary figure sitting in a chair in the middle of the room. Slumped, head down, matted black hair covering his face, Loki made not a move upon their entering. Tori wondered if he was asleep, or possibly drained from torture. Whatever the reason, he looked weak and frail. The room was not dark. Windows, laid about every twenty feet encircled the tower, letting in plenty of light, giving the room an open and airy feeling.

Tori scanned the room. No one was visible, but she knew they were not alone. She was paralyzed as to what to do. This wasn't like slashing demons, this was god magic. And what did she know of that, nothing. She closed her eyes and concentrated, trying to see the plan. What did the god expect her to do? Tori started to shake, her mind threatening to slip into oblivion from fear. Fear. When had she ever known fear? All of a sudden she felt something on her arm. Opening her eyes and looking down, she saw Percy starting to encircle her wrist. The snake had an instant calming effect. Her heart started slowing and her mind was clearing.

Tori looked curiously at Percy. She remembered the first time they had encountered the viper many years ago. She and Cleo were just getting ready to ride out on patrol when they noticed a snake sitting in the middle of Cleo's saddle. How it got there was a mystery, especially since snakes and horses are not overly fond of one another, yet these two animals acted like they were old friends with the docile way Cleo's horse was behaving. Cleo had a choice of either sitting on the snake or physically removing it. As she went to grab it, the snaked hissed and tried to bite Cleo. Several times she tried reaching a hand around to grab it by the neck with no success. Finally, Cleo leveled her sword at it, attempting to just chop it in half. Upon seeing the lowered sword, the snake had lowered its head at the bare blade, and as if it were the most natural thing in the world, slid along the length of the naked flat and curled itself around Cleo's wrist. Neither of them had ever seen anything like this and decided to keep him as a mascot. Tori named the snake Percy. She didn't know where the name came from, it just popped into her head.

Looking at him now, Tori felt something magical surrounded the snake. In all the years they had ridden into battle Percy had never once been injured, not even scratched. Also, she didn't think snakes lived that long. It didn't really matter to Tori if he was magical or not, she was grateful for his calming presence in any case. Tori looked over at Dain.

"I have no idea what to do," she told the wizard.

"That's because you are thinking with your mind," Dain told her. "The power in you is Fallon's power. It's about the raw energy and heat of battle. That emotional side that comes out when the fight is hottest. That is where you must go Tori."

Tori nodded and cleared her head. Her body and mind knew how to fight without her even thinking about it. She slowly started to walk towards Loki, her swords held forward, eyes sweeping back and forth. She was not more than three paces from him when the air suddenly went cold, the hairs on the back of her neck standing up. Tori's battle sense told her the fight was imminent as she came in contact with an invisible barrier. It was then that it felt like a hand grabbed her, lifted her up and threw her, causing her back to slam against the far wall.

"Tori!" Cleo yelled as she rushed over helping her shield sister to her feet.

"I'm okay," she said shaking her head. It was then that the melee began.

A sharp crack split the air and the room was suddenly filled with demon possessed soldiers, with several demon lords among them, including the hooded figure that stood in front of Loki. The being pushed back its hood.

"By the goddess," Leah exclaimed. "He looks like Pan!"

"Dain," it said.

The mention of Dain's name by this creature sent a chill through Tori. It seemed to her as if it were marking Dain.

"How do you know me," Dain said. Tori saw Dain had his hands raised, energy of the source dancing between his fingers. The being did not respond. All of this happened in a matter of seconds as everything exploded and the soldiers rushed them.

Leah's wings were a blur as she jumped into the air, circling the tower looking for targets. Cleo's blades were singing as she held her own against those that attacked her. However, these were not ordinary demons that turned to vapor when killed. Blood sprayed everywhere as the Border Lands warrior's blade cut to bone, the floor starting to get slick.

The demon lords who possessed magic had engaged Dain. The wizard/general wasted no time taking the offensive. Tori knew if he took up a defensive position he would find it difficult to break out of it. The demon lords were doing a very good job fending of Dain's lightning strikes though, the air burned from it.

Tori turned her attention to this Pan look alike. "I guess your mine," she said.

Tori's eyes blazed as she started to draw heat from everything around her, her intent to set it on fire. Before she could finish, the thing had sent a fireball of its own. Her concentration was broken as she hastily crossed her swords in front of her. What she hoped this would do she didn't know. She was operating on instinct now. Her instincts were proven true as her swords effectively blocked the assault. The thing howled in frustration as it sent fireball after fireball. Now Tori was in the very position she wanted to avoid, being on the defensive. The moment she dropped her sword shield, she would be incinerated.

"Tori!" Dain yelled. "You know what to do, it's in you." Dain was put on the defensive now. A cut across his brow was bleeding and dripping into his eye. Cleo was starting to give ground as well. Leah was still effectively impaling soldiers as she swooped down to attack.

Dain had said she would know what to do. What he had said about Fallon had come back to her. Letting her mind clear again she reached down deep into her battle emotions, those feelings that come out during the battle frenzy. When she did this, she found a pool of energy in the center of her being. Tori pulled from it, causing it to move in her body. Rage, excitement, anger, vengeance and triumph started to run through her blood. Her body was becoming super-hot, beads of sweat running down her face. She suddenly felt more alive than any time in her life. She focused that power up her arms and into her swords. The blades turned a blazing white, with tongues of fire leaping out from the edges, incinerating several soldiers close by. Tori's eyes narrowed as the fury of battle descended upon her. With a feral growl she started running straight for the Pan look alike, giving an ear shattering cry as she leaped into the air, swords poised to slice the thing in two. The being's eyes went wide as it threw its hands up and suddenly disappeared.

She came down, and her white-hot blades impacted with the dome. The explosion from it sent a blast of air that leveled everyone to the floor, including Loki. Scrambling towards him, Tori picked Loki up, his head lolling to the side.

"Leah!" Tori yelled to the faerie.

Leah flew to Loki and grabbed him under his arms. Lifting off she flew towards the door.

"Let's get out of here," Dain shouted. "Follow me."

They raced down the stairs to where Leah was waiting with Loki.

"What do we do now?" Cleo asked.

"This way," Dain said as he ran out the door.

They made several turns as the came to a long hall that headed west, coming to another tower. They all followed Dain inside as the ascended another stair case and another door.

"I know where we are," Tori said. "This is the tower with the portal to Andros and Donella's world."

"Yes," Dain confirmed. "And to other places as well."

Once inside, Dain led them to the center of the room, where etched into the floor was the symbol of a dragon in flight.

"Hold tight!" he said as he threw his hands up.

There was a bright flash and Tori felt like she was suddenly free-falling as everything went dark. What seemed like only moments, Tori felt her face pressing onto a stone floor, her head splitting in pain. She closed her eyes as she sat up, rubbing her head. As the pain started to subside, she took in her surroundings. They were in an immense cave, the floor was white marble, and the ceiling hundreds of feet high. A huge stone hearth was built into one side of the cave.

This is a cave for dragons, Tori thought to herself.

A stone ring filled with water stood in the center of the cave. Tori looked towards the entrance to the cave, the opening was enormous. Yes, this was a cave for dragons.

"Dain, where the hell are we?" Tori asked. She looked over and saw Cleo getting up and shaking her head. At least Tori wasn't the only one with a headache.

"I would like to know that myself," Cleo echoed.

Dain and Leah were laying Loki down on a bed against the wall.

"We are in the Macedon Mountains," Dain responded. "In the cave of dragons. This is where Loki lives and the dragons of course."

Tori walked over to the bed. Loki looked like he was asleep.

"That was quite the route we took," Tori said rubbing her head. "How did you know of it?"

"Loki told me," he explained. "It was how he got Andros away from Devon when he first came to Vasara."

"What now?" Leah asked her love.

"I will go to the source and see if I can reach Loki. Now that he is no longer shielded, it's possible his spirit may be there."

"I will go outside and keep watch while you do," Tori said drawing her swords. "I should be able to see if anyone approaches."

Dain nodded as Tori left the cave and came to stand by a wall on the cliff. The cave was very high up on the mountainside, the air crisp. Watching the hawks circling far below her, she imagined this must be where Andros first learned to fly. She wondered what he and the others must be up to at this moment.

Chapter 12

Andy couldn't believe how fast he was ascending. With Emma holding one arm and Bella on the other, they cleared the demon hoard in a matter of seconds. Looking down he judged he was high enough.

"Let me go!" Andy told them.

Bella and Emma instantly released him and peeled off to get out of range. Andy began his free fall. Turning his thoughts inward he reached for his dragon self and poured his being into it. Where once a young man had been, the fearsome black dragon had opened his wings slowing his descent.

He gave two powerful thrusts as his long neck swept back and forth trying to locate everyone. Abby and Rhyan were nowhere in sight. He spotted his father just in time as he was pulled from his horse, with a hulking demon about to cave in his skull. Letting out an ear shattering roar he tucked his wings and started his dive. Andy didn't want to rake everyone with fire for fear of hurting the others. Taking a more targeted approach he threw his claws out in front of him, shooting lightning bolts at the demon. Scoring a direct hit, the demon vaporized as his weapon fell harmlessly to the ground.

Dad, where are Rhyan and Abby?

Leading some of the demons away from here. Torch the ones that remain, I will shield myself.

Andy looked up and saw Emma and Bella engaging several flying demons, their spears striking without mercy. They seemed to be holding their own, so Andy gave his attention to the ones below. Reaching deep inside himself he brought forth his heat. Opening his mouth, fire spewed out as he swept his long neck back and forth, igniting and vaporizing scores of demons.

I can handle the rest, Redlin told him. *Go find Abby, she's headed down the trail.*

Andy broke off his attack and flew among the tree tops. Swaying his flight back and forth, looking for any sign of his beloved.

Abby, can you hear me?

Yes. I need some help. The ones left can fly and I'm having a hard time hitting them.

Andy had no idea what that meant. *What was she hitting them with?* he wondered.

I can't see you. Where are you?

Just then a lightning strike shot up right before his face, making him pull up abruptly.

Could you see that lightning bolt?

Umm, yes. It nearly blew my nose off.

That's me. Hurry Andros, they are almost on top of me.

I'm coming love.

Andy plunged into the forest, knocking trees down left and right. Some of which took out a few demons. He could see the ones following Abby. He would need to calculate this just right. Using his dragon sight, he judged the distance to just behind Abby and let his fire go. It gave him great satisfaction to see these hideous monsters vaporize into nothingness.

Abby, you can slow down. I got them.

Abby pulled back hard on the reigns and turned around. Andy had just changed his form back and was running towards her. She jumped down and rushed into his arms as he held her tight to himself.

"You certainly took long enough mister," Abby said pulling her head back to look him in the eyes.

"What? I…" Andy stammered but never finished as Abby grabbed both sides of his head and pressed her lips to his. He decided he was never going to understand this woman and it was folly to try. So he did the only thing he could do under the circumstance and returned her kiss with a fervor.

Abby and Andy found the others waiting back where the fight had originated, just as Rhyan came galloping in from the woods.

"How did it go?" Redlin asked her as she dismounted.

"They are probably halfway to Kensington," she said smiling, taking a long drink of water from the skin on her saddlebag, and passing it around to the others.

"How did you manage that?" Emma asked her.

"Once I knew I had them totally disoriented in the woods, I created the illusion of hoof beats heading off to the west."

"You can do that?" Andy said surprised.

"When it comes to things involving horses, my sister and I have various talents. The illusion of horse sounds being one of them."

Andy was watching Bella's butterflies, when one with brightly colored yellow and orange wings landed on her pointed ear. Bella titled her head listening.

"Redlin, we should go soon. My little friend tells me a scouting party is headed this way."

"I never knew butterflies were versed in military terminology," Redlin said with a raised eyebrow.

"Oh yes," Bella told him. "There is very little butterflies don't know. They have a collective mind, and all memories are carried down from generation to generation."

Redlin let that pass. "Rhyan, can you lead us through the woods?"

"No problem," the priestess answered.

"Okay, let's get out of here."

Rhyan thundered through the underbrush while the others followed in her wake.

After a week of hard riding, they found themselves riding across the Wizard's bridge. The bridge would disappear whenever a ship sailing along the Tear River approached it. Andy also remembered how the bridge would disappear whenever enemies tried to cross it.

"How did you do it Dad?" Andy asked his father.

"What do you mean?"

"The bridge. How did you do it? What makes it disappear?"

Redlin gave him a sly look. "You are my son, but there are some things we don't tell dragons," he said giving him a wink.

"Oh come on," Andy exclaimed. "You can tell me. I won't tell anyone."

"I know you won't, because I'm not telling you."

Abby busted out laughing.

"I will tell you this though," the wizard said seriously. "The bond the three of us shared was never stronger than in that moment we created it." He looked sadly at his son. "I never would have believed that bond could ever break, but it did."

Andy could see the pain that Devon's betrayal had on his father and his heart went out to him.

"Riders are approaching," Rhyan said pointing and pulling an arrow.

Andy watched as three riders came galloping out of the woods. They wore light mail. Capes, dark with white trim around the edges, adorned their shoulders. On their breastplates was the symbol of a raven. Andy found this curious and his mind drifted to his own raven brand that Devon had marked him with. Andy did not remember a cavalry in Albion, but he supposed things could have changed in the time he had been gone.

As the riders pulled up, the oldest, but certainly not the largest of the three, brought his horse to a halt and hailed them.

"Welcome back Lord Dragon," he addressed them. "I am Tol, captain of the Baron's cavalry."

His hair was dark, but lined with streaks of grey. Andy guessed his age to be in his forties.

"Do I know you?" Andy asked him puzzled. He was sure he had never met this man before. Tol smiled and it seemed to give him a kindly countenance. He also radiated confidence. This man knew his business.

"I don't wonder that you should not know me," Tol replied. "I was but a lad of seventeen and one of many who joined the army of Andros the Black in throwing off the yoke of Devon's oppression. These other two with me are Anwell and Dayvn."

Anwell and Dayvn were young, twenty-five at the most. They seemed almost shy and unsure. Tol laughed.

"Take no mind of the lads my Lord Dragon," Tol said. "They are just dumbstruck to be seeing a living legend. All they know of that time is from the tales the bards sing. And that alone has made you seem to be almost a god in their eyes."

"Please Tol, just call me Andros. I try to keep things simple. It is well to meet you Anwell and Dayvn."

Andy then proceeded to introduce the others. If Anwell and Dayvn were dumbstruck at meeting Andy, they nearly fell off their horses when Andy introduced his father, including Tol.

"Astonishing, isn't it?" Bella chuckled as butterflies circled her head. "Seeing the stuff of legends in the broad light of day."

"Bella pleased," Redlin groaned. "It's really not all that amazing Tol."

"If you say so master wizard," Tol said still wide-eyed. Redlin just shook his head in resignation.

"Who governs in Albion these days?" Abby asked. The

wind off the river had picked up and started blowing her hair wildly. She reached behind and tied it into a ponytail to keep it out of her face.

"Aidan's son, Stefan," Tol replied. "Aidan died five years ago. He's son is just like him, and we are fortunate for that. Stefan is kind and just. Paolo himself appointed him. Stefan had apprenticed at the White Castle for many years, so Paolo had a good idea of the path his governorship would take. Even though he is but a lad of twenty-five, the youngest Baron ever, his mind is like no other I have ever encountered. He can read a book in an hour and recite the whole thing back to you without error."

"Excellent," Redlin exclaimed. "Can you take us to him? We have an urgent matter to discuss with him."

"At once master wizard."

"Tol, please," the wizard told him. "Redlin is just fine. I am no king or nobleman, and I have little use for titles."

"Yes, sir," Tol apologized, "Redlin, sir."

Redlin just shook his head as Abby and Emma burst out laughing.

Stefan was seated at a large dark mahogany desk rifling through papers when Tol entered with Andy and the others. Andy took a moment to take in the man who had resumed the duties of Albion's stewardship. His hair was dark as was the pointed beard that adorned his face. Andy could see the resemblance the son had to the father. Although Aidan's hair had been white when Andy had met him, Stefan had the same merry-like disposition that was imprinted on his face. The similarity ended there though as Tol cleared his throat to introduce the travelers.

Stefan looked up and arose upon seeing he was not alone anymore. Where Aidan had been short and round, Stefan was tall and well-muscled.

"What are you about today Tol?" the Baron asked cordially.

Tol introduce everyone to the Baron, who, like Tol was astounded to be in such exalted company.

"Friends, you are most welcome," Stefan said expansively. "I am at your service."

"Your welcome is most gracious Baron," Redlin said. "We could use your help on a most urgent matter."

"Of course," the Baron replied. "Let's go into the library where we will be more comfortable."

"If you no longer need us sir, my men and I will return to our watch," Tol said.

"Certainly Tol," Stefan said.

"Thanks for your help Tol," Andy said.

Tol raised a fist to his chest in salute. "I am still a member of the Lord Dragon's army. I stand ready should the need arise," Tol replied as he turned with Anwell and Dayvn as they left the hall.

Stefan's brow knit together as sat in a high back charcoal grey cloth covered chair. His wine glass half empty sitting on the small table next to him as he concentrated on all Redlin had told him regarding their quest.

"Samara, I have heard of," Stefan began, "most of it the stuff of legends and I therefore did not put much stock in it." The sun was low as it streamed into the west facing arched window. "I do believe she has great power. Traveling to Dragonsgate, I came across a vagabond who claimed to be a slave to Samara, but not in the sense you might think."

"What do you mean?" Andy asked.

"He claimed he had been transformed into a hawk and forced to spy for her." Stefan looked over at Redlin. "You have heard of frendrawl?"

"Truth drug, yes," Redlin replied. "But the plant that is

used died out several hundred years before I left, and even then, it was very rare."

Stefan pulled a small vial out of his breast pocket and held it out to the wizard who took it to examine. "That has been handed down to every Baron since the founding of Albion. Something told me I needed to verify the truth of what the man was telling me. I put a drop in some water and had him drink. He repeated his story without variation."

Redlin handed the vial back to Stefan. "Wizards can change themselves, but we don't have the power to change others in that manner. Samara has skills I know nothing about."

This troubled Andy more than anything else. The fact that there were things out there that his father had never encountered made him slightly uneasy.

Abby and Emma were over in one corner of the library scanning the titles of the books on the shelves, taking one down now and again to glance through it. Bella had left to take her butterflies to the beautiful gardens in the rear of the manor house. Rhyan was inspecting, quite intently, the fletching on her arrows. Andy sat in a high back chair next to his father, directly across from Stefan.

"Stefan," Abby called to him. "Do you still have the book written by the Alfar, Lorcan?"

Stefan pointed to the opposite side of the room to a pedestal. "It is there. I've actually been spending a couple hours each week combing through it. It's quite fascinating."

Abby and Emma walked over to it and started leafing through the pages, taking their time so as not to miss a thing.

"Wait," Emma said to Abby, pausing her in mid-turn of the page. "Go back one, there," she said pointing.

Abby started reading, *"The blood forest erupted in light and sound, as the red sorceress raked her vengeance on the unsuspecting creatures of Parma. "*

"That has to be Samara," Emma said.

"Does that mean we are heading for Parma?" Andy asked.

"No," Redlin said in aggravation. "Why can't things be easy for once?"

"What do you mean?" Abby asked.

Redlin didn't reply right away. Stefan replied instead.

"The blood forest is akin to the grove of the Unicorns. It moves around," Stefan explained. "However, whereas the Unicorn grove is never in the same place twice, the blood forest moves in a pattern. This I had read in an ancient scroll in the library in Kensington. Which at the present time, is inaccessible to you."

"Why is it called the blood forest?" Andy asked.

"Because of the trees," Emma answered him. "Their bark, the leaves, even the fruit they bear are the color of blood." She looked over at Redlin. "I only heard of one tree ever speak of it to me. The oldest tree in Laurel Hollow. I was young at the time and pestered him with tons of questions about magical groves and the like. I think he told me about the forest just to shut me up." Emma smiled at the memory. "He absolutely refused to explain anything else about it, and I never asked him again. I think that is our next destination."

"I believe you're right," Redlin said.

The next morning, they bid Stefan goodbye as they rode out of Albion, heading towards Laurel Hollow. Andy continued riding his horse. No need to tip any demons off to their current location. It was rainy when they set out, and continued so for the next two days.

"I'm absolutely water-logged," Abby exclaimed. "I've never seen so much rain."

Andy looked over at Bella. She had donned a light gossamer

cloak that was see-through. All variety of color shimmered beneath it. Apparently this is where Bella's butterflies took refuge when the weather turned foul.

It seemed no time at all when they had reached the boundaries of Laurel Hollow. The path they took brought them into the glade where Andy and Emilia had first trained together. He pulled his horse to a stop as he gazed around. It felt like yesterday when Braylynn had challenged them to defeat her in a test that would let her know they were ready to face Devon.

"Memories?" his father said as he pulled up beside his son.

Andy merely nodded.

Redlin scanned the glade as well. "I remember coming here once and watching Velda, the Dragon Summoner at the time, and the nine dragons practice combat together. It was a sight to see."

Andy could not imagine what it must be like to have nine brothers. One thing had been gnawing at him with each passing day. Abby had noticed and remarked upon it once, but he had been reluctant to say. As if thinking about her called him to her, Abby appeared by his side as the others started to continue to Emma's tree friend.

"It's bothering you again, isn't it?" Abby asked him with love and sympathy. "Can you not tell me what it is?"

Andy didn't keep secrets from the woman he loved, but it had just been so hard to voice his concern. On some level it felt childish to him, but in dragon years, perhaps he still was. He figured the only thing to do was just say it.

"What if they don't accept me?"

"Who?" Abby asked perplexed.

"The other dragons."

"Oh, I see," Abby said understanding.

"They have lived thousands of years Abby. Living and fighting together, and here I come along, about to usurp that order."

Abby could see he was really struggling with this. She put her hands on the sides of his face. "This is your destiny my love. You were able to get a whole world to follow you into overthrowing an evil wizard. The gods made you for this, and I'm sure the other dragons will feel it as I do." She stared into his eyes lovingly. "And if some have doubts, I know in time you will win them over." Leaning in, she pressed her lips gently to his.

Andy marveled at the blessing in his life that allowed him to have such an amazing woman love him. "Thank you, Abby. Once again, you have rescued me from myself."

She mussed his hair as she took up her reigns. "Come on, let's catch up with the others."

They finally reached the tree on the utmost south-east border of Laurel Hollow that Emma spoke of. It stood upon a grassy knoll in solitude. Its trunk was massive, with sweeping broad leafy branches. Looking up, Andy estimated its height at about a hundred feet. A carpet of deep green moss encircled its base.

"Wait here," Emma told them. "He's very temperamental."

Emma flew up the knoll. Placing her hands gently on the bark, her wings beat out a slow rhythm. Andy felt like he could almost hear her singing to it. Several minutes went by when Emma motioned them to join her.

"He wants to speak to you Redlin," she told the wizard.

"I assume he can facilitate this?" Redlin asked her.

"I can," a booming voice came from the upper boughs. Everyone looked up startled.

"How do I address you?" Redlin queried.

"You may call me Arsa," the tree responded, its leaves rustled even though there was no wind.

"Can all trees talk as you do?" Redlin asked Arsa.

"None but I, for I am the first tree. I alone stood next to the goddess as she created this land she loved. Also, the prophecy has ordained that I converse with you. Listen carefully, for your time grows short. Emma tells me you seek the Blood Forest. Though she pestered me once to reveal its location, the time had not yet come."

"You could have at least told me that," Emma shouted up at him.

Andy could have sworn he heard the tree laughing. Emma stuck her tongue out at Arsa.

"If you leave from this spot right now and travel north for four days you will come to a circle of hills, five to be exact. It is called the circle of the gods, I'm sure you can guess why. It is invisible to most, and enchanted. Many have ridden right by it, never knowing it was there."

"I fly up that way all the time and I know I have never seen it," Bella remarked.

"In four days' time, the Blood Forest will be in the valley of those hills. If you are late getting there, the forest will next be beyond the Mistral islands. You will never reach the spot in time and your quest will fail."

"I really hate being on a time schedule," Rhyan said.

"That makes two of us," Andy agreed.

The tree started to sway violently.

"Arsa, what's wrong?" Emma asked alarmed.

"Demons on the northern border of Laurel Hollow! You must go now."

"We have to help them," Andy exclaimed.

"No!" Arsa commanded. "That is their intent, to delay you. They must know your time grows short. Ride hard master wizard and do not stop. If you do, all of Vasara will be lost."

Arsa went silent and his branches were still once more.

"Mount up, we need to go," Redlin said urgently.

Like an arrow released from a bow, four horses and two faeries shot through the woods at break-neck speed, wondering if a wall of demons would meet them as they broke free of the trees of the faerie realm. Andy held his connection to the source. No matter what Arsa said, he was not going to sit idly by and allow any demon to bring harm to the ones he loved. He put his head down and charged forward, praying to the Five that they would succeed.

Chapter 13

"Ala?" Emilia asked in disbelief.

"Donella!" the brown-haired, Black River healer and priestess of Raphael exclaimed.

Emilia could not believe Ala was here in Diminitus's house. She looked like she hadn't aged a day, which puzzled Emilia greatly. So many questions were running through her mind, but she put all that aside as she looked down at Ava.

"Ala, we need your help. Our friend was shot with an Alfar arrow. I've stopped the poison from reaching her heart, but I cannot hold it back much longer."

Ala was all business as she leaped into action. After a brief inspection of Ava's eyes, and feeling for a pulse, Ala ordered them all inside.

Walking into the foyer, they turned into a small sitting room with a couch.

"Lay her down there," Ala told Emilia. "Dim, get out here!"

"What the devil is all the shouting for?" Diminitus said crankily as he entered the room, stopping himself short as he took in all the various races that have suddenly populated his house. "Donella, what the…?"

"No time Dim, this girl has been shot with a poisoned Alfar arrow."

Diminitus ran out of the room muttering to himself. Emilia thought she heard him say something like, "Why do these things always get dropped at my doorstep." Emilia couldn't help smiling to herself. She knew Diminitus well enough to know that all his bluster was for show.

Ala walked about the room lighting various candles. Emilia knew these candles were not for illumination. Some of the candles remained unlit for one thing. Also, these were not the tall thin white candles you might see. Some were short and fat of varying shapes. Others tall and knotty looking, like the trunk of a tree. The flames were sometimes normal and at other times changed hue. No doubt they had some healing agent in them. Breathing deeply, Emilia could feel the weariness leaving her body.

Emilia looked at Ava. Her breathing was becoming labored.

"The poison is moving," she told Ala.

"Dim, hurry!" Ala shouted.

"I'm coming, I'm coming," Diminitus said entering the room with a vial and a long bone needle.

"By the gods!" Lyson said looking at the needle. "What are you going to do with that?"

"Calm yourself general," Diminitus told him. "This is the only way to save her life. We need to inject the serum into her heart directly."

"Are you mad?" Tera exclaimed. "You'll kill her!"

Ala looked compassionately at Tera. "Do you remember how you once thought I was killing Donella?" Ala asked her.

Tera was pulling on her pointed ear, the memory of that day at the Inn, when Ala gave Emilia dragonroot to burn out the skull-spider venom came rushing back to her.

"In the hands of a healer, that which seems like certain death is in fact the most potent of cures. Lyson, open her shirt. Trust me dear Tera." Lyson quickly unbuttoned her shirt, exposing the white skin just above Ava's heart.

"I trust you," Emilia told Ala making eye contact. "Do it quickly. I can't hold it back any longer."

"Now Dim," Ala said.

Diminitus quickly filled the needle with the serum, and placing it over her heart smacked it down with his palm.

Ava's eyes went wide in shock, and the scream that tore from her throat was deafening. As Diminitus pulled the needle out, Emilia placed her hand over Ava's heart. Allowing her healing power to flow, the hole in Ava's chest began to slowly close. Ava was whimpering and tears leaked out of the corner of her eyes and slid down her cheeks. Emilia then placed her hand on Ava's forehead, putting her into a deep sleep. Lyson re-buttoned her shirt, pulling a blanket over her to keep her warm.

"She will sleep for a while," Emilia said. "How long do you think before she can travel?"

Ala looked closely at Ava.

"A lot will depend on her. She suffered a major trauma to her heart, not to mention the weakness her body is going to feel due to the poison. I've seen some laid up for a month or more."

"We may have to leave her here," Luel told her daughter.

Emilia didn't like the thought of leaving her friend behind, and she was pretty sure Ava would resist having to stay.

"Can you stay a couple of days? We should know by then the extent of her injuries."

Emilia looked at her mother who nodded. "We will stay."

"Come," Ala said. "Let's go into the kitchen. We will prepare a meal and you will tell me what has brought you back to us, although I think the present crisis has something to do with it."

Everyone followed Ala to the rear of the house that opened into a wide airy kitchen. The ceiling was easily fourteen feet high with visible twelve by twelve support beams. The walls were painted a light blue color, like that of a sky on a cloudless day. A large oven stood against one wall and a stand-in fireplace adorned the other. A thickly carved oak table stood in the middle of the room. Emilia could tell it would easily seat twenty people, although there were currently only ten chairs divided among both sides of the table. There was a door off to the side that led to a root cellar, for keeping food items cool.

After everyone had hugged and greeted one another, Diminitus pulled a chair out at the head of the table and sat down. His grey hair seemed to be neatly trimmed, making his facial features seem somewhat less stern. Ala took the chair next to him, placing a hand affectionately on his shoulder as she sat down.

"I suppose you are all wondering why I am here," Ala said looking at Diminitus who returned her gaze.

"That was my first thought," Emilia said smiling.

"Don't you start gloating now missy," Diminitus said wagging a finger at her.

"Diminitus, would I do that?" Emilia said, clearly enjoying this.

"Do you remember the wish I made at the source of the Five gods, when Dain was chosen as the new wizard," Ala said.

Emilia did remember. Diminitus had made some sarcastic comment after Leah and Dain were rejoicing and hugging, and Ala had said in the presence of everyone,

"Dim, I am going to make a wish in this place where all the power of the gods, and goddess, have currently come together and maybe it will come true," Ala said mischievously. "I wish for you to meet a woman, that you are so smitten by, you will not be able to think of anything else for the rest of your long, long life."

"You don't mean…?" Tera said bursting out laughing. Diminitus glared at her. Ala's cheeks had a slight blush.

"Yes," Ala said. "I had no idea that it might rebound on me." She looked to Diminitus and smiled. "But I have never been so happy in all my life."

"Oh," Emilia said with a catch in her voice as she went over and hugged Ala.

"Okay, we don't need to get all mushy about it," Diminitus remarked. Emilia could tell he did not mean it. His voice had not the heat and sarcasm that is usually characteristic when Diminitus talks of emotional topics.

"What brings you here Donella," Ala asked.

The hours seemed to fly by as Emilia told Ala and Diminitus everything from when the left Vasara after Devon's defeat to the moment they arrived at their door step bearing the dying Ava. Diminitus seemed to be pondering all that was said and seemed a little troubled.

"What is it Diminitus?" Luel asked him.

Diminitus smiled at her. "You look exactly the same from the last time I saw you," he said.

"Why thank you, kind sir," Luel said inclining her head. "I'm taking that as a compliment."

"Well of course it's a compliment," he said crankily.

Everyone laughed, which made him harrumph even more and cross his arms.

"I'm sorry, forgive me," Luel said smiling. "But tell me, what has you troubled."

"Pan," Diminitus said in all seriousness. "I haven't seen him since you all left. I can't even find his grotto anymore."

This bothered Emilia greatly. "What of the fauns, has no one asked them?"

"They seem very skittish," Ala put in. "Whenever we would get close to a herd, they would run and disappear over the nearest hill."

"Anyone have any ideas how to find him?" Lyson asked.

Emilia thought on it, when an idea came. "Tera, do you still have your pipes?"

"Yes," the silver haired faerie said as she reached into the folds of her dress. "I always carry them."

"What do you have in mind?" Luel asked her daughter.

"We are going to the ruins. The ones we came to when I first entered Parma. That place has a connection to all of this, and to Pan. Tera will play her pipes to call him." Emilia looked over at her faerie sister. "If he would come for anyone it would be Tera."

Two days later found Emilia walking the flower garden behind Diminitus' house. The sun felt good on her outstretched wings. She found it amazing that someone as cranky as Diminitus could create such beauty. A grassy path wound its way among the flower beds and various plant species that dotted either side of the path. The sights and smells brought back her sojourns among the gardens of Vassar College. All of a sudden she was missing her home. She was wondering what her classmates and friends might me doing at this moment.

"Donella," Lyson called.

Emilia smiled to herself before turning around. She missed her past, but her future was here before her. With this man she loved with all her heart. When Lyson caught up with her, she wrapped her arms around his neck and fiercely pressed her lips to his. They were both breathless when they broke their embrace.

"I will never be apart from you again," Lyson told her as he stroked her hair and pushed it behind her pointed ears.

"There will never be a need," Emilia told him, drawing his eyes into hers. "I've made up my mind, whatever happens, my home is where you are." Lyson leaned in to kiss her again.

"Ava is awake," he told her.

"Come," Emilia said taking his hand as they walked back to the house.

They found Ava sitting in a chair, bent over lacing up her deerskin boots. She looked up when Emilia and Lyson walked into the room. Emilia could see some dark circles under her eyes, but she looked whole.

"Are you sure you should be up?" Emilia asked her concerned.

Ava smiled tiredly. "It will take more than a poisoned arrow to keep me down for long. And you forget my advantage." Ava reached into her shirt and pulled out her medallion of Aditya. "The god saw fit to help his priestess when I called upon him."

Emilia smiled back. "Yes, I had forgotten you had that access." Emilia looked over at her mother who seemed to be concentrating. "Anything wrong Mom?"

"I was just thinking. Never in my life had I known who were the priests of the gods, and in this very room there are two," she said looking over at Raphael's priestess, Ala.

"Do you think it significant?" Lyson asked.

"I do," Luel responded. "If my husband were here, I'm sure he would say the same."

Emilia wondered how her father and the others were faring. She only knew they were somewhere east of her, based on the pull she was feeling from her Summoner link with Andy. Her mother's observation had merit, but only time would tell if there would be any other priests of the Five crossing their path.

"If Ava is ready to travel, I think we should leave at first light tomorrow," Luel said.

"Ala and I will come along," Diminitus said. "I know a shortcut to those ruins." He seemed uncomfortable in his generosity. "Besides, I don't want to chance you getting stuck with another arrow and having to drag whoever back here."

Emilia just smiled at him.

They spent most of the next day traveling to the ruins. Arriving just before sunset, they walked through what was left of the tunneled archway. More vines seemed to be climbing up either side of the arch from what Emilia remembered. She thought on what Dain had said, that this was probably once the capital buildings of the functioning government of Parma. Closing her eyes, she could still feel the open wound, the betrayal that must have happened here to cause all of this. The others were milling about, looking around at the various structures and debris that littered the place. Most of which was covered in grass and lichen.

"Should we try and call Pan now?" Lyson asked her.

Emilia thought about it. "No, let's wait until morning. I don't want Tera's pipes alerting unwanted visitors to our location."

"Ava and I will clear a place to spend the night and get a fire going."

Emilia placed a loving hand on his cheek. Lyson placed his hand on top of hers. He leaned in and kissed her before walking away to go get Ava.

"That's a fine man you've chosen," Luel said coming up behind her daughter.

"Thanks Mom," Emilia said smiling at the retreating figure of her beloved.

Luel put her hands on either side of Emilia's face. "I know how hard it is to make this choice. To love a mortal man can cause excruciating heartbreak. I never had to face that eventuality with your father since he is a wizard. But my own mother knew the hazards of that choice."

"Did she ever tell you why she chose to love a man?" For some reason, Emilia desperately wanted to know.

"Yes. She said the alternative of not sharing a life with him was too bitter to contemplate."

Emilia could certainly understand that. Whatever time she would get with Lyson she wanted and would be grateful for it.

The sun was bright as it crested the horizon, shining

through the boughs of the trees. Ava was already up and had a fire going. She had placed an iron grate across the flames. Where on earth had she found that, Emilia couldn't guess. A closed-lid iron pot was resting on top, steam emanating from the hole in the top.

"Is that coffee I smell?" Emilia asked surprised.

"Yes it is," Ava replied smiling. "The best Fenner blend you will ever find." Ava poured her a cup.

"Cream and sugar?" Emilia asked hopefully taking the offered cup.

"You won't need it, trust me."

"Is that Fenner honey coffee I smell," Tera said flying over, "I'll take some of that."

Ava laughed as she poured Tera a cup.

Emilia hesitantly sipped it. The taste was amazing. Ava had been right, cream and sugar were not necessary. It had the bitter coffee bite that Emilia loved while being sweet at the same time.

After breakfast everyone gathered around Tera as she stood on a stone pillar, her pipes raised to her lips. She played her song of calling, that Pan had taught her. It was a complex melody that drifted on the air and floated through the forest. Everyone seemed transfixed as the music wound around them.

Tera played steadily for the first half hour with no appearance by Pan. She then played once every hour until sunset. Still, Pan did not come.

"I don't get it," Tera said slightly downcast looking at Emilia. "I was certain he would come."

"You did your best," Emilia told the silver haired faerie. "Tomorrow I'm going to try something."

"What are you going to do Donella?" Tera asked concerned. "You're not going to make Pan mad are you?"

Emilia laughed. "It will be alright." Truth be told, she was not entirely sure about that. She was still working on what she wanted to do and prayed she wasn't making a mistake.

The next day, Tera once more took her place on the pillar. Emilia stood next to her, the staff of the goddess in her hand.

"Just what do you have in mind," Luel asked her daughter.

"I did this once with Andy," Emilia explained. "I remember he didn't like it very much, but the circumstances warranted my actions."

"What did you do?" Ava asked her.

"She had overridden his will, and forced Andros to come to her," Diminitus answered for Emilia, remembering the day Tera was stabbed by Zana and close to death. The only way to save her was to have a dragon fly her to Laurel Hollow, where Braylynn could heal her. Andy had been the dragon Emilia had forced to come. He raised an eyebrow at Emilia. "You try that with Pan and you are likely to have an army of fauns stampeding down on us in no time."

"Don't worry," Emilia said. "I can only supplant a dragon's will. My hope is to compel Pan to listen to Tera's song. That is all. Go ahead Tera, play."

Tera put the pipes to her lips once more and played out the melody that would hopefully bring Pan to them. Emilia had her eyes closed, the pearl-white sphere atop her staff started to pulse and glow, her mind reaching out. She touched a hand to her necklace, which strengthened her connection to the earth and all living things. She reached further, and just when she was about to give up she found him. He was resisting her call. She focused harder, bringing all her Summoner powers to bear on the King of the fauns. Now she could feel him reluctantly start to head in their direction.

"You can stop Tera, he's on his way."

"Okay, great. You don't mind if I make myself scarce for a few days?" Tera asked.

"I'll come with you," Diminitus replied.

"Both of you stay where you are," Emilia said firmly. "You're being ridiculous." For some reason, she had the sudden urge to flee as well.

About a half hour had passed when the sound of a hundred hoof beats could be heard coming over the hill.

"He brought his whole bloody army," Lyson said, his hand resting on his sword hilt.

"Don't worry love," Emilia said placing a hand on his shoulder. "Pan is a friend, he would never hurt us."

The fauns thundered down the slope and into the ruins, encircling the travelers, their spears lowered in a defensive posture. Coming down the hill in a gliding trot was Pan himself. The circle parted to allow him entrance. He strode up to Emilia, his face like a thundercloud, his eyes occasionally darting towards Tera, since it was her song that called him. Tera had taken up refuge behind Ava, peering around and ducking back as Pan's black eyes alighted on her.

Pan glared down at Emilia, his red horns seeming to changing hue to match his fury. "How dare you Summoner." Pan's voice was low and ice-cold. Emilia did not flinch as she returned his stare.

"Oh stop being silly," Emilia said, talking to him like a petulant child. Diminitus groaned. "It didn't hurt you. And you were purposely not answering Tera's call, when you promised you would always come."

Pan's features softened slightly along with the stiffness in his shoulders. Most of the anger had dissipated, but he wasn't ready to be overly friendly just yet. "What is it you want?" he asked.

"I think you know," Emilia said.

Pan didn't answer. His glance roamed around at the others, stalling Emilia thought. Not wanting to dig down and answer with the information they needed. He finally let everything go. His entire demeanor changed before their eyes. He looked shrunken, his shoulders slumped. "Follow me," he told them.

They followed him deeper into the ruins, coming to what was once the palace audience chamber. The remains of a large stone chair sat back against a ruined wall. Pan climbed the steps and sat down. As he did, the scene suddenly changed. Everything looked as it did when this place was first built. The hall was awash with people running on various errands, some passing through the startled visitors. Tears were streaming down his face as he spoke. "Welcome to my kingdom," Pan said in anguish. Emilia looked at him in wonder. No longer did he have the horns and legs of a goat. His eyes were blue and his hair a golden yellow as it cascaded down his back, a silver circlet adorned his head. Around his neck was a silver necklace with a medallion attached to it. Stamped on the medallion's face was forest pool with various magical creatures sitting down or bending their heads to drink. Emilia thought the detail was incredible. It was much like Ala and Ava's, which led Emilia to suspect the Pan was the priest of Cael.

"Pan, what is this?" Tera asked a little frightened.

"Fear not dear Tera. I'm just allowing you to see things as they once were, it is all illusion and will not harm you. It will be easier to explain things to you."

"Does that medallion mean what I think it means?" Emilia asked him.

"Yes, although the real one is hanging in my grotto. I stopped wearing it long ago. I'm too ashamed to be Cael's priest, however he refuses to appoint another, I do not know why."

"You were human then?" Luel asked.

"No," Pan replied soberly, "a warlock. There were eleven of us, and though we may look alike, I assure you, we were all very different, each having his own set of gifts. I ruled over all."

"Pan," Luel said gently. "Tell us what happened."

Pan looked kindly down on Luel. Emilia could tell he was dealing with emotions buried deep inside. A faun carrying a tray of food stopped directly in front of her, swinging his head back and forth in indecision, as if he had lost his way. The constant activity she was seeing was starting to become distracting.

"Pan, do you suppose we could reduce the number of beings in the hall?" Emilia asked.

"Of course," Pan said giving a negligent wave of his hand.

Once the scene changed, Emilia's eyes were instantly drawn to a far corner of the chamber.

"Look out!" Lyson yelled drawing his sword.

"Easy General, they are not real. They are shades, as the others were."

What had drawn Emilia's eye and caused Lyson's outburst were ten figures dressed in red flowing robes. Intricate silver designs covered the outside of the robes from collar to feet. It was spectacular and dizzying to look at. At first glance, Emilia thought them identical to Pan. Staring longer at their faces, Emilia could start to see the differences in each one.

"These are my brothers," Pan began. "Do not ask their names, I have vowed to never speak them again. Besides, those who I once held as kin ceased to exist on that fateful day."

"What day was that?" Tera asked.

"We were a brotherhood of knowledge, and we sought it in all places. I never strayed very far from Parma, being consumed with its daily issues, which relied heavily on my wisdom and advice." Pan suddenly laughed, but not in a happy way. "Forgive me, it just struck me how ironic that my so called wisdom failed me, and to no small degree my pride blinded me, else I would have seen the danger signs."

Emilia watched as Ava walked over to examine the warlocks more closely. Slowly pushing an arrow through one, as if to verify they were not real.

"What do you mean?" Lyson asked him.

"They would be gone for years at a time, but we would always come together to share our knowledge, both mental and magical. We did not draw power from a godly source, our power came from the earth and all living things. I could tell from the knowledge they were sharing that they were delving into areas best left alone."

"What kind of areas?" Luel asked.

"We borrow our magic from the life force of plant and animal, but it is only borrowed and taken from many different sources at once. My brothers were experimenting with taken energy and storing it." Pan hung his head. "I should have forbidden it right at that moment, but I thought us all responsible, and everything we did was without malice or greed, only for the greater good. What I didn't know is they had sought the knowledge of demon lore, which Cael specifically forbid us from studying. The darkness seduced them with promise of power, and they bathed in its blackness. I was so blind. Hundreds of years passed before I saw them again. They were totally possessed by the strongest demon lords ever spawned in hell. The sulfur stench that emanated from them was almost unbearable. They were sucking the life force out of everything within their mental reach. Magical beasts were dropping dead as their energy was drained from them. I had to act quickly. I caused a fissure to open beneath their feet and they fell in. I then closed it on top of them, sealing them inside the earth." Pan paused a moment as he gathered his thoughts. Tera had come to sit on his lap and he wrapped his arms around her.

"I thought I had trapped them. But I didn't realize how strong they had become. The earth exploded, and every building in the capital was razed to the ground. They walked out of that hole, drawing energy from the lives that had survived the explosion. I shielded myself and was unharmed, but it took a while to dig myself out of the debris. Once free, I followed them, which was easy. Bodies lay on either side of the trail they walked. By their direction, I knew where they were headed, the holy mound of the Alfar."

Emilia looked over at her mother. Luel's body stiffened and her face turned grim at Pan's mention of that place.

"Once in the mound, they could go anywhere," Pan continued. "I followed them inside. It was then that I took out my medallion and called Cael to me. Together we were able to trap them."

"Where?" Emilia asked. Something told her she needed to know.

"It was a cave, enormous, with a lake. In the middle of the lake is a mile-long rock island. There was nothing else. It took all of my power and Cael's aid to seal them there forever. When it was done I collapsed on the shore. I do not know how long I was unconscious, days, months, perhaps years. But when I awoke, I was in what is now my grotto and in the form you all know me as. My time as a warlock was over, my powers gone. The god had transformed me. Cael told me this was the only way to save my life. "

"If you sealed them in there, how did they get out again?" Ava asked him.

"When I heard of the being that attacked Andros, I knew it had to be one of my brothers. I left the battle against Devon and journeyed straight away to the Alfar mound. I searched many years, but I was never able to find the cave. I think Cael did this so I would never be tempted to seek them out, even if only to make sure they were still there. But I do believe another had found that cave," Pan said addressing Ava's question. "I believe Devon, with the help of the demon lord inside him, made his way down there."

"Why would he seek them out?" Lyson said.

"To strike a bargain. I think the dragons are held captive there. Somehow, Devon was able to penetrate the barrier and free my brothers, their task, to hold captive the other nine dragons and deny them to the Summoner. But now they are free to roam again, with an army of demons to aid them."

"Are the dragons dead then?" Tera asked.

"No," Emilia said. "Braylynn told us they were still alive for the present. We must hurry however; I feel their time growing short."

"You cannot defeat them Summoner," Pan told her gravely.

"Tori killed one," Tera put in. "They can't be too difficult to beat."

"No," Pan said shaking his head. "When I heard the tale of her encounter, I knew the only thing that died was the demon lord inside. As soon as the blade touched its skin, the warlock disappeared, wounded perhaps, but not dead. He will find another demon to inhabit his body. You can't win Donella."

"By myself, no, but I think that is another reason the dragons need to be freed." Emilia looked to her mother. "I guess we know where we need to go, the mound."

Luel nodded her head soberly. "We already knew we had to, now we need to find this specific place."

"Anybody have any ideas?" Lyson asked.

No one had a clue.

Chapter 14

Dain walked the path that eventually came to where the source rotated on its five axis. It was quiet, save for the occasional chirping of some of the smaller birds that frequented this place. He stood still for a moment, holding his arms up, palms turned out as if in supplication, allowing the wave of the source to wash over him, calming his spirit.

"You look mighty holy standing there like that," a voice said behind him.

Turning quickly, Dain saw a figure approach; he already knew who it was.

"Just getting my bearings old man," Dain said to Loki smiling, rushing over to embrace him.

"I know what you did," Loki told him. "Thank you brother."

"You would have done the same for me," Dain replied.

Dain told Loki everything that had been going on, from Redlin's return to the escape from the tower. Loki listened without interruption.

"So our errant brother has returned," Loki said smiling. "That pleases me more than you know. And it all makes sense now."

"What's that?"

"Andros. Long had I wondered how he came to be."

"I don't understand," Dain said puzzled.

"He was not created the way the other dragons were. His spirit obviously was, but not his body. The others were hatched in their dragon eggs. They came into this world first as dragons and learned to transform into their human counterpart. With Andros, it was the opposite. It makes sense that he was born to Redlin, since dragons and wizards share the same power source."

"So what now?" Dain asked him.

"We need to meet up with Redlin and Andros. A major confrontation is coming with many players, and we have to make plans."

"Are you fit to travel?"

"I will be. Let's go," Loki said as turned and started walking back the way he came with Dain following.

The wind had picked up, blowing Tori's dark hair crazily back and forth in front of her face. Gathering it, she tied it off in a ponytail as she continued to gaze down the mountainside. Something moved. Her head snapped to the left as she heard several small rocks bounce down the mountain.

She pulled her swords. Her red eyes focused, piercing the twilight. Whatever had dislodged the rocks had stopped moving. Even with her enhanced vision nothing seemed to be out of the ordinary. But she knew something was there.

"Cleo!" Tori yelled.

"What is it?" Cleo came out, swords drawn, looking down to where Tori was staring.

"I'm not sure. I know something is there. Should we have Leah fly out and take a look?"

"She's watching over Dain and Loki," Cleo told her.

Together they scanned the cliff face. Nothing moved. Nothing, which bothered Tori even more. She should be able to hear the normal sounds of nature. All was still. If anything was there, it perfectly blended with the rock. Or, something was preventing her from seeing.

The shrieks suddenly came from their left, five hundred yards down the stone path. As in Fenner, there was a hole in the air and demons were pouring out of it.

"Leah! We are under attack!" Cleo yelled into the cave. "Tori wait!"

Tori was moving too fast to check her speed. The battle frenzy was on her as she rushed to meet the devil spawn, screaming her battle cry which alone would make normal troops pause in their fight.

As before on the bridge, her movements were lightning fast, cutting down swaths of the monsters. She looked up and saw Leah engaging some of the flying demons, taking on two or three at a time, her talon spear dealing death. Tori knew Leah wouldn't last long up there by herself. Sheer numbers were going to destroy them. Looking back, she saw Cleo backed against a rock wall, holding a score of them at bay.

"Back to the cave! Now!"

Tori turned. Loki was standing at the door to the cave. Somehow this gave Tori enormous relief. She thought if anyone knew how to get out of this mess it was the wizard. She started making her way back, cutting her way towards Cleo. Once she reached Cleo, they raced back to where Loki was.

"Inside, quick," he commanded. Leah came swooping in behind them as Loki lifted both hands, many lightning strikes, like branches on a tree came streaking from his palms. Dain was standing next to him, obliterating his own line of demons coming up over the cliff face.

"Get ready to shut the doors," Loki said as he and Dain started inching their way backwards. Once they cleared the threshold, Cleo and Tori, with Leah pushing one side from the top, slammed the doors into place. Loki was speaking an incantation as they shut. The demons shrieked in frustration as they banged against the door.

"Good to see you back with us wizard," Tori said smiling.

"Was there ever any doubt Tori," Loki said smirking. "Come, we need to get out of here. That door won't hold forever."

"This was not a random attack, was it," Dain said. "No one comes here by accident."

"What do you mean?" Leah asked, drawing her lavender wings into her body.

"He means, something or someone drew them to this cave." Loki seemed to ponder that for a moment.

"I think it's me," Tori said.

"Why do you say that?" Cleo asked as if it were the most ridiculous thing she heard.

"Think about it Boss. The way they attacked here was just like on the bridge, and Fenner too for that matter." Tori's shoulders slumped. The more she thought about it, in her heart she knew it was true. She was a danger to whoever was around her.

"Tori," Dain said noticing her posture and where her thoughts would lead. "Whether you are marked or not, it doesn't matter. You are not going off by yourself."

Tori looked sharply at the former Border Lands general. How had he read her thoughts? He was a wizard after all. "How…"

Dain smiled compassionately. "I am no mind reader," he said holding his hand up to forestall her. "I was once a soldier as you are, and I know the difficulty of putting your friends in danger."

"I am a magnet to these things."

Loki walked over and placed both hands on her shoulders. "Then that is a good thing, saves us time from having to track them all over Vasara."

Tori couldn't help busting out in laughter. These were true warrior brothers and sisters.

"Come on, we're getting out of here."

"Where are we going?" Leah asked as they started running down a corridor.

"The wizard's alcove, you will understand when we get there. Hurry."

They ran through a labyrinth of tunnels for about five minutes when they suddenly found themselves in a spacious room with dizzying symbols drawn all over the floor and walls. Tori looked up, the ceiling had wizarding marks as well. The room was aptly named.

"Now what," Cleo said.

"We create our own portal," Loki told her as he scanned the floor looking for a particular spot. "Here," he pointed.

Everyone came to where a circle was etched into the floor. Inside the circle was a large tree with sweeping branches, and the image of faeries around it.

"Where will this take us?" Tori asked.

"Laurel Hollow," Loki replied. "I can feel Redlin to the south. And whenever I sense my brother in that region I always assume he is there. Being the romantic, love struck wizard that he is, I would always find him at the home of his beloved. Let us hope my assumption is correct. Something tells me he is going to need us."

They all stepped within the circle as Loki began his magic. Tori could feel a sensation building in the pit of her stomach, telling her this mode of travel was not going to be pleasant. As Loki clapped his hands, her feeling was validated as she felt like someone had reached inside her, grabbed her spine and pulled her across many miles. She wished she could just pass out and wake up when they reached their destination. But it was not to be as she heard her own voice screaming in her ears.

Chapter 15

Andy tried hard to keep pace with Rhyan. But her superior mount and expert horsemanship had her outdistancing everyone. She had unconsciously appointed herself scout on their quest. Andy didn't really mind. His own horse was fast, but he could feel it starting to labor. The white flecks on the shoulders of the other horse told him they were all in pretty much the same situation, and they would soon need to give them a breather.

Rhyan, my horse is almost spent, Andy mind spoke to her.

Yes, I know. We are trying to just get past this next rise where there is water, she replied.

They came down over the hill and the forest path turned sharply to the right, opening up into a glen with a good size pool. Everyone dismounted and led the horses to the water's edge where they began to drink noisily.

"Dad, there is no way we can ride these horses non-stop for four days," Andy said cupping a handful of water, dousing his head to cool off. "I could fly you, Abby and Rhyan the rest of the way."

Redlin shook his head no. "You would be too visible. The demons would be on us like flies." Redlin was rubbing his horse down when he had a thought. "Rhyan, how far ahead can you sense wild horses in the area."

"About fifty leagues in any direction," she replied while fletching an arrow.

"We want to change horses as frequently as we can. Is it possible to have four waiting for us every thirty leagues?"

She thought about it for a moment. "Yes, but I will need a moment," she replied as she walked to a nearby tree and sat on the mossy side in a lotus position. Placing her hands in her lap she closed her eyes and pulled her priestess medallion out to lay on her chest. Andy could see it starting to glow around the edges.

"What do you think she's doing, Dad?"

"I assume it has something to do with contacting the horses we need."

After several minutes she rose and came to where they were standing.

"It's all arranged," she told them.

Every thirty leagues, as Rhyan had promised, fresh mounts greeted them to take them on. On the morning of the third day they could hear battle sounds. As they crested the hill, their worst nightmare greeted their eyes. A contingent of faeries and Border Lands warriors were engaged in a pitched battle with a host of demons and very badly outnumbered. Andy felt bile rise in his throat as he noticed the number of faerie and warrior dead. He reached for the source. Emma and Bella had their spears out, ready to join their sisters in battle.

"Stop! Andy, no!" his father said, sensing what he was about to do.

"Dad, we can't leave them all to be wiped out!"

Redlin looked over sympathetically at his son. "Arsa would not lie to us. His words are prophetic and should be taken as such. If we delay, this quest will fail. Vasara will fall."

Anguish was written all over Andy's face. The desire to transform was strong, but he knew his father was right. Suddenly he loathed himself for what they were about to do. Leaving these brave souls to be butchered.

All of a sudden lightning split the sky and landed not two feet from where they stood. The white flash had temporarily blinded them. When they could see again, Loki, Dain, Cleo, Tori and Leah were standing in front of them. Andy noticed Tori was having difficulty of some sort the way she was shaking her head. His father was off his horse in a flash and ran to embrace his brother.

"So the errant wizard has returned," Loki said pounding Redlin on the back.

"It's so good to see you brother," Redlin said smiling big.

Andy also jumped down to embrace the man who was like a second father to him. Tears were running down his cheeks as he realized how much he had missed the old wizard. Loki smiled at him knowingly. "I've missed you too, lad," Loki said placing both hands on the sides of his face. Andy had a lump in his throat and couldn't speak.

"I don't want to interrupt this happy reunion," Rhyan said, "but there is a contingent of demons coming this way."

Andy looked and saw Rhyan was right. A hoard of demons, some flying, were heading in their direction.

"What now Dad?" Andy asked.

"I think the time for stealth is over," Redlin said. "Can you fly us all to the Blood Forest?"

"We will take care of the demons here," Loki said. "You go."

"Don't get yourself killed, now that I just got back," Redlin told his brother.

"Not a chance," Loki said smiling wickedly. Redlin burst out laughing as he smacked his brother on the back. Andy was already running for a clear space as he changed. He watched as Tori drew both her swords and jumping on the horses left behind, she started riding hard towards the oncoming battle. Cleo, Dain and Leah following in her wake.

"Meet us at the source in two days' time," Redlin said.

"Dain and I will be there," Loki replied.

Redlin, Abby, Rhyan and the faeries jumped onto Andy's back. Leaping into the air he beat his wings hard, gaining altitude. Looking back, he could see the others had engaged the enemy. Loki and Dain were blasting their way through with fire and lightning. Cleo dealt death with every blow. Leah was engaged by several flying demons, her spear a blur as she soared through one demon then another. Tori on the other hand was lightning herself. Fire emanated from her swords as she cut a path right down the middle of the hoard. Seeing his friends had the situation well in hand he started heading north. He dared not fly too high for fear of missing the five hills. It was Abby who spotted it first.

"There it is, off to the left," Abby exclaimed.

Andy looked in the direction she indicated. Sure enough, there was a ring of hills. Five to be exact, and nestled in the center was a forest of trees the color of blood.

"I think we found it," Redlin said. "Andy, bring us to the edge of the forest. I'm sure Samara has erected a barrier to prevent us from landing right in the middle of her forest."

"You think so?" Emma asked.

"I'm certain. I can feel the warding magic from here."

Andy started to spiral down and landed at the beginning of what looked like a well-worn trail. After everyone had climbed off, Andy transformed.

"Emma, walk to that nearest tree and tell me what you sense," Redlin told her. "Bella, now would be a good time to send out some scouts."

"They are already on it," Bella said as three of the larger dark butterflies took off.

Emma walked over to the first tree she encountered. A tall

oak with a wide trunk. It's bark and leaves the color of blood. She reached a hand out and came in contact with a barrier. "I can't push through master wizard," Emma told him. "I think she's blocking us."

Redlin closed his eyes and held out his hand. With the other he pulled out the medallion Trystan had made for him. Everyone stepped back as a blue glow started forming around the wizard. Making a shoving motion, Redlin pushed the light into the barrier. There was a loud audible crack and the acrid smell of acid as the barrier shattered. Somewhere in the distance they heard a woman shriek in great pain.

"Dad, what did you do?" Andy asked shaken.

"I played a hunch," he replied.

Bella's butterflies came flying back and whispered in her ear.

"My friends are saying to beware, Redlin. There are eyes watching everywhere."

"Everyone be ready for anything," the wizard said holding onto the source.

Just then a figure in red came flying down the trail. Samara's face was livid in anger. Flecks of blood had pooled at the corner of her eyes as if something had exploded behind them.

"How dare you!" She screamed at Redlin.

Redlin was one of the three original wizards of Vasara. He's lived thousands of years and come across many adversaries. Not one has ever cowed him. And Samara would be no different. Andy knew his father could make himself look very intimidating when he chose it, and he did so now.

Samara blinked twice and lowered the hand she had raised as if she were about to strike.

"Wise decision," Redlin told her.

"One day you will pay for this wizard," she said through clenched teeth.

"Well until that day, can we get on with why we are here."

Samara smiled then. Feeling she had regained some form of control, she turned and started walking back up the trail. "Follow me," she told them. "And do not touch the trees." Samara looked directly at Emma when she said this.

"Fine," Emma agreed looking longingly at the massive giant just off the path.

What's the deal with the trees? Andy thought to his father.

My guess is they know her secrets, and Emma might be able to pick that up.

"You are in the borders of my domain now," Samara rounded on them. "I may not understand what you are saying, but I know you are using mind speak. I sense it in the air. Do so again and our agreement is off and your brothers can rot for all I care."

Redlin was not ruffled if that was her intent. "We will refrain. But trust me when I tell you, the prophecy set us on this path, and if we are meant to have the skull dagger, rest assured we will leave here with it. So we may as well all just relax."

"Well said master wizard." Samara smiled, but Andy could tell it did not reach her eyes. Trust was still withheld as far as he was concerned.

They walked for maybe ten minutes before coming to a clearing. In the center was what looked like a miniature castle, not unlike the White Castle, but on a much smaller scale. And the white walls of this castle was a stark contrast to all the red. The gate was raised and two sentries stood guard on either side of the entryway.

"I would love to know how they came to be in your employ," Redlin said.

"These two are working off a debt to me. Don't bother asking what incurred that debt, it doesn't concern you."

"I wouldn't dream of asking," Redlin replied.

"Most that are here are working off a debt, though some have sought to be here of their own free will. I do not keep slaves as some have rumored about me."

Andy sorted through all this. Samara, he decided was a complex individual. The castle and the people seemed at odds with the person he imagined her to be. Solitary. No contact, no friendships. He felt it might not be a bad idea to keep an open mind. Andy could feel all the eyes upon them from the woods that the butterflies had sensed. They would need to be careful here.

"Andros, look over there," Rhyan said pointing off to their left.

Andy saw a corralled fence with a very large barn in the center. Eating grass and drinking at a nearby watering hole were the most magnificent looking horses Andy had ever seen. They were completely white except for the mane and tail, they were the color of fire, which danced like flames when caught by the breeze. But even that is not what struck Andy. These horses had wings.

"They are Sonipes," Abby said from behind.

Andy turned to look at his beloved. Sometimes he forgot that Abby was a scholar from Dragonsgate. She knew every animal by sight it seemed. He smiled at her.

"What?" Abby said suspiciously.

"I was just remembering something," he said planting a quick kiss on her lips.

"Really? You're going to do this now?" Bella said smirking as one of her butterflies landed on Abby's ear. Andy was just now wondering how they made the trip while he was flying.

"That is my first time seeing them," Rhyan said bringing everyone's attention back to the horses. "In Fenner, they are the stuff of legends."

"There are only six," Samara said walking back towards them. "They are under my care and protection."

Suddenly the ears of the Sonipes perked up, and they were staring straight at Rhyan who had her eyes closed and a hand on her medallion.

"No!" Samara screamed so loud it shattered Andy's ears. "Stop that now!"

It was too late. Rhyan had seen everything in the Sonipes minds and her eyes went wide as she looked at Samara.

"Out! All of you! Get out!" Samara shrieked as she pulled lightning down from the sky to dance around everyone's feet.

Redlin had quickly erected a shield so no one would be hurt.

"Leave! Leave now!"

"Samara stop this!" Redlin commanded. "No one will give away your secret."

"Dad, what's going on? What secret?" Andy asked.

"Liar! You would never keep this from your family!"

"I swear by Trystan; I would never reveal a thing without your leave."

Samara softened a little at this. "And what of Aditya's priestess?" she said looking at Rhyan.

"How did you know who I am?" Rhyan said shocked.

"I could feel you mind link with the Sonipes. Only Aditya's priest could do that."

"Rhyan will not reveal anything either," Redlin said.

"I will hear her oath from her lips," Samara said raising her hand to the wizard.

Rhyan locked eyes with the witch. Andy thought she might actually refuse.

"As a priest of the god, I swear by Aditya to never reveal what I have learned."

Samara visibly relaxed. She seemed to accept this and proceeded to move into the castle. Andy so badly wanted to ask his father what he knew. But Redlin had given his promise, and Andy would not put his father in the awkward position of having to refuse his son.

The witch led them through a maze of rooms and corridors. Andy seriously wondered if they would be able to find their way out again. Finally, they came to two very large gold colored doors. Samara made a gesture with her hands and the doors opened. The room was circular, with shelves running from the floor to the ceiling which was easily twenty feet high. Every bit of shelf space was covered by books. Andy couldn't imagine how many books there must be. Abby and Emma couldn't contain themselves and started to randomly run their hands along various books, reading their titles.

In the center of the room was a marble pedestal with a glass dome sitting on top of it. Within the glass, suspended as if floating in midair was the death dagger pendant. Andy traced the outline of the brand on his palm, it was identical to what stood before him. He started to walk towards it.

"Stop!" Samara said firmly. "There is the method of payment."

"What is it you want?" Redlin asked, his eyes narrowing.

Andy felt the tension in the room jump up two notches. Something told him this would not be good. But good or bad, they needed the pendant. It suddenly dawned on Andy, they had no idea what exactly this thing was supposed to do.

"If we accept this deal, what are we supposed to do with this death dagger," Andy asked.

Samara softly chuckled. "Very clever, lord dragon. Had you not asked that I would have taken my payment and vanished. Leaving you to flounder in what to do."

"So why tell us now?" Abby asked with an edge to her voice. She was still wroth with her for branding Andy. "You know that we have to have it regardless."

"It is part of the magic of the death dagger. Any question asked about it must be answered."

"What is the answer?" Redlin asked.

"There are two barriers surrounding the dragons," Samara began. "You must defeat the one put in place by the warlocks. The skull dagger will help you in doing that."

"What warlocks?" Rhyan said.

"The warlocks of Parma, and that is all I'm required to say."

Andy and his father exchanged a glance. They both knew who these warlocks must be. The hooded figures that have dogged their every step since this quest began.

"And what of the other barrier?" Redlin asked.

"That must be breached by your daughter and your wife," Samara answered as her eyes narrowed. "That is Devon's magic."

Andy was watching Samara closely. He felt she didn't want to reveal that, but something had compelled her.

"Be warned," she continued. "Because Devon is dead, his magic is totally uncontrolled and unpredictable."

Andy opened his mouth to speak. "No more questions!" Samara said raising a hand. "It is time to pay."

"Very well, Samara," Redlin said. "What is it you want."

Samara's smile was almost wicked, sending chills down Andy's spine. He knew this wouldn't be good.

"The dragon wears it about his neck," she answered.

Andy's hand instinctively went to his chest. The medallion felt warm for some reason. Most of the time he felt nothing when he touched it, even though the power of a god resided inside. He was torn as to what he should do.

"Paolo entrusted this to me. I don't know that it is mine to give."

"Then your brother's will die. That is my price."

Andy looked at all his friends one by one, his eyes pleading for someone to help him decide what to do. He couldn't leave his brothers to die, but nor could he deliver up the power of a god to Samara.

"Dad?" he asked his father.

Redlin had not taken his eyes off Samara the whole time and now they had narrowed to slits.

"Give it to her," Redlin said.

Andy seemed puzzled. "You sure?" he said as he slowly drew it out from under his shirt.

"Yes," the wizard replied. "Samara may think she is controlling things here, but it is the prophecy that is guiding this quest. I have to believe it knows what it's doing."

The young dragon started to take the medallion from around his neck.

"Andros, wait," Rhyan said. She walked over, taking her own medallion out and placed her hand on his. A green glow surrounded them both as Rhyan closed her eyes as her mouth moved silently.

"What are you doing?" Samara yelled.

"I am not changing it in any way," the priestess replied. "What you hope to gain from this I do not know, but should the power within ever be released, I will know."

"As if that is going to help," Samara sneered taking the medallion from Andy.

Andy couldn't help feeling a sense of loss in giving the medallion up. He remembered how concerned Braylynn was that he and Emilia even had them. Now he had given it away to a person he had no idea was either good or evil. He prayed to the gods that he just didn't make a colossal error. But he trusted his father. Once Samara had the medallion, Andy started walking towards the glass dome. He could feel a power emanating from the death dagger. As he lifted the dome off, the eyes in the skull burned red.

"Andros, beware!" Rhyan shouted as she drew an arrow.

Andy stared into the eyes. There was a presence in it. A living presence that was softly speaking to his mind in a language that he could not understand, but he felt that presence was not evil.

"Lower your arrow, Rhyan. It will not harm us," Andy told her.

"It speaks to you?" Redlin asked.

"Yes, but I cannot understand the language."

"Can you describe it?" his father asked.

"It is almost like birdsong. Very musical but animalistic."

"It is the ancient language of Parma," Abby told them.

Andy turned towards her. "How do you know?"

Abby looked at him tenderly and with a trace of pain. "You know my love of music?"

"Yes," he said reaching a hand to her shoulder.

"My father taught me everything about music. All I know is because of him. One of the last things he taught me was the musical language of Parma, spoken by the ancients that ruled there long ago. There is a book of translation. A very special book. Magical you could say."

Redlin looked intently at Abby. "Do you know where he got this book?" the wizard asked her.

"No."

"What makes it magical?" Andy asked.

"You speak words, and they suddenly appear on the page. The word you spoke, along with its meaning and translation."

"So you are saying, if I speak, or rather sing, the words the pendant is saying in my mind the book will show us what it means in our language?" Andy said.

"Exactly."

"I'm afraid to ask, but where is the book?"

Abby paused before answering. "Dragonsgate."

"I had a feeling you were going to say that," Andy said shaking his head.

"Let's go," Redlin said, "We have no time to lose."

Chapter 16

"There! Do you see it?" Brayton exclaimed.

"See what?" Cathal asked. "All I see is the fog we have been sailing through for the past week. I have to agree with Colton this time, I think you are slipping."

Brayton knew he wasn't. His horn had been glowing steadily in the direction they were currently heading. Every now and again he would see what looked like a silver star rising out of the fog. He also started hearing whispers in his head. Where it was coming from, he could not tell. Nor could he decipher any words.

"Two fathoms!" A sailor cried out

"Your highness, we are going to run aground soon," Colton said walking up to the two men.

"What do you suggest, Captain?" Brayton asked not looking away from where he saw the light.

"That we anchor here and proceed in long boats."

"But what if we have leagues to go?" Cathal said. "We can't row that far?"

"No," Colton said, "but we could see if this shelf we are on opens up again into deeper waters."

Brayton pondered that. He kept staring through the fog. Something told him he was close. But he didn't know if that was intuition or just wishful thinking. Running his fingers through his hair he made up his mind.

"We will take the long boats, Captain," Brayton decided.

Cathal looked sidelong at him. "I hope you plan to take a turn rowing."

"I wouldn't have it any other way," Brayton said slapping him on the back. "Cheer up, Cathal. This is a grand adventure."

"No brother, a game of dice and a pint of beer at the Bard House is an adventure. This is work."

Brayton burst out laughing as he pushed him over towards where the boats were secured.

The water lapped against the side of the long boats as the oarsmen beat out a rhythm propelling them through the mist. Sound was muffled and Brayton couldn't hear a thing, except for the whispers in his head that got louder the longer they rowed. Soundings were taken every five minutes and the depth of the water had not changed at all. Cathal snapped open his pocket watch and looked at it.

"Two hours your highness," he said slapping the lid shut. "Time to turn back before it starts getting dark."

"By the gods!" On sailor in the lead boat exclaimed.

Brayton and Cathal sat with their mouths open at what seemed like an impossibility. Suspended in midair was a horse's head poking out of the fog. Of course what set it apart was the long and deadly pointed horn protruding out of its forehead. One could not doubt that this was anything but a unicorn. Both long boats suddenly stopped as if hitting an invisible shield, causing everyone to lurch forward.

"Land ho!" the bosun shouted.

"You think?" Cathal remarked sarcastically.

Brayton was transfixed by what he saw before him. Suddenly the mist started to lift. He couldn't help wonder if the unicorn was causing that. The beast stood before them on a rock shelf that ended right at the water's edge, which is why the head seemed to be floating in midair. It was a stallion standing tall and proud. The unicorn turned its head slightly so it was looking dead on at him. The continued whispers in Brayton's head were getting louder. He looked down at the pendant. It was warm to the touch and shining brighter than he had ever seen it. Clasping his hands around it suddenly made him gasp. He could understand the whispers. He locked eyes with the unicorn and realized it was he that was speaking.

How are you able to find our grove? the unicorn asked. *Who are you?*

Brayton wasn't sure if he should respond aloud or with his mind. He figured he would try aloud first.

"I am Brayton, son of Paolo. Descended from Tayio."

"Um, your highness?" Colton asked. "To whom are you speaking?"

Tayio we know. You we do not.

"Do you know this?" he said holding the pendent aloft.

The unicorn just stared at Brayton for what seemed like an eternity.

Follow me, he told him as he turned and started heading inland.

"Can you tell me your name?"

Tilmin, came the reply to his mind.

"Brayton, what is going on?" Cathal asked with concern as he gripped his friends arm.

"He wants us to follow him. His name is Tilmin."

"How are you talking to him?"

Brayton watched the slowly retreating animal as he cast sidelong glances over his rump. "He speaks to my mind when I hold the pendent," he said. "I can understand his words. I'm not crazy my friend," he said smiling. "We have found what we seek. Let's go ashore."

"Should we all come ashore, your highness?" the captain asked.

"You and the sailors stay here. Cathal and I will see what's afoot."

"Oh joy, thanks a lot brother. I thought I was the one supposed to lead us into trouble," Cathal said laughing as he slapped his friend on the back.

Brayton and Cathal followed the unicorn through a densely wooded forest. Even though the sun was past midday, its rays were hard to penetrate the thick foliage. It seemed almost twilight. As they emerged from the woods, Brayton shielded his eyes until they got use to the light once more. Once he could focus, he saw standing on a grassy hill in the middle of a glade the largest equestrian he had ever seen. It was a unicorn of course, a mare as black as midnight with a black horn to match.

"By the gods!" Cathal remarked astonished. "I thought all unicorns were white?"

"That doesn't seem to be the case here," Brayton said clearly as astounded as his friend.

Wait here, Tilmin told him.

Brayton looked around at his surroundings. The herd was scattered all throughout the glade but looking not so much like a herd as friends gathered together talking about who knows what. Tilmin trotted back.

The queen will see you now, Tilmin said. *Her name is Savano.*

"Savano," Brayton said.

"What?" Cathal asked perplexed.

"It's the name of the queen of the unicorns," he said casting his head towards the black mare.

Walking over to her, Brayton could really take in her size. He would need a step stool if he were ever to climb on her back, not that he would ever dream of riding a unicorn. Savano was like a shadow, her blackness drawing in all the light around her making her appear even more stark. Her eyes however were red in the center surrounded by black rings.

What is your business here? Savano asked. *Tilmin says you are descended from Tayio.*

Brayton couldn't help thinking the voice she projected was of a woman his own age. He truly wasn't sure what to expect, but that surprised him. It was soft and musical, but there was a tone of command there that left little doubt that Savano ruled here.

"She say anything?" Cathal asked clearly puzzled.

I see your friend cannot hear us. I will make an exception for him. The black horn on the top of her head started to hum, causing an inner light to pulsate, giving off an eerie glow. *What is your name human?*

"By the gods!" Cathal exclaimed.

"Just answer her," Brayton told him. "Let's not insult anyone."

"Cathal, umm, your majesty," he replied a little nervously. Brayton smiled to himself. He had never known Cathal to be nervous, ever.

I will ask again, what is your business here?

"Do you know this?" Brayton said holding up the pendant.

Of course, I gave it to Tayio.

"Wow! How old are you?" Cathal asked shocked.

Brayton elbowed him into silence.

"Then you know what it means," Brayton said.

Savano looked at him for what seemed like hours, but knew it must have been only a few moments. She seemed to be searching his mind. Images of his past flashed before his eyes in no particular order.

So, you think you are the Summus Re'em, Savano said.

Brayton held her eye. "If I were not, I don't believe the horn would have led me here."

Hmmm. Well said son of Paolo. But just because the horn

216

seems to have chosen you, there is another test you must undergo. Once you accept to undertake this test, there is no turning back.

"I don't like the sound of that," Cathal whispered to Brayton.

"Neither do I, but do we have a choice?" Brayton rubbed his chin before directing his question to Savano. "What is this test?"

The queen craned her neck to two large white birch trees that stood close together just behind her. *You will be bound between the two sacred trees. I will attempt to pierce your heart with my horn. If you are the Summus Re'em, you will be protected. If you are not, you will perish. Your friend will bear witness.*

"What? Wait, no!" Cathal exclaimed. "Brayton you can't be considering this?"

A calm had descended over Brayton. His friend's protestations were barely audible to him. The air suddenly felt warm and charged, every nerve in his body was alive. Either his body knew his death was imminent or he was where he was supposed to be. There was only one way to find out which.

What is your answer, blood of Tayio?

"I will submit to the testing," Brayton said with resolve.

Four unicorns immediately surrounded Brayton and led him to the trees. Another three surrounded Cathal as they led him off to the side to watch dumbfounded. Vines snaked out of the trees and wrapped themselves around Brayton's wrists and ankles, pulling tight and lifting him off the ground forming a human X. Savano trotted over to him and barely touched her horn to where it lined up with his heart.

Prepare yourself human. Know this, whatever the outcome, you have earned my respect. And I do not give that lightly.

Savano trotted about fifty yards away and turned. The wind blowing her black mane in all directions. Brayton could see what looked like a bright star shooting out of the top of her horn as she started her gallop. Savano was not holding anything back. She meant to impale him if at all possible. Brayton closed his eyes and slowed his breathing, waiting for that fatal impact. "Why was it taking so long," he thought to himself. He should have felt something by now. He strained his ears to listen. He could no longer hear hoof beats. As a matter of fact, he couldn't hear anything. He had to open his eyes. Once he did that, the realization hit home, and he felt his chest explode as darkness took him.

Chapter 17

Emilia looked hard at the opening before her. Everything led them here. But what waited beyond was anyone's guess. So much of her own family history lay through the opening. She looked over at her mother who seemed to be in deep thought as she was. There were no Alfar in the area. Pan had given her the pendant from her first visit that guaranteed safe passage through Parma, for which she was grateful. More for her mother's sake than anyone else.

"Well? Are we just going to stand here or are we going in?" Diminitus asked sourly.

"I'm not sure if we all should," Emilia said. "Mom, if I remember right there were spots where you had to fly."

Luel looked around at the others. "I think when you enter the mound, need takes over."

"What does that mean?" Ala asked her.

"The mound knows who enters and why they are there, and accommodates itself to that need." She smiled and winked at Ala. "That's just a guess of course. I'm sure if my husband where here you would get a much lengthier explanation."

"That's for certain!" Diminitus chimed in. "I never met a man so in love with the sound of his own voice. Ouch! What did you do that for?" He said scowling at Ala who had just smacked the top of his head.

"You don't need to be so disagreeable, Dim," Ala said with hands on hips.

Luel burst out laughing. "I must agree, he does like to talk."

"I kind of wish he were here now," Tera said,

"You and me both, sister," Emilia said wrapping an arm around her shoulder.

The air seemed to be getting hot and thick. Emilia could hear insects buzzing all around them. Once in a while she would catch a very faint rustle way back in the woods, but if it was the Alfar, they were for all intent and purposes, invisible. They couldn't delay this anything longer. No word needed to be spoken. Pulling the pearl comb out of her hair, Emilia transformed it into the staff of the goddess. Illuminating the crystal, she stepped inside. Even with the light, the cave felt very oppressive. She wondered how her mother ever summoned up the courage to step inside.

Single file they walked for what seemed like an hour. The staff casting its light only a few yards in front of them. The first drop came without warning. But it wasn't that they fell into a hole, instead, it was like the floor had detached from the walls and started sinking down, like a platform being lowered by some giant machine.

"Where do you think it's taking us, Mom?" Emilia asked.

The glow from the staff gave Luel a ghostly pallor. "I don't know dear. I didn't know the last time I was here until I arrived."

The platform they were on finally hit bottom. But instead of more tunnel, they came to a door. Emilia seemed to recognize it.

"Is that..?" Emilia started to ask.

"Yes," Luel answered staring at the door with an intricate design that was all too familiar. "It's my father's door."

Emilia looked sympathetically at her mother, clearly seeing the pain and anguish this door represented written on Luel's face. Luel didn't hesitate. She traced the symbols of her father's door, and once complete, the door opened onto a sunny green valley with a lake and a house the color of black obsidian. Everyone passed silently through the door and stood on the grass as the sun warmed their skin.

"Where are we?" Ava asked in awe.

Luel responded in a quiet subdued voice. "This is Trystan's forge. It is here that…" she couldn't finish as she looked grim faced, tears standing in her eyes.

Emilia finished for her and told the others what had transpired here long ago. Tera flew over and gave Luel a hug. Luel smiled and hugged her back fiercely.

"Mom, look," Emilia said pointing at a tall black stone down by the lake. By its arched shape it couldn't be anything other than a gravestone. "Do you think..?"

"Let's go check," Luel said in resignation.

Once they reached the stone, Emilia read the words etched there.

Eriyn
Here lies the culmination of his life
Beloved Husband, Master Craftsman, Loving Father
Redeemed by his daughter
T

"Did you bury him?" Ava asked Luel.

"No, after I took his crown, I have no other memory of this place."

"Could "T" be Trystan?" Emilia asked.

"It must, I don't know who else it could be."

"He is in paradise now," Lyson said tracing the etching on the stone.

"Yes he is," Luel said softly. Emilia could see the tension visibly leaving her mother. She imagined Luel must have been wondering about the afterlife outcome of her father. And now she knew. If there was no other reason for coming to this place, then this was worth it.

Luel started walking to the forge with a puzzled expression on her face. She suddenly stopped and raised her hand behind her, motioning the others to halt. Changing her skin to the surrounding colors, Luel all but disappeared as she blended in. Emilia watched as she flew low to the ground and hovered near the forge's entrance and peered inside. All of a sudden a bolt of liquid fire shot out of the opening. Emilia whipped out the staff of the goddess as she flew up to help her mother.

"Watch out!" Luel yelled.

Flying out of the door was one of the hooded beings from Pan's memories. The warlock pushed his hood back and the resemblance to Pan was remarkable. He hovered ten feet off the ground with his palms upraised, creating a sphere of energy that was acting as some sort of shield. Emilia flew slightly above him, raining lightning bolts down on him, but to little effect. She didn't dare stop though, because the moment she did she felt he would attack, and brave as everyone was, Emilia didn't think they would be a match for this being.

"Summoner," the warlock said as he looked to where Emilia was flying. Then it seemed like the sun had exploded in Trystan's valley, sending everyone onto their backs.

"Is everyone all right?" Emilia asked.

"Do you mean aside from the fact that we can't see?" Tera said sarcastically.

"Has anyone else been blinded?"

"I think all of us, love," Lyson said staring around sightlessly.

"How are you not affected?" Luel asked her daughter.

Emilia went to each in turn, and using Braylynn's staff, healed every one of their temporary blindness.

"Using the dragon crown, I turned my sight inward, much like I did when Andy and I blinded Devon."

"What was that thing doing here?" Diminitus asked angrily. He didn't appreciate being thrown on his back and blinded.

"It was looking for something," Luel said walking into the forge. The others followed and watched as she went from place to place scanning for something. Suddenly she stopped in front of the wood carving that once held her father's crown. Scorch marks were made in anger on its face. "He was looking for the crown."

"But you hid that," Emilia said. "What would draw him to look here."

Realization suddenly dawned on Luel's face. Going to the wall she grabbed two shovels. Throwing one at Lyson, she flew back to her father's grave, the faeries flying close behind while the others ran. Luel started digging.

"Mom, what are you doing?"

Luel directed her daughter to the writing on the stone. Emilia was puzzled as she read each line several times over. "I don't understand," she said.

"Here lies the culmination of his life's work," Luel recited. "Trystan wasn't talking about the man himself. He hid the crown here. Somehow it got back here from the place where I had hidden it in Vasara, and he buried it here, I'm sure." She paused for a moment and looked at her daughter. "I can feel it."

Lyson helped her dig and two feet down they hit a metal box. Digging around it they were able to loosen it. It had handles on each side. Emilia grabbed one and Tera the other and together, used their wings to pull it free of the earth and set it on the grass. On the lid were symbols not unlike the ones on the door to this place. Once again, Luel traced the pattern and the lid opened. A thin gold crown with a blue crystal embedded in the center lay on a burgundy color cushion. No one made a move to touch it. Luel just stared at, her eyes welling with tears.

"What do you want to do Mom?"

Luel looked at her daughter. "I cannot touch it. I will not touch it."

Ala, who had been quiet the whole time since entering the valley spoke up. "As a priestess of the god, I will take it up and carry it, but I will not wear it." She bent down and hovered her hand over it and closed her eyes. "This is not a crown for just anyone to wear." Her eyes connected with Luel. "This crown has but one master."

Ava had a shoulder pouch that she emptied and handed to Ala. "Here, you can carry it in this."

Ala picked up the crown and deposited it into the pouch and slung it over her shoulder.

"I want to leave this place," Luel said casting one last look around.

"Ok Mom," her daughter said given her a hug. "I think this is why we were brought here."

Luel looked at Emilia with tears standing in her eyes. "I am not wearing that thing again."

"Maybe you won't have to. Maybe it is meant for another."

Luel gave her a look that said that was highly unlikely.

"Enough of this," Diminitus said in his usual gruff manner, more to dispel the melancholy that had descended on the group. "Are we going to go save some dragons or what?"

Luel smiled, grateful for this crotchety old man. Planting a kiss on his cheek she started moving towards the door. Tera also flew over and covered Diminitus in kisses.

"Will you all stop that!" Of course everyone knew his protestations where just for show. Ala came over and tenderly kissed his lips, which he didn't mind at all.

Emilia looked back towards the opening in the forge. For a moment she thought she saw a flash of bright light, but it never came again. Shrugging it off as a trick of the eye she followed the others out of the door.

He watched them as they walked away, cursing himself for letting his brilliance show. His sister's Summoner almost saw him. But all was good. The prophecy had pulled him back to fulfill this one piece of the quest. She had the crown. Now if she only had the courage to use it when the time came.

"Will she be able to do it Lord?" the man standing next to him said.

"Your daughter is strong, Eriyn. We will have to rely on that."

Chapter 18

It was late at night and the streets were quiet. Andy looked down a side street to see a soft yellow glow coming out of one of the establishments. A sign of a red bull swung in the slight breeze that was blowing. He suddenly felt a pang of loss as he remembered this is where he first met Bart.

Keep your eyes on the target lad.

Andy turned his head sharply back and forth,

"What is it?" Redlin whispered.

Andy didn't answer, he just kept looking around. Had he actually heard the words or was it just in his head because he had brought his friend to mind. It was something Bart would say he thought. "Nothing, I just thought. Never mind."

"Abby, do you know a more unobtrusive way to the library?" Andy asked.

"Yes, follow me."

Andy flew them straight from Samara's home to Dragonsgate. If anyone happened to see them, it couldn't be helped. Time was running short and stealth had to be abandoned. Abby now led them through deserted back alleys to come upon the side door of the library that butted up against a hedgerow. Rhyan brought up the rear, arrow on bow while Emma flew in and out of the woods. Bella's butterflies did reconnaissance of the immediate area. So far no one seemed to have noticed them. Once everyone was caught up, Abby ran her hands along the wall, her fingers searching for a certain spot. Finding it, she pulled a loose brick back to reveal a key. She was about to open the door when Redlin grabbed her wrist.

"Wait," he told her. "After you left, we have no idea who watches over the library or where their allegiances lie."

"What do you want to do Dad?" Andy asked.

"Abby, where would the book be?" the wizard asked.

"There is a hidden panel in the small alcove near my bedroom. My old bedroom," she amended. "I am the only one who would be able to open it."

"Why do you say that?" Andy asked her.

She lowered her eyes, almost afraid to speak. "A certain pattern has to be pressed against the door to make it open. I had a craftsman make it for me to hide things I wanted secured."

"What pattern?" Rhyan asked.

Abby took a deep breath and looked at Andy for the comfort in his eyes. "The one on my back."

Andy put a reassuring hand on her shoulder. "We will do this quickly, grab the book and get out."

"Follow me," the wizard said. "If I remember the layout of this library, there is a secret door close to where your bedroom would have been."

"Let me guess, you put it there," Andy said.

His father smiled and winked at him.

They circled around to the extreme rear of the building to a solid wall with no opening. Redlin traced the design of a tree on the stone with his fingers, the lines quite intricate and silver. "For mom?" Andy asked guessing the tree was a talon tree.

"Yes," his father replied as he gave a slight shove causing a door, that had not been there before, to silently open inward.

One by one they moved with stealth, Emma protecting the rear this time. Her talon spear out and extended, ready to impale any would be attackers, Bella stood next to her in support. Redlin led the way, creating a sphere of light to go before them. They heard no sounds.

"Abby, you lead the way," the wizard said.

After two quick turns, they came to an alcove. "My bedroom was just down that hall," Abby said pointing.

Redlin turned the sphere of light to illuminate the direction that Abby had pointed. On the floor by the door was a dark shape.

"What is that?" Andy asked with apprehension.

They all walked over and their worst fears were realized. It was the body of a man. Andy turned him over. He wore brown trousers with a burgundy colored vest. Attached to the breast pocket was a pin of a feathered quill.

"He was the curator," Abby said sadly.

"How do you know?" Rhyan asked.

"That pin was once mine. It's handed down from curator to curator. My father had given it to me."

"How did this man come by it?" Emma asked looking around for possible would be attackers.

Abby looked up from her study of the pin. "I had left it here in my flight with Andros, when we were fleeing from the Raptors."

Andy remembered well that fateful night. Again it was Bart who had saved their lives. Andy felt he needed to get out of this town. Too many memories of his departed friend was starting to affect him.

"I wonder what killed him?" Abby asked.

Emma bent down and examined the body. Her eyes scanning, she found a puncture wound on the neck.

"Alfar!" she exclaimed. "He was hit with a poison dart."

Everyone started looking around anxiously.

"Quickly," Redlin said. "We need to get out of here. Get the book."

Abby reached down and unclasped the curators pin and put it in her pocket. Then running back to the alcove she turned her back to the wall. "Shield me," she told Andy.

Using the source, Andy created a dark curtain as Abby took her shirt off and pressed her branded skin against the wall. There was an audible click as a recessed panel opened. She grabbed the book and placed the curator's pin inside, then closed it again as she put her shirt back on.

"I got it."

Just then out of nowhere, darts came flying from several directions. No few bouncing off Andy's shield around Abby.

"Dad! We got trouble!"

"I know," Redlin replied creating a shield of his own to protect the others. "Quick, into the bedroom."

Keeping their shields up, everyone quickly retreated down the hall and backed into the room. Andy pulled the dead curator in and slammed the door shut, driving the dead bolt home. Running footsteps could be heard as well as pounding on the door moments later. Whatever was there had an ax and began to splinter the door.

"Ok master wizard, what now?" Emma asked.

"We are going out the other door."

"What other door?" Rhyan said.

Redlin turned to face the back wall. Holding both palms up he closed his eyes and concentrated. His hands started to glow red, like iron in a forge. He released the energy he was holding and beams of liquid fire exploded through the brick and mortar of the library's wall.

"This one," Redlin exclaimed as he dashed through the hole that was the size of a horse, the others following closely behind. "Get clear and change," he told his son. "We need to get out of here."

Andy took the lead looking for a spot to transform without causing too much damage.

"Andros, over here!" Bella called out from his left.

Running down a side street they came out near an empty corral on the edge of town. Quickly making the change, and after knocking down a few barns, the black dragon spewed fire. Looking down the street the way they had come, Andy could see figures running towards them. Small and like shadows they were. He knew it must be Alfar. Rhyan was shooting arrows as fast as she could draw, but there were too many. Having an idea, instead of fire, Andy spewed ice between the buildings, making an effective wall from the ground to the roof line. It bought them the time they needed.

Jump on, Andy sent to everyone.

Running up his wing and settling on his back, everyone held fast. With a thrust of his powerful wings Andy leaped into the air, creating a rhythm to give them altitude quickly but not without multiple arrow strikes bouncing off his scaly iron hide. Once airborne, he headed south, putting as much distance between himself and Dragonsgate as he could.

"Down there," Redlin pointed after flying for most of the day.

Andy spiraled down landing in a large field surrounded by woods. After everyone had jumped off, he changed back to human.

"This seems like as good a place as any," Redlin said as he scanned the woods for any movement. "Emma, if you please?"

Emma nodded. "Be right back." She streaked into the sky, but not above the tops of the trees as she disappeared into the woods, her multi-colored autumn wings blending in with her surroundings.

"Where is she going?" Andy asked.

"Just checking the area for likely trouble," his father replied. "Let's look at that book Abby."

Abby took the book out of the satchel she hastily grabbed while in the curator's bedroom. It was bound in black leather, with no design or markings on it. Abby tenderly rubbed the cover as if resurrecting memories from long ago. Andy had no doubt she was remembering her father.

"Aistriu," Abby spoke.

"By the gods!" Andy exclaimed.

Golden scroll work started to appear around the edges and along the spine. In the middle was the picture of a closed door with the words:

Labhair le nochtadh

"What does it mean?" Rhyan asked.

"Watch," Abby said.

To their astonishment letters started to change and rearrange themselves into their own language.

Speak to reveal

"Well that's plain enough," Andy said.

Just then Emma came flying back towards them.

"All clear," she reported landing next to Andy.

"Good," the wizard said. "Alright son, I guess the rest is up to you."

Andy opened the book after Abby handed it to him revealing page after page of blank parchment. Grabbing the death dagger he focused his sight inward. All of a sudden an image of a man stood before him. He was hooded and the face was shrouded so that he couldn't see any discernible features. Tied to his waist was a belt with a dagger sheath attached to it. The hilt sticking out looked like a replica of the one on the pendant. Suddenly the voice spoke in that musical language Andy heard before. The ancient language of Parma. He kept repeating the first phrase and nodded at Andy. Taking his cue, Andy started singing the words he heard. As he spoke, words started to appear on the page in golden script:

If you seek to break the barrier you must pass through the door of the dead. If you are allowed out on the other side, the barrier will come down. Be prepared to pay the price demanded of you. It can go as high as the life of one of thy companions. Heed, the death dagger cuts two ways. This is your warning as well as your possible resurrection. In the mound all will be clear. Death speed you on your journey first dragon.

Andy looked up from the page, visibly shaken by what he saw written there. He looked around at his friends. His father. His beloved Abby.

"I can't do this. I won't do this!" he said vehemently. Suddenly he felt his blood pressure rise, his face going red with anger. Fire shot out of his dragon eyes as he sprayed the forest in frustration and sorrow.

"Andros no!" Emma screamed.

Redlin was already there, releasing water and ice from his upraised palms, quenching the fire.

"Son, stop!"

Andy released the source and crashed to his knees. Abby ran over and cradled his head to her breast. Andy looked up at her with tears running down his face.

"I almost lost you to Devon, I'm not going to risk your life again. Any of you," he told them looking up at his friends.

Redlin came over and squatted next to him and placed a hand on his shoulder.

"Andy, we could all lose our lives at any time. If we don't free your brothers, that will be a certainty. We all know the risks here."

"But this is different, Dad. This will be with an action I

take. If I do this, it is certain one of you will die."

"That is not true Andros," Rhyan said folding her arms. "The words only say the cost could be as high as that, not that it would be." Rhyan took the book from where Andy had dropped it and gave it to Redlin. "Look here master wizard, would you say this almost reads like prophecy?"

"I thought the same thing when the words started to appear," Redlin replied.

"And what does this mean, 'the death dagger cuts both ways', that could mean anything," Rhyan said.

Abby put her hands on both sides of Andy's face. "Andros, I love you, and together we will face anything. Do you know what Bart would say?"

Andy smiled at this young woman he loved. She always knew how to bring him out of his despair. Suddenly he laughed, because he knew what Bart would say.

"He'd say, 'Get up off your ass lad, there're demons to fight don't you know'."

Everyone burst out laughing and the gloom the settled over that place dissipated.

"I guess we know where to go now," Emma said.

"Yes we do," Redlin replied. "You ready to fly us to the mound of the Alfar?" he asked his son.

Andy got to his feet with determination in his eyes. The dragon was staring back at them as he made the change and let out a dragon's roar. He was ready, and he was focused. They would free his brothers or die trying.

Chapter 19

It felt like days that Emilia and the others spent wandering the tunnels in the mound of the Alfar, with only the sphere of the goddess to give them light. Once in a while the tunnel would open into a vast gallery. In one such gallery, with walls like polished marble, in the very center stood a large white stone coffin resting on top of a dais. There were no inscriptions. On the lid of the tomb were the images of a faerie and a man in armor, holding the hilt of a sword.

"I wonder who they were?" Emilia asked.

"The man was obviously a Border Lands warrior," Lyson remarked tracing the image with his hand.

"How do you know?" Ava asked.

"The sword," he said pointing. "See the design on the hilt."

They all looked, and worked into the image of the sword was a raised palm under a sphere. "That is the family's coat of arms. Only Border Lands swords have such designs."

"Do you know what family that is?" Emilia asked.

"I do not," Lyson answered. "They must have died out hundreds of years ago."

"A little over fifteen hundred years ago," Luel said quietly.

"How are you so sure?" Tera asked flying up and down its length, investigating every scratch for clues. "Wait, are you saying..no."

"Yes," Luel said. "It was my father's crest. It was on the door to Trystan's forge as well, but it didn't come to mind to comment on it."

"Do you know the faerie?" Emilia asked her mother.

"No. I don't know who the man is either, only that he was a sire on my father's side."

Diminitus was circling the tomb, his eyes furrowed as he concentrated.

"What is it Diminitus?" Ala asked him as he completed another circuit.

"I'm not sure," he said looking up at his beloved. "Something is nagging at me. It seems strange that Luel's father's family seems to be connected to this place. I think we need information."

"And how do we get that?" Emilia asked.

Diminitus smirked at her. "Come now missy, has age addled your memory?"

It suddenly dawned on her. "Oh! I did forget. You're a necromancer!"

"As you of all people should know," he said winking.

"What exactly are we talking about?" Tera said hovering just off the ground.

"I believe Diminitus is about to raise the spirit of this Border Lands warrior," Lyson told her.

A sudden hint of a breeze seemed to come into the gallery. Ava spun around, arrow on string facing the way they had come.

"What is it?" Emilia asked her.

"I don't know," she replied. "I felt something."

Lyson came over to stand beside her with his sword drawn.

"Whatever you are going to do, I suggest you do it quickly," Ava said. "We are no longer alone."

Diminitus took out a coal stick that he used for writing on stone. Drawing a circle and the necessary symbols, he stepped inside of it and sat cross-legged. He chanted the incantation, being careful not to get it wrong and raise something he didn't intend. Suddenly a sinuous image was rising out of the coffin, vaguely resembling the shape of a man. Diminitus spoke louder and faster, willing the shape to become more visible. Now they could make out the features of the man. His hair was shoulder-length and he had a bushy beard. His brow was large and hard. Then he spoke.

"Who are you, and why have you summoned me from my sleep?" the apparition asked.

"I am Diminitus, a son of the god Cael. I've summoned you on behalf of others. Might we know your name my lord?"

"I do not know thee son of Cael, and am under no obligation to answer your question. Release my spirit."

"I am of thy kin sir," Luel stepped forward.

The spirit turned towards her. "And just who are you?" he asked her.

"I am Luel, daughter of Eriyn of the house of Caster."

The ghost hesitated as if searching her mind.

"House of Caster?" Emilia whispered to her mother.

"It is the name of my father's house," Luel replied. "And his."

"I sense familiarity in you, and the name you mention is the very name of my house and lineage. Have you any other proof."

Luel looked around helplessly at the others. She had nothing but her word. She was about to speak when Ala spoke up.

"What about this?" Ala said holding up the crown Luel's father had made.

The spirit's eyes went wide and he screamed. "Treacherous! Treason! Where did you get that?" he shouted.

Everyone looked startled at his sudden outburst.

"My father was a master craftsmen and armorer. He made that crown out of godstone, and something else."

"Not the crown! The jewel embedded in it! It is the most prized possession of my house, handed down through generations. You have no idea of the power that rests within."

"I do know," Luel said. "I have worn the crown and seen things I would like to forget."

"You have touched the jewel and suffered no harm? Then you must be of house Caster, or you would not be standing here."

The ghost warrior paused a minute in thought. He seemed to have come to a decision.

"My name is Callan, first of my house and Lord General Supreme of the Border Lands warriors."

"My Lord," Lyson said bending a knee.

Callan smiled at the homage paid to him. "I see you have a Border Lands warrior of your own in your party. Rise general, for I sense that is what you are."

Lyson stood up amazed that he knew what he was.

"I can hear something moving out there," Ava shouted over her shoulder.

"Ask your questions Dim," Lyson told him.

"Do you know how to successfully navigate these tunnels?" Diminitus asked.

"I should, it was my people who built the mound. Maybe I should put that another way. Everything in the mound already existed, we just opened the galleries and connected the tunnels. Is there a specific place you are trying to get to?"

"I think this is where you come in lass," Diminitus said to Emilia.

"And who might this be? I sense a power here."

"I am Donella, Dragon Summoner of the goddess Braylynn, daughter of Luel and also your kin."

The ghost was suddenly taken aback.

"Show me the mark," Callan said.

At first Emilia wasn't sure what he meant, but then she remembered the mark that identified her as the Dragon

Summoner. She turned her leg so that he could see the red twisting dragon. Callan looked long at it.

"It is the same as the one that adorned the leg of my Thea. Braylynn's first Summoner."

"The first Summoner?" Tera exclaimed. "That was thousands of years ago."

"Has it been that long then," Callan said wistfully.

"Lord Callan, our time is short," Emilia said. "In your sleep, the evil wizard Devon seized power and imprisoned the dragons somewhere in the mound."

"Devon! I should have known. I never trusted that wizard," Callan said.

"You knew Devon?" Ala said. "How?"

"He's always been around since my time, but continue on with your question, Summoner."

"We seek a cave. In it is a lake with an island of stone in the center. That is where the dragons are, surrounded by a barrier of some sort."

"I know of the place you speak. We were sorry we ever uncovered it."

"Why is that," Lyson asked.

"Evil taints it. I don't know how or why, but a score of my people went mad upon entering. We sealed it with a stone door." Callan turned to Luel. "As a kin of the house Caster, you will know how to open it. There is another door in this very chamber that opens onto a tunnel that leads to the level of that cave."

Every one turned their heads looking for a door amongst a seamlessly looking wall.

"I don't see...Where did he go?" Lyson said.

"I couldn't hold him any longer," Diminitus said panting from the exertion.

"That's not important right now," Ava shouted. "I can hear running feet."

"Everyone quickly look for the door," Luel said.

While everyone began running their hands all over the wall, Ava took out a small tinder and lit an arrow on fire. Drawing it back to her cheek, she held her breath and let it fly. A cry went out as she heard it strike something solid. For a moment as the fire was sailing through the tunnel, she could see its light reflect off numerous eyes.

"Donella, I need you!" Ava called as she started to loose arrow after arrow.

Emilia rushed over. Leveling her staff at the tunnel's mouth, she created an energy shield to prevent anyone from entering. Suddenly there was the pounding of many fists on it. Emilia could make out what looked like children.

"Alfar!" she exclaimed. "Don't worry, they won't be able to breach the barrier. Ahhhhh!"

Emilia fell to a knee. Something had struck her shield with enormous power.

"Something else is out there," she said trying to catch her breath. It took all her concentration to make the barrier hold. "Where is the door! We need to get out of here."

"It's here," her mother said from the far side of the coffin. "It's not on the wall, it's on the coffin."

Luel quickly traced the pattern that would open the door. Once complete, the coffin started to slide forward, revealing a stairway going down.

"Quickly, everyone inside now!" Luel shouted.

Tera quickly darted down, followed by Ala and Diminitus. Luel went next with Ava and Lyson backing down slowly to protect the rear.

"Emilia! Come now!" her mother shouted.

Focusing her will and using every power element in the arsenal of the Dragon Summoner, Emilia shot an angry red energy bolt towards the opening. A high-pitched wail pierced her ears, so she took that as signal to leave. Somersaulting backwards and using her wings to give her more arc, she aligned herself with the opening as she dropped to the darkness below. After she was in, her mother traced the pattern that started the coffin sliding back into place. Emilia lighted the way as they descended a staircase that wound down many levels.

Suddenly the staircase stopped at a rounded door.

"Who makes a round door?" Tera asked.

"Obviously the House of Caster," Ava replied.

Luel ran her hands over the door, ready to start the pattern.

"Mom wait!" Emilia said.

"What?" she asked.

Emilia closed her eyes. The dragon crown on her head was glowing.

"They are there," Emilia said. "I can just barely feel them. There are eight."

"Eight?" Diminitus said. "There should be nine."

"Oh no," Ala said. "You don't think..?"

"Mom, open the door, now."

As Luel traced the pattern and the door swung open, everyone's jaw dropped at what waited on the other side.

Chapter 20

Andy and his father stood by the source as they watched the multi-colored beams of power rotate on its axis. Andy wasn't sure, but he felt like everything seemed a little more serene somehow. The trees felt softer and the grass a bit greener. Was it this place, or was it just him. This place was a haven, a respite. It was here that he could stop thinking and just be, if only for a moment. His thoughts were jumbled since his encounter with the being who told him one of his friends or loved ones would die if he chose to enter death's door. He ran his fingers through his sandy brown hair and let those thoughts go for the moment.

"Where do you suppose they are?" Andy asked.

"Who's to say with Loki?" Redlin responded. "For all we know he could be off on some side quest. He was always flighty."

"I heard that," a voice said from behind.

Andy and Redlin snapped their heads around in the direction of the voice to see Loki and Dain striding towards them, smiles spread wide across their faces. After much embracing and back slapping, the two senior wizards spent some time catching up after their hurried encounter just outside of Laurel Hollow.

"Where are you now?" Redlin asked.

"We are just outside Albion, close to the wizard's bridge," Loki answered. "Redlin, something is wrong."

"What is it?" he asked eyeing his brother.

"There is no way these monsters could be traveling by normal means. There are too many appearing in so many places at once and disappearing just as fast. The warriors are running all over Vasara engaging them whenever they appear."

"Normally, the only entrance into Vasara for demons has been through the corridor in the Border Lands." Dain chimed in. "Since Cleo and Tori had replaced the stone of Fallon that Devon had stolen, the corridor has been relatively quiet."

"So you are saying these demons are not coming in by that route?" Andy asked.

"That is correct," Loki replied.

"The gods setup the corridor, forcing any demons who want material form to come through there," Redlin said.

"Apparently the rules have changed," Loki said stroking his beard. "It can only mean there is another god in play."

Redlin looked hard at his brother. "You realize who that has to be, right?"

"Meliakken," Loki replied nodding. "Dain and the others told me about the shriker after they rescued me. His prison is weakening."

"So you think he is free?" Andy asked running his fingers through his hair.

"No lad," Loki said. "But I do believe he is no longer locked in the cave the Five put him in. He's moving around in the underworld and somehow managed to punch holes in the fabric between us, but I don't believe he is able to pass through himself, or he would have done it by now."

"How do we defeat a god?" Dain asked.

"We don't," Loki said soberly. "All we can do is hope to contain him. The shrikers however are another matter. Meliakken created them to offset the power of the dragons."

Loki looked over at Andy. "You better get ready for a fight."

Andy looked thoughtful. "At least there is only one loose so far," he said.

"Don't count on that lad," Loki said. "You just happened to see one. Whether the others are out or not is anybody's guess now that the evil god can deposit his monsters anywhere he wants. What are your next steps brother?"

Redlin scratched his chin in thought. "I don't think we have any choice but to release the dragons as quickly as possible. We are at the mound now looking for death's door." Redlin filled Loki in on the being involved with the death dagger pendant.

Loki put both hands on Andy's shoulders. "You have been in this spot before son, you know you can do this right?"

Andy's eyes welled as he looked at this man who was a second father to him. "I had doubts, and I don't want to think of the possible price needed to be paid, but I can't be any readier than I am."

Loki slapped him on the back and sent him reeling. "That's the Andros I know! Good spirit there lad!"

Everyone burst out laughing as Andy rubbed his throbbing shoulder.

"Where will you be heading?" Redlin asked.

"I am not sure yet. With Tori's new-found abilities, I think it best to use the portals to travel to where the fighting is the hottest. One thing for certain, we are taking back the White Castle."

Dain started to laugh.

"What?" Loki said.

"I was just thinking of what Tori's going to say when she learns how we are going to move about."

"I take it she didn't like it very much."

"That is an understatement. She may have the power of a god flowing through her, but she still has a hard time keeping her food down when we use the portals." They all laughed out loud. Somehow it was poetic justice Andy thought, given the prankster personality of Tori. It was almost like karma.

"Be careful brother," Redlin said, "both of you."

"Don't worry, we will. You two try not to get yourself killed."

"We will do our best," Redlin said winking.

Andy opened his eyes to see Abby staring down at him. He always liked to have his head in her lap while he traveled to the source. He wanted her to be the first thing he saw when he came back. It always amazed him the depth of the love he had for this woman. The shared a connection both physical and on another level, spiritual. Andy felt his life was full and complete whenever they were together.

"Where you successful?" she asked as she kept stroking his hair.

Andy filled her in on everything they discussed with Loki and Dain.

The door opened and Redlin poked his head in.

"Time to go," he said as he closed the door behind him.

"I guess we're not wasting any time," Andy said jumping up and planting a kiss on his beloved before they both exited the room of the empty house on the edge of Parma.

A day later brought them to the heart of Alfar territory, but for some reason, they were not harassed by its inhabitants. As they entered the mound of the Alfar, Andy suddenly felt very closed in. There was no way he could transform in here without bringing the whole ceiling of the cave down on top of him.

"Where do we go?" Rhyan asked.

"Straight for now," Redlin replied. "It's the only way we can go." Redlin created a sphere of light to proceed them.

Just as they started to walk forward, the eyes in the skull of Andy's pendant light up, shooting two pencil beams of red light in front of them.

"Dad look!" Andy exclaimed.

"I guess we have our compass," Redlin said. "Lead the way son."

Andy took the point. Whenever they came to a choice of tunnels, he would turn and face each opening, letting the beams of light to point the way. They couldn't tell how long they traveled. Time did not seem to have meaning here. After the last right-hand turn, they came to a solid wall.

"Now where?" Emma asked looking around.

Just then, the platform they were standing on began to descend rapidly.

"This way," Redlin said smiling.

"You think?" Abby said giving the wizard a glare as she tried to regain her balance.

Eventually they reached the bottom of wherever this thing was taking them. They all gasped as they turned around at the enormous cave they had just entered. The walls had veins of color that looked like intricate scroll work whenever the wizard's light hit them. He made the light brighter and caused it to go higher.

"By the gods!" Andy exclaimed. "A host of dragons could fit in here."

"Look," Emma said pointing upward.

Everyone strained to see.

"What?" Andy said. "I can't see anything."

"Look all the way to the top," she told him.

Andy thought he could see something, but he wasn't sure.

"Dad, turn your light out for a second."

As soon as Redlin did that, a bright white beam of light shot down.

"What is that?" Andy asked.

"Moonlight," Abby said in wonder as she went to stand under it.

She looked almost ghost-like as the moonbeam washed over her. It made Andy shiver as if he were suddenly cold.

"That opening must be thousands of feet up," Redlin remarked.

"That can't be the top of the mound," Emma said.

"In this place, that could be anywhere," Rhyan said.

Bella's butterflies were instantly attracted to the moonlight and tried to fly up it.

"Get back here," Bella said stamping her foot. "You can't fly that high." Reluctantly they all came back and settled back down.

Redlin illuminated the cave once again with his own light.

"I see something," Emma said flying over to the far wall. Once the others got there, they saw what was obviously a large black door in the shape of a large tombstone with a gold colored depression in the center.

"Well, that seems fitting," Andy said looking the door over. "Any doubts this is death's door?"

"How does it open?" Abby asked.

"Try the pendant," Redlin said pointing at the spot in the center of the door.

Andy leaned forward and pushed the pendant into the door. There was a click, followed by the sound of a large bolt being drawn back, setting everybody's hair on end. The door swung inward, but nobody moved to walk through. It was dark and all light seemed to be swallowed up right at the edge of the door. Andy squared his shoulders and took a deep breath, sweat dripping down his brow as he wiped it away with a hand.

"Well, we've come this far, we might as well go all the way," Andy said.

He took a step forward and crossed the threshold. A sudden blast of cold air blew his hair in all directions. He looked back at the others, whom didn't seem to be following.

"Aren't you coming?" Andy asked.

"It's not letting us through," Redlin said. "I think because you wear the pendant, you are the only one allowed."

Andy looked over at Abby, concern written all over her face.

"I love you," she mouthed, just as the door slammed shut, plunging Andy into totally darkness.

Fear seemed to clench Andy's heart and squeeze. He directed his thought inward to touch the source and let it calm him. Raising his hands and cupping them as if he were making a snowball, he crafted a sphere of energy much like his father's. He could only hope the others were okay.

He suddenly heard several low growls. He quickly got a shield up just in time as what appeared to be three large wolves the size of elephants leaping out of the shadows, slamming him back against the door knocking the wind out of him. Keeping his shield intact, he struggled to get his breath back while three mouths with large fangs snapped ineffectively at him.

Andy knew he couldn't just sit there forever. He reached into his bag of tricks for his default standby, fire. If they were like most canines, they should be afraid of fire. He quickly dropped his shield and shot huge wide spread flames at them. He didn't focus the heat in hopes it would just scare them away. He didn't want to have to kill anything here, especially not knowing what the repercussions might be. The price he had to pay was still in the back of his head, and he wanted to give himself every advantage he could to keep the cost low.

The fire eventually worked as the animals turned and fled down a side tunnel. He started walking forward, the eyes of the pendant guiding him once again. Now and then he would pass a door, but resisted the urge to open it. He would hear scrapings and screams from some. Laughter and singing from others. This place had no rhyme or reason he thought as he kept moving on.

Andy couldn't help thinking of the others, and more than once found himself standing in the middle of the walkway about to turn and head back. But if his brothers were to have any chance he had to do this. Suddenly he could go no further. Another door stood in his path. Touching the pendant to it, the door swung inward.

Inside it looked almost like a throne room with three chairs made out of bones. As he looked at the walls, he was taken aback in revulsion. From floor to ceiling, the walls were constructed of skulls, one on top of the other. Sitting in the chairs were three robed figures, exactly like the one singing to him when he was translating the song of the pendant. Their robes were the color of midnight with stark gold trim around the edges. Their hoods were drawn up with deep cowls, hiding their facial features. He was wondering if this was such a great idea after all. Actually, the way he looked at it, he didn't really have a choice.

Suddenly they spoke and Andy found he could understand them.

"What does it want?" they said in unison.

"It has the pendant," the one on the left said which Andy decided to call thing 1, after the Dr. Seuss characters, subsequently naming the others thing 2 and 3. Somehow by doing that they seemed less scary.

"Give it back!" thing 3 said flying over towards Andy.

Andy threw up a shield around himself that it couldn't penetrate. Thing 3 pounded on it to no effect.

"It has power," thing 2 remarked sitting calmly. Andy thought out of the three, this was the most dangerous. He also had a feeling if he were to have the pendant taken from him, his life would be over.

Thing 3 sat back down. Again in unison they repeated the question. "What does it want."

Andy paused to gather his thoughts and frame his response. "Somewhere in this place is an island surrounded by a lake where the dragons of Vasara are held captive," Andy began. "A shield of death is over it."

Thing 2 leaned forward just ever so slightly. "Yes, we remember this. The price was paid."

"The price was paid," the other two chimed in.

"Wait, what..? I'm not.." Andy stammered.

"What does it want?" the three said again.

"I want the damn thing removed!" Andy said with some heat. He was clearly getting frustrated with these three.

"The request has been made!" they said.

"It cannot be taken back," thing 2 said.

"What are you talking about? I don't want to take it back."

"Of its own free will," thing 1 and 3 said.

"Has the price been paid?" Thing 2 asked.

"What is the price?"

The three tilted their heads to the side as if listening.

"Has the price been paid?" Thing 2 asked again.

Thing 1 stood up. "The price has been paid."

Thing 3 stood up. "The price has been paid."

Andy was getting a very sick feeling in the pit of his stomach.

Thing 2 stood up. "The price has been paid."

"Hey! Alright, what is going on? We haven't even talked about a price. I don't underst..."

Andy never got to finish. The three clapped their hands together and far off he could hear a loud detonation. Just then the door to the chamber opened and a wind with the force of a gale picked Andy up and started to propel him backwards. He thought for sure he would be crushed against the outer door when that one opened too, causing him to tumble end over end across the cave floor as the door slammed shut. Andy got to his feet and saw everyone huddled around something on the floor. The sound of the door crash made everyone look in his direction. His father ran over to him.

"Andy are you alright?" Redlin said.

Before answering, Andy could see his father's cheeks were wet from tears and his eyes were still full of them.

"Dad, what happened? What's going on?"

Redlin couldn't respond but looked to where the others stood, looking downcast. Andy spotted it immediately, Abby was missing. Then Rhyan and Emma moved to the side and Andy saw her lying still on the cave floor. "The price has been paid," kept echoing in his head over and over.

"No!" He screamed as he ran over sliding on his knees and pulling Abby onto his lap, cradling her as her arms hung limply at her side. Bella's butterflies had covered Abby's body like a colorful blanket, but scattered once Andy had pulled her to him. "Abby, don't go, please don't go! Oh god, oh god! Please, please, Abby…" Andy kept caressing her hair and face, trying to will her back to him.

"Please," he said looking at his father. "Dad, please I beg you. Oh god please."

"Son," Redlin said placing a hand on Andy's head. Redlin couldn't get anything else out, pain and helplessness written all over his face. Andy looked at Bella, Emma and Rhyan for help. With tears streaming down their cheeks they shook their heads in indication that there was nothing they could do.

Andy was rocking and sobbing with utter despair. For how long he did not know. There was no pulse, no warmth. No life. Abby was gone. The price has been paid. Every memory he had of Abby played out in his mind. From the first time he saw her as he walked into the ass end of a horse, until she mouthed the words, I love you, as death's door closed him in.

After what seemed like forever, Andy laid his beloved down, smoothed out her hair and kissed her brow.

The price has been paid.

He could feel himself going hollow and numb, as if concrete had hardened around his heart. Everything was shifting out of focus and his face felt hot. He thought he heard someone speaking to him. He turned towards his father who was mouthing words but Andy couldn't hear him. There was a loud buzzing and ringing in his ears and he felt like he might pass out. He heard them in his mind again. The price had been paid.

In that moment, Andy's mind snapped. His pupils went wide and he could see fear and concern on his father's face. He was on autopilot now. He reverted back to his basic animal form. Andy the man was gone. Andros the black dragon stood in his place and roared a sound of grief and longing, fire spewing up the walls. Andy leapt into the air, with the cave as large as it was he was able to fly straight up. He was flying up the shaft of moonlight. He needed to get out, he needed to get away. Faintly from far below he thought he heard his father calling. But then he could hear nothing.

Lost. I am lost. All is lost. The price had been paid.

Chapter 21

As they looked up all they could see was darkness, then as if a door had been open, the moonlight shone down on Abby's body once more. Andy was gone. Their grief was raw.

"What do we do, Redlin?" Emma asked in a hurt voice, her cheeks still moist with tears at the loss of her friend.

"Emma, for the first time in my life I do not know," Redlin replied grimly. "I've lost someone who would have been my daughter-in-law, but she was just as much my daughter as my own. My son has succumbed to madness. Needless to say, I don't trust my own judgement right now." He looked up at Rhyan. "Can you sense your sister?"

Rhyan closed her eyes and clenched her medallion. She shook her head. "I sense her in many places at once. I think this place is interfering somehow. She's traveling in darkness, I could see that much."

Redlin pondered for a moment. "Well, one thing I know we are not doing. We are not going to leave Abby here. I will carry her to the top myself if I have to." The others nodded soberly in agreement. Just then they heard a clicking sound echoing off the floor near the entrance.

"Someone is coming," Bella said wiping the tears from her eyes.

It was hard to see from this distance, but they could tell it was a tall figure walking towards them, and it was not footsteps they were hearing. More like hoofs.

"Pan?" Redlin said stunned.

As he got closer, they could see it was Pan. The leader of the fauns quickened his pace when he realized who it was.

"Redlin? What are you..." then he noticed Abby. "By the gods! What monstrous deed has happened?"

Redlin told him everything that had transpired. Pan listened without interruption his features getting grim and sad with each word. Pan in turn told Redlin about the visit of his wife and daughter.

"This is my fault," Pan said looking down at Abby. "Me and my family's. Those beyond death's door are soul collectors. They have no problem granting requests because of what they crave. Makes me wonder what soul my brother's gambled when they put their death shield around the dragons."

"Pan, how did you find us?" Redlin asked.

"I wasn't actually looking for you," he said. "Cael visited me in spirit. He told me it was time to put my grief aside and take up the mantle he placed on me as his priest. He directed me to come here, but he did not say why. This must be why," he said looking at Abby once more, tears standing in his eyes.

He took out his pipes and played a heartbreaking melody as he slowly walked around Abby's body three times.

"That was beautiful, Pan," Emma said. "And a beautiful tribute."

"Thank you, but it was not for tribute. The song I played is magic. It will keep her body whole and free from decay." He looked over again at Redlin. "Your son will reclaim his mind once again, I am certain. When he does, he will want to say a proper goodbye, or he will regret it for the rest of his life."

"Thank you, Pan."

Pan reached down and picked Abby up as if she weighed no more than a feather. "Come, we will take her back to my grotto and place her in a hallowed place. Then we will take counsel together."

Redlin took one last look towards the hole where his son had flown, his heart breaking at the loss this day had brought. But he knew he had to set grief aside for the moment or all would be lost, and Abby's death would be in vain, and he wasn't about to let that happen.

"Let's go," the wizard said grim faced.

***

Emilia and the others did not know what to expect when they opened the door. The last thing they expected was a woman in an ice blue dress, with hair the color of dancing flames standing before them. Just then there was a loud crashing sound, as if a thousand windows had broken at once.

"You have no time," the woman said drawing every eye to her. "You must hurry or all is lost and everything done is in vain."

"Who are you?" Emilia asked her. She was certain this was the being Leah had encountered in their flight to save Fenner.

"No time Summoner of Braylynn, no time!" she said urgently. "You must bring everything to bear. You must release YOUR dragon!"

Then she turned and looked at Luel. "You must do that what you fear most, or the quest fails here."

"Now look here, missy!" Diminitus started approaching from the rear.

The woman just smiled at the cranky old man. "Should you complete your task, make your way to Pan's grotto. Much will be revealed there." Then putting her hands together in a thunderous clap, she disappeared in a cloud of white vapor.

"Well that was short and to the point," Ava said easing the tension off the bow she had drawn.

"Let's go!" Emilia said running down the tunnel, approaching what looked like a cave mouth opening. She had the feeling this was all going to come down to a matter of seconds.

As they burst into the cave, everyone spread out to meet any threat that might emerge. Tera zig-zagged around rock formations with lightning speed, making sure no one was hiding behind any rocks. Lyson and Ava were keeping a close watch on their rear. They had little doubt this cave had only one entrance.

They all came to the edge of the lake and looked out at the rock bound island. Nobody moved. It seemed nobody breathed. Staring straight back at them, un-moving were eight dragons in a semi-circle around a man lying on a boulder. Their stares were flat, even angry.

"I think this part is up to you, dear," Luel told her daughter.

Just as the dragons surrounded their fallen brother, everyone surrounded Emilia in like fashion.

"Do you think that one is dead?" Diminitus asked Ala.

"I cannot tell," she told him. "But by the way his arms and legs are splayed out, and the fact the Donella could not sense him does not bode well."

Emilia drove her staff hard into the rock, standing straight without the aid of a hand, it's power radiating outward. Closing her eyes, she focused all thought into the dragon's eye in her crown. Names started coming to her mind; Caleb, Daragh, Elek, Finn, Gael, Herve, Irwyn and Jace. By process of elimination, she knew the man lying on the rock must be Brion. What she could not tell is if he were alive or dead. She brought all the power of the Dragon Summoner to bear. Drawing on all the elemental forces around her she began probing the barrier that surrounded the dragons. She had encountered this magic before and it filled her with dread. This was Devon's magic. Just the thought of that evil wizard made her shudder. She pushed on it, and without warning a lightning strike was heading straight for her heart.

"Donella!" Lyson yelled.

Quickly, she raised a shield just in time to absorb the strike, the force driving her back several yards, knocking her over. Lyson ran over and helped her to her feet.

"Are you ok?" he asked, concern written all over his face.

"Yes. This is going to be harder than I thought," she said leaning on his shoulder.

"What happened?" Luel asked coming over.

"It's Devon's magic, and it is very unstable. I believe I can punch through it, but I am not sure what will happen when I do."

Emilia walked back to the edge of the barrier. Raising her palms, she closed her eyes to better see the pattern in the magic with her mind's eye. What she saw was total chaos. There was no rhyme or reason to it. Nothing to grab onto and unravel. Chaos. Something was nagging at her mind. Chaos. She titled her head as if listening with her pointed ears for something. Chaos.

"Of course!" she shouted when all at once it hit her.

"What?" Ava asked.

"Chaos," Emilia answered. "I must release my dragon. Everyone stand back!"

Emilia knelt on the cold stone floor of the cave. Arms stretched out, she started to concentrate, drawing everything inward. The dragon tattoo on her leg started to glow. Plunging into that raw elemental power of herself that was every emotion, good and bad, that brought joy as well as great loathing, she communed with her dragon. She had released it into Andy once through the connection of blood. Now she was going to release it totally separate from herself. She imagined a splitting apart. The pain ripping through her was excruciating. She was not expecting this. Every nerve ending in her body was screaming out in pain. Finally, after she felt like she hit the point of not being able to bear it any longer, the pain stopped as her head slumped to the floor and her chest heaved trying to catch her breath. Pushing herself up she got to her feet. She glanced at the others who stood with open mouths at the dragon that had suddenly appeared before them. Tera was flying all around it, from head to toe, babbling a mile a minute.

"Is this yours? What's his name? By the goddess, how does he fit inside you?"

"Tera, come down and leave it alone," Luel called to her.

The dragon just looked at her impassively. Emilia thought it might have even smiled. It was not as substantial as the real dragons, appearing luminous as if you could walk right through him.

Emilia spoke to his mind. *You know what to do. Please don't get yourself killed, if that is even possible.*

Emilia's mind was suddenly filled with images of destruction and fire. *So this is how you communicate. Not that way,* she told him. She filled his mind with images of what she wanted. He lowered his head in acknowledgement of what she said.

The dragon leapt into the air, skimming along the surface of the barrier. The other dragons watched in amazement as he flew back and forth. To those watching, it seemed like he was seeking something. Suddenly he stopped and hovered. Looking back at Emilia, he nodded.

"Ok, here we go," Emilia said to the others. Sending her dragon some more images, she knelt on the ground. Her ring and necklace started to vibrate and glow. Drawing all the forces from around her, Emilia was gathering her will to unleash everything at once into the barrier. Sweat was running down her brow until she felt she could hold no more. Sending one final image, she unleashed her power as her dragon raced to the edge of the cave before turning and flying headlong into the spot he was previously hovering by. Shooting like an arrow he pierced the shield, sinking halfway in before he could go no further. Emilia did not expect him to go all the way through, that was not the plan.

Now! she sent to her dragon. He suddenly became a ball of pure energy in the shape of a dragon. The barrier started to change colors, convulsing and shedding lightning strikes worse than any storm. Emilia created a shield around the others while sending lightning strikes of her own at the barrier. It was a conflagration of color and light as all those forces came together. Stress cracks started to appear. Emilia could feel it was almost ready to burst, but she had nothing left to give. She could tell she was at the limit of her power, and yet she couldn't give it that fatal punch to make it shatter. Looking at her dragon, she could tell he was at his maximum as well. She was locked in now and couldn't pull back, but knew she couldn't keep this up forever. Beads of sweat were running like a river down her face. She looked back at Lyson who was trying to get past her shield to help, but there was nothing he could do. Emilia started to worry she would burn herself out. If only she had just a little more to give.

***

Luel was watching her daughter intently, worry creasing her brow. She knew the barrier wasn't going to break.

It is your turn daughter, a voice said in Luel's head. *My Summoner, thy daughter needs you. You must put on that what you fear most.*

Luel knew who it was. The goddess, Braylynn.

Mother please, I am not strong enough to bear what comes with that.

You are much stronger than you know, Braylynn told her. *For now, I will block that sight which causes so much pain, but in time you will learn to control it on your own. It is your destiny to be the bearer of the jewel of your father's house, as well as the crown, for I mean you to be queen of my people.*

Luel did not trust herself to speak. The enormity of what was just placed on her almost put her on her knees. But then she looked at her daughter. She saw Emilia nearing the end of her strength, and yet still not giving in. Suddenly Luel felt ashamed of herself. A moment of weakness had entered her soul, but the sacrifice of a mother for her daughter left no doubt about what she had to do. She thought of the sacrifice her own mother made so that she might live. The weakness and fear were gone and in its place, iron resolve.

"Ala, give me the crown," Luel said to Raphael's priest.

"Are you sure?" Ala said opening the pouch in which she carried it.

"Yes." Luel reached in and drew it out. Closing her eyes, she placed the crown on her head. The jewel in the crown blazed forth, and she was not prepared for the power that ripped through her body.

***

Caleb, what is happening? Finn said, moving his golden neck higher for a better view of the strangers on the shore. *I'm not liking this at all.*

Nor I, not after all we have been through, Caleb responded. Caleb watched as a faerie knelt on the ground and lifted her arms.

She praying to Braylynn or something? Jace chimed in. *What is that staff?*

Caleb was beginning to have some suspicions as his dragon eyes narrowed to slits. He could see this faerie had power.

Daragh, Caleb called his brother. *Did you sense anything when they showed up?*

Out of all his brother's, the one most empathic and able to sense things unseen, whether good or bad was Daragh. He was the first one that told Brion he felt something was not quite right with Devon. If only they all had heeded his gift then, but even Daragh wasn't a hundred percent sure anything was amiss.

I did, Daragh replied. *They are not hostile to us. And look, the faerie kneeling, she is wearing Layla's crown. She must be Braylynn's Dragon Summoner.*

Caleb mentally smacked himself. *How the hell did I miss that?*

I think she is trying to bring down the barrier, Daragh said. *But will it be in time to save Brion? His heartbeat is almost nonexistent, and a long space between beats. I can sense his spirit getting ready to depart.*

Caleb looked down at his brother. Brion had collapsed after Jace woke up, who was the last. He had not been able to connect to his mind since then. His body still lived, just barely, but where had his mind gone?

By the gods! Elek exclaimed lifting his golden dragon neck higher to follow the flight of a red dragon. Although this one seemed ghost-like by its transparency and the way it shimmered. Everyone followed his gaze.

Did that come from her? Finn asked.

It must have, Caleb said. *But I have never seen Layla do that.*

What followed next had every dragon on their feet. Talons scratching the rock in anticipation. The ghost dragon, as they thought of it was buried in the center of the barrier, lightning shards striking everywhere, including on their side of the barrier.

We could sure use a shield right now, Irwyn said. *Can anyone touch the source?*

Caleb suddenly had a thought. *Gael, get up here.*

Gael, a gold dragon of medium size compared to the others, moved to the very edge of the rock.

I assume you want me to use my gift? he asked.

You are the only one of us who can without needing the source.

It was easy to forget Gael's gift because under normal circumstances any one of them could create a shield with the source. Gael however had the ability instilled within him since his creation.

Gael erected his own barrier just in time as a dozen lightning bolts struck hard. He winced at their impact but was able to keep the shield intact.

What's that other faerie doing? Finn asked.

By the gods! Caleb exclaimed.

***

It took everything Luel had not to sink to her knees. It felt as if something had unlocked inside of her as she connected with the jewel of her father's house. She did not remember feeling this much power the last time she adorned this crown. She looked quickly at the others. True to her word, Braylynn had blocked the horror of having to see how her loved ones would die. How she would ever learn to block it on her own was something she didn't want to think about right now.

Luel brought her focus back to Emilia and the barrier. Emilia's dragon seemed to be phasing in and out, as if it were nearing the end of its strength and energy. Bringing all her focus to bare on the center of the barrier, she could feel the energy building. Every nerve in her body was alive as her eyes turned ice blue. She raised her hands palms out. She let that force travel through her body, stopping it at the hands as it continued to build. When she felt she could contain it no longer, she released it in one long continuous surge, a scream being torn from her throat as she hit the barrier.

The sound of the barrier cracking was like a high-pitched shriek, causing everyone to throw their hands over their ears. Emilia slumped to the ground. Her dragon, now free, had sped towards the rock where the dragons were, some who had lifted off as soon as the barrier was down. The red dragon seemed to shrink in size as it sought its target. Dropping like an arrow, he pierced Brion's breast. Brion's arms flailed as his back arched and eyes opened wide. He yelled in pain, before becoming unconscious once more.

***

Emilia pushed herself up from the floor, her head spinning. She saw specks flying as if flies were in front of her face. Once her eyes focused she realized what she was seeing, dragons flying towards her. A red dragon, carrying the man that was unconscious on the rock alighted just in front of her. After setting him down, the dragon transformed. A young man with red hair and dark brown eyes stood before her, wearing the kind of clothes Andy wore when he transformed back to human. For a few moments they stood looking at each other, neither saying a word. Their minds connected.

"Caleb," Emilia said. "Your name is Caleb."

"And you are the Dragon Summoner," Caleb answered warily. "What is your name?"

"Donella. Braylynn sent us here to rescue you."

Emilia looked behind Caleb as seven other men in dragon clothes came walking up from the shore. They all stopped in their tracks as Emilia's mind connected with all of them, the link of fifteen hundred years that had been broken was whole again. The first time she linked with Andy was like nothing she had ever felt before. Linking with these nine just about brought her to her knees with the amount of power flowing between them.

The other's started to come closer, no one really speaking. Mostly because they never really knew if they would succeed or not. It was a stunned unbelievable silence. Caleb, as was his way was the first to speak.

"What did you do to Brion?"

"I sent my dragon into him, in the hopes that it's power could save him."

"Daragh!" Caleb yelled not taking his eyes off Emilia. "What do you see?"

Daragh, with auburn hair and blue eyes and a scar on his cheek, walked up and knelt down placing both hands on the sides of Brion's head.

"He's alive and his spirit is intact for now."

"Can you wake him up?" Caleb asked.

"Now that I have the source coursing through me I probably could, but there is something else hovering over his spirit that I have never seen before." He looked up at Emilia. "There have been other Summoners before you, and even your predecessor, Layla, did not have the same measure of power I sense in you. I think this is something you must deal with."

Emilia grabbed her staff. The pearl on top was glowing white. Grabbing the top of the pearl, she disconnected it from the staff.

"Whoa, I didn't know it came off!" Tera exclaimed.

Emilia gave her a knowing smile. Holding the sphere above Brion's chest she let it go and allowed it to hover, slowly moving from head to toe. The jewel in her dragon crown started to glow as she closed her eyes and focused.

Brion, she whispered to his mind. Emilia could see the dark force that surrounded him. It was like an impenetrable cloud.

Brion. She brought every power of the Dragon Summoner to bear as her mind reached through that wall. Suddenly a light exploded in her mind as Brion sat bolt upright, taking a deep gasping breath.

Caleb started to pound his brother on the back.

"Easy Bull," Brion exclaimed. "You're going to knock my heart right out of my chest."

Emilia grabbed the sphere and attached it to the staff. Then, turning it once more into the pearl comb she put it in her hair. "Are you ok?" she asked. "Can you stand?"

Brion blinked several times at her, taking in everyone standing around him. "I take it something momentous has happened here," he said.

"You could say that brother," Caleb said with tears in his eyes. "Our imprisonment is over, and our vengeance is just beginning. Can anyone tell me where Devon is? I'm kind of hungry and I would very much like to eat out his heart."

"Gross!" Tera exclaimed. Everyone suddenly burst out laughing.

"You should all sit down," Emilia said. "There is so much to tell you."

Emilia introduced everyone and then proceeded to give a very high level summary of the time when they first set foot in Vasara until this very moment. To say the dragons were stunned would have been an understatement. The hardest thing for them to grasp was the amount of time that had passed. Many were chagrined at being denied their vengeance against Devon, but they would be content to take it out on Parma's warlocks.

"Where is Zana," Finn asked suddenly.

Emilia looked at him sharply. He had said that with a note of familiarity.

"There has been no word of her since Devon was defeated," Lyson said. "If she is smart, she will take the gift of her life and live in exile somewhere, never to return."

Finn looked slightly downcast for a moment, but quickly recovered.

"So where do we go next?" Caleb asked.

"Pan's grotto," Luel said. "Things will be revealed there that we need to know."

"First things first," Caleb said. "I need to eat!" Eight other dragons echoed that sentiment.

Chapter 22

Nothing moved on the Palatine Bridge, that much Tori could see with her enhanced vision. In returning to the White Castle, their original point of entry when they set out to free Loki was no longer there. They rode back and forth over the spot where the cairn was, but any trace of it was gone. Not even a bent blade of grass.

"Well we know an empty bridge means nothing," Cleo said. "Tori?"

"I see nothing, Boss," Tori responded. "But I can feel them there." The red around her eyes were blazing as she probed further into the castle itself. High on a top turret she could see men walking about. Demon possessed men no doubt.

"Well wizard, this was your idea," Cleo said to Loki. "The five of us take on the hoard in there. What do we do now?"

"We could sure use the dragons right about now," Leah said tying her hair in a ponytail. "I wonder how the others are making out?"

"I was wondering the same myself," Loki replied.

Suddenly they heard a sound they were never likely to forget. Everyone looked up at the direction of a grief stricken roar of a dragon.

"There!" Dain said pointing.

High above the castle spewing flames as he went was a dragon heading out over the sea. Its color was too hard to make out.

"Do you think that was Andros?" Dain asked Loki.

"It's hard to tell from this distance," Loki responded, but I fear it might be. "By the gods! What's gone wrong now?" he said not expecting an answer.

"Should we turn south and see if they need help?" Tori said.

"No," Loki responded sadly. "Whatever has happened is already done. We need to deal with what is in front of us." Loki was silent for a moment and closed his eyes. *Lad, can you hear me*, he sent to Andy. There was nothing. Loki knew in the pit of his stomach, something had gone terribly wrong.

"I believe we are at a standstill," Dain said, his tactics as a general kicking in. "They are not going to come out and attack us, and we are sure to be overwhelmed if we take the fight to them."

"I believe I can help," a woman's voice from behind said, causing them all to turn with weapons drawn.

Tori went a little further than the others and channeled the full power of Fallon, both of her swords red-hot and aflame.

"You will not need those Cath Priomh of Fallon," she said.

"Samara!" Loki exclaimed. "By the gods woman! You didn't need to sneak up on us like that."

Samara laughed but her smile did not reach her eyes.

"What are you doing here?" Loki asked her.

Samara looked at him soberly. "The reason just flew overhead."

Loki's eyes narrowed as he looked at her. "What do you know?"

"It's not what I know, but what I can guess," she replied.

"Speak plain witch," Leah told her with heat.

"One of your friends is dead," she said soberly.

"What? Who?" Cleo asked.

Samara continued to look toward the direction where Andy had flown. "I cannot say for certain, but those who guard death's door do nothing without exacting payment."

Loki let out an exasperated sigh. "This is getting us nowhere; you probably should start at the beginning."

Samara told them everything from when Andy entered the blood forest to when they departed. "I knew once he had Death's Dagger there was going to be a heavy price to pay. The fact that Andros shrieks a sound of grief and loss tells me that either his father or his beloved has paid the ultimate price."

"Oh no," Dain said sadly. "It was Abby."

"How do you know," Leah asked him.

Dain looked silently at Loki.

"Because we can still feel Redlin," Loki answered her. "We know if one of us dies. That poor boy."

"We need to go help him," Tori said fiercely, running her fingers through her dark hair. "After all he has done for us, we need to be there for him."

Loki shook his head sadly. "He is too far now, and I have no idea where he is going. I don't even know why he is heading out to sea." Loki looked to Samara. "Do you know?"

"No. Even a witch doesn't know everything," she replied.

Loki continued to gaze where Andy had flown. Indecision written all over his face as to the next course of action. Andy was beyond his help. The liberation of Kensington stood before him.

"You mentioned help earlier," Loki said. "I assume it is with our current dilemma?"

Samara looked towards the castle. The sun reflecting off its stark white walls. "Yes. You are having trouble figuring out how to cross that bridge, and only one of you can fly," she said nodding towards Leah.

"What do you propose?" Dain asked her.

Samara smiled as she pulled up her sleeves. "I've asked some friends of mine to come lend a hand." Samara raised up her palms and started to quietly chant under her breath. Then she blew out a continuous whistle, modulating the tone every couple of seconds.

"Is she summoning birds?" Cleo whispered to Tori.

"Your guess is good as mine boss," Tori replied.

A beat of wings could be heard as everyone turned their heads to the west, astounded at what they saw coming at them.

"By the gods!" Loki exclaimed. "Sonipes! How did you come to find them?"

Five Sonipes glided down and formed a semi-circle behind Samara as her whistling ended. She walked over and gently stroked one of their flanks. "That is a long story master wizard. And no, they are not my pets or slaves to my whims if that is what you are thinking. They are my friends, and they have agreed to help you in your cause."

Loki let one the flying horses nuzzle his palm with its nose. "Why are you doing this Samara?"

"Always the cynic Loki. Can't I do anything out of kindness."

"Of course you can," he replied looking side-long at her. "I've just never seen it."

"Fair enough. Let's just say, for the time being our purposes happen to coincide. And also for him," she said pointing at the now vacant sky in the direction Andy had flown.

They all looked once again where she had pointed, sadness mirrored in everyone's eyes.

"So what's the plan?" Leah asked bringing their attention back to the situation at hand.

"Well, now we have a means to get to the castle," Loki said. "But our troubles will only have just begun once we land. Tori, anything?"

Tori gazed once more at the castle, her eyes penetrating from the bridge to the city. "They are there," she said, "and they are many."

"If I am not mistaken you are not alone," Samara said looking back across the plains. Everyone turned to where she was looking.

"I can't see anything," Cleo said confused. "What do you... hey! Where did she go?"

They all turned their heads back to where Samara was standing. She had vanished.

"Typical," Loki said.

"Do you think she actually saw anything?" Dain asked.

"Wait, I hear something," Tori said straining.

Cresting over the rise was a wave of white, with a spot of black in the very center. The sound of thousands of pounding hooves shook the earth like thunder.

"By the gods! Unicorns!" Tori exclaimed. "Who is that!" she said pointing at a rider on the lead black unicorn.

***

"Brayton," a voice called. "Brayton. Can you hear me?"

Brayton opened his eyes, the bright sun stinging them. Lifting a hand to make some shade to see, he could make out the form of Cathal standing over him. Why was Cathal standing over him he wondered. It was then he realized he was flat on his back in the grass. The ends of the vines holding him were burned off at the ends.

"What happened brother?" Cathal asked. "When Savano hit you, there was this brilliant white light that blinded all of us. Once we could see, you were lying here on the ground."

Brayton sat up and shook his head, running his fingers through his hair. "I was taken somewhere," he said.

"Where?"

"I don't know where it was."

Brayton went on to explain how he felt an explosion in

his chest when Savano pierced him, and she did pierce him. He felt it in his heart. He was certain he had died. But as the horn penetrated his heart it was followed by a soothing warmth. Once his mind cleared he could see he was in a rich and vibrant glade. The trees surrounding it had leaves and flowers of all kinds of colors. Brayton imagined that if there was a unicorn paradise, this had to be it. A crystal clear stream was running through it, so clear he could see the rocks and schools of fish in striking detail. It came to his mind that he was very parched and the desire to drink was overwhelming.

"You may drink if you wish," a voice out of nowhere said.

Brayton looked around trying to find the source of the voice. Over on the other side of the stream in a copse of trees, resting on the ground was the purest white unicorn that he had seen yet. It's horn however was the color of the rainbow.

"Am I dead?"

"What is death?" the unicorn said. "It is but a door to another existence, just like birth is. I guess you would be just as correct in saying this is a birth."

"So I am dead," Brayton said. It is not at all how he imagined it would be.

"Dead is a relative term really. For most, when they leave their former body behind, death is but a one-way door. They cannot go back. Such is not the case for you."

Brayton took a moment to bend down and take a drink from the stream. The water was cold and incredibly refreshing. He sat cross-legged on his side of the stream, processing what he was seeing as well as the unicorn looking at him with dark-liquid eyes.

"Are you the god of this place?" Brayton asked.

"No. Cael is god here. I'm the guardian of this gate."

"Do you have a name?"

"Call me Caomhnoir."

"What did you mean, 'such is not the case for me'?"

Caomhnoir just looked at him. The sound of the stream and bird life seeming unusually loud in Brayton's ears as he waited for him to speak. "Are you allowed to answer?" Brayton asked him.

"This is a question only you can answer," the unicorn said.

Brayton pondered that response. What makes him different from anyone else crossing death's threshold he wondered. Caomhnoir eyes held no answer. Then the only reason he could cross back came to him.

"Because I am the Summus Re'em," he answered confidently.

"Now you are," Caomhnoir said. "Until you spoke it in this place you were not. Now a choice is before you. You can go through the gate behind me and leave all the sorrows and pains of the world you left, forever. Or you can go back. You may think this is an easy choice, but it is not. Ponder this awhile, time has no meaning here."

Brayton didn't have to ponder. But he did take a moment to walk along the stream and let the peace of that glade rejuvenate him for what was about to come. He held in his mind's eye every person that was important to him, as well as all the people who would one day look up to him as king. The weight of that responsibility could be crushing. But as he thought of his family, his friends, he knew he was not alone. He found his way back to Caomhnoir.

"I'm ready to go back," Brayton told him.

Deep in the woods a gong sounded that continued to echo for some time.

"And now, Summus Re'em, this place is bound to you."

"What does that mean?"

"If ever you need respite or a question asked, you can always journey back here. However, the gate behind me is closed to you forever. You have chosen another resting place when your mortal life reaches its end. But that is not necessarily a bad thing." It almost looked like to Brayton the Caomhnoir winked.

Cathal looked at him in stunned disbelief after Brayton finished his tale. "What now?"

Brayton stood up and looked over to where Savano stood. She lowered her head in acknowledgement. Brayton did likewise. "Now we ride."

***

The lead unicorn stopped short of where the other's stood. Loki squinted as he looked closely to who was on the back of this black unicorn.

"Brayton?" Loki said.

Brayton and Savano trotted apart from the herd to meet Loki. Brayton jumped down and embraced his friend that he has known since childhood. "It's true then," Loki said. "You are the Summus Re'em."

"It appears so," Brayton responded smiling. Loki noticed a drastic change in Brayton. He had the air and demeanor of a man who has seen things other mortals have not.

"So Savano, it appears you and your unicorns have come down off the fence and taken a side," Loki said aloud for the other's to hear.

Savano looked at each person in turn, doing for them what she did for Cathal so all could hear as she spoke.

Our fence, as you call it master wizard, was imposed upon us by Cael himself, and only the Summus Re'em can move us from it, as you well know.

"Actually I didn't know, Savano. Dragons are my specialty, not unicorns. Tayio knew more than I ever did."

Which is probably why we are closely linked to his heirs. What is your plan?

"Simple," Loki started to respond. "Now that we have the Sonipes to help us, we will fly to the high tower in the castle. It is there that we feel we will encounter the strongest demons, as well as their hooded masters."

"How can we help?" Brayton asked. "The paramount objective for me is getting to my parents."

"I figured it would be," Loki said soberly. "How do you feel about rushing the demons on the bridge and securing Kensington?"

"I see no demons," Brayton said shielding his eyes against the sun.

They are there Tayio's heir. I can sense them, Savano said, her horn starting to pulse from black to white.

"How many of your herd is here?" Dain asked.

All of them, she replied.

"The entire unicorn population?" Leah asked stunned.

Yes, from what I understand, Vasara is in its greatest need, hence the appearance of the Summus Re'em, Savano said looking at Brayton.

"All right," Loki said. "This is a cleansing, pure and simple. One thing that I am hoping is when we defeat the demon lords, their hold on the soldiers still in there will break. Keep from killing humans as much as possible, if we can neutralize them, so much the better." Dain and the other's nodded their agreement.

"Are we ready then?" Tori said.

"Yes, mount up," Loki told her. "Brayton, once we are airborne, you and the unicorns mount your attack. Hopefully that will distract them enough for us to fly through unmolested."

"You got it," Brayton responded climbing back onto Savano's back.

"Once the dust has settled, meet us in the castle courtyard."

Brayton and Savano rode back to where Cathal and the rest of the unicorns waited.

"Well?" Cathal sitting astride Tilmin asked once Brayton was next to him.

Brayton quickly outlined the plan.

"I was never a fan of these do or die charges," Cathal said once he finished.

Art thou afraid lad, Tilmin said looking back up at him.

"Not at all Tilmin, I just like a little bit more strategy that's all," he said shifting his weight to sit up straighter.

There is very little use for strategy when it comes to demons, Savano remarked.

"There, they are lifting off," Brayton said pointing at the Sonipes as they flew straight up. "Let's go now!"

The charge of the unicorns began. Never in the history of Vasara had they been called to war. It was a thunderous roar as the unicorns formed in ranks of ten, enough to span the width of the Palatine Bridge. Brayton looked up and saw the Sonipes and their riders veer off to the right. Now was the time to draw all attention to themselves to give Loki the time he needed. As they got closer to the bridge it seemed as if a dark cloud had enveloped it.

"By the gods!" Cathal exclaimed with sword drawn pointing.

What they thought was a cloud was in actuality the swarm of demons. Climbing over each other like ants on an ant hill, the demons had whipped themselves into a frenzy. There were many flying demons that were circling above and below the bridge forming a tunnel of death. Brayton suddenly had doubts as to their chances.

Take heart Paolo's son, Savano said sensing his unease. *You have never seen unicorns fight. I think you will be in for a surprise.*

The horn around Brayton's neck suddenly became very hot and blazed with a brilliant white light. The light started to pulse and created a sphere around him and Savano.

"Umm, I don't suppose you have another one of those?" Cathal shouted over to him.

Don't worry Cathal, I will take care of you, Tilmin said.

Tilmin's horn started to glow. Brayton looked to the unicorns on either side of him and saw their horns were glowing as well. Glancing back, he saw a barrier being erected by every glowing horn. As the lead element met the first row of demons on the bridge, there was a sound like an explosion. The unicorns didn't slow. Rank after rank of demons vaporized in a cloud of smoke as they tried to beat against the barrier. Brayton thought surely the demons would never be able to penetrate.

But the demons seeing the futility of their actions tried another kind of attack. Every demon on the bridge vanished.

Stop! Savano commanded. Every unicorn stopped as they were about three quarters of the way across the bridge.

"Where did they go?" Cathal asked.

"I don't know," Brayton responded looking around, "and I don't like it."

Surely it is a trap of some kind, Tilmin said.

Most definitely a trap, Savano agreed. *Be prepared for anything.*

Suddenly the middle of the bridge exploded causing a huge gaping hole to appear. The unicorns standing over the hole fell through to their deaths waiting below. Brayton sat frozen in disbelief. The shield the unicorns projected obviously did not protect from an attack below. Now the demons swarmed again and the battle on the bridge turned into a melee.

Attack! Savano yelled.

Horns were lowered and the unicorns were impaling every demon that came in range. With two-thirds of the unicorns cut off from Brayton and the others, the only way they could go was forward.

"Quickly!" Brayton shouted. "To the other side!"

Savano reared and darted forward. Demons came flying in as her horn dealt out death while Brayton slashed his sword at any demon fool enough to come within reach. His mind was numb at what was the sudden death of a score of unicorns. Deaths he took upon himself as his fault since he had called them to war. His face was grim. He no longer cared about his own safety. Taking huge risks, he engaged multiple enemies at once from Savano's back.

"Brayton, watch out!" Cathal shouted, seeing that Brayton was recklessly battling demons. The warning came too late. Out of the many pounding hooves rose up a brute of a demon with a wicked looking sword. Slashing in front of Brayton's face, the tip of the blade caught his left eye. Letting out a painful shriek, Brayton covered his eye with one hand while raining down sword strokes with the other. Blood was streaming through his fingers as he took out the demon who blinded his eye. He felt himself starting to swoon. He couldn't allow himself to faint now. Praying to the gods he did the only thing he could do and fought on. In the end he hoped that would be enough.

Chapter 23

Out of nowhere, there was Tori. Screaming her battle cry as she stood on the back of her Sonipe, twin blades a blur as they dealt out death to every shrieking demon she encountered. Her eyes were blazing and fire shot out of them, sweeping the edges of the bridge. She didn't want to injure any unicorns, so she kept her focus there. After several passes, two more Sonipes joined in. On their backs were Dain and Loki.

"Dain, we need to seal the breach in the bridge," Loki shouted. "Tori, cover us!"

Tori came back and engaged every demon trying to thwart the wizards. She was limited however to the speed of the Sonipe and couldn't bring her true advantage to bare in the air. She was able to keep most at bay. But the demons that could fly sensed what the wizards were up to and doubled their efforts. Tori would not be able to hold off all of them.

"Loki, you better hurry," she yelled.

Suddenly there was the movement of wind on either side of her. Looking up, she could see Cleo and Leah had circled back to help. Leah's staff was a blur as she impaled demons left and right. Cleo was holding her own as she came beside Tori.

"Any ideas, Boss?," Tori asked her.

"Yes, create a flying circle around the wizards, forcing the demons to the outside. This should give them time to work."

Tori flew to on side while Cleo flew just opposite. Together they started flying in a clockwise circle around Dain and Loki,

278

striking any demon that came in their path, clearing the center.

"Now Dain!" Loki said hovering just above the breach.

Dain held out both hands as Loki did the same. Shooting out of their palms was what looked like colored light, but solid like a bar of metal. Laying it on the hole, Dain started filling one side while Loki took the other. The hole kept getting smaller and smaller until nothing could be seen but a solid patch of multi-color crystal.

"It's done!" Loki shouted. Loki quickly flew down to where Brayton was, landing beside him.

Erecting a shield around them, Loki came over to have a look at his eye. Loki saw him take the sword strike.

How is he master wizard? Savano asked concerned.

"I'm fine," Brayton said, blood still pouring between his fingers.

"You are as stubborn as your father," Loki said pulling his hand away. "Your eye is gone lad."

"Can you patch it up? There is fighting to be done," Brayton said fiercely.

Loki looked at him concerned. "Be careful highness," Loki said as he pushed his palm onto Brayton's burnt out eye socket. "This is going to hurt."

Brayton let out a gut wrenching scream of pain. Once Loki pulled his hand away, a leather patch covered his left eye.

"Can you get off this bridge?" Loki asked.

Now that the breach is fixed, yes, Savano said.

"Good, go now," Loki said as his Sonipe launched into the air.

"Unicorns! Barrier up!" Brayton yelled lifting his sword high looking every inch a pirate with his patched eye.

Every horn ignited and cast the shield that disintegrated any demon that came in contact with it. Galloping as one, Savano lead her subjects across the bridge into the city of Kensington. If they thought the amount of demons on the bridge was overwhelming, what they encountered on the streets was beyond belief. These demons however were not coming within range of the barrier, knowing now that it meant instant death. Their posture was totally defensive, willing to wait the unicorns out. Brayton held up his hand causing everyone to stop right in front of the Kensington library.

Well Summus Re'em, what is your plan? Savano asked him.

It felt strange to Brayton to only be able to see out of one eye, it would take some getting used to. Looking around at the various cross streets and the demons lining them just waiting, he felt they were in a stalemate. Neither being able to move. But move they must.

"Brayton?" Cathal asked looking at his friend.

Brayton cast his eye back towards him. He knew there was only one course of action. He did not want to think of the casualties it might incur.

"The only thing left to do now is fight," he responded. "We can't just sit here, and who knows what kind of demonic power resides in the castle."

"This is suicide; you know that right?" Cathal said.

Brayton just looked at his friend, there was nothing he could say to that. He started to think, taking in his surroundings and the best possible positions it could offer. This was his city. He knew it well, not to mention all the misadventures Cathal and himself had trying to elude the palace guards for fun. Suddenly he started to smile.

"I don't like that look brother," Cathal told him. "What are you thinking about?"

"Eight square," Brayton said.

"You're not serious! Last time we did that I remember your father and mine being furious."

Would you mind sharing with us what you are talking about,

Tilmin said.

Brayton told them how when they were young they would try and out maneuver the guards assigned to protect them. Up in the north section of the city were cross streets that if you navigated them in a certain way it resembled the path of a figure eight. You could be pursued by someone, but if you took the right cross street at the right time while having your pursuers take a different cross street you would eventually meet up again, only now you have become the pursuers. The palace guards hated being bested in this manner and would take great pleasure in making their discomfort known.

How does this particular plan help us? Savano asked

"We will drop our shields," Brayton began, rubbing at his eye patch. He knew it would be awhile before he got used to it. "This will force the demons to engage, we need them to follow us. We will head to the north side of the city where there are streets that Cathal and I know that we can use to our advantage. Cathal will take Tilmin and half the unicorns down one street while we lead the demons down another. If this works, the demons will be the anvil between two hammers."

And you have used this tactic before? Savano said.

"Not with any success," Cathal remarked.

"It will work," Brayton said smiling. "The key will be getting enough distance between us and the demons, so they don't realize they have put themselves between the two hammers."

Very well. Lead on Summus Re'em.

Brayton and half of the contingent of unicorns took off through the center of the city, taking a large portion of the demons with them. Cathal took a more westerly route before he turned north. There was a large fountain in the middle of the street which Brayton started to circle around before he entered the first street that began the diagonal for the figure eight. Upon hitting the center of the four cross streets, Brayton quickly looked down one and saw it empty. This was good. It meant Cathal was timing it correctly, the demons following him wouldn't see them cross.

"Savano, we need every ounce of speed now!" Like a burst of black lightning, Savano and the unicorns shot along the avenue at an incredible pace, the demons just disappearing around the turns as they tried to keep up. They were coming back to the cross streets now, and Brayton prayed Cathal wasn't there yet. They shot through and so far so good. Now they were at the bottom half of the eight and made their turn to the cross streets once more. If this was timed right, there would be a pile of two groups of demons colliding together from opposite streets. They were on the straightaway now. They could see the demon horde in disarray, stumbling over each other.

"Now!," Brayton said. "Drop the shield!"

The unicorns dropped their protective shield and lowered their horns as they made impact. From the opposite side, Cathal and Tilmin had slammed into the demons, vaporous smoke ascending to the heavens as the unicorns slashed and kicked every demon they encountered. The demons though did not sit idle to allow themselves to be slaughtered. It became a melee. Horns connecting with swords as the battle raged. Brayton could see unicorns dropping, being covered by demons like ants on a sand hill. They could sorely use some aid.

As if the gods had somehow heard him, Brayton felt something speed past him in a flash of red. Then another from the opposite side. Suddenly coming over the rooftops, the sky was filled with faeries. Brayton saw one that he knew well and had become a friend over time. He raised his sword in salute.

"Brie!" he yelled to the red winged faerie.

Brie dove quickly to where Brayton was, her talon spear slashing at every dark creature she connected with.

"I heard you could use a little help, highness," Brie said smiling, wiping sweat from her brow. "Is that a new look?" she said pointing at the patch.

"Nothing worth talking about now," he said winking with his good eye. "By the gods! It's good to see you Brie, Yes, we need your help desperately. Help us dispatch this lot, then we will focus on sweeping the kingdom clean. How many faeries did you bring?"

"Close to a thousand."

"Excellent! Shall we?"

"Yes," she said giving her spear a spin. "They have occupied this city long enough."

Brie jumped up, her wings beating a steady rhythm as she climbed to do battle with her sisters, all had their hair pulled back in a ponytail as is the nature of faeries when doing battle. Brayton led Savano and the unicorns on a circle of death as they created a ring around the demons, going faster and faster, taking them out one rank at a time. Cathal, seeing Brayton's maneuver followed suit and fell in behind his line with Tilmin and the rest of the unicorns. All the flying demons were occupied by the faeries, so Brayton did not fear an aerial attack. The demons howled in frustration, but their swords were not idle. The center of the cross streets were covered with the blood of fallen unicorns and some faeries. Brayton burned every death in his soul as he and Savano moved as one, evening the score, making sure those deaths were not in vain as they dealt death with each strike of horn and sword. After what seemed like an eternity and also a matter of mere moments, the streets were suddenly quiet with the heavy breathing of unicorns, faeries and two men. The faeries landed as Brie alighted on the ground next to Brayton and Cathal.

"Where to now highness?" Brie asked him.

"We fight our way to the castle," Brayton answered.

"What should we do if we encounter any possessed soldiers?" Cathal asked him grim-faced.

"Avoid hurting them if possible. My hope is once the demon lords are dispatched their possession will end."

Cathal nodded. There was nothing more to be said, and they rode off to begin the grim business of cleansing the white castle.

***

Loki brought up his Sonipe short as he hovered over the topmost tower. They had managed to avoid most of the fighting. The few flying demons that had chosen to engage were quickly killed. The sun was bright and hot and to their backs, blinding anyone who should happen to look up in their direction. Dain had suggested this tactic to help give every bit of stealth they could manage. Dismounting, Loki led the way to the edge of the tower and looked down. He could see where Brayton and the others were fighting. Just then he saw the faeries flying in from the east over the water.

"Yes!" he shouted. "Looks like the goddess, wherever she is, has taken a hand," Loki said pointing. "That makes me feel better. Now I can concentrate on our task."

"What's the plan master wizard," Leah said pushing a stray hair behind her pointed ear.

Loki looked over at the tower where he was held, which wasn't too far away. He picked this tower to land so as to make his approach unknown.

"We descend to the next level. There is a passage way that

only soldiers use when going to their places on the battlements. There will be fighting, but I believe it will be less than if we try to go down any main halls."

Lifting the hatch in the floor of the tower, they quickly went down and slowly opened the door of the room they came to. Loki peered out, then quickly closed the door.

"Well?" Cleo said.

"There are two sentries. I will take care of them." Loki closed his eyes as he concentrated. "We can go now."

Tori opened the door and drew her swords. Stepping out she saw two figures slumped on the floor.

"Did you kill them?" She asked.

"No," Loki said. "They are just asleep."

Quietly they ran down the corridor, being careful not to raise any alarm before they came to an ornate wooden door which Loki knew well. Placing both hands on either side he concentrated.

"They are in there," Loki said after a few moments.

Cleo also had her twin swords drawn. "What's our plan."

Loki paused for a moment as he ran his hand through his hair and looking at each person, weighing in his mind what the best course of action would be. These things had immense power, he knew that first hand. They also knew they were coming.

"I think Dain and I should distract them. Cleo and Leah will protect our backs."

"What should I do?" Tori asked.

"I want you to wait out here," Loki explained. "Once everyone is fully engaged, come in. They have felt the brunt of your power before, so I must assume they have thought of some way to counteract it. Maybe we can keep them busy long enough that they forget about you."

"Let's stop talking and just do it," Leah said extending her spear.

Dain smiles as he looks over at his beloved. "My thoughts exactly."

"Ok, here we go," Loki said. There was no sense for stealth now. Loki lifted both palms up and blasted the door inward as they rushed inside. Standing in the center of the room, three of those hooded things formed a triangle in their stance, a visible shield of translucent red encircling them.

"Don't touch that shield!" Loki exclaimed.

Just then a contingent of demon possessed soldiers came running out of the shadows. Leah and Cleo immediately started to engage. Cleo's swords, though not as fast as Tori's, were a blur as every swing came in contact with a body or blade. There was enough room from floor to ceiling for Leah to command an aerial assault. Dain and Loki stood side by side as lightning strikes flew out of their hands to impact with the shield, but to little effect. The beings in the center of the room, eyes glowing red from under their hood were returning the wizards strikes, causing them to erect a shield of their own.

"Any ideas?" Dain shouted over the din of battle.

"We are not getting through," Loki said. "Tori!"

Tori had been poised, both swords ready, the power of the god flowing through her. Suddenly she heard Loki's call. Bursting into the room, all focus of the three warlocks had turned to her. Everything seemed to slow down as she entered that other state. This time however they were prepared. She could feel their hatred of her, as if they knew what she was. They saw her as the biggest threat and focused all their power on her. The air was alive with energy. Suddenly three bolts of lightning came streaking towards her. Tori quickly dived out of the way. Even though her speed was enhanced, she was still not fast enough to out run a lightning bolt, and it wouldn't be long before she was struck. The only thought she had was to dive sword first into their shield in hopes to shatter it. She quickly started to push herself up.

Not that way, a voice inside her head said. She looked around quickly to see who spoke. More lightning bolts were headed her way. Suddenly a shield was thrown up in front of her. She looked over at Loki and Dain and saw that they were throwing everything they could into protecting her. Even at the risk of making themselves vulnerable to attack. Tori saw one of the warlocks start to focus his attention back on the wizards. There was no more time. Time. It struck her mind like a bell. Then the voice was back.

Look there.

Tori looked to her right and saw what looked like an angry red slash, suspended in the air that ran from the floor to the ceiling. But the slash was no ordinary red. It was her red. Fallon's red.

Go! the voice commanded.

Tori didn't hesitate. Running, she dove head first through what she saw in her mind as a rip in the fabric of reality. Coming out the other side she rolled and got quickly to her feet, stunned at what she saw. She was still in the tower, but not a thing moved. All the colors where enhanced and hyper vibrant. As if she were seeing color for the very first time.

She could see Dain and Loki still holding their shield, but they were frozen. Lightning bolts were spewing from the warlocks, but those too seemed frozen in midair. She could walk around them. She quickly touched one, but its energy did not flow into her. She looked up and saw Leah, her flight suspended as she locked with a demon twice her size. Cleo was frozen in the act of driving her sword through a soldier against the wall. She was able to move within the warlocks shield and circle them one by one. She took her sword and tried to push it into one of them. She might as well have been trying to push through stone. Wherever it is she had found herself, there is not very much she could do here. She raised her sword high, getting ready to swing as if she would chop off the head of one of these beasts.

"That will do nothing but injure your arm."

Tori spun around, both swords leveled at the person who spoke. It was a man unlike any she had ever seen. He was well over seven feet tall, and dressed for battle. He wore a leather kilt with gold lining running along the edge. His breast plate was a dark burgundy with gold greaves on his legs and arm bands around his biceps to match. Strapped to his back was the largest broadsword she had ever seen and doubts even she could lift. His flaming red hair ran down and over his shoulders. But what struck her the most was the raw energy of battle she felt emanating from this being. She realized now he wasn't human, which left only one other possibility as the color drained from her face.

"So you figured it out my daughter."

"Lord Fallon?" Tori said shaking.

The god started laughing long and loud, which made Tori even more frightened as she sank to her knees.

"Stand Tori, you have no need to fear me."

"My Lord," Tori said slowly getting to her feet.

"Fallon is fine, Tori. I'm not as stuffy as some of my brothers," he said winking. Placing both hands on her shoulders, the god made Tori feel instantly relaxed. "You are also my Cath Priomh, and I am very proud of you my daughter."

Tori's heart broke as she fell into the god's arms and wept. She no longer felt alone and outcast, a freak. Fallon waited for the tears to run its course. Tori looked up a little embarrassed and smiled sheepishly.

"Sorry, not the way a captain of the once mighty Vipers to behave."

"It's alright," the god told her. "You could not be a warrior if you did not understand suffering and grief. It's what comes after that proves your mettle. And you have proven yourself time and time again, Tori." She was happy to hear that from her god. It was as if now it all made sense.

"We cannot linger long here," Fallon told her. "Some things I must tell you."

"Where exactly are we?" she asked looking around.

Fallon ran his fingers through his hair. A typical human thing Tori thought. Or maybe it was humans imitating the gods.

"We are inside a frozen moment," he explained to her. "You could stay here for years and the world would not have moved on a single second. Of course you would probably starve if you did that since you can't even move a single blade of grass. But this place does come in handy when you want to travel and you need time to stand still while you do."

"Can anyone come in here?"

"Other than you, yes, but they would not be able to get out again unless they maintained contact with you. Do not bring your friends in here if you can help it. Should you get separated they would wander until they died."

Tori shuddered at the thought of someone like Cleo being lost forever in here. She looked up at her god.

"What am I to do?"

"For right now, you need to cleanse my brother's city of this filth," he said nodding towards the three warlocks.

"How can I do that?"

"Stand in the center of them. You will be able to slide back into time, but now you will be inside their shield. But you must strike quickly and plan your strikes ahead of time."

"Will it kill them? Last time I struck one of these creatures it dissolved like a demon."

"No, you cannot kill them. But once you strike down the forms they are wearing, they will have to flee. In essence, they are not truly here. You would need to go where they physically are to destroy them."

"Do you know where that is?"

"I am not permitted to answer that my daughter; it is part of the quest that you all figure that out. That's all the questions I can answer for now. I must leave, and you have a battle to win." He reached under his breastplate and drew out a medallion on a golden chain. "Lower your head Tori."

Tori did as she was told as the god slipped the necklace over her head. Taking it in her palm she studied it closely. The edge was tinged with red and gold, looking like an autumn fire when she moved it. In the center were two crossed swords, not unlike the ones she wore on her back.

"From this day forward you are my priestess, Tori. This will allow you to call me. It also gives you the ability to make the doors into the frozen moment. Just visualize the doorway and step through."

Tori didn't know what to say. The emotions were running rampant through her. Fallon saw her conflicting expressions and pulled her towards him in a final embrace. Cupping her face in both hands he told her, "Serve me well my child and fear not, I am always with thee."

And with that the god disappeared, leaving Tori feeling very alone for the moment. She gripped the medallion tighter and the strength and confidence of Fallon flooded her being. The fire around her eyes lit up as she slowly walked to the center of the triangle formed by the three warlocks. Forming the image of the 'rip' as she came to call it, she had her swords at the ready. Her medallion burned red-hot against her chest. Her entire being was alive and the fire in her eyes were spinning. Jumping through the rip she could tell her adversaries were totally bewildered to suddenly see her appear before them. That hesitation gave Tori all the advantage she needed. She thrust her swords at the two warlocks in front of her, then completed a back thrust to the one she knew to be directly behind her. A great scream went up as three very powerful demon lords were evicted from the host bodies the warlocks controlled. Their robes fell to the stone floor, empty. Suddenly the sound of battle stopped. The soldiers also found themselves released from their possession as they looked around as if in a daze, unsure as to what had been happening. Cleo and Leah immediately had sheathed their weapons to prevent any accidents or misinterpretation of who was on who's side.

"What? What is going on?" a soldier remarked.

Loki walked over to him and put a hand on his shoulder. "What is your name captain?"

"Logan, sir."

"Logan, you and your men have been under the control of demons for quite some time now. Please, just take your men to your barracks. Someone will come along to explain things further."

The captain saluted Loki and lead his men down out of the tower. Loki then turned towards Tori with wonder and amazement on his face.

"Would you like to tell my how by the gods you did that? And what exactly was that?"

"By the gods is correct," Tori said, "or rather one god to be more precise."

Tori went on to explain everything that had happened from when she jumped through the rip to when she dispatched the three warlocks. Everyone was silent as she told her tale, astonishment clearly written all over their faces.

"This gives us a great advantage," Dain said.

"True," Loki agreed. "But it does have its drawbacks. I don't recommend traveling by the frozen moment unless necessity absolutely demanded it."

"Where should we go now?" Cleo asked wiping the sweat and blood from a cut on her brow.

"Let's go and see if Brayton needs a hand. The soldiers of Kensington should be free of their possession now, but there is still a host of demons out there."

"I'm going to find Brie and see if my sisters need a hand," Leah said. "I will meet you in the throne room when all is done."

"Be careful," Dain told her with a raised eyebrow.

"Always my love," she responded after kissing him and launching herself out of the tower window.

The battle for Kensington raged for the remainder of the day. The soldiers once possessed were now able to fight for their city. The casualties were high, but realizing the things they did while possessed, they were ready to sell their lives if it meant ridding them of the demonic scourge. Leah came soaring down to stand next to Brie on the castle steps.

"How did we fare?" Leah asked her sister.

"Too many lost," Brie replied nursing a cut on her arm. "Most during the fight helping Brayton." She looked sadly at Leah. "Do you ever get tired of fighting?"

"All the time," Leah said looking over at the smoke rising from the burnt out buildings by the south wall. "Hopefully some peace will be coming soon. Have you heard anything from Donella or any of the others?"

"When we left Laurel Hollow I had heard they were deep in Parma, but nothing more. Andros we saw flying over the sea." Brie said worried. "I had a bad feeling in the pit of my stomach."

Leah told Brie what Samara had said about Abby. Brie looked grief stricken and near tears on hearing that news.

"What happens now sister?" Brie asked.

"Loki, Brayton and the others are coming, we will soon find out."

As they mounted the steps, Leah could tell Brayton had suffered a dramatic change in his psyche. His bearing and his look were more intense, and that wasn't because of just the eye patch. Leah thought that for the first time, he felt responsible for the death of others. She hoped the weight of that grief didn't overwhelm him.

"We are headed to the crypt," Brayton told them. "I need to let my parents know it is safe to come out."

It was quite the procession that descended into the bowels of the castle to the one place where only the King and his firstborn could enter. Placing his hand on the clear orb above the door, there was a momentary white flash as the door opened inward. Stepping inside, Brayton can feel something was wrong. When he placed his hand on the orb it showed him the last person to enter, and it was not his father. It was a man, very tall wearing a hooded cloak. The hood was down, and he could see the man had red hair braided into a ponytail.

"Mom? Dad?"

There was no answer. The crypt was as silent as the tomb.

Chapter 24

Emilia was numb. She just stood there. She couldn't tell if it was minutes, hours or days. She looked upon the body of the person who was not only her friend but sister as well. She felt hollowed out inside as her eyes ran up and down the flower bower where Abby's body rested. Abby looked like she was just sleeping. Emilia couldn't understand why her own body couldn't move. It's like her muscles wouldn't obey her command to walk back to where the others were. There was a lot of crying and sorrow when everyone arrived at Pan's grotto. Her mother and father were devastated, but they seemed to be able to handle it better than she could. And what about Andy? Her father had told her he had fled upon seeing Abby struck down for the price of lowering the death shield. She looked over to where the brothers of Andros stood. She could feel their empathy through the Summoner link, Brion's most of all. He seemed to be staring at her, concern written all over his face.

"Donella,"

Emilia turned to her left, and coming out of a side alcove was Lyson. Suddenly she could move again and flew into his arms sobbing.

"Oh Lyson, I lost a part of my family," she cried. "Devon tortured and nearly killed her because I pulled Andy away from her." She looked up into his eyes pleading. "She already paid a price once, this isn't right." She buried her face in Lyson's chest.

Tears were also running down Lyson's cheek. He tried to think of something comforting to say, but no words would come. He did the only thing he could do. Held her in his arms and let his love pour into her. After their grief had run its course for the moment, Emilia heard a footfall behind her. It was Brion.

"I'm sorry if I am intruding," Brion said.

"It's alright," Emilia said placing an arm on his shoulder and wiping her eyes.

Brion looked sadly at Abby. "I can't help but feel responsible. If I wasn't so foolish as to let Devon trick us, her sacrifice would never have been necessary."

"There is no blame here," Lyson said. "Except for Devon and the warlocks, if you are looking for a villain. The gods know it was they that set this all in motion long ago."

"I will redress this wrong," Brion vowed.

"Come, let's head back," Lyson said. Lyson, Emilia and Brion walked over to where the others were gathered.

"Are you alright, dear?" Luel asked hugging her daughter.

"For now Mom," she answered. "We need to make sure Abby didn't die in vain."

"We will make sure," her mother said fiercely.

Emilia looked around at all her friends, new and old. It looked like a small invasion force had come to Pan's abode. Pan himself sat in a stone chair, slightly elevated making him seem a king once more, and not just king of the fauns. Taking up his mantle once again as Cael's priest had started to change him. The grief and pain of his life was still there, but now something else as well. Hope.

"I think it is time to discuss our next course of action," Pan said.

"The next course of action is Andy," Redlin said. "Not just because he's my son, although that alone is reason enough,

295

but without him the prophecy fails, and Vasara with it. And the death of that beautiful soul laying over there," he said pointing, "will have been for nothing."

"But we have no idea where he went," Emma said, her wings stirring a gentle breeze.

"I may know," Brion suddenly spoke up, looking at Redlin.

"Where?" the wizard asked him.

"That I cannot tell you."

"And why is that?" Redlin said stepping closer to him, his eyes showing impatience.

"I mean no disrespect Redlin," Brion said. "It is a sacred place for dragons. And only dragons can go there. I cannot even tell you its exact location. Need always guides us, and I am certain the death of his beloved is driving Andros there, and he probably isn't even aware of where he is going in his madness."

Redlin put both hands on Brion's shoulders, holding his eyes with his own for a very long moment. "Go then, and find him, and be careful yourself."

"You speak like a father," Brion said smiling.

"Well, you are my son's brother," he said with a raised eyebrow.

"So you are the father of dragon's now?"

"Who's to say," Redlin said winking. "Now go."

Brion took off at a run. Once he had the space he needed he made the change and everyone watched as the red dragon took flight over the tree tops, the sun glistening on his scales as he veered towards the east.

***

Brion could feel the pull already from the sacred island of the dragons as he flew over the Scio Ocean. Looking down he spotted a ship. He decided to circle and land and see if they had seen Andros fly over. As he got lower, he could see all the sailors staring at him with mouths open wide in astonishment. Hovering just above the mast, Brion changed form and allowed himself to drop into the crow's nest.

"Permission to come aboard!" he shouted below.

"Looks like you already gave yourself permission laddie."

Brion looked down at the man who spoke. Tall with dark curly hair. Streaks of grey lined the sides of his head giving him the impression of a seasoned sailor. Climbing down the rigging he dropped to the deck by the man who had spoken to him.

"Welcome aboard the Grey Morning. Captain Bowen at your service," Bowen said shaking Brion's hand.

"Thank you Captain. I didn't mean to startle you and your men. Brion is my name."

"You might have if you weren't the only dragon we've seen recently."

"You have seen another I take it," Brion said.

"Aye," Bowen said sadly. "Andros the black. I assume you know him, being a dragon yourself and all."

"We have never met," Brion told him. "How did he seem when you saw him?"

Bowen took out his pipe and walked over to the port side rail. "Look there," Bowen said pointing.

Brion looked down in the water. Swimming frantically and over top of one another were four Tagen. Their dragon-like heads banging occasionally into the side of the ship.

"Why are they doing that?" Brion asked.

"Andros," the captain said sadly.

Bowen told Brion how Andy had come aboard ship just like he did a couple of days ago and told them what had happened. The captain looked at Brion grief stricken.

"He's mad, Brion. The lad I knew was gone. He spoke erratically and very fast." Bowen lowered his head. "Then he told us of Abby, and what was left of his heart was ripped out of his chest as he fell to the deck."

Bowen looked back down in the water.

"That's when the Tagen came. They know Andros and probably wanted to greet him. He went to the rail with a wild look in his eyes." He looked up at Brion again. "His mind must have linked with theirs. They have been doing that ever since he flew away."

Brion could see tears starting to roll down Bowen's cheeks. "I'm so sorry, Captain."

"My heart broke for that lad. And poor Abby..." Bowen couldn't continue. Brion looked around at the crew and realized to a man, they all had tears standing in their eyes.

"Aye, the crew loved Abby," Bowen told Brion noticing his reaction to the sailors standing on deck. "There is not a man here that wouldn't lay down his life in exchange for hers, there would not be a moment's hesitation I promise you that," Bowen said fiercely.

Brion filled the captain in on everything that had happened after Andy flew away and how he took up the task to try and bring him back. Suddenly Bowen's eyes widened.

"Wait here lad," Bowen told him as he ran below decks. When he emerged, he was holding something in his hand.

"Now I don't know if this be prophecy or what, but when Andros and his family were aboard ship, Abby came to see me."

Bowen deposited what he held into Brion's hand. It was a bracelet or anklet, Brion wasn't sure which. It was silver with miniature black dragons every third link.

"Keep this safe for me Captain," Abby had told me. "It is precious to me."

"Did Andros give it to her?" Brion asked.

"I assumed so. I didn't think to ask."

Brion slipped it into a pocket. "Thank you Captain. I must get to Andros before it's too late."

"The gods speed to you lad. I've not been much of a praying man, but I would pray to the gods, and the goddess herself if it will help you. Of course if I start praying to Braylynn she will never let me forget it."

"I think that is a safe bet that she won't," Brion said laughing. It felt good to laugh he thought. He needed all the positive energy he could gather in his coming confrontation with Andros. Brion knew what he was up against, because he had been there himself. Before leaving, Brion looked down at the tagen. Joining his mind with theirs, he could see and feel their agitation. He started sending them images of peace and calm seas. Eventually their thrashing slowed. They looked up at him, staring. Then as one they jumped up, somersaulted in the air and calmly swam away as they broke the surface of the water.

"I hope you manage the same with Andros," Bowen said shaking his hand.

"I hope so too, Captain," Brion said as he leaped over the side and into the ocean. Once he was a distance away from the ship he made his change, his wings beating a steady rhythm as he climbed high in the sky.

Brion wasn't sure how long he had flown, but looking to the north, his dragon sight caught of what looked like a smudge on the horizon. He veered towards it, gaining altitude as he did so. He could definitely feel the strong pull of the dragon's island. As he got closer, he started to see familiar landmarks from the last time he was here. Like Andros, grief had driven him here. Brion decided to descend and approach from the beach before heading into the mountains where the caves were. Suddenly, shooting out from the island a ball of liquid fire came hurtling towards him. He dove quickly, the fireball barely missing him. This was going to be harder than he thought if Andros was already trying to kill him. Landing on the beach he changed back to human. He figured he would make a smaller target. Again, another fireball came shooting out of the woods. Brion barely managed to get a shield up in time.

"Andros stop!" He shouted.

At first, it seemed like Andy must have heard him. All around was quiet. Then Brion started hearing a tearing sound, as if hundreds of trees were being uprooted and shredded. Without warning a thousand wooden missiles came streaking towards him. Brion quickly raised a shield of fire and pushed it forward, incinerating the wooden stakes before they could impale him.

Andros, please. Stop this madness, Brion spoke to his mind.

Leave me, Andy responded. *Leave me or I will kill you. Leave me.* The last almost seemed to come out as a sob, Brion thought.

I can't do that.

Then you will die.

Wait, Brion said. *Can you see this?* He said holding up Abby's bracelet.

With a scream of rage, Andy practically flew out of the woods even though he was in human form. Before Brion could react, Andy had him by the throat as he snatched the bracelet out of Brion's hand.

"Where did you get this?" Andy screamed with a frantic, wild look in his eyes. "Tell me or I will crush your windpipe."

Brion struggled to pull Andy's fingers apart to allow him to speak. "You need to let go," he managed to get out.

"Very well." Andy made a twisting motion with his hand. Brion instantly felt a pressure in his chest. "My hand is around your heart now. Try anything and I swear to the gods I will squeeze."

Brion stared at his chest in amazement. Never had he heard of such a thing and wondered how Andros learned to do this.

"Now tell me how you got this."

"Bowen gave it to me. He said after he had picked all of you up on the island, Abby had come to him. She asked him to keep it safe for her."

"Liar! She would never part with this. Never!" Andy's eyes had a feral look. Brion thought for sure the heart squeezing would commence any moment.

"Andros, you need to listen. I know your mind is sick right now, but please hear me out."

Andy started to snarl.

"Andy, please. Listen to me brother."

The use of his common name was not lost on Andy, and Brion used it as a long shot to try and pierce some of his insanity. Andy blinked, confused and startled. He probably didn't realize it, but Brion saw tears starting to roll down Andy's cheek.

Andy's whole demeanor suddenly changed. He sank to the sand, hugging his knees as he rocked back and forth sobbing. Brion could still feel Andy's hand around his heart. He didn't move to comfort him. Instead, he let him release his immense grief.

"Please go. Leave," Andy said not looking up.

"I can't. We need you. Vasara needs you. The prophecy will fail without you."

Andy looked up with hatred in his eyes. His hand made a twisting motion, making Brion gasp and his eyes grew wide at the pain he was feeling in his chest.

"Do not speak to me of prophecy. It is because of the prophecy that Abby is dead! Oh God..!" Andy buried his head,

301

releasing Brion as the sobs wracked his body once more. Brion felt the hand disappear from around his heart as he quickly raised an inner shield to prevent Andy from regaining contact like that again.

Brion waited patiently as the sobs started to lessen, Andy's body seeming to relax from sheer exhaustion if nothing else.

"Please leave me alone," Andy said quietly. "I can't do this anymore. I'm tired of losing people I love just to fulfill a prophecy. I'm done."

Brion seized on this bit of clarity that was coming through. With most of Andy's rage and grief spent, now would be his only chance.

"Andros, I know your pain."

Andy's eyes suddenly flared red. "You could never know my pain!" He shouted.

Brion remained calm. He knew he walked the knife's edge now, and he couldn't afford to push Andy off one side or the other. If it came to a full-blown fight, Brion didn't feel too good about his chances. He knew he had the experience, but the raw power that Andy demonstrated was immense.

"I do know. I suffered a loss just like yours, but worse." Brion hung his head at the wound he was about to rip open. "At least you didn't kill your beloved," he said to Andy.

Andy blinked several times as the words penetrated his brain. "What do you mean?" Andy's eyes bore into Brion's, seeking any deception he might play. Brion stared right back and allowed Andy to see into his soul.

"It happened in the first millennium of Vasara's creation." Brion took a deep breath, steeling himself for what he was about to reveal. "There was a man. An illusionist who would go from town to town, tricking people out of their money with visions of riches and glory. The dragons, when we weren't fighting together, would roam the various kingdoms, helping wherever we could."

"What was his name?" Andy asked getting caught up in the story. Brion smiled inwardly. He knew he had Andy's attention now.

"Makala," Brion answered. "He was a tall man with jet black hair with clothes to match. He was very good at what he did. He could create visions and illusions to make people believe almost anything."

"Even you?" Andy asked.

"Not at first," he replied sadly.

Brion told Andy how he had chased Makala, finally catching up with him in Albion. The confrontation was short-lived as Brion was able to expose him for what he was. Word went out to all the kingdoms and Makala was deemed an outcast. From what Brion had learned Makala had sought refuge in the Parma Wilds.

"I thought he would live out his life in exile and to leave the world in peace."

"I'm guessing he didn't," Andy said.

"I never guessed how deep his hatred of me went. It drove him to make a pact with the king of hell himself." Brion looked sadly at Andy. "He gave up his soul and humanity for the power to make me suffer."

"I still don't see how your situation is anyway similar to mine," Andy said getting frustrated.

"Because I haven't told you about Ciara," Brion said as a tear slid down his cheek. That name had not been spoken aloud in thousands of years, though it was ever present in Brion's mind. Her image would be there forever, as well as how she died.

"Is she the woman you loved?"

Brion couldn't speak at first. His chest was tightening, and he wasn't sure he would be able to continue. The pain was too much. He had made a peace with himself thanks to the gods and Caleb, who had pulled him out of his insanity. Now he was diving back into it.

Damn it Bull, where are you when I need you, Brion thought to himself.

Andy waited expectantly. Brion knew this was the only way he could bring Andy back, so he opened the wound wide and plunged in. He told Andy how he had rescued Ciara from a band of robbers in Dragonsgate.

"She was so beautiful," Brion told him. "Golden hair like the sunrise with eyes as blue as the sea." He smiled as he looked at Andy. "And the way she could sing, Andros. It was like listening to angels."

"I know what you mean," Andy said sadly.

"I knew it was folly to fall for a human given their so short lives. But I fell, I fell hard in love every moment we spent together. We even talked of marriage." Tears were streaming openly now down Brion's face. "She wanted to have children with me, Andros. She said if it were not possible for her to live forever with me, she wanted a family line born from our love that would stretch down the long centuries to always remind me of her, and to know that our love is eternal."

Andy's eyes were clear. Brion could see him slowly coming back to reality.

"What happened?" Andy asked.

"Makala happened," Brion said in snarl. He could feel the bile rising in his throat. "I was away with my, our brothers, when Makala sneaked into Dragonsgate. I could feel something was wrong, so I flew back as fast as I could. But I was too late, so I thought."

"What do you mean?"

"When I got to the door I burst it open with a thought. My mind couldn't comprehend what I was seeing. There on the floor was Ciara, her body twisted and broken. It was like my body would not obey my commands to move. Then I heard that cackle of a laugh that I knew was Makala. Without even thinking I followed it deep into the woods of Dragonsgate. I found him standing in the middle of a clearing. His arms across his chest as if locked in position, his head down. I had no idea of what he might try. I didn't think, I didn't hesitate. With palms outstretched I shot two lightning bolts at his chest, killing him instantly." Brion paused in his narration. His bottom lip was quivering. Andy placed a hand on his shoulder. Brion looked at him and knew he was almost back. He had to go on.

"Everything was silent. Even the animals made no sound. And then I heard it again. Fading in the distance was that maniacal cackling laugh. I quickly ran over to the body to make sure he was dead. To my horror, there was my beloved Ciara. Arms bound across her chest, her eyes staring up at me emptily. Accusingly. My blindness was complete."

Andy looked at him confused.

"I never stopped to remember what he was. A master of illusion, and even more so since his power was enhanced."

Brion stopped talking and looked out to sea. The surf was rough, but no match for what was currently stirring inside of him. He had to keep telling himself, this was for Andros. He hoped it wasn't in vain.

"Did you kill him?" Andy asked.

"I never saw him again. Although, I still hear his cackle in my head to this very day." He brought his attention back to Andy. "My mind snapped. I flew to this island, at the time

I didn't understand why. A hundred years, Andros. For a hundred years I was mad."

Andy gasped at that.

"I laid waste to this place. I'm glad to see everything came back," he said scanning the countryside. Brion felt emotionally drained and all he wanted to do was lay down and sleep for a month.

"How did you make it back?"

"In the end, Caleb found me and helped me. Before that, the gods would visit during my madness, though at the time what they were telling me didn't really register. At some point Trystan came to me to tell me Ciara was with him, and she would be waiting for me for as long as it took. That took seed in me, and I believe it was that kernel of knowledge that grew until Caleb found me and brought me back. I still see what I did to my beloved in my mind's eye every day, but now hope is there to help make the pain bearable."

Brion watched as Andy sat quietly, absorbing everything he had told him. Tears were still escaping from the corners of Andy's eyes, but his body had a relaxed state of letting go.

"I feel so lost," Andy finally said. "I have no clue what to do."

"There is no shame in admitting you are lost brother, or asking for help. We will not leave you to face this alone. The love of your family and friends is a powerful force. It's all about connections, for the ones that are here and also the ones who have journeyed on."

"Where do we go now?" Andy asked.

"To Pan's grotto, where you will say a proper goodbye to your beloved. After that, we will put forth all our efforts to insure Abby's sacrifice was not in vain."

Chapter 25

"Set the mainsail, we are getting underway," Bowen yelled to his crew.

The Grey Morning leapt to the task as a good wind started pushing her east.

"Captain, there be dragons here!" a sailor shouted from the crow's nest.

"Where?" Bowen yelled back looking around.

"Port side, two o'clock high, sir."

Bowen searched the sky in the direction his crewman had indicated. There, flying high were two dragons, one black the other red, their long steady strokes taking them towards the mainland. Bowen's face split into a grin from ear to ear.

"Well done laddie," he said aloud. "Well done indeed."

Bowen quickly ran up to the quarter deck and grabbed the ships wheel.

"All hands on deck!" He said changing course. "Lay out all the canvas we have! Look sharp lads!"

"What's going on Captain," his bosun asked running up.

Bowen pointed at the dragons retreating figures. "If I am not mistaking, battle will be coming soon. And the Grey Morning is not about to be left out of this fight."

***

Brion kept a close eye on Andy as they flew towards the Parma Wilds. Andy and Brion had talked all day and through the night. When the sun came up, they began their flight. Brion knew Andy was feeling hollow and shattered, but clarity was back in his eyes. It was enough. His mind started reaching out for Caleb.

Bull, can you hear me?

After a few moments, his brother's thought came back to him.

I hear you, Brion, Caleb responded.

I have Andros with me. Prepare the others, you know what to do.

Yes, I do. We will be ready when you get here. Be careful.

I will, see you shortly.

Brion didn't have to tell his brother what he needed. He already knew. They all did. They needed to be ready to help Andy once he saw Abby. His madness could so easily return.

***

Andy felt so tired and emotionally drained. He looked over at his new-found brother as they winged their way to Pan's grotto. He still felt very fragile and shattered, but he also felt he wasn't alone. Brion knew what he had been through. Knew what it meant to have your heart cut out, chopped up into bits, and then have it put back into your chest. They passed a ship sometime back, Andy assumed it was the Grey Morning. He would have to apologize to Bowen when he got the chance. Looking down he could see the edge of the jungle that marked the boundary of the Parma Wilds. Another hour of flight found them descending. Once on the ground, they changed form right by the water that ran past the grotto. A flood of people suddenly came running out of the grotto's entrance. Family, friends and some he hadn't met yet, but all ready to lift him up and support him. He fell into the arms of his mother and father letting the cleansing of his emotions take him as everything turned bright white before his eyes and his head slumped on his father's chest.

After Andy found the strength to stand again, he made his way to where Abby lay. The place where Pan had placed her was so vibrant with color. He was trying hard to not look at her body. What if he couldn't handle it he thought. What if the madness returned? But he had to look at her, which he did. What was left of his heart lurched in his chest. She looked so serene and peaceful, as if she were just taking a nap. The tears hadn't stopped running since he entered the alcove. She still had that look of a pirate about her. And not so much the way she was dressed he thought, but her adventurous spirit. She never flinched from adversity and she knew no fear.

"How do I go on, Abby?" he said to her. "How do I do this without you?"

He was trying to hold the sobs back, but his body started to wrack with them. He leaned over and cradled her head to his chest. Surprisingly she didn't feel cold. Andy wondered if this was part of Pan's magic.

He whispered in Abby's ear. "I'm lost, love. Lost and broken and I don't know where to turn. Abby, can you hear me? I need you to hear me," he pleaded. "I have to finish this. By the cruelty of the prophecy, I'm forced to go on without you. Hold me tight in your heart, please."

Andy lay her head gently back down on the pillow. Moving to her right leg he took out the anklet that Brion had gotten from Bowen and put it back on her ankle. In so doing he turned to her one last time.

"Goodbye my love. When everything is achieved, I will be back." He gently started stroking her hair. "We will see each other again I promise. In a far better world where we will never be separated again."

Andy's shoulders started to heave as the sobs started again. He could feel his mind starting to slip. "Gods, please no," he said through clenched teeth as he lifted his face skyward.

Suddenly he felt an enormous amount of energy enter his body, a warm heat spreading from head to toe. Every positive emotion imaginable was swarming through his mind. He turned to look behind him. In a semi-circle around him, his brothers stood with palms stretched forward. Light of all the colors of the gods shot from their hands and into himself, plus one more. Standing off to the side stood Tori. Her eyes were red, her body surrounded by an aura that she had pushed forward to encompass Andy. He could feel the power of the god Fallon, filling him with focus and determination. Andy was so humbled by this display of support and love. Tears were still streaming down his face, but it was a good release. He felt the strength to move forward. His brothers were free, but that was only the first half of the problem. There were ten warlocks to deal with.

Redlin assembled everyone together. Loki and the others had arrived shortly before Andy and Brion. Loki had told them about how Paolo and Acacia had gone missing and that Brayton and the unicorns were scouring the countryside for them, engaging demons in the process. They had honored their dead as best they could. Now it was time to make sure those deaths were not in vain. There was a lot of information sharing and everyone was pretty much on the same page.

"I guess the big question now is where do we find these warlocks?" Redlin asked.

Everyone turned to Pan.

"It is not in Parma, I can tell you that much," Pan said.

"I wish Abby were here," Emma said with new shed tears. "She would not stop searching the books until she got a hint of a location."

"That's true," Redlin said with a half-smile. "But we must find another way."

"I think I know who can help us," Rhyan said looking intently at Redlin.

"Who?" Andy asked.

Rhyan didn't answer but kept staring at Redlin.

"I think I know who you mean," Redlin said, "and I believe I know why."

"Who?" Diminitus said crankily. "We don't have time for your riddles master wizard."

Redlin smiled at him. "I sure have missed you Dim."

Diminitus just grunted and crossed his arms in reply. "Can you find her?" he asked Rhyan.

"Yes. The enchantment I put on the medallion will lead me to her. If one of these brave dragons would give me a ride I could be there and back in no time."

"I will take her," Finn replied.

Redlin looked at Finn, surprised at his sudden offer to help. The wizard always remembered this dragon as being a little reticent.

"Do you want me to come with you?" Ava asked her sister.

"I would love that, but I think two priestesses of the god would upset her."

"Who are we talking about," Luel asked her husband.

"Samara," he responded.

Andy, Emma and Bella looked at Redlin knowingly. They all knew Rhyan had seen something when her mind connected with the Sonipes.

"Go," Redlin told Rhyan.

"Where should I meet up with you?" Rhyan asked.

"Laurel Hollow," Redlin said.

"Why there, Dad?" Andy asked.

"Because you and your sister need to train with your brothers."

Chapter 26

It felt good to be back home. Or at least the place she called home in Vasara. Emilia looked around the cottage she had lived in when she first discovered she was Braylynn's Dragon Summoner. There were more books here than she remembered as her hand ran along the spines. This was Lyson's touch. He had told Emilia that Braylynn made him study the faerie mysteries. She was certain that Braylynn had plans for him, and she wasn't really sure how she felt about that. The sun was cascading through the window illuminating the circular green carpet with a white dragon symbol emblazoned on it. Tilting her head, her pointed ears could pick up the sounds of footsteps and knew someone was approaching. Her thoughts were confirmed when she heard her brother's voice call out.

"Hey sis, you ready for this?"

Emilia smiled, although it was also mixed with sadness for the one that was no longer there. She was amazed at how her brother was able to come back from that. If something similar had happened to Lyson, she didn't think she would make it. Stepping outside she met Andy, along with eight of his nine brothers. It felt like her own small private army. She looked at each face in turn, as if memorizing their features. Finn had taken Rhyan to find Samara, she would have to train with him separately. Finn disturbed her. Not his mannerisms or any distrust that she felt from him. But because he had some connection to Zana. She saw it in his eyes when he had asked about her in the caves. She would have to deal with that later. It was time to see what she could do with a host of dragons. They all walked to the dragon's glade. That wide open expanse where Emilia and Andy had first trained. Braylynn had seen to their training then, but now she was on her own.

"I must confess, I'm not really sure how to begin," Emilia said. "It's one thing connecting with Andy, being my brother and all."

"Perhaps I can help," Brion said stepping in.

Emilia was grateful for Brion. She knew she would eventually bond with each one, but she already felt a bond with him when her dragon had plunged into his body.

"I would appreciate that."

"It's not really difficult," Brion began. "We will each open our minds to you as you open yours to us. The trick is make the connection one at a time, but hold each one before moving to the next. Make sense?"

"I think so," Emilia said.

"Connect to Andros first, then to me and see how that goes."

Emilia closed her eyes. The dragon eye on her crown started to glow as she concentrated. Connecting to Andy was easy. Holding onto him as she reached out for Brion proved a little trickier. Once she had Brion, her connection to Andy would drop. She tried several times and it kept slipping away.

"You are maintaining full contact with Andros while trying to connect fully with me," Brion said sensing her frustration. "Picture a glass of water. The totality of the water represents your full connection. Right now you are giving it all to whomever you connect to first. Instead, release just a fraction. Hold it. Then release a little more to the next connection and so on."

"Yes, I think I can see that," Emilia said.

Once again she closed her eyes. Opening up her mind she

made a slight connection to Andy. She measured it and held it. Holding her breath, she reached out to Brion. The temptation was strong to just flood him with her consciousness. She slowly let the connection between her and Andy split as she connected to Brion. She latched on and held them both, allowing herself to feel this new experience. It started flowing both ways and images started to flood her brain. The heart wrenching grief of Abby's loss from Andy, as well as a profound loss from Brion. Everything Brion had revealed to Andy was suddenly opened to her. The connection dropped immediately as her eyes flew open, the hurt evident on Brion's face.

"I'm sorry, I didn't mean…," Emilia stammered.

"No, that was my fault. I should have warned you," Brion said. "Just as you have the power to override our wills, you can also pull out our thoughts. I know it wasn't intentional. It probably seemed natural to you with Andros since he is your brother by blood. Just exclude those thoughts from your connection. We also in turn can seal those off from you. I must admit I was not thinking, and we haven't linked with a Dragon Summoner for over fifteen hundred years."

"I won't ever bring up what I saw," Emilia said sadly.

"I know you won't," Brion said smiling, letting her know everything was alright. "Let's keep going."

Emilia re-established her connection to Andy and Brion. It was much easier the second time.

"Now connect to Caleb," Brion told her.

"Don't worry about seeing my thoughts, Summoner," Caleb said. "I wear my heart on my sleeve anyway."

Emilia smiled to herself at his comment and proceeded with the link. One by one she finally had them all. The emotion and energy she felt was massive and raw. It made her feel a thousand feet tall. She carefully closed herself off to their private thoughts. Emilia started to relax. It felt like she held the reins of a team of nine horses, although it was much more intimate than that. It was like they were all an extension of herself.

"Are we ready?" Andy said.

"I think we are," Brion said. "If you would do the honors, Summoner."

Emilia knew what he meant. Taking the pearl comb out of her hair, she transformed it into the staff of the goddess. It made a loud crack as the staff slammed against the stone at her feet and a hundred demons filled the glade. As Braylynn had done when her and Andy first trained, these demons weren't real, but they can hurt.

"Nice! Let's go!" Caleb said excitedly. "Been a long time since we had a good scrape."

He started running into the glade as he transformed, the sun reflecting off his red scales as he started to climb high into the sky, followed by eight other dragons.

It was an aerial circus as Emilia flew up to join them. All the demons she created were flying ones, all of various sizes and horribleness. She could still feel all the connections, but it took some concentration to maintain them.

Let it flow naturally. Try not to think about it, Brion spoke to her mind.

Emilia emptied her mind of thought and just allowed herself to feel. She totally opened herself up to these nine dragons and realized she had been holding back. Once she let go, everything clicked into place. Like watching an acrobatic dance, she could see what all of them were doing all at once as well as where her powers would be most effective. She settled onto Andy's back as he crisscrossed amongst the demons, spewing fire and ice as he went. In her mind Emilia could see Caleb and the trajectory he was taking. Running down Andy's back, she somersaulted as he flew out from underneath her, allowing her to drop straight down onto Caleb's back as he was about to engage ten large demons at once. As fire roared out of his mouth, it split as it sped towards its intended targets. Emilia followed suit with streaks of lightning chasing behind the fire. The demons never stood a chance as they were suddenly vaporized.

Well done, Donella, Caleb said. *I could feel you see what I was about to do. Your timing was perfect.*

Thank you, Emilia said a little proud of herself.

We should save some for the others though, Caleb said laughing in that infectious way of his. *We can't be too greedy.*

Just then a flash of lavender went streaking past Emilia's field of vision. She looked behind her and saw Leah impaling two demons at once on her talon spear. Emilia laughed out loud. You can't keep Leah out of a fight, even if it isn't totally real.

After several hours of practice and eliminating every imaginary demon, Leah and Emilia lay on the grass staring up into the sky. The dragons had flown off to search for food and talk, so Andy had said.

Emilia looked over at her sister and remembered a time not that long ago from her reckoning where she and Leah were in this exact position. Leah had just finished giving her some first-hand training in aerial combat. After, they had talked about the hurt and sadness that comes when a faerie loves a human. Things had obviously worked out for Leah and Dain since he was now a wizard. He was likely to outlive Leah, assuming of course he didn't get himself killed. Emilia smiled to herself. She knew with Leah, her sister was never going to allow that to happen, by sheer will if nothing else. That brought her thoughts around to Lyson. Now she was in

Leah's shoes before Dain became a wizard.

"What are you thinking about?" Leah asked looking over at her.

"Lyson," she responded.

"I thought so. If you truly love him, take each moment as it comes."

Emilia smiled at her sister. "As I recall you didn't always think that way."

"Very true sister. And I was wrong."

The bond Emilia had with Leah was deep and strong, and she would be forever grateful for it. Her mood turned a bit melancholy. She couldn't bear to lose anymore sisters, faerie or human. She tried not to think of Abby, but Leah's bond with her made her think of the sister bond she shared with Abby.

Just then there was a flood of color that caused Emilia and Leah to jump to their feet. There standing before them was the goddess of the faeries in all her glory. The crown of flowers adorning her golden hair cast a glow about her whole body. Both Emilia and Leah ran to her open embrace, and for the moment, let the sweet release of tears to flow.

"It's alright my daughters, I have you in the palm of my hands always."

Emilia felt safe and protected in the arms of her goddess. She could feel the warmth of her presence spreading through her body. Stepping back, they looked into Braylynn's eyes and saw peace there.

"Are you truly here?" Emilia asked.

"Of course," Braylynn laughed. "Why wouldn't I be?"

"I imagine it's because no one has seen you in quite some time," Leah answered. "Tera has been beside herself with worry."

Braylynn looked thoughtful. "I will speak to Tera. There were reasons for my being away."

"Care to share?" Leah asked smiling.

"Not this time, daughter," Braylynn said winking. "I came to tell you everything is on a precipice as far as the outcome of your quest." She looked hard at Emilia. "Keep an eye on your brother. The hurt he has is only buried for the moment. Something will happen that will require all of your strength to get him through."

Braylynn cupped a hand to both of their cheeks. "Protect each other, my daughters, and know I am very proud of you."

With a bright flash, she vanished, Emilia still feeling the warmth of her hand upon her cheek.

Chapter 27

Andy and Caleb were walking through the talon woods in Laurel Hollow. After spending some time with his brothers, Andy felt a strong connection to each one of them. It was almost like he had always known them. Their footfalls were muffled as they walked the lush green paths of the woods. Caleb was filling him in on everything that had happened since the creation of dragons. Their history and their struggles, although a very much abridged version. Andy in turn told him of his life and the unexpected turn it took when he landed in Vasara.

"It makes me happy that it was one of us that brought Devon to ruin," Caleb had told him. "I only wish I had been there to help you rip his heart out," he said fiercely.

"Emilia and I were able to bring out the demon lord that was inside him," Andy said, "but it was Valencia who eventually killed him. Sacrificing herself in the process."

"It is amazing to think she was the Phoenix," Caleb said. "I knew her in one of her earlier incarnations," Caleb said a little sadly.

Andy looked over at his brother and sensed there was a tender wound there. Of course that immediately brought Abby to mind, not that she was ever out of his mind. He took two shuddering breaths. Caleb quickly grabbed his wrist.

"Steady brother, I'm right here with you."

Andy visibly relaxed.

"You knew what I was thinking?"

"We can usually feel one another's mental state. I'm just more sensitive to it than most, except for Daragh of course."

Suddenly a shadow passed overhead. Looking up they caught a flash of gold.

"It's Finn and Rhyan," Caleb said following his flight to the center of Laurel Hollow. "Let's go."

They didn't bother changing, but sprinted back to the hall. Two more figures went flying overhead. It was Emilia and Leah. They must have seen Finn fly over as well. Upon reaching the hall they saw a sizable crowd already gathered.

"Ah, there you are," Redlin said. "We were just about to send someone for you."

Looking around, Andy realized it was quite the little army that had assembled in the faerie kingdom. Tera seemed agitated for some reason as she flew from one person to the next demanding hugs. Andy wondered if she sensed what was about to come. How many of his friends might he lose to this battle. He couldn't think of that. His mind was still fragile and it wouldn't take much to push him back into madness. He closed his eyes and centered himself. Reaching slowly and deliberately he reached for the healing energy of the source in the same manner he had seen his brothers do when they were supporting him in Pan's grotto.

Redlin was talking to Rhyan when he calmed himself down.

"Was Samara able to help?" the wizard asked Rhyan.

Strangely, Andy noticed Finn standing close beside Rhyan, as if he were protecting her.

"Yes, though she was reluctant. You're not going to like where we have to go."

"Where?" Loki asked.

"She said seek them on the island of the shrikers," Rhyan said.

"You mean that thing that flew over us in Fenner?" Cleo asked.

"Yes," Redlin said grimly. "Looks like it won't be just warlocks to fight."

"But I thought you said they had to come through the corridor in the Border Lands to take physical form," Tori said sitting on a stump as she sharpened her swords with a whetstone.

"I believe these warlocks are making it possible for the demons to enter anywhere in Vasara at will. I'm sure they could do the same for a shriker," Redlin replied.

"Does anyone know where this island is?" Emma asked.

"I do," Redlin said. "But there is a problem."

"Oh great," Andy groaned. "What's the problem."

"The island they are on is Meliakken's. The five and Braylynn put a barrier around it to prevent anyone from venturing onto it and trying to claim its power. The shrikers and Meliakken can go there, or the gods of course."

"So who will solve this god riddle," Diminitus said angrily.

"Perhaps I can help," a voice behind Diminitus' ear said as he jumped up in the air in fright.

"Braylynn!" Diminitus said crankily. "Can't you announce yourself instead of just popping in and out of thin air like that.

"I do not believe you would have heard me regardless my old friend," the goddess said smiling.

"Did you have to say old?" Diminitus said crossing his arms.

"Dim, behave," Ala said kissing him on the cheek. "How can you help, Braylynn."

"Funny that you are the one to ask, Ala. Because the solution involves you, and others."

"Dim is right," Loki said. "Out with the god riddle, or goddess riddle in this case."

"There is someone here who has been hovering on the edge of it since the quest began," the goddess said.

"That's why!" Luel exclaimed.

Braylynn smiled. "Very good, daughter," she said proudly.

"What, Mom?" Emilia asked her mother.

"Remember back at Diminitus and Ala's house, how I thought it unusual that priests of the gods were relatively unknown, and yet we were traveling with two of them, Ala and Ava."

"I remember," Emilia said.

"This is why. It's the priests of the gods that will get us through."

"But you will need the priest of each god and goddess to be allowed to pass the barrier," Braylynn added.

"Well, looking around we have four priests of the God's," Redlin said.

"We do?" Ava asked.

"You and your sister for Aditya. Pan for Cael. Ala for Raphael, and though she told only me, Tori for Fallon."

"That just leaves Trystan and Braylynn," Dain said.

"My priestess has always been the Queen of the faeries," Braylynn said.

"But we have no Queen," Tera remarked. She had flown into Braylynn's arms some time ago and didn't seem to be leaving anytime soon.

"Yes we do," Luel said stepping forward.

Braylynn beamed at her, her pride in her daughter visible for all to see.

"Do you take up this mantle freely my daughter?" the goddess asked in all seriousness.

"I do, Mother," Luel responded.

Andy had a lump in his throat. He never thought of his mother as a queen, although in his eyes she was so much more. He must have been half asleep not to remember his mother's linage. In a strange way, he felt he was losing a part of himself. No longer would his mother's attention be solely on Emilia and himself. Although Emilia being a faerie, she would garner more than him since she was a part of the faerie kingdom. Andy suddenly felt ashamed of himself. There is no way she would treat him any less than she ever had. Even if she were empress of all Vasara, she would still be his mom first. He looked up and saw his mother looking at him. He wondered if she sensed what he was thinking. Suddenly she winked and smiled at him, and everything was alright again.

"There is one more thing," Braylynn said. "You must wear your father's crown as you sit the throne. Henceforth, all the queens of Laurel Hollow will wear it as the symbol of their power and authority."

Luel's eyes went wide and she started to shake. "Must it be so Mother? It took everything I had to put it on to help save the dragons, but I don't know if I have the strength to continue to wear it."

"You have the strength my daughter," a deep male voice said from behind Braylynn.

"By the gods!" Diminitus shouted. "If people don't stop popping out of mid-air I'm going to start having seizures!"

"Father?" Luel said hesitantly.

Andy saw his mother didn't immediately rush over to his grandfather, whom he couldn't believe was standing there. He knew it was him from the vision cast in the fire by his father back in New York when his mother told the tale of how she had fought and killed him. He could understand her hesitancy.

Eriyn smiled and held his arms open.

Upon seeing that, a sob escaped Luel's throat as she flung herself into her father's embrace. She closed her eyes and let the tears flow as she rested her head on Eriyn's shoulder. Andy saw his father had tears in his eyes upon seeing all the pain and anguish his mother bore for many years, finally swept away.

Luel lifted her head and stared into her father's eyes.

"How is it you are here?" she asked him.

"Trystan arranged it. But I can only stay mere moments. Already I can feel the pull that will bring me back."

"No, please. There is so much I want to ask and tell you."

Eriyn placed both hands on the sides of his daughter's face. "Not now my daughter. When your work in this world is finally complete, we will have all of eternity to talk. Your mother awaits you there as well. She told me to tell you it is time to lay your guilt down. Nothing was ever your fault."

Luel closed her eyes as fresh tears rolled down her cheeks, but they were good cleansing tears.

"I have one last task to perform. Redlin," Eriyn called.

Redlin walked over to the father of his wife. Eriyn embraced him and patted him soundly on the back. Andy saw tears also roll down his father's cheeks. What could he say, he was born into a very emotional family, and they never held back.

"I know we barely said two words to each other when I walked the land, but thank you for being the best life partner my daughter could ask for."

"She is my love and my life, sir."

"I know she is. And for that I am eternally grateful that you have one another."

Eriyn reached into his pocket and drew out a black ring. Holding it up to the light of the sun it looked as if a blue flame traveled through it. He took Redlin's right hand and placed the ring on his finger. The wizard's eyes suddenly went wide.

"I made that ring, shortly before I made the crown that my daughter now possesses. But I hadn't finished it at the time, which was strange since I never begin anything new until I finish what I am working on, and at the time I had no idea why I had set it aside. Now I do. Trystan and I finished it not that long ago. The blue flame you see traveling around the band is his power. He bade me tell you he wants you to have this to augment your power. For you are his friend as well as his priest."

Andy felt something shift, as if two puzzle pieces had locked into place with an audible click.

"Trystan also said the ring has many powers, but it will be up to you to discover them all. Oh, and he said, try not to kill yourself trying to figure it out."

Redlin burst out laughing. "He knows me so well," the wizard said.

"My time is up and I must leave. Will my grandchildren do me the greatest honor and give me a hug?"

Andy and Emilia didn't hesitate as they ran over to their only grandfather and embraced him tightly.

"Please know I love you both. And whatever blessings a grandfather can bestow, they are yours. If you ever make it back to Trystan's forge, I left something there for each of you."

Eriyn started to fade and Andy could feel his form getting less solid. "Farewell, grandfather," Andy said.

"We love you," Emilia added. They said this quietly and were certain that only Eriyn heard them.

There was silence for what seemed like the longest time. Nobody moved. Nobody wanted to dispel that wonderful energy that lingered in the hollow.

Andy wondered what his grandfather might have left him. He would leave that for another time. If he was not mistaken, the time had come to take that fatal step into battle. He looked around at everyone and never in his life had he seen such resolve. A sudden pang ripped through his heart. He would have given anything to have Abby meet his grandfather.

Chapter 28

Emilia sat on Andy's back as he winged his way across the ocean. They spent three days in Laurel Hollow. Her mother's coronation was unbelievable. Emilia had never seen the crowning of a queen except in a documentary back in New York. And never had she seen the crowning of a faerie queen by a goddess. Her mother had spent two of the three days locked up with Braylynn. Part of that time was to learn to control the inner sight of her grandfather's crown. Looking over at Brion, she could see her mother and father astride his back, the crown of the house of Caster firmly upon her head. Ten dragons beat a steady rhythm across the water, each with multiple riders. Lyson and Emma were on Andy's back with her. It seemed fitting somehow, to have Emma with her, since she and Tera were responsible for getting them all back to Vasara, and now she was here for the final battle. Emilia knew it would be final, because either the warlocks would be vanquished or they would. There would be no retreat. It was quite the assembly of faeries, dragons and humans with incredible powers she imagined.

Do we have a game plan? Emilia asked her brother speaking to his mind.

Not really, he responded. *I have the feeling we are going to be making a lot of this up as we go along.*

You two don't inspire very much confidence, Emma remarked. *Perhaps the mighty Redlin has some ideas.*

Also Emma, do not underestimate the battle prowess of the Border Lands warriors, and you have four of them with you, Lyson told her.

Emilia looked over at her father. Loki, Leah and Dain were close by on Caleb. *Well, let's hope between those three wizards over there that someone has an idea or two,* Emilia said. She looked to her left and saw Ava and Rhyan catching a ride with Finn. She had not tried linking with Finn since he came back with Rhyan. The compulsion to search his thoughts for Zana was too strong.

Lyson saw where she was looking.

"You are thinking about her again aren't you?" he asked her. She knew who he meant. They had talked about it many times.

"Yes."

Lyson was sitting behind Emilia and was able to speak directly into her ear.

"Donella, if she decides to show, she would be no match for all the power that is assembled here at this moment."

He turned her head around to look in her eyes. "You are not alone my love; you are never alone."

Emilia closed her eyes and rested her head on his chest as he held her. She felt like the luckiest faerie in Vasara to have such a man love her.

Suddenly the island came into view. Surrounding it was a cloud with a multi-colored hue.

Those are the color of the gods, Andy said.

Makes sense, since they put it there, Brion said a few wing strokes behind Andy.

Look to the left, Caleb remarked.

Emilia could see extending into the ocean a long wide jetty that seemed to be outside the cloud barrier.

Are you thinking what I'm thinking? She asked Andy.

Yep, like planes at an airport.

What exactly is that? Brion asked.

We will land one at a time, changing just before we hit the ground. The faeries can lift those that can't fly off our backs and lower them to the ground.

That's a workable plan, Caleb said.

Andy led the way. As they got close, Emilia grabbed Lyson under his armpits as her and Emma lifted off of Andy's back and alighted on the jetty. Andy came in low and just before making contact with the ground he changed, having to run a few steps to slow his momentum as his feet hit the rocks. One by one all the other dragons followed suit until everyone was on the ground.

"Ok," Redlin began, "Braylynn told me as long as we maintain physical contact with one another we should be able to pass through the barrier. Priests of the gods, and goddess, will go in front. Everyone else put a hand on someone's shoulder."

"What do we do once we are through?" Tera asked.

"Any ideas, Pan?" Redlin asked.

The king of the fauns looked towards the barrier. "If you are asking what I think my brothers might do master wizard, I haven't the slightest idea."

"None at all?" Loki said.

"Loki, I have not seen or communed with them for thousands of years. The last time I saw them was when Cael and I imprisoned them on that island the dragons were rescued from. I can tell you this by way of warning. For some of you, they spoke your name, which means they have marked you and gives them a slight power over you."

"What does that mean?" Andy asked.

"Just that they may be able to manipulate you in some fashion. Be wary of them."

"Can we just move along," Diminitus said. "Ocean spray is soaking me to the bone."

"You didn't really need to come old friend," Pan said laughing.

"Are you kidding? You think I would let Ala face something I wouldn't face myself."

"Oh Dim," Ala said kissing his cheek.

"Besides, you may need a necromancer," he said, his tone softened somewhat after Ala's display of affection.

Just then the shriek they heard in Fenner echoed over the island.

"Well I know at least one creature on this island is looking for a fight," Jace said.

Emilia looked over at the man who is silver in his dragon form. Jace had hair the same color as his dragon skin, and the same as Tera's, which did not necessarily follow with the other dragons and their hair color. In her training with him, Emilia knew he was a scrapper and loved a good fight. Brie was standing next to him. She insisted on coming along, and over the last several days, her and Jace had struck up a friendship.

"You boys are going to have your hands full with that shriker," Redlin said.

"Caleb, Herve and I will deal with him," Brion said. "The rest of you can deal with the warlocks.

"There is something I don't think we are calculating in our strategy here," Dain said.

"What is that?" Loki asked.

"Demons."

"Do you think there are any?" Andy asked.

"I do," Dain said soberly. "Even though I am a wizard now, my Border Lands instinct tells me they are there, or will be."

"I feel the same," Cleo said agreeing as she re-tied her hair in a ponytail.

"Whether they are there or not, there is only one path for us," Loki said. "We will deal with what comes, as they come."

"There is no point in trying to cover every possible scenario," Redlin said. "Let's move forward."

"By the gods!" Diminitus exclaimed. "I'm getting really tired of this."

Emilia looked over at what caused Diminitus to jump. Standing in the middle of the jetty just behind him was a woman in an ice-blue dress, with hair the color of dancing flames. It was the same woman Emilia saw in the tunnels of the Alfar, warning them to make haste, lest their quest fail.

"Despair will enter your hearts today," she said. "If it takes hold everything is in vain. Look for help unexpected."

"Why is it you always tell us that we are on the edge of failure?" Diminitus said grumpily.

The woman looked sternly at Diminitus. Emilia was concerned some form of ancient magic was about to be unleashed on the world's oldest living man. To everyone's surprise, the woman laughed.

"Thousands of years may go by, worlds will come and go, but one constant in all the universe is thy crankiness old friend. One day it will go up in flames."

There was an ear-splitting crack, and when everyone looked again she had vanished.

"Ha! I knew it!" Diminitus said.

"Knew what?" Ala asked him.

"I know who that was," he said. "I had a suspicion the first time we ran into her. Saying my crankiness would go up in flames has been said to me by only one being, the Phoenix."

"Are you saying that woman was Valencia?" Leah said.

"No. Valencia is gone," Diminitus said sadly. "The Phoenix is not any one person. In this incarnation I don't know what she is, or who."

"Andy and I have had the same suspicion when Leah first told us about her," Emilia said. "One thing I do know, her advice has not been wrong yet."

"I don't believe it is possible for her to lie to us," Tori said soberly. "If she says it, I believe her.

"I think it's time" Redlin said.

No other explanation was needed.

With the priests of the gods and goddess taking the lead, everyone else maintained physical contact as they pushed through the barrier. Emilia had her hand on her mother, who also was now her queen, but she would always be her mother first. Her whole body electrified as they passed through, but the feeling was not unbearable. Once everyone was on the other side, it became eerily quiet. The only sound were sea birds circling overhead and the sound of the surf hitting the shore. The barrier didn't seem to pose a problem for the birds as they passed in and out of it.

"Do you think we should slip into Tori's frozen moment?" Leah asked. "It would allow us freedom of movement."

"I don't think that would be a good idea just now, without knowing where everyone is," Loki replied. "They could be in a dimension of their own, and we would wander aimlessly."

"Any idea where the shriker thing went?" Tera asked.

"No," Brion said, "and that bothers me."

Emilia suddenly felt the ring on her finger start to pulse, it's dark red stone giving off an eerie illumination. The air was charged, and she could feel the raw energy building all around them.

"Brace yourself!" Dain shouted. "Something is about to happen."

***

Without warning, four portals opened up, one in front and back and one on either side. Demons in the hundreds poured out. Andy quickly assessed their situation and the odds against them.

"Shields!" Andy shouted.

All ten dragons plunged themselves into the source and created a shield of energy around the entire company. The demons swarmed it like bees in a hive, covering them.

"Would now be a good time to enter that frozen moment, Tori?" Diminitus asked. "I currently don't like our odds."

"It's too late," Tori replied.

"Why?" Emma asked.

The shield was so thick with demons that the sun was no longer visible, plunging them into darkness. Redlin created a sphere of light that floated over their heads.

"Because," Tori began, "they have in effect created a shell around us. In that space where nothing moves, we would not be able to push past them. We might as well try and move the moon."

"We could try and blast our way out," Caleb said.

"I think first we need to figure out how to close those portals," Andy remarked. "Mom, are you okay?"

"Luel?" Redlin said concerned.

Andy was looking at his mother when her face seemed to go blank, as if she were suddenly someplace else. Slowly her eyes started to come into focus as she turned her gaze towards Andy.

"I don't know how he did it," Luel said, "but my father just pulled me out of my body and took me to a totally different place."

She caressed her husband's stubbled cheek. "I know how to close the portals."

***

Luel was looking around trying to find an answer to the predicament they were currently in. The demons were in a frenzy now and there was no telling how many were pouring through the portal every second it was open. Suddenly she felt a tugging deep in her body. Then it felt like her spirit was separating from her physical form as she was pulled upward. Looking down she could see herself standing next to Redlin as Andy and his brothers kept the focus on the shield they had erected around them. Still, she kept going up until all around her the scene changed. She was racing through the stars, faster than light. Coming into view was an island that seemed to be floating all by itself in the universe. As she touched down, the brightness of the stars made it look like mid-day. There was a quiet little stream coming out of the woods when she heard her father's voice calling her. Stepping out of the woods he came into view and she ran towards him and his welcoming embrace.

"Father, how is this possible?"

"You wear the crown, with our family's jewel affixed to it. It is that which makes this possible, as well as the permission of the gods. It can only be done when need is great. And I would say the predicament you are in now is great indeed," Eriyn told her.

"What must I do?" Luel asked. She knew her time was probably short and wanted to get right to the point.

"In my madness, the demons wanted me to make this crown in order to create the portals they are now using. I did that, but I also put a part of myself into it. I think some clarity came through as I was forging it and I put the ability to close the portals in a particular place without the ability to reopen."

He looked seriously at his daughter, thinking as she, that their time was short.

"The warlocks have figured out another way to open the portals. You will need to destroy whatever it is they are using. Once you close the portals on the island however, they won't be able to open anymore there."

"Show me," Luel said urgently. She could feel the pull back to her body starting.

***

"What do you mean?" Redlin asked her. "How?"

"I will explain later," Luel said.

Closing her eyes, she made the symbol of the sun with her hands. Focusing as her father showed her, the jewel on her crown started to blaze. With the inner sight she was able to see the four portals. The edges were ragged as her father said, because the time and space fabric had been ripped open. She began by smoothing the edges.

"Think of steel," Eriyn had explained. "Make a ring and draw it close."

Luel thought of a ring her father had made for her mother. It was flawless. Fixing that image in her mind she started to draw the portals closed. She could see the demons still frantically trying to pour through as the opening got smaller and smaller. Many demons were destroyed as the holes closed shut on them. She could now feel the warlocks using whatever power they had to open them again. She now put her father's final touch on it. To seal the portals, her father had told her to affix the image of the symbol of their house in the very center. Luel did that. Placing a gold image of the house of Caster, upraised palms under a sphere, she sealed the portals. Opening her eyes, the ground started spinning as if rising up to meet her face.

Redlin grabbed his wife before she fell face first on the ground.

"Mom!" Andy yelled as he rushed over. Letting his part of the shield drop.

334

"Andros!" Brion said. "They are getting through."

Fifty or so hulking demons dropped through the hole where Andy's part of the shield had been. To his credit he quickly grabbed the source again and patched the hole. Rhyan and Ava had their bows singing, dispatching as many demons as they could. Tori's and Cleo's blades were out, cutting down any monster dumb enough to come in range of their weapons. No magic was used giving the close contact of everyone under the shield. Some of the demons were fliers, and every faerie in the company was in the air, their spears making short work of them.

Redlin had gently lowered Luel to the grass. "Emilia, quickly!"

Emilia flew over to where her mother lay after the last demon had been vaporized. Taking the staff of the goddess, she slowly passed it over her mother's body, the healing energy restoring the queen of the faeries. Luel started to stir, Redlin helping her to sit up.

"Are you alright?" her husband asked, concern written all over his face.

"I'm fine, dear. Thanks to our daughter," she said pressing a hand to Emilia's cheek. "The portals are closed now. They cannot be re-opened."

"Someday you will have to show us how you did that," Loki said astonished.

Luel just winked at him.

"It's all well and good that Luel has closed the portals," Diminitus said, "but we still have this little problem at hand of several thousand demons or so preventing us from lowering our own shield."

No one said anything for several moments. Luel thought it a puzzle near impossible to solve without personal loss of those here.

Suddenly there was a loud roar from the demon hoard.

Then like water washing mud off of glass, the demons jumped off the shield to meet some unseen threat.

"What the…?" Diminitus began.

"Wait, listen," Dain said silencing him. "Can it be?"

Luel turned a pointed ear and started picking up what sounded like hoof beats thundering over the ground.

"It is," Dain said pointing.

Luel followed the direction he was pointing, astonished at what she saw.

"The unicorns!" Tera said excitedly. "The unicorns! The unicorns!"

"How is that possible?" Andy said to his father.

"I have no idea," the wizard responded.

Chapter 29

Where to now?" Cathal said to Brayton.

They had crossed the Palatine bridge and were standing next to Savano and Tilmin. The city had been cleansed of demons, and all the soldiers had returned to normal. One thing that bothered him most was where his parents might be. The image in the orb above the crypt's door had troubled him. Did that man take his parents, he wondered? He didn't even know where to start looking.

"Perhaps I can help you with that?" a voice from behind spoke, startling the small company.

"What? Who are you?" Cathal said drawing his sword.

Brayton looked long at this woman in an ice-blue dress, with hair the color of autumn. Something about her seemed familiar and yet not.

"Cath, put your sword away. I don't think we need to fear her. What might your name be madam?" Brayton asked her.

I'm not so sure I trust her, Savano said to Brayton.

There is no false in me, queen of the unicorns.

"You could hear that?" Brayton asked astonished.

"No time," the woman said. "You must make haste, or your friends are lost. All will be lost."

"What are you talking about?" Cathal said hotly. "Haste where? Sire, I don't think we need to listen to this. Your parents are out there; we need to find them."

"Your parents are safe, Summus Re'em. Your friends

337

however are not. On an island where the final battle has already begun."

"And how are we supposed to get there in time?" Cathal asked.

The woman looked at Savano. "You must invoke dodhéanta."

Savano just stared at her, not saying a word as the breeze gently blew against her mane.

No, you cannot do this! Tilmin said.

"What is dodhéanta?" Cathal asked.

In essence, it would be the death of the unicorns, Tilmin answered.

That is never certain, Tilmin, Savano said.

"What exactly is it? Brayton asked.

The grove of the unicorns moves at its own will, and never in the same place twice, Savano said. *It is what protects us and keeps anyone wishing us harm to readily find us.*

Dodhéanta changes all of that, Tilmin added.

"How so? Cathal asked.

As queen, I can invoke dodhéanta once in my lifetime. It overrides the will of the grove and places it in a place of my choosing. Savano looked long at Brayton. *But there is a cost. It will remain in that spot for a thousand years.*

A thousand years! A thousand years of vulnerability, Tilmin said.

There is something else, Savano said for Brayton alone. *Not even Tilmin knows. At the end of the thousand years, my life will end.*

No! Brayton said to her horrified. *We will find another way.*

The woman looked at them both knowingly Brayton thought. As if she had heard their mind speak.

"What is your decision, unicorn queen?" the woman asked.

Everyone looked at Savano.

The Summus Re'em must decide, Savano said after some thought.

"Me? Why me?" Brayton asked shocked.

This is your final test. If you are truly to be the master of unicorns, the choice must be yours.

Brayton closed his eye and quickly journeyed to that place where Caomhnoir the guardian dwelt. During his trial to become the Summus Re'em, Caomhnoir had told him he could journey back here for respite or questions. He found himself back by the stream.

"Caomhnoir," he called out.

Back so soon, Caomhnoir said stepping out from under the woods. *I see you have already had some sacrifices,* he said noticing Brayton's missing eye.

"I need your wisdom. I have a question."

Ask your question, the guardian said as he polished his rainbow horn on his flanks.

"How can I bypass the rules of dodhéanta?"

Caomhnoir lifted his head quickly at the word and the muscles in his flanks started to flex and ripple with tension.

So, it has come to that. I assume the queen told you of the price to be paid.

"She has."

This is an easy question to answer Summus Re'em. You cannot get around it. It is our oldest magic. The only one who might be able to offer an alternative is Cael. To contact him, you will need to find his priest.

"Who might that be?"

That is hidden from me. What is not hidden is that your time here is up. You must go back now, and for good or ill, make your choice.

Brayton opened his eye.

"Have you decided, Summus Re'em?" The woman asked.

Brayton turned and looked at Savano as a tear slid down his cheek and he spoke his choice.

***

Andy waited until the last of the demons had slid off their shield to meet the threat. The shield dropped and the melee began.

"Em! Take me up!" Andy shouted.

Emilia knew what he meant as she flew over and grabbed him under his arms. Her wings beat strong as she ascended high into the air. Several demons spotted them and started the chase.

"Are you ready?" she asked.

"Now!" Andy said. Emilia let go and Andy began his free fall. Turning everything inward he made the change. Two huge black wings banked to the left as Andy's talons ripped apart several of the demons in his path. Emilia descended on his back and took her comb out to transform it into her staff. Lightning strikes emanated from the pearl sphere to blast into nothingness the remaining monsters on their tail.

Andy looked below and could see the battlefield quite well. He had never seen so many demons in one place, but sweeping through them was a white tide of unicorns, trampling and impaling everything in their path. But he knew they would need help. Looking to his left he could see Brion, Caleb and Herve following his lead as Leah, Brie and Emma flew them to a height to begin their fall. Once they made their change, he could feel Emilia linking with each of them. The rest of his brothers remained on the ground, using the source to wreak havoc on the earth bound demons.

You ready Em? Andy asked his sister.

Yes. Let's do this, she replied. *Herve is coming up. I'll be back shortly, be ready.*

Andy watched as she leapt off his back to land on the silver back of Herve. Andy had learned that when it came to speed and maneuverability, Herve was the best. The turns and banks he made with his wings seemed to defy physics for a beast his size. He and Emilia were in an aerial acrobatic dance as they engaged demon after demon. Herve was like a jet ski cutting the water as he weaved in and out. Sensing Emilia's pull, Andy drove straight down, flames spewing from his mouth as he opened a path for his sister who was streaking like a comet. She hit his back so hard when she landed, that Andy winced at the impact.

Damn, sis! Did you have to hit that hard?

Andros, a familiar voice called to Andy's mind.

Andy's flight faltered and his path skewed to the right.

What are you doing? Emilia asked incredulously.

Abby? Where are you? Andy said. He knew it was her voice.

Andros, why did you let me die? Why did you not protect me? I thought you loved me.

Andy's mind started to scream at him. But he couldn't hear it. He couldn't hear anything except the accusation of the woman he loved.

Abby, I'm sorry, so sorry.

He could feel himself starting to lose control

You lied to me. You betrayed me.

The overwhelming guilt started to bury Andy.

"Come see what you did Andros."

Andy looked to where he now heard the voice coming from. Above him and to his left standing on a cliff face was his beloved. Looking exactly as she did the first moment he saw her.

Abby!

He started to fly towards her. With his dragon sight he was able to see the accusations in her eyes. His mind continued to scream and send out warning bells. Andy was numb to it all. Just before he reached her, she suddenly burst into flames.

No! No! gods, please no! Abby!

He watched as his beloved turned to ash. His mind was on the abyss as he turned and started to fly back towards the barrier. Someone was screaming his name, but he could not hear them.

***

Brion watched in horror as Andros' beloved burst into flames. It immediately brought back his own pain since it was fresh in his mind. He knew it was an illusion. The logical part of his mind took over, allowing him to separate from the pain. He watched as his brother started to wing his way from the battle. He also felt Donella's link drop.

Andros! Stop! It's not Abby!

Suddenly an ear shattering screech echoed off the cliffs.

Brion! We got company, Caleb exclaimed.

A grey shadow flew past him, sending him spinning out of control. After righting himself before crashing against the rocks on the shore, he sped in the direction of the shriker. Brion was able to get a good look at him. It was definitely dragon like. Its neck was shorter and body thinner, and the horns on its head were like a ram but spiked at the end and jutting straight out. Plus, he had two sets of wings, all in a ghostly grey color, making it hard to see at times. Brion imagined it could probably maneuver extremely well. He watched in horror as liquid fire spewed from its mouth, setting unicorns and demons a flame.

Herve, try and draw it away, Brion said.

If anyone had a chance of out flying that thing it was Herve.

Bull, any ideas? Brion asked as he flew close to his brother.

Nothing is coming to me. Unless…By the gods! Where did he go? Caleb exclaimed.

Herve, stay alert, Brion said. *That thing just up and disappeared.*

342

Brion saw Herve banking left then right so as not to be an easy target. Then out of nowhere, it appeared right in front of Herve, its talons reaching out. Herve dove down, but not before the shriker's claw ripped through his wing. Herve spewed fire as he roared in pain. He started to spiral out of control, the ground coming up dangerously fast.

Herve, change back now, I'm coming, Brion said. *Bull, keep that thing occupied.*

With claws extended as he flew, Caleb shot lightning strikes at the shriker, scoring several direct hits as Brion began his suicide dive, trying to get to Herve before his body was dashed against the rocks. Brion saw Herve return to his human form, which slowed his descent considerably as he stretched out his arms and legs. His back was a mass of blood.

Brion was able to get underneath him, Herve landing heavily on his back. Skimming just above the heads of the unicorns and demons, Brion started to rise again. He spotted a faerie he recognized.

Brie! I need your help.

"What happened?" she said seeing Herve unconscious on Brion's back.

No time to explain. Get him to safety and tell Jace we need him.

"I will," she said lifting Herve from under his arms as she flew him to the ground.

Brion banked hard to the left, several spears from ground level demons bouncing off his scaly hide. Jace was already winging towards him.

We need to help Caleb with that thing, he told him.

What happened to Andros and the Summoner? Jace asked. *We need them.*

Brion was thinking the same thing, but they both had disappeared over a mountain to the east. Whether they would make it back in time was anybody's guess. Brion started to feel the edges of despair.

***

Emilia flew as hard as she could. She could see Andy ahead of her, disappearing over the tallest mountain on the island.

Andy! Stop!

Whether he heard her or chose to ignore her, Emilia couldn't tell. In either case he wasn't turning around. The image he saw shattered his mind and his madness was returning. She could feel despair trying to creep up on her. The words of the phoenix came back to her. That if they let despair take hold, all would be lost. She closed her eyes and hovered for a moment as the battle raged around her. Finding her center, she found her resolve. She knew what she had to do. She didn't like it, and she hoped Andy would forgive her.

Andros, she called. The dragon eye in her crown was blazing. A field of energy surrounded her, keeping any demons trying to attack at bay. She could feel Andy's reluctant thought drifting back to her.

Andros, you will come back.

Now she could hear him quite plainly.

You promised you would never do this! Em, let me go! he snarled.

No, you need to come back now.

Emilia could see him reappear over the mountain. His anger and hurt were raw as she supplanted his will with hers. What came down the link was an inferno of rage. Andy opened his mouth. Emilia erected a quick shield. In his current state she didn't know if he would actually rain fire down on her. But then suddenly the rage was gone, and in its place she felt hopelessness. Andy suddenly changed back to his human form and fell like a rag doll. Emilia lost no time and flew like a comet to get underneath him, catching him just in time.

Dad, I need help! Emilia sent reaching out to her father.

When she touched the ground and laid Andy down, Redlin and Loki were suddenly there.

"How did you do that? She asked.

"Another time, what happened?"

Emilia quickly summarized all that took place. Looking at her father she noticed he had a cut across his brow as well as black smudges on his cheeks as if he had been near an explosion.

"Is there anything you can do? His madness has come back."

"Battle is not really the best place to experiment with this ring Trystan gave me, but there has been very little choice in the matter. It's already proved very valuable. Let's hope so again. Loki, erect a shield around us."

"You got it brother." Loki spread his hands wide and formed a dome that settled over their little group.

Emilia watched as her father placed the hand with the ring of the god on Andy's forehead. Redlin's features started to change. His eyes went wide and wild, his breathing becoming very rapid and labored. Andy started screaming and thrashing. Emilia sat on his legs as her father straddled his chest, pinning his arms, never once losing contact with Andy's forehead. Redlin gave an earth shattering shriek. Suddenly Emilia and her father were thrown back by an incredible force.

When they picked themselves up they rushed backed to Andy. He was sitting up. He was shaken but his eyes were clear.

"Oh Dad," he sobbed as Redlin pulled his son up and crushed him to himself.

After his grief had run for the few moments the battle provided, Andy looked into the eyes of his father.

"I saw what you did," Andy said, "and what you took onto yourself."

"It was the only way to reach you," Redlin replied.

"I know now that wasn't Abby." For a moment Andy looked grief stricken, but Emilia saw no despair in his eyes. "Abby is dead, and she is never coming back. I need to find acceptance for that somehow, someday."

The way he said that made Emilia's heart clench. Then she saw resolve written all over Andy's features.

"For now, there is some demon ass to start kicking," Andy said grimly.

"Yes!" Loki shouted.

"First, we need to deal with that shriker," Emilia said. "Your brothers need help. It seems that thing can disappear at will."

"Any ideas?" Andy asked her.

"I have one."

"Be careful," Redlin told his children, hugging them both.

"Don't get yourself killed laddie," Loki said, "or you, lass. Your mother will kill me otherwise."

"We will try not to," Andy said as he set off running for space, blasting demons with fire bolts to clear a path as he made the change.

Emilia flew up and landed on Andy's back as he passed underneath. She sat crossed-legged and closed her eyes, focusing while she established her link with the dragons once more. Her body felt like it was growing larger with each dragon she connected with. Quickly, they caught up to Brion who was scanning the sky for the elusive shriker.

Welcome back Summoner, Brion said. *You too Andros.*

I'm sorry I let you down, Andy said.

The warlocks deceived you. Had it been my beloved, I don't think I would have fared any better.

Thank you brother.

Hey, you guys going to help us out here, Caleb said.

They looked down and to their right as they saw Caleb and Jace engaging the shriker with fire and ice. The shriker had magic of its own as metal shards shot out of its claws, racing towards the two dragons. Jace and Caleb split and dove barely missing the incoming missiles. The shriker then promptly disappeared.

Damn! Brion said. *How do we defend against that?*

Em, whatever your idea is, I think now is the time to try it, Andy said.

Might we know what you are going to do, Summoner, Brion said.

I'm going to release Chaos, Emilia said.

Who? Andy asked.

It's what I call my dragon, Emilia said a little sheepishly. *I had to call him something,* she said at their silence.

I'll call him anything you want, Em, if he can lend us a hand with this thing.

That is a most fitting name, Brion said knowingly.

Emilia felt Brion would know, given that Chaos had penetrated his very being. She closed her eyes and made the symbol of the sun with her hands, the red dragon tattoo on her leg blazing in sharp contrast to Andy's black hide. As in the cave when she was freeing the dragons, Chaos was separating from her, once again making Emilia feel as if she were being ripped in two. Then he was there. Flying next to them, his red form phasing in and out of reality, giving him a ghostly appearance. Emilia sent her need to him.

Can you do it? Emilia asked him. He nodded once as he peeled off and flew straight down.

What exactly is he doing? Andy asked as he followed the flight of the red dragon.

You notice how he is both here and not here, Emilia said. *It's because he can move between this world and another, giving him the ability to see things we can't. He's going to mimic the flight of the shriker, because Chaos can follow him. Follow his flight path and you will be right on top of the shriker when he appears.*

Brilliant! Brion exclaimed. *Bull, follow that dragon!*

Already on it, Caleb replied.

Emilia watched as Caleb followed Chaos' path. Suddenly, Chaos did a half loop and turned, heading in a straight line for Andy and herself. Which meant only one thing, the shriker was going to collide with them, and it was too late to move out of its path.

Then, out of nowhere, a red beam of energy struck the air in front of them. An ear splitting shriek penetrated their heads as they felt the beat of a wing brush inches past them. Another energy bolt followed by lightning, wrapped itself around the now visible shriker. It was writhing in agony as it tried to break free.

Hit it now, everyone at once! Andy said.

Brion and Caleb hit it with fire, while Andy and Jace sent energy bolts from either side. Emilia, leveling her staff and aiming at the shriker's gaping mouth, shot liquid white energy down its throat. The thing started to expand, fire pouring out of its eyes and mouth. Unable to contain the power of everything hitting it, the beast exploded, spraying gore and body parts everywhere.

Everyone stared in disbelief. They had destroyed it.

Who hit it with that first assault? Jace asked.

Emilia looked in the direction the lifesaving strikes came from. Her body went cold as she saw the familiar figure standing on the rock jutting out from the cliff face.

Is that who I think it is? Andy said his wings steadily beating to hold him in a hovering position.

Yes, Emilia said not looking away. *It's Zana.*

Emilia jumped off Andy's back and flew up to where Zana was standing. Zana wore her typical black, a gold band, almost like a crown adorned her head. A black raven perched on her shoulder. It must be one of Devon's ravens that had flown south during the battle for the White Castle, Emilia thought. She also held a staff of black ash, with an orb the color of black obsidian on its top. Zana had certainly grown in power, which Emilia found very troubling. As they stood facing one another, a jumble of emotions was running through Emilia's mind and body; fear, sorrow, anger, hatred and even pity. The dragons flew closer and hovered in a semi-circle around Emilia.

You have nothing to fear from me, Andros the black, Zana said contemptuously. *Today anyway.*

"Why are you here, Zana," Emilia said mastering her conflicting emotions.

"What's the matter, Donella?" she sneered. "To proud to appreciate a little help?"

"I'm sure your help is due to no love of me, or anyone here."

"In that you are correct," Zana said seriously. "I almost didn't come."

"You have been watching us? How?"

"Wouldn't you like to know. Don't waste your breath on it, I won't tell you. The only reason I am here is to repay a debt. You spared my life and saved me from Devon. Now we are even. Plus, no one gets to kill you but me," Zana said coldly. "And in that interest, that which you seek is in the center of this island." She paused as she looked at the dragons surrounding her. "You spared my life, but you destroyed my world. I will repay that debt as well. Farewell Summoner," She said as she turned to fly away.

"Zana!"

Everyone turned towards the battle floor. Standing on a boulder, a shield visibly around him stood Finn. He was using the source to make himself heard. Emilia watched Zana's features as regret and anguish fleetingly played across them. Her mouth drew down into a grim line as she leapt into the air and flew over the mountains. Emilia looked down at Finn and saw his head drop in resignation. She knew without a doubt that Finn had once loved Zana. Her heart went out to him. The pain and suffering he was feeling must be unimaginable knowing what she has become.

Chapter 30

The battle of demons seemed to be winding down. Tori was everywhere, dealing death with each sword strike, Cleo and Leah fighting right by her side. The unicorns had turned the tide. If it were not for them there is no way they would have been able to handle the sheer number of demons. Demons do not leave any bodies behind when they are killed, so all those lying dead were their own comrades, the unicorns. Tori felt broken up inside that the unicorns had borne the casualties of this fight. But their task was done. Now there were ten warlocks to deal with. Tori had taken on three, and even that required the help of a god to achieve. She knew they would be ready for her tactics this time and would have come up with some form of countermeasure.

"What are you thinking?" Cleo asked her, walking up as she sheathed her sword.

"You know me Boss," Tori replied. "The next step."

"Yeah, me too." Cleo couldn't help looking over at Tori and smiling. "You still insist on calling me Boss."

Tori couldn't help smiling back. "You are always the boss, and I always rely on your leadership skills, no matter what I've become. That will never change."

Cleo hooked an arm around her neck and drew her in for a quick hug. Tori knew the bond between them would never break, and it would never change.

"Look, Brayton is coming," Cleo said.

Tori watched as Brayton riding Savano and Cathal on Tilmin came galloping towards them, accompanied by two unicorns.

"You saved our lives," Tori said as they reached them.

Your lives were the paramount goal in this quest, Savano said. *But now we are also fighting for our home.*

"What does that mean?" Tori asked.

Brayton dismounted from Savano's back and told them of how they were able to get to the island as well as the cost of that path.

So if we are bound here for the next thousand years, you need to clean out these irksome warlocks, Tilmin added.

"That's the game plan," Cleo said.

"We bring word from Dain," Brayton said pointing. "There is a small council of war happening over by those huge cluster of boulders."

Tori noted it was no small distance.

"These unicorns have consented to bear you on their backs to take you there," Cathal added. "The rest of the unicorns will handle the cleanup of the remaining demons."

"Well, there is no point in waiting," Cleo said mounting a unicorn.

Tori followed suit. Being on a unicorn was a far different experience than being on a horse. She would not even think of directing this unicorn on where he should go. He consented to let her ride, and ride was all she planned to do. It wasn't long before they reached the others in a clearing surrounded by the huge rocks. The ground was grassy, green and lush. If this island had to be the home of the unicorns, it wasn't such a bad place to live in regards to the beauty of the landscape.

"Ah, Cleo, Tori, there you are," Redlin said. "We are ready to begin."

Tori dismounted and walked into the circle and sat down next to Andy.

"What's the plan master wizard," Cleo asked sitting next to Tori.

"It's time to end this," Redlin said.

"I'm in!" Caleb agreed. "This is payback time for fifteen hundred years of imprisonment."

All the other dragons muttered their agreements to that sentiment.

"I would say they are pretty pissed," Andy whispered to Tori.

Tori chuckled quietly. "Sometimes the things you say Andros, makes no sense at all."

"Does anyone know where we are going?" Diminitus asked.

"Inland," Emilia answered. "To the very center of the island."

Emilia explained to them everything Zana had told them. Tori watched as Lyson stood protectively near his beloved. The encounter with Zana had him slightly furious, especially since he was not there when it happened.

"I guess this means we are going dragon riding again, Boss," Tori said.

Cleo nodded in acknowledgement.

The flight was not a long one, a couple of hours at most. Upon reaching the island's center, they came upon what looked to Tori like an ancient stone keep. As they circled above, in the very center was something resembling a temple, all in black stone with blood-red wooden doors.

As before, the faeries lifted everyone off of the dragons backs and onto the ground as the dragons made their change. The unicorns would not be coming to this fight, although Tori secretly wished at least some would cross the terrain and journey here, but Brayton wouldn't hear of it.

"They have sacrificed enough," he had said. Although he and Cathal did make the trip on the back of one of the dragons.

"I think we need Tori for this next part, brother," Loki said once everyone had assembled near the front gate.

"What did you have in mind?" Redlin asked, raking his fingers through his thick mane of dark hair.

"Kind of wondering that myself," Tori said raising an eyebrow at the old man.

"I think now is the time for you to go into your frozen moment and see what awaits us."

"You can't be serious!" Cleo exploded. "There is no telling what she will encounter in there."

"This is our best hope, our best advantage," Loki explained. "I don't want you to engage anyone, just see if you can discern what they are planning and come back."

"I don't like this at all," Cleo said.

Tori had been rubbing her chin as if pondering.

"I think it will be alright, Boss," Tori said.

Cleo looked at her and realized her mind was made up. "Then I am coming with you, and that is not up for discussion."

Tori smiled at her friend. "Okay."

"Mind if I come too," Andy said.

"Alright, but no more. If anyone gets lost in there you could wander around until you die."

"No problem with that," Diminitus said. "I'm fine right here."

Tori had to laugh at that.

"Andros, before you go," Pan said putting his hands on his shoulders. "One of my brother's called you by name. That gives at least one of them some measure of power over you."

Andy looked grim faced at the king of the fauns. "I think he already used that power on me," he replied. Everyone knew he meant the illusion of Abby. "I won't let them pull me in again."

"Let's go then," Tori said.

"Wait!" Luel said.

"What is it Mom?" Andy asked startled.

"That building you are thinking of entering has no windows, and the doors are closed."

"I don't know where my head is at," Tori said smacking herself. "Of course we can't open the doors in the frozen moment."

"So much for our element of surprise," Dain said.

"There is a way," Luel said as she pondered the problem. "I must open the door."

"Why you?" Redlin asked his wife with some amount of concern.

"Because dear, I am the only one that can render themselves almost invisible by changing my skin color to match my surroundings." She looked long at the door before speaking again. "And also, I am the only one with the knowledge to open it."

"What do you mean, Mom?" Emilia asked.

"Can you see the markings on the door?"

They all looked, squinting to try and see what she saw.

"Looks like some kind of designs," Brayton said.

"Are those designs...?" Emilia started.

"Yes, those are your grandfather's designs, or rather of the house of Caster."

Tori was watching Luel closely, and before anyone could say anything, she vanished.

"Where did she go?" Brion exclaimed.

Everyone was looking all around for the newly crowned faerie queen.

"She went to open the door," Redlin said.

"I can't see anyone heading for the door," Caleb said.

"That's the point," Redlin said with a small hint of pride for his wife.

After some moments they could see the doors open and the silhouette of a faerie barely visible.

"Let's go," Tori said opening the rip in the fabric of reality.

Tori led the way as Cleo and Andy placed a hand on her shoulder. She was still amazed at the vibrancy of color when they passed over into that other place.

"By the gods!" Cleo exclaimed.

"You took the words right out of my mouth," Andy agreed.

As before, everything was frozen. Tori looked over at Diminitus. He had this frozen startled expression on his face. Probably from the moment they stepped through the rip.

"This is unbelievable," Andy said walking up to his father, tapping him lightly on the forehead.

"He probably can't feel it," Cleo said, "but I don't think we want to chance that do we?"

Andy looked over at her. "You are probably right."

They came to the doors Luel had opened. Even in this altered state, it was still hard to see her.

"This is so freaky," Andy said.

They continued into the building. A long hallway stretched before them with some kind of sconces that had glass milky white spheres on top that illuminated the place. Many doors opened off the main hallway.

"How are we supposed to know what is behind these doors?" Andy asked.

"We don't," Tori said. "We can only observe wherever we can get to."

"This place is very limited," Andy said.

They were halfway down the hall when they noticed a very ornate door. Tori examined it closely. It appeared to be made out of solid gold. On its face was an emblem. A circle of shrikers, connected snout to tail around an embossed letter M.

"Are you thinking what I am thinking?" Cleo said.

"Yes," Andy answered. "I think when we come out of this

frozen moment, we make it a point not to open that door."

"We don't really know if that door leads to Meliakken's prison, or the source of his power for that matter," Tori said. "It could be a weapon to help defeat him and his shrikers."

"Too many puzzles here," Andy said. "I hate puzzles."

"Let's keep going," Tori said. "There is an opening at the end of this hall."

They eventually came to an arched entryway. Peering in, it was a large circular room that had darkened alcoves along the wall. In the center was an altar with three of the warlocks, frozen like statues in the act of performing some ritual. One had a raised knife, and another a bowl, while the third seemed to be holding a brazier with something burning, like incense. They walked closer to the altar and then everyone froze when they saw what lay upon it.

"It's a faun!" Cleo exclaimed. "Monstrous!"

"We need to get back," Andy said urgently. "Whatever they are doing is aimed right at Pan."

Tori agreed. "As soon as we step back into real-time, that knife will fall. We will barely have time to take action. Any ideas?"

Everyone was silent, trying to think of what to do.

"We either have to try and shield him from whatever spell they are conjuring, or isolate him after he is hit," Cleo said.

"There might not be any shield that will protect him here," Andy said.

"Then maybe we need to send him somewhere else." Tori said scratching her chin as she pondered. "We need your father."

"If we had time, he probably could lend some insight," Andy said, "but we only have seconds once we step through."

"I have a plan," Tori said. "Let's go."

They turned and started to head back the way they had come when they froze in their tracks. Blocking their way with swords drawn were two warlocks, blades swinging back and forth menacingly. Their hoods were thrown back. Tori still thought it uncanny how much they resembled the king of the fauns, minus the horns of course.

"How are they here?" Cleo said stunned, "and how are they moving?"

"They must be drawing on the power of a god," Tori said drawing both her swords. Cleo followed suit.

"What the...?" Andy began.

"What's the matter?" Cleo said.

"I can't use the source. I can feel it, and I can use it internally, but I can't direct anything outward. It has to be this place. I'm sorry, but I can't help you. Why didn't I bring a damn sword?" Andy said frustratingly.

"Can you protect yourself?" Tori asked.

"Yes. I can create a shield for myself, but that's it."

"Okay," Tori said. "Don't get separated from me. Ready, Boss?"

"Yes," Cleo responded. "You come from the left, I'll go right."

Tori and Cleo split the warlocks, steel on steel echoing in the chamber, and even though they were considered the best with the sword in the Border Lands, the warlocks were matching them stroke for stroke. Andy walked in between them, moving towards the other side of the entryway, closer to the exit. Tori never lost eye contact with her opponent. His eyes had an orange-golden ring around them, letting her know that a demon resided in this man.

"We are not getting anywhere, Boss," Tori said. "We need to get out of here."

"I have an idea," Andy said. "Cleo, you help Tori after I engage your guy."

Andy stepped in front of Cleo just as the sword was descending. The warlock looked stunned as his sword ricocheted off Andy's shield and nearly took his leg off. The other warlock now having to fend off two attackers was completely overwhelmed and fled back towards the altar. Cleo and Tori, turned to help Andy, but it was unnecessary as his foe was limping after his comrade.

"Let's go!" Tori said.

The three of them raced down the hall and out the door past Luel. After exiting the main gate, they stood in front of Redlin.

"Okay," Cleo said. "What's your plan?"

"I plan on opening a rip, pulling Redlin in and closing it again."

"Will there be enough time to do that before the blade falls?" Andy asked.

"With my enhanced speed, I believe I can. You two watch behind us in case those guys get any bright ideas," she said inclining her head back towards the warlocks.

Tori stepped a few feet back from Redlin. She didn't want to open the rip to close. Closing her eyes, she took several breaths to calm herself. It was crucial to open and close it in the space of two seconds at most. She felt the rip forming and coiled herself. As she opened it further she darted out, grabbed Redlin and yanked him through. The speed in which she did this caused a momentum that threw them both to the ground.

"By the gods!" Redlin said sputtering as he pushed himself up off the ground. "What was that all about, Tori."

"I'm sorry master wizard, but there was no time to explain anything," Tori said.

"I assume there was a need for it," the wizard said.

"There is Dad," Andy said.

Andy went on to explain what they saw in the temple and the danger it presented to not only Pan, but the entire quest if his mind should be enslaved somehow.

"They could wind up controlling him," Cleo said. "Maybe even turn him against us."

"That's why we brought you here," Tori said. "We need your wisdom on this."

Redlin was silent for a moment as he thought. Tori and the others kept looking back for any unexpected attack.

"I have an idea," Redlin said. "I will take him to the source."

"Is that possible?" Andy said skeptically. "I thought only dragons and wizards could go there, unless under special circumstances. Like when Dain was chosen as a new wizard."

"Pan is the priest of Cael. I think the gods will allow it."

"Next question, how do you get him there?" Cleo said.

"With this," Redlin said holding up his hand with Trystan's ring on it.

"Can it do that?" Tori said.

"I'm starting to get a real feel for this thing," the wizard said. "Although I'm sure I've only just started scratching the surface of its power."

"What do you need me to do?" Tori asked.

"I'm going to stand just in front of Pan. When I tell you to, open the portal or whatever it is you call it. I will take it from there."

Redlin walked over and stood just to the left of Pan because there was more room and no one was in a direct line, removing any chance of getting hit accidentally. The wizard closed his eyes and started to focus. Tori could see a multi colored hue circling around the ring on Redlin's hand.

"Okay, Tori. Now."

Tori's eyes went red as she saw the pattern in the fabric of reality. As soon as it opened, time would flow again. She couldn't afford a slow rip from top to bottom. It had to open all at once if they were to have a chance.

"Get ready," Tori said. "Now!" she yelled as she brought her hands together in a loud clap. Redlin was jumping through, his ring leveled at Pan who had just started turning his head towards them.

"Redlin, what…" Pan started to say before being hit with the full force of the wizard's ring.

It looked like a small tornado of color and light had descended around the king of the fauns. And so quick that it was hard to tell how it happened, the tornado elongated skyward and disappeared, taking Pan with it.

"By the gods!" Lyson exclaimed startled since he had been standing next to Pan. "What the hell just happened."

Tori, Cleo and Andy jumped out right after Redlin.

"It's alright, Lyson," Redlin said. "I just sent him somewhere safe."

Cleo told everyone what they had discovered in the warlocks' lair and the threat that was posed to Pan.

"I'm wondering if this wasn't their intent all along," Loki said.

"What do you mean?" Dain asked.

"Pan was once one of them," Loki explained. "It's possible they wanted us to remove him, thereby removing any advantage we had into their psyche."

"Why don't we just go to the source and ask him," Brion said.

"Get ready!" Luel shouted, flying up from the temple. "Their coming, and there's a hoard of demons with them."

"The doors," Andy said to Cleo.

"Yes," Cleo answered. "One of them must have been a portal to bring them through. Probably the one with the M on it."

"So much for going to ask Pan," Caleb said.

Andy took command. "Brother's, to me!"

***

Andy watched as ten warlocks hovered above the ground. There was no use in transforming into dragons, it was going to be close up fighting. First thing to deal with were the demons. It was not as many as the initial assault when they landed on this island, but it was enough.

"Dad, can you guys keep the warlocks occupied while we handle the demons." By guys, Andy meant his father, Loki and Dain.

"We'll keep them off your back lad," Loki answered. "Let's go brothers."

The three wizards formed a triangle. A pyramid to help focus their power. Lightning shot out of their palms as it created a dome over the warlocks. It wasn't enough to destroy them by a long shot, but it would keep them busy Andy thought.

"You boys ready for a brawl," Andy asked his brothers. Since Andy had accepted the reality of Abby's death, a cold efficiency had entered his soul, and all he thought about was ridding Vasara of every last demon filth and their masters that brought them here.

"Let's do this," Caleb said.

Just then the ground erupted at their feet, hurtling the dragons backwards several yards.

"What the hell?" Caleb exclaimed sputtering.

"They have demon lords with them," Brion said getting up with the others and brushing himself off.

"I've marked them," Gael said. "There are ten, standing on that low ridge," he said pointing.

"Of course there are ten," Caleb said sarcastically. "How do we deal with them and this hoard."

"As best we can," Andy said. "My worry is those warlocks."

They all looked over at the wizards who were having trouble keeping the warlocks in check. The containment was weakening. Andy absently scratched the stubble of his beard that was forming as he thought quickly.

"Change of plans," Andy said. "We need to transform and take out those demon lords."

"I agree brother," Brion said putting a hand on his shoulder. "Faeries?"

"Yes," Andy replied.

Andy called for Emilia and his mother and every other faerie in their company. The demon lords were shooting lightning and fire as the faeries flew the brothers up high to release them so they could transform. Suddenly the air was filled with dragons. But that wasn't the end of it. The demon lords also transformed, and they were able to fly as well. The final battle had begun. As Andy banked to the right to engage his demon lord, he heard his father shouting.

"Loki! Watch out!"

***

Lyson had his sword drawn, ready to meet the foe streaking towards them. He really wished he was mounted, but he would make use of the terrain to his advantage. Suddenly he heard Redlin yell and saw Loki fall. He started to run over and help when everything went still and silent. Nothing was moving. He looked around nervously wondering if he had slipped into Tori's frozen moment, or maybe his mind was slipping.

"You are not going crazy, general," a voice said from behind.

Lyson whipped around, leveling his sword, ready to thrust. Then he realized who it was. Standing in front of him was the goddess of the faeries, an aura of flame colored light surrounded her.

"Braylynn," he said incredulously. "Are you here? Can you help? Loki just fell."

"No, I am not here," she answered. "I have stopped this moment for just the amount of time I need to give the help you asked for. Put your eyes back in your head, general. My brother isn't the only one who can manipulate time."

"What are you going to do," he asked nervously.

"Something I've been waiting eons to do since my brothers created wizards, but the time was never right, until now," she said looking at him possessively.

Lyson did not like that look at all.

"Um, Braylynn, I'm not sure I'm ready for what's coming."

She laughed, but it sounded more mischievous than funny.

"Trust me, you are not ready. But after, you will be."

"After what?" he said looking unsure of the raised hand above his head.

"Brace yourself, General. A large amount of power and knowledge is about to flood into you. To say this is going to hurt would be an understatement."

"Braylynn, wait!"

It was too late. Her hand connected with his forehead, and the scream that tore from his throat seemed to go on forever. Everything went black as he felt himself falling. Just before he landed face down in the dirt, Braylynn scooped him up and set him on his feet.

"Easy, Lyson. I've got you. Now just let the power flow slowly through your body."

He could feel an energy so vast, that the urge to let it run wild was intense.

"I don't suggest you do that," Braylynn said reading his thoughts.

"What did you do to me?" Lyson asked with a small hint of fear at the power and knowledge he now possessed.

"I made you what you were born into this world for. To be my wizard," she said proudly, smiling big at what he thought was her own personal creation.

"I'm surprised Fallon didn't put up a fight," he said starting to relax.

"Oh he did. But he owed me a favor," she said winking.

"I have never felt more alive."

"That's good my wizard, because you are going to be alive for a very long time."

Then it hit him. "Donella!"

"Yes," Braylynn said feeling pleased with herself. "It would not do to have my Dragon Summoner wallowing in grief at your death as a human. I will not have it."

Lyson felt like everything in his life had finally clicked into place.

"Now, General, it's time to go help your brother wizards. Even though you do not pull from my brothers' source but mine, you are still brothers in the common cause you serve. The protection of this world."

She leaned down and whispered in his ear. "You do have one advantage. You my wizard, can fly."

Lyson's eyes went wide. The knowledge of what to do was already there as he made the wings sprout out of his back. The wings were black and shaped like a falcons', but translucent like a faerie. He started them moving as he began to lift off the ground.

"Go now, and turn the tide of this battle," Braylynn said, and with that she promptly disappeared.

Lyson turned to face the warlocks. With grim determination he started to pick up speed as he flew straight for them.

***

Emilia had just let Andy drop and watched him transform as she heard her father cry out. She could see Loki on the ground. All of a sudden a figure had lifted off the ground and started heading towards the warlocks.

"Now that goddess has gone too far!" she heard Loki shout out as he started to rise. Apparently he wasn't seriously injured.

Her mouth dropped open as she realized the source of his outburst.

"Lyson?" she said aloud to herself.

Leaving all thoughts of the battle behind she flew over to him. "Lyson, what has happened?"

Lyson quickly flew in front of her and quickly raised a shield just as two energy bolts came flying in their direction.

"In a word, Braylynn happened. The rest I will tell you later love, right now, care to help me with these troublesome monsters."

Emilia couldn't believe what she was seeing, and the implications of that when it finally hit her made her smile real big. Taking the comb out of her hand she transformed it into her staff. "What did you have in mind?"

Redlin, can you hear me?

I hear you, Lyson. You have some explaining to do.

When all is done. Donella and I will fly above these guys and keep them occupied, while you hit them from below.

That's a sound plan. Be careful brother.

You too brother.

Even in the midst of battle, Emilia had never been happier.

***

Andy craned his neck to see where his sister had gone. His dragon eyes went wide as he saw her flying alongside Lyson.

What the hell? Lyson? he exclaimed.

It appears the goddess has been meddling again, Brion said falling in just below Andy.

You boys want to focus on the task at hand, Caleb said weaving back and forth with a demon lord hot on his heels.

Andy soared higher, making a loop that brought him up right behind Caleb and his attacker.

He remembered this tactic in a movie where an enemy was on the tail of fellow fighter jet while his comrade came up from behind unnoticed and attacked from the rear.

Caleb, don't make any sudden move, Andy said. *When I say, go straight up.*

You got it.

Andy gauged his distance and the path Caleb would lead his target.

Now, Caleb.

Caleb gave a powerful thrust of his wings and propelled himself vertical. Andy timed his shot perfectly as lightning flew out of his claws and connected with the demon lord, causing it to disintegrate into a vaporous cloud of black and sulfur.

That's one, Caleb said triumphantly.

It was an aerial dog fight with the dragons weaving in and out of each other's path. Baiting the monsters into positions to be obliterated. The dragons didn't escape unscathed however. Herve took a shot to the head temporarily disorienting him, causing him to collide with a cliff face and falling unceremoniously in a heap at the foot of the cliff. Luckily, he was able to shake himself out of it and rejoin the fight.

What the hell was that? Finn said.

Don't judge, Herve said. *Could happen to anybody.*

Andy laughed to himself in spite of what was going on around them. They were brothers to the core.

Andros! Brion shouted in his mind just as he narrowly missed being hit by a lightning bolt. Are *you wool gathering or something?*

Sorry, just lost focus for a minute.

The battle was full on, as the wizards kept the warlocks occupied while the dragons and faeries battled the demons. The demon lord count was down to four. Herve, Irwyn and Jace split off to engage the demons on the ground. The last of the demon lords were very smart. They didn't engage head on. Now they were the ones doing the bait and switch, causing Andy to take several direct hits on his scaly hide.

Where is your sister? Caleb asked. *We could sure use her right now.*

I believe she is still helping Lyson, Andy said.

Suddenly there was a tremendous roar as a gale wind and a flash of red flew between dragons and demon lords, causing their flight to falter.

I would say Chaos is back, Gael said, the sun reflecting off his gold scales as he used that reflection to blind his opponents.

I thought you boys could use a little help, Emilia spoke to their minds.

Thanks sis! I have an idea. Everyone follow me.

Andy followed in Chaos' wake while six other dragons followed in his. The demon lords were confused by this and had no idea what was going on or what kind of creature had joined the fight. They stupidly formed a line like a wall. What they thought to achieve by this maneuver Andy didn't know, but he knew what he was going to do.

You thinking what I'm thinking? Brion said flying directly behind him.

Yes. Get ready.

I see it too, Caleb said.

For some reason, flying in single file had confused the demons, and they left themselves totally vulnerable as they tried to withstand the might of dragons in flight. Just before Chaos impacted with the center of the demon line, Andy veered right, strafing the demons with energy bolts as Brion did the same to the left. Caleb followed Andy as Daragh banked left behind Brion, every subsequent dragon doing the same. Unleashing energy bolts in rapid succession. The demons had no chance as they tried to erect hasty shields only to be blasted into oblivion.

As the black vapor cleared, the dragons hovered for a moment to ensure none had escaped.

Shall we tidy up down below, Gael said.

Yes, Caleb agreed. *Then we can turn our attentions to the real monsters,* he said turning his long neck in the direction of the warlocks.

***

Emilia was hitting the warlocks from the left while Lyson occupied them from the right. It was still unbelievable to her the implications of what Braylynn had done to him. She couldn't really concentrate on that right now. These beings were taking all of her focus. She could see the demons on the ground were being systematically destroyed by the dragons. Her mother was also using the power of her family stone to great effect. She basically was able to create invisible shields around all the faeries and humans that were fighting on the ground. The shields were not all encompassing, but they did provide some measure of protection given the odds that were arrayed against them.

The pearl on the top of her staff was blazing white as she kept a barrage of energy bolts aimed at the warlock's shield. Lyson had formed a bubble of lightening around them while her father, Loki and Dain hit them from below. Even with all that firepower, they were unable to penetrate their defenses. Suddenly, without warning, the warlocks disappeared. Both her and Lyson had to quickly erect shields, because the energy shots from the wizards came streaking through the space the warlocks occupied and headed straight for them. They were both propelled back as a conflagration of light, color and sparks ricocheted off their barriers.

Emilia, are you alright? her father sent worried he had almost killed his daughter.

I'm ok Dad. Lyson, are you hurt?

I'm fine love, let's go down.

They both flew down and helped with destroying what demons remained, and everything was strangely quiet. The wind stirred warmly and it gave Emilia that feeling of a calm before a great storm.

"Is everyone okay?" Andy asked when they assembled in front of the gates. All the dragons had returned to their human form.

"I don't believe we suffered any casualties," Loki said. "And I find that to be quite miraculous."

"Where did they go?" Brion asked.

"My guess is they retreated back to their strongest position," Redlin said, "their temple."

"And I believe it's time to end this once and for all," Caleb said. "Time for all accounts to be settled. And I have been waiting over fifteen hundred years to settle this one."

Emilia looked sharply at Caleb. His tone was so cold and fierce. She could tell this was payback for him. Vengeance for all those years imprisoned. For all the friends and loved ones now long gone that he never had a chance to say goodbye to through the normal passage of time. Suddenly she could understand what he and the other dragons must be feeling. It would be like if she had come back to Vasara only to find Lyson hundreds of years in his grave. Thankfully she will never have to know what that would be like now.

"Let's go," Redlin said. "I can't think of any reason to put this off any longer."

"What's our strategy?" Dain asked.

"Stay alert and prepare for anything," Loki answered.

"At least let me take the lead," Tori said. "I have certain advantages."

"Very well," Redlin said.

Emilia walked next to Tori as everyone else filed in behind them.

"Any words of wisdom, Summoner?" Tori asked her.

"Yes," she said. "Don't get killed."

Tori smiled at her. "I will make it a point not to."

"Where's Percy?" Emilia asked. She hadn't seen the Viper mascot in quite some time.

"He's with Cleo. I was worried he was being subjected to too many dangerous situations riding with me."

They were walking down the hallway with the many doors off of it. Tori had stopped in front of the one with the 'M' marked on it.

"Did you want to see what is inside?" she asked the wizards.

"Let me check," Loki said.

The old man closed his eyes as he ran his fingers along the face of the door, pausing occasionally as if he were listening.

"There is definitely an energy in there. I'm not sure it's something we want to tackle just now though," Loki said.

"Let's deal with the warlocks first," Redlin said. "We can always try it later."

Emilia and Tori continued to lead the way until they came into the inner sanctum.

"Is it my imagination, or does this place look bigger than it did before?" Tori asked Cleo.

"It's definitely bigger," Cleo said. "There also seems to be a lot of darkened alcoves along the walls."

"No!" Tera shouted as she flew to the altar.

"Tera! Get back here," Luel shouted.

Swords and spears were drawn as everyone rushed to the altar to try and protect Tera from any sudden attack. The silver haired faerie was sitting on the top of the altar with tears running down her cheeks. In her lap was a dead faun, a ragged gash in his chest where his heart had been.

"Did you know him, Tera?" Redlin said gently. She nodded her head.

"His name was Clovis," she said. "One of Pan's top generals. He taught me how to shoot a bow, and would practice with me on the pipes." Her words came out in choked sobs. "How did he get here?"

"I don't know," Redlin responded, speaking more urgently. "Tera, let him rest here, and we will come back for him and make sure he is buried properly. We are in a lot of danger right now."

Tera knew the truth of his words and gently laid Clovis down as she flew off the altar and into Luel's waiting embrace.

"Everyone get ready," Dain said. "Defensively I think we are in the worst possible position we could be in."

"I'm sorry, Dain," Tera said. "This is my fault."

Dain smiled tenderly at his longtime friend. "No it isn't, Tera. If anyone is to blame, it's those ten monsters who forced us here."

Suddenly there was an ear shattering crack as lightning lit up the chamber. Everyone that could erect a shield had one up surrounding everyone else.

"Emilia, surround us with a barrier, everyone else drop out," Redlin said.

"I got it, Dad," Emilia said.

Just then a bolt of liquid fire, white-hot, came shooting through Emilia's barrier and headed straight for her. Quick as thought, Luel jumped in front of her daughter. Crossing her arms, the jewel of her house blazed as she absorbed the impact of her hastily thrown shield. The impact propelled her back into Emilia, knocking them both to the stone floor. Out of a darkened entry way demons started coming into the chamber.

"You've got to be kidding me," Caleb said preparing to meet the new threat.

"Scatter and attack!" Loki shouted.

Emilia helped her mother up.

"Mom, are you okay?"

"Yes, come with me, quickly!"

Emilia and her mother sprinted out of the main area and down the hall. Stopping at the door with the M on it, Luel closed her eyes and started to concentrate. Her hand hovered over the knob as she slowly made a twisting motion. Emilia could see the knob was actually resisting. Whatever was in there did not want them to come in. Luel exerted even more force. Suddenly the knob turned and the door flew open. In the center of the room was what looked like a man, but Emilia knew he was not human. His hair was white and cut short like a buzz cut with a neatly trimmed white beard to match, and his eyes were a penetrating ice blue with white centers. His robe was black with all kinds of gold thread designs on it. He was sitting at a table with a black pyramid in front of him. He spoke, and his voice was so overpowering, Emilia found herself almost wanting to obey immediately.

"Please come in," he said. "My name is Meliakken."

Emilia's mind was screaming to run from the evil god, but found she lacked the will to do so. Both her and her mother walked inside as the door closed behind them.

"No need to introduce yourselves. I know who you are Summoner. And you Luel," Meliakken said turning towards the faerie queen. "Your father spoke often of you in his ravings."

"How do you know my father?" Luel said.

"Where do you think his dark power came from? I gave them to him. The same as those twelve fools out there. They believe they are using me, but I assure you it is the other way around."

Emilia didn't know if she entirely believed him. Looking at her mother she could tell she was enraged.

"Mom, he's safe now."

Luel's features softened as she looked thankfully at her daughter. Emilia knew Meliakken was trying to bait them for some reason.

"You can't be truly here," Luel said. "You are imprisoned in the underworld."

"Am I?"

"Yes. I seriously doubt you would be sitting in this room otherwise, and also try to prevent us from entering."

"But I let you enter. It is my will that you are here."

"No, I don't think so," Luel said her eyes narrowing.

Emilia could feel the air starting to charge with energy. Whether it was her mother, the god, or both, she couldn't tell. She started tapping into her own power.

Donella, not yet, and not that way.

Emilia knew it was her goddess speaking. She looked at Meliakken. He didn't seem to register that he sensed or heard anything.

When I tell you, join your power with the one in the medallion.

Emilia felt the power resonating from the medallion resting against her chest. The power of a goddess resided in it. How was she supposed to join with that? As if sensing her thoughts, Braylynn answered her question.

I will briefly open that doorway that will allow you to join. Once you do, direct it all at Meliakken. Then your mother must destroy the pyramid.

"You are strangely silent, Summoner," the god said. "Please don't feel like you can plot against me. Your powers are quite feeble compared to mine."

"You sure are an arrogant S.O.B.," Emilia said reverting back to her New York dialect.

Luel suddenly burst out laughing. It was as if that little stand of defiance was enough to break his over-powering influence.

"You insolent witch!" He shouted getting to his feet. "I will destroy you."

Now! Braylynn's command echoed in her mind.

Emilia sought the door in her mind as she connected with the medallion. Standing in a white marble archway was perhaps the most beautiful woman Emilia had ever seen. But the beauty was not in her physical form, it was the aura the radiated from her. Her smile was bright like a sun while at the same time her eyes were fierce, almost frightening. She held out a hand. Emilia took it and suddenly felt like her whole body was going to fly apart.

Focus! Braylynn shouted.

Emilia took all the energy she felt she could handle, then with a closed fist, raised her hand to point directly at the god's chest. Opening her hand, she let it all fly. The impact slammed Meliakken against the wall behind him.

"Don't let up!" Luel told her daughter.

Emilia kept the energy flowing. Instead of waning, she felt it increase. As if the goddess whose power she tapped into recognized the threat and wanted to obliterate it. Problem was, it just might obliterate herself as well. Then Meliakken's form started to crack. Dark lines like vines appeared on his face. He was screaming in agony, causing physical pain in Emilia's ears and mind. All of a sudden, his body exploded. But instead of body parts flying everywhere, pieces of him floated towards the ceiling like paper from a fire, disappearing until there was nothing left.

It was eerily quiet as Emilia looked at her mother astonishingly. Once he was gone, the door to the goddess whose power was in the medallion closed, leaving Emilia feeling very drained.

"Mom, you have to destroy the pyramid," Emilia said quickly.

"I know. This is what they were using to open portals for the demons."

Luel placed her hands at the base of the pyramid. Her eyes were wide as she focused all her mental energy at the very tip. Once again the jewel on her crown started to blaze as a fine razor like beam the color of blood connected with the pyramid. Like with Meliakken, cracks began to appear on its surface.

"Shield us," Luel said as the pyramid detonated and exploded into a hundred shards, most of them embedding into the walls and ceiling after ricocheting off of Emilia's shield.

"You alright?" her mother asked her.

"Yes. How did you know to come in here?"

"When we first passed by this door I felt an energy similar to the portals I had already closed. Once the demons started to appear in the temple, I was sure the device was in here. I had no idea Meliakken would be here. How did you do what you did?" Luel asked in wonder.

"Braylynn helped me to join with the power in my medallion," she said as she drew it out to look at it. It still felt very warm to the touch.

"It's a good thing she did. We would not have beat him otherwise."

"Did we kill him, Mom?"

"No. It's as I said, he was not really here. At least not in his full power. I've no doubt you gave him enough pain to give him pause. Come, we have to get back."

With that they both went sprinting back towards the temple.

***

The demons coming through had suddenly stopped as Andy and the others proceeded to make short work of the ones that were left. Thanks to Tori and her enhanced speed and battle skills, the amount of demons was not enough to overwhelm them. Suddenly a fire bolt streaked out of a darkened alcove and grazed Andy's shoulder, knocking him to the ground. An unbelievable rage descended over him. His eyes narrowed to slits as he roared his defiance.

"Enough!" he shouted. He threw his hands to the ceiling and white light shot out illuminating every dark crevice. The warlocks were visible now. In a ring around the outside wall they began their final assault.

"Dragons!" Andy yelled.

They knew what to do. They formed a circle, each dragon facing off against a warlock with all of their friends inside the circle. Emilia and his mother came running in and joined the others inside the ring of dragons. No word was spoken. At precisely the same moment, dragons and warlocks thrust their hands towards one another as their energy beams collided and locked. The air was charged and hot. Everyone could feel the heat in their nostrils as they breathed. Andy could hear his father behind him talking to Loki.

"We need to help them," Redlin said.

"Their energies are locked," Loki told him. "I wouldn't even know where to begin. If we throw anything in there we could possibly destroy them both, and us with it. They have to overcome, or be overcome."

Andy focused on the warlock directly in front of him. It was like they were standing nose to nose. Normally the dragons would have the better advantage, but these warlocks were drawing on another power. He could feel his beam starting to be pushed back. He drew on more of the source which halted the warlocks advance. He looked over at his brothers and saw they were having similar issues. Some of those hurt earlier, like Finn and Herve seemed to be struggling the most. They were committed now. If they stopped, they were dead. He could feel despair slipping into his heart. In that moment he thought of Abby. Her face appeared to float before his eyes. The kindness and tenderness in her eyes started to relax him. He thought if he just let go he could go and be where she was. To finally rest and be together. Then a hundred images started to flood his mind. And not just Abby. Bart was there as well. Every adventure, hurt, laughter and trial they shared came to him. Then he heard Bart's voice.

"You going to finish this lad? We got other stuff to do don't you know."

Andy's whole body started to expand with the love that was pouring in, and right behind that was hope. He looked down and saw that the warlocks beam was only inches from his chest. With renewed purpose he pushed back, almost obliterating the warlock, but his enemy was able to bring it back to the middle.

"You had me worried, brother," Brion said through clenched teeth.

"Me too," Andy said. "We can't hold this forever. I'm tapped out as far as the source goes."

"As am I."

"Speak for yourselves," Caleb said breathing deeply. "I can do this as long as it takes, although I'm not sure if they can."

Andy saw the warlocks were straining just as much as they were.

All of a sudden there was an explosion and the entire roof of the temple shot upward. Sunlight poured into that chamber for the first time ever. The dragons and warlocks kept their focus on one another as everyone else looked up. Something was descending. Something with power. Andy risked a glance upward as the being started to get closer. The sun was directly behind it and he couldn't get a clear view. An aura of blue surrounded it. Andy's eyes went wide as he suddenly realized who it was.

"Pan!" Tera shouted.

The king of the fauns made a loud impact as his hooves connected with the ground. It seemed like everything was in slow motion as Andy saw Pan. He looked the same and yet at the same time vastly different. Andy glanced at the warlock facing him and saw fear in his eyes. Pan was carrying a staff with a decagram, a ten pointed star, on top. With a wave of his staff, Pan brought it down with a loud crack. Blue light shot out of each point in the star and into the backs of the dragons. Andy felt that incredible power filling his body up. He saw his energy beam start to take on a deep blue color as it shot straight at the warlock. There was no resistance as it connected with their chests. The warlocks' energy couldn't overcome the added might of the source and whatever it was Pan was feeding them. Each warlock started to smoke, their skin turning black and papery as they screamed in agony. Andy wanted to look away but found he couldn't. He made the energy even hotter. For Abby. For Bart. For every person and creature that had died because of their murderous schemes. Andy could feel something coming from Pan through the link he was sharing with him. Pain, regret and loss. Pan was using Andy and his brothers to destroy his own brothers, for good. When the last molecule of their existence ascended upward, Andy and the others released the source and slumped to their knees. His ears were ringing and buzzing and he could barely hear his father asking him if he were alright. He really didn't know if he would ever feel truly alright ever again.

Chapter 31

A breeze was blowing through the alcove in Pan's grotto where Abby lay. It was warm and gentle and felt good on the skin. Andy was sitting on a rock just at her head. How long he sat there he didn't know. Hours, days, months; time lost meaning for him. When first seeing his beloved lying there he threw himself on her and cradled her in his lap as the tears flowed. He didn't know how he could go on without her, but he knew he must. He knew once he took that step away from her he would never come back. That thought alone was gut wrenching. Pan said she could lay there in that perfect state for as long as he still had magic. Andy didn't know if he could do that to Abby. The thought of her in the ground seemed abhorrent to him for some reason as well. He stopped thinking about it for the time being and just looked at Abby. Her hair was fanned out under her body, her face just as beautiful as the first day he saw her on the library steps at Dragonsgate.

He looked over to where the king of the fauns was standing with his father, mother and the other wizards. Actually not king of just the fauns, but king of the Parma Wilds. After the battle Pan had told them what happened to him. When Redlin had whisked him away to the source, Cael was there, and not just in spirit. He gave Pan the decagram staff as well as his power to overcome the warlocks. Pan had explained that since Cael was their god, it would take an enormous amount of power, his power, to destroy them. That's why the color of the energy was blue. Just like red is Fallon's color, blue is Cael's. Cael also told Pan his self-imposed exile was over. He needed him to rule, and not just passively.

Lyson was also with the wizards, although now he was a wizard himself, but of a different stamp. Andy smiled as he remembered all the bluster Loki had pretended to put up about that, especially the fact that he could fly. He was happy for his sister, who had locked arms with Lyson as she listened in on their conversation.

Brayton and Cathal had walked over to join the expanding group. Andy and Brayton had spoken before coming to the grotto. He learned of the hard decision he had to make in order for the unicorns to make it to the battle in time. But that too had turned out somewhat alright. Brayton had told him how Pan, being king and priest to Cael, was able to give the unicorns a way to travel from the island to the mainland. How they could do that he was not allowed to reveal. The unicorn grove would have to remain on the island for a thousand years and they could never be long from it, but at least they were not complete prisoners. There was some other aspect to the decision Brayton had made, but he was very reluctant to speak of it. Only that he and Pan were working on a solution. Whatever it was seemed to be causing Brayton no small amount of anguish.

"What of your parents?" Andy had asked him.

"I have had no word," Brayton had replied. worriedly "As soon as we get back, we will launch a kingdom wide search for them."

The grotto was large but at the moment very full. Everyone had come here that had been at the battle, minus the unicorns of course. It was a good place to rest. And also, everyone wanted to say a last goodbye to Abby, whom to everyone she had meant so much.

"Ho Edward!"

Andy couldn't help smiling at the voice that hailed him. Bowen had arrived several days ago, navigating a very small river in one of his long boats with several of his men. When they saw Abby they were inconsolable. The fact they couldn't join in the battle and help avenge her had them extremely put out. That part they had gotten over, but her passing they never would. Every sailor to a man would have traded their lives for Abby at any time on any day. Andy had such a love for this man.

"Are you heading out, Captain?"

"As soon as we see our dear friend off laddie," Bowen said choking back a sob and wiping his nose with a kerchief.

"Thank you for being here," Andy said clasping his arm. "You have no idea what this means to me."

"I think maybe I do," Bowen said soberly pulling him into a crushing embrace.

As if Bowen coming over had broken the ice, everyone else had started to gather around. Andy had that feeling it was time. It was time to say goodbye to his beloved and begin his journey alone. The tears started flowing, and he couldn't stop them. He didn't want to stop them. They were a testament and witness to their love, and he would not betray his Abby by holding them back and pretending to play tough.

"Have you decided Andros?" Pan asked him.

He knew what Pan meant. What did he want to happen to Abby's body.

"I don't know if I can make this decision, Pan. I am very conflicted."

The other dragons had circled around Andy, his brothers feeling his anguish and lending their strength. Andy realized his brothers had never heard Abby speak, never heard her sing. But they knew that if it weren't for her sacrifice, they would not be standing here today.

"I would welcome any guidance in this," Andy said.

"Perhaps I can help," a voice said right next to Diminitus' ear.

"By the gods!" Diminitus yelled after jumping three feet forward. "Braylynn, you did that on purpose!"

Braylynn smiled fondly, even affectionately at the grumpy old man, as if imprinting him in her mind for all time.

"I am sorry my old friend. Next time I will blow a fanfare I promise."

"Hmmm. See that you do missy!"

The air in the grotto suddenly turned light. The oppressive gloom of sadness and death banished for the moment to its own dark corner.

Andy was always in awe of the beauty of the faerie goddess. The colors of her hair and the aura surrounding her body seemed extra vibrant today. She hugged and greeted all her daughters, as well as Lyson. Andy thought this odd. He felt like he was watching some kind of ritual. Tera was the last one to let go before bestowing multiple kisses all over her deity's face.

Then, Braylynn came to stand before Abby. After giving her a kiss on her brow she turned to face Andy.

"I know thy hurt Andros. The magnitude of it reaches across the heavens, even to the ears of my brothers, and they have asked something of me. But first I would know, what would you give to have your beloved restored to you."

"My life," Andy replied without hesitation. "But since that means she would be without me, I would give my life to be where she is."

"Your life is required here," Braylynn said. "Would you let someone else offer their life; your parents, your sister, or perhaps one of your brothers or friends, or even an enemy."

Again, without hesitation, Andy answered, "No. I would not allow that and neither would Abby. If I must go on without her I will. I thought you were here to help me," Andy said getting frustrated by her questions.

"Easy lad," Bowen said putting a hand on his shoulder.

Braylynn however took no offense and smiled lovingly at him. "You have grown immensely my young dragon. Although this has always been a part of your character. I wanted you to hear it for yourself. Your heart is true, right and pure, and you have the strength to go on, alone if need be. Hold out death's dagger."

It took a moment for that to register in Andy's mind. He lifted the chain from around his neck and placed the pendant in his open palm. He was hesitant to give it up at first. It had become the symbol of Abby's sacrifice, of the ultimate price that was paid.

Braylynn made a pulling gesture, making the pendant float over to her outstretched hand.

"The dagger cuts both ways," Andy thought he heard Rhyan mumble.

Braylynn put the necklace around Abby's neck. She then placed both hands on her body. Her wings started moving in a specific rhythm that was so intricate and complicated Andy couldn't follow it. She started singing a soft quiet melody. And even though it was soft and quiet, there was a power in it. It was as if everyone were holding their breath, wondering what was going to happen.

Andy watched as Abby's color started to come back while at the same time, Braylynn seemed to be growing more and more insubstantial. He could see right through the goddess now, as if she were more spirit than physically here.

All of a sudden Abby gasped. Taking a deep breath as if she just broke the water after being underneath it for many minutes, sucking in that life giving oxygen, her chest heaving and her eyes wide in shock. Andy ran to the stone slab and scooped her up and held her tight to his chest. Two things he noticed right away. Abby's body was warm from the life blood flowing through her veins. The other was when he picked her up, his hand had passed right through Braylynn.

"Andros?" Abby said weakly.

Andy looked into the face of his love. She looked totally drained, but her eyes were clear. She was alive, and tears flowed freely down his cheeks. He couldn't believe she was back. He was so afraid to move for fear this was all just a dream and he would wake up if he took a step in any direction.

"It is no dream, lord dragon," Braylynn said, sensing he thoughts.

Andy looked around. All his friends and family were shedding just as many tears as he was. Tera and Emma flew over and crushed them in a group hug, which was followed up by the entire company.

Andy sat down with Abby on a stone bench next to them, Abby's strength starting to come back.

"Can you sit?" Andy asked her.

"Yes," she answered wearily. "But I feel like I've been run over by ten Mack trucks."

Andy laughed hard at that. Besides himself and his family, Abby was the only other person in Vasara who knew what a Mack truck was.

"Do you remember what happened?"

"I saw you enter through death's door," Abby began, "Then it felt like I was hit hard in the back of my head. A bright light exploded behind my eyes as I fell into darkness. When I could see again, I was sitting on a bench by a dirt road under a tree in a forest. Then a man came along."

"A man?" Redlin asked. "What did he look like."

"This will sound strange, but he was dressed like one of those conductors on the train we use to take to the city."

Andy remembered the men and women of the railroad who use to collect their tickets when they would travel to New York City for shopping or a ballgame. It all seemed like another life ago.

"Did he say anything," Emilia asked.

"He looked at his watch and said I would be moving on soon. I asked him when, and he said once the choice had been made. Then he disappeared as he went beyond a turn in the road. I don't know how long it was, but after that I woke up here feeling battered and bruised. I don't know what the choice was."

Andy looked over at the goddess.

"I think Braylynn just made it," Andy said.

Braylynn came walking over towards them. "Very astute Andros. I did make the choice. My existence here for Abby's life. This is the favor my brother's asked of me."

"What does that mean mother?" Luel asked. "Your existence here?"

"I will no longer be here in body. Crossing death's barrier to bring someone back comes at a cost." She looked tenderly at Abby. "But I was more than willing to pay that cost. I was never meant to be here forever my daughters. My brothers have been waiting for me, there are other worlds to make."

"Does that mean we will never see you again?" Tera asked in tears.

"Absolutely not dear Tera. My priestess can always call me. Plus, you have a wizard now, who can draw from my source of power." She directed this last at Loki with a raised eyebrow.

"Lyson, do not let your brother wizards push you around."

"I'm hurt Braylynn, that you would think that of us," Loki sputtered.

"Besides, Lyson and I are both brothers as wizards and as warriors, and those bonds never change or break," Dain said.

Braylynn laughed. "I merely tease General. I know you will all look after one another. She turned her attention once more to Abby.

"One more thing Abby. I will not be able to come back to Vasara physically; you may never leave it. The birthplace of Andros is closed to you. Should you try and go back there you will die."

"That's alright Braylynn," Andy said. "We can make a fine life here."

Abby looked startled. "But what about your life and friends on the Hudson River? You would never see them again."

He put a hand on Abby's cheek. "My life is where you are, and it always will be for as long as you draw breath."

"That could actually be quite a long time, Andros," Braylynn said.

"What do you mean?" Emilia asked.

"You really didn't think a goddess could bring a mortal back from death without changing them a little. Your experience with Tori should have taught you that," she said with a wink.

"You mean I will live forever?" Abby said astounded.

"No child," Braylynn said. "But pretty damn close."

"Does she have powers too?" Rhyan asked.

"Who's to say priestess. Maybe in time she will discover some. Also Abby, you are the owner of death's dagger now. There is a power in it. Guard it well. Now I need to move apart for a while with my queen and Summoner."

Braylynn turned and walked to the far end of the grotto followed by Emilia and Luel.

Everyone else was rejoicing at Abby and Andy's good fortune.

"You don't know how lucky you are brother," Brion had said to him smiling and slapping him on the back. "Treasure this gift that has been giving to you both."

Andy jumped up and fiercely hugged him. He knew the pain and madness they had both shared in losing someone they desperately loved. "I will treasure this gift brother, I promise."

"I know you will," Brion said.

"Where will you go from here? Now that it's over," Andy asked him.

"I use to have a home in Albion, I will be very surprised if it is still standing," he said laughing. "The others have homes in the various cities and towns as well. We usually get together several times a year at our cave in the mountains above Dragonsgate. I assume you have been there."

"Oh yes," Andy replied remembering his time first training with Loki. "I know that place well. When are you leaving?"

"I think most of us are flying out in the morning. Finn was going to stay, but now that Abby has been restored to you, he wants to leave this evening." Brion looked over to where Finn was standing with Jace and Herve.

"Is he alright?" Abby asked.

"Yes. You don't know since you weren't there, and I'm sure Andros will fill you in later, but Zana was at the battle."

"No!"

"It turned out okay," Brion said, "but the way Finn had called out to her let us know that he once had some form of relationship with her. How deep or involved I do not know."

"You think he is going to look for her?" Andy asked.

"Either that or word of her. We will need to keep tabs on him to make sure he is alright." Brion smiled at both of them. "I've taken up enough of your time. I know you will have much to discuss and also others that will want to speak with you."

With that he left them on the bench alone. Everyone seemed to be in conversation with someone else, so no one was in a hurry to interrupt them.

"Where shall we live, Andros," Abby asked him rubbing a hand on his stubble chin.

Andy leaned in and kissed his beloved tenderly. He was on an emotional high. He still couldn't believe she was sitting right here next to him. And not only that, she would live as long as he would.

"Wherever you want to," Andy responded kissing her again.

Abby mussed his sandy brown hair as her eyes held his. "Dragonsgate? I know they need a curator, and I have so many memories there. If you would rather be near your parents and your sister I would understand," she said quickly.

Andy placed both hands on the side of her face, kissed her one more time, although there will be a lot more to come. "Abby, I think that would be a perfect choice. It is our beginning and everything about that just feels right."

Abby hugged him tight and rested her head on his shoulder, the tears sliding down her cheeks. She didn't show any signs of ever letting him go.

Chapter 32

The Grey Morning was making good headway as it sailed the Scio Ocean up towards Kensington. Emilia looked across the deck which seemed quite crowded. After she and her mother finished talking with Braylynn, the goddess simply vanished. What they spoke about was for the ears of the queen and the Summoner alone. She was not even allowed to mention it to Lyson. At least for now she had said. Emilia decided not to think on that and delighted in the company of all those she loved. Those that lived in Laurel Hollow and the Wilds made their own way home, the dragons leaving the next day, after Abby's restoration. Except for Finn, who left that same day. She knew they would have to talk about Zana at some point. For the rest of the company, Bowen would take them up along the coast. Dropping Brayton and Cathal off in Kensington. Then he would sail up to the port in Fenner, where everyone else would make their way across by land. After the dragons had all flown off to various parts of Vasara, Emilia could still feel each and every one of them. Brion told her she would see them periodically, but probably not all together unless there was a crisis, or for their yearly training, which her predecessor had always insisted on.

Suddenly a voice was raised in song. Emilia looked towards the bow to see Abby standing by the ships wheel above everyone on the quarterdeck. Every sailor not on watch or performing some duty sat cross-legged on the main deck and listened raptly. Abby looked every inch the pirate in her long sleeved white flowy shirt with her leather pants and boots. Bowen had always kept clothes for Abby on board ever since their first voyage together. She always had a permanent berth on the Grey Morning. There didn't seem to be a dry eye as she sang of sailors and lovers. Even Andy, standing at the far rail with Bowen, Rhyan and Ava, seemed to be batting away a few tears. Emilia and Abby had talked long into the night after everyone else had gone to sleep. To have the person she considered a part of her immediate family back was nothing short of a miracle. Braylynn had gone into more detail of what she had done, but she gave strict instructions that Abby never know. Abby had asked her if she were going back to New York, even though that was no longer possible for her.

"No," Emilia told her. "My life is here with Lyson, with the dragons."

As if thinking about him summoned him, Lyson came flying over to her.

"Show off," Emilia said laughing.

Lyson winked at her. "Just trying to get under Loki's skin."

Emilia looked over at Loki who seemed to be frowning in their direction.

"What were you thinking just now?" Lyson asked her.

"About when Abby asked me if I was staying here."

"Love, if you ever feel…"

Emilia put her hand on his lips. "Hush. I'm never leaving you again. Our lives are together, end of story."

Lyson just smiled and kissed her.

"I will need to build us a house."

"Why can't we just use the Dragon Summoner's house."

"No offense love, but I don't think it will be big enough to hold all my books from Lyonsdale, not to mention the maps and scrolls in the palace library that I will need to have for further study."

Emilia gave him a dangerous look.

"Or...I could just expand your house," Lyson said catching on. "Maybe add an addition that could house everything."

"Good thinking my darling," Emilia said satisfied, patting his cheek. "You'll do just fine."

"You two seem to be getting along well," a voice from behind said laughing.

Emilia and Lyson turned around to see Redlin and Luel walking up to them. The plan had been to travel to Dragonsgate with Abby and Andy, then along with Leah and Dain, take one of the portals in the dragon cave back to Laurel Hollow. Tori and Cleo would travel onto the Border Lands. Tori said she would rather forego any portal travel.

"Yes, I believe I'll keep him," Emilia said slipping her arm under his.

"I never got to ask how you were holding up with your new position in life, Lyson," Redlin said.

"I'm still not very comfortable with all this energy and power that seems to be right at my fingertips," Lyson responded. "Not to mention these wings I can make appear at will," he said as he moved them back and forth.

"Time will help with all of that my friend. And we are always here ready to assist should you need us."

"Thank you, Redlin," Lyson said grasping his hand.

"Thank you, son, for making my daughter so very happy."

Emilia couldn't argue that point. She was very happy indeed, and she looked forward with great joy to spending the rest of her life with this man who totally owned her heart.

The shores of Kensington came into view. Bowen lowered his sails and coasted into the harbor, pulling up to the dock that was always reserved for his ship. Brayton and Cathal jumped off, promising to keep them all appraised on the search for his parents. Their wives and children were waiting for them as Brayton ran to them and scooped them all up in fierce embrace. They all waved as the ship pulled out and pointed her prow towards Fenner.

To say Lily was overjoyed to see her daughters was a gross understatement. And no one was allowed to leave at least for two days while they celebrated their safe return. For those going on, the best of their horses were provided for travel.

"Thank you Rhyan," Redlin said as they made ready to depart. "Tell your mother and sister we will see the horses make their way back here."

"No problem master wizard. And I will let you know if I sense anything with Samara," Rhyan said.

He nodded once. Emilia knew of the bargain struck with Samara in order for Andy to obtain the death dagger. The cost being his god medallion. After feeling just a fraction of that power, she can't imagine what would happen if Samara succeeded in releasing it all at once. Even though they had just won a major victory and there appeared to be a lot of happy endings, Emilia didn't think they were done. For herself, there was at least on more matter she would have to deal with at some point. Zana.

***

No one seemed to be in any hurry, as if they didn't want the company to totally break up just yet. A couple of days later found them entering Dragonsgate. Andy had told Emilia all the stories, but she had never seen the place where the adventure had started for himself and Abby.

"What do you think, Em," Andy said riding up beside her.

"It's smaller than I imagined, but in a way it reminds me of our town on the Hudson."

Andy smiled knowingly. "I felt the same way when I first stumbled my way in here as a new human/dragon."

They kept riding until they came to the Red Bull Inn. Now that everything was over, there was a peaceful air about the town. As they went inside to the common room, Andy turned towards the fire where he saw the chair by the fireplace. A man was sitting there, stirring up the embers. As he leaned back and turned, Andy felt a pang of loss. He half expected to see Bart sitting there.

Abby came up behind him and wrapped her arms around him.

"Remembering?" she asked him.

"Yes," he answered. He turned to look at her. "This is the center of everything for us. It's right that we begin to build our life together here. There is one thing I need to do though. Come with me."

Andy grabbed Abby's hand and led her out the doors and down the street to the library. As he mounted the steps to the place where he first saw her, he dropped to a knee. Abby's eyes lit up and her body started to shake. Andy concentrated as he made a twisting motion with his hand, then closed his fist. When he opened it, laying in his palm was the most amazing ring Abby had ever seen, she gasped when she saw it. The ring was silver and the wrought image of the band was a twisting dragon biting its own tail to complete the ring. Its eyes were two diamonds which shined brilliantly.

"Abby, we have been destined for each other since the first day we met, and when you died I thought that destiny had died with you. Now that you have been restored to me, I don't want to miss this chance. Will you marry me, Abby?"

Abby took the ring, felt the weight in her hand, felt the

metal and the warmth that radiated from it. With tears running down her face she slipped it on her finger, then bent down to kiss his lips tenderly.

"Of course I will my dragon. My heart has been yours since the first day, and I will spend the rest of my life with you or no one."

Andy stood up and lifted Abby in a crushing embrace before cradling her to him.

All of a sudden the area in front of the library lit up with a terrific brilliant light accompanied by the sound of clapping and cheers.

Andy set Abby down as they held each other. As their eyes adjusted from the temporary blindness, they could see that their family and friends had followed them out but kept a respectful distance as Andy professed his love. He could see his parents, arm and arm, never looking happier. Emilia and Lyson likewise were holding each other as they smiled big. Loki was the most raucous, whistling and shooting off fireballs. His family and friends were all there. This was perfect. This is his family, Andy thought to himself, and he was home. He turned back to his bride to be and kissed her soundly.

"You will have to tell me where you got this ring," Abby whispered to him after breaking from the kiss.

Andy smiled and winked at her. "That my dear is a whole story unto itself," he said as held her tight, his heart glowing as he thought to himself, this is the first day of a brand new life.

Epilogue

The wind blew across the blue waters of the hidden lake near the southern most border of the Parma Wilds, although it was not exactly in the Wilds. And not just anyone could find it. Zana would never have found it if not for Devon's ravens. She followed them here after Devon had tried to kill her along with everyone else. The Summoner had saved her life that day.

In the very center of the lake was an island, and on that island was a stone doorway, that if you looked through, all you saw was the other side of the island and the water beyond. But if you were allowed to pass, you came to a different place altogether. She spent her years in exile discovering all of its secrets, and there were many.

Zana stood on the steps with the doorway beyond.

She felt it. She felt that the Summoner and Andros had succeeded in defeating the warlocks. The last obstacle to increasing her power was removed by her enemy. She also knew that Braylynn was gone. Anyone with a sense of magic could have felt the goddess' departure. It was time to align herself with another god. She had approached him once, but he said the time wasn't right. She was sure it was now.

Finally, she would have her revenge against the so called Dragon Summoner. Yes, Donella had spared her life, but not before destroying her world and all she had worked for. The scales were even now. It was time the Dragon Summoner shared her pain. And with no gods or goddess in Vasara, it was time for her power to rise.

Zana cast her gaze across the lake. All was still and quiet except for the occasional caw of the ravens sitting atop the stone lintel. She felt she was being watched. She always felt like she was being watched, but it really didn't matter. There wasn't anyone to challenge her power now. Yet still an unease had entered her spirit.

"Why did he have to be there," Zana said aloud. She hadn't thought of him for over fifteen hundred years. She couldn't afford to. She thought him dead to her, now she realized he was very much alive and a chink in her armor. She hated that. It meant she had a weakness, and his name was Finn.

Her feline eyes narrowed to slits. She would grow in power. She would put her own King on the throne in Kensington. That plan she had begun long ago. And finally she would make her enemies worship her as their new goddess. There would be only one answer for those who did not. Death.

The ravens took wing as they circled the lake once before following Zana through the gateway, each one disappearing as they flew under the lintel of the gateway.